A Scholarly Pursuit

Book Four ⁓ The Ellsworth Assortment

by

Christina Dudley

Copyright ©2023 by Christina Dudley

All rights reserved. This book, or parts thereof, may not be reproduced, stored in a retrieval system, or transmitted in any form or by any means, electronic, mechanical, photocopying, recording, or otherwise, without the written permission of the publisher.

Cover design: Kathy Campbell,
https://kathryncampbell.com/

Print ISBN: 9798858902515

Chapter 1

I will not shew my Anger against this Word-man.
— Matthew Prior, *Poetical Works* (c.1721)

It was Warden Gauntlett's firm opinion that there were too many Ellsworths at New College. The number of undergraduate spaces at The College of St. Mary of Winchester in Oxford had dwindled in the last ten years to fewer than twenty-five, as the graduate fellows hung on far too long, occupying space and consuming precious college resources. And here were these Ellsworths—three of them, by the Lord Harry! Messieurs Benjamin, Austin, and Tyrone Ellsworth. Would New College never be rid of them? Too often, gentlemen fortunate enough to come into a fellowship chose not to marry, that they might keep the handy income, and Warden Gauntlett feared this applied to the two elder Ellsworths. For Benjamin and Austin hailed from a poorer branch of the Hampshire family, and if livings could not be found for them somewhere, he suspected they might never be struck from the rolls. But their cousin Tyrone—surely he could be got rid of? His father was wealthy enough. If Tyrone Ellsworth chose to be idle, therefore, it were better he did it at home in Winchester.

Even as the reverend doctor grumbled to himself, he saw that same Tyrone Ellsworth emerge from the library to cross the quadrangle, his head in a book, as ever. In fact, after four years Warden Gauntlett had no very precise idea what the young man looked like because he was forever reading.

"You there!" He pushed the window open to glare down at the offender. "You there—come up here. I would like a word."

The undergraduate halted and glanced up, surprised. The warden saw a tall, golden-haired fellow with intelligent, regular features and a firm jaw, but discovering Ellsworth's good looks only added to the older man's crossness. New College did not exist to support and house handsome, wealthy young men who might easily support and house themselves!

"Me, sir?"

"Yes, you! Do you see any other person in the quadrangle whom I might be addressing? Come up here at once." He shut the window smartly and threw open the door to his parlor, clearing his throat and tapping an impatient foot.

Not that Tyrone dawdled. The warden soon enough heard his quick step on the stairs, and then there he was, filling the doorway, his black silk gown with its tufted tassels billowing around him from the haste of his movements. Tyrone had indeed never in his four years at Oxford been called into the warden's office, and he had a few things in his pocket which made him not eager to appear there now.

"Sir."

"Sit down, Ellsworth." The warden's parlor was full of commodious, comfortable chairs, but in this instance he pointed to a hard wooden one bare of upholstery.

Tyrone colored, a guilty hand even touching the guilty pocket, but he took the proffered seat.

The warden himself merely leaned against his desk, preferring to maintain the advantage of height. "Ellsworth, you have been at New College four years now, have you not?"

"This is my fourth year, sir, yes."

"And what plans have you got, now that you have completed or have nearly completed your undergraduate studies?"

Tyrone hesitated.

"Do you wish to become a clergyman?"

"No, sir."

"A tutor?"

"Er—not particularly, though I have enjoyed my studies."

"Do you intend on remaining at New College, then?" persisted the warden, his eyes narrowing with each successive question behind his tiny spectacles until Tyrone thought they might blink out altogether.

"Er—my cousins have encouraged me to, but I have not yet decided."

The warden heaved a long-suffering sigh. "Yes. Your cousins. That is another matter I would question you about. Mr. Ellsworth, rumors have reached me that your cousins, Messieurs Benjamin and Austin Ellsworth, have been recently more flush with cash than of yore." Now Dr. Gauntlett had no hope that the young man before him would "peach" upon his cousins, but to his surprise Tyrone Ellsworth straightened suddenly in the uncomfortable chair, taking hold of either side of the seat with his hands.

"Yes. You see...there's been a little more—family money coming their way, sir."

At this the warden's eyes opened to their normal size again. Family money? Would it be possible to rid New College of all three Ellsworths and to present the electors with *three additional* places in the coming year? But—and here his spirits sank from their brief exaltation—if this family money was righteous Mammon, why did Ellsworth look so self-conscious?

"What...sort of family money? I understood their father, your uncle, was the mathematics instructor at Winchester. An honorable position, but, if I might say, not a lucrative one."

"No," agreed Tyrone. "Not a lucrative one." Squaring his shoulders, he met the warden's gaze directly. "Sir, if Benjamin and Austin seem to be a little more in clover at present, it's because we have started something of a...family business. Ben and Austin—they're well connected here in Oxford, after so many years. They—find the business, and I—provide the product."

Business? *Product?*

Abruptly Dr. Gauntlett abandoned his height advantage to sink into the nearest armchair, one with such squashy cushions that he sank to a lower level than his student. Removing his handkerchief from his sleeve, he passed it over his brow. "Good heavens! What sort of dreadful 'product' can you refer to?" he demanded. "You are not distilling liquors in your room, are you? Pushing laudanum cordials or Dover's Powder or ether tonic on other boys?"

"What? No, sir!"

"Holding laughing parties, then?"

"No! Though I confess to be curious about them."

"Paying the porter to look the other way, then, while you sneak young ladies into the college?"

"No!" cried Tyrone, unable to prevent himself leaping to his feet, in his earnestness. "Nothing of the kind, sir—nothing of *any* of those kinds—and I am not certain what we might have done that you should so instantly suspect us of such—such—" He broke off. "Depravity" seemed too strong a word, and "tomfoolery" too weak.

But the warden was moaning now, still imagining all manner of gambling and intoxicants and general mischief, and Tyrone found his indignation giving way to amusement. How his sister Minta would laugh when he wrote to her about this!

"Sir," he began again, more quietly as he resumed his seat, "I repeat: my cousins and I are engaged in no activities which would harm our fellow students or the safety of the college. It is something altogether different. I am helping others improve their lives and situations by writing things for them."

"Papers? Reports? Translations they ought to be doing for themselves?"

"No, sir." A note of impatience made itself audible. "I write personal items, not academic ones. Poems, you see. Or notes. Or *billets doux.*"

Rather than appearing reassured by this declaration, Dr. Gauntlett clapped a hand to his chest, sputtering. "This—you—you mean to say—on the very grounds of New College! Literary—*pandering*—for money!"

Then Tyrone did flush, and there was a dangerous glint in his usually mild blue eyes. "Sir, with all due respect, I do object to such a word being applied to my—to our—activities. There is nothing immoral being encouraged or arranged. Nothing intended for the purposes of seduction. Sir, if I write a sonnet for a schoolmate or help him...pay his addresses with some little elegance, it is only to forward his honorable intentions, I assure you." He reached in his pocket and withdrew several folded scraps of paper, holding them out to the warden. "See there. You may look at any of those you please, and you will find we have done nothing to be ashamed of. If I hesitated in speaking of it, Dr. Gauntlett, it was because you will understand these writings are of a…sensitive and confidential nature, and the revelation of my hand in them would not be appreciated by any young man hopeful of winning his love. He may be given full credit for the sentiment behind the words, sir, if not for the words themselves. And I promise you, I am not personally acquainted with any of the young ladies addressed."

The warden made a rumbling grunt, backed into a corner by the young man's seeming frankness. It would never do to read another person's correspondence, of course, but did this qualify for that protection? Was he not responsible for the conduct of every young man at New College, as well as everything which took place within its walls?

He was, he decided.

Taking the papers, he retreated behind his desk and unfolded them one by one.

"'My dearest Miss Kemp,'" he read aloud, "'pardon my daring in addressing you, but I have been able to think of little else since you first gazed upon me Sunday last in St. Cross Church. In that blessed moment when our eyes met, yours "shone sweetly lambent with celestial day," and my heart has never since been my own.'"

Tyrone pulled a face. "It's wretched, I know, and the bit from Pope's *Eloisa to Abelard* a little much, but Johnson would go on about Miss Kemp's 'radiant orbs,' so Pope was at least an improvement. I still hope to convince him not to frighten her away at the first go and to let me toss that draft in the fire."

"Mm," said the reverend doctor. He set the page aside and unfolded the next. "'There once was a lady from Gloucester/Who made her swain's heart beat the faster./It went off at a canter,/Whipped up by her banter,/So rich with Donne, Spenser, and Chaucer.'"

Tyrone grinned. "Sorry, sir. That one is from Pinchbeck to Miss Browne, the daughter of the bookseller in Broad Street. She likes jokes, he says."

"I see. Though I am not certain well-bred young ladies should make use of such oftentimes ribald or frank authors in their banter."

To this Tyrone had no answer, and the older man continued, "And how much do you charge for these…efforts, Ellsworth?"

"A half-crown, sir. Generally. Unless they want something longer. But a proposal of marriage is a full crown."

"Heavens! And if he be refused?"

"I have, in pity, granted some partial refunds, though I persist in maintaining that refusals are not an indication that the work was deficient."

Astonishing. Not simply the young man's self-assurance, but also his failure to grasp the weightiness of his crime.

The situation was unprecedented in New College history, and the warden was determined to think it through. He made a pretense of reading the other items, but he did not truly take them in. Ellsworth must be punished, of course. And how convenient that his punishment corresponded with the school's need to reduce the roll.

"I'm afraid this is a very serious matter, Mr. Ellsworth," sighed Dr. Gauntlett. "Very serious. Grave, even."

Tyrone swallowed.

"To allow it to continue would signify that New College condones the enterprise, which, of course it does not. It cannot. Why, this business of yours depends entirely on the practice of deception, with respectable people as its unwitting victims."

"But sir—"

The warden held up a finger. "*Even* deception in the name of laudable ends—and I have not yet decided if this qualifies—even deception for such purposes could not be excused or overlooked because deception, by its nature, is at odds with an institution founded upon honor and truth. 'Manners maketh man,' the good bishop told us, and we at both Winchester and New College have taken Wykeham's motto for our own. *Lying*, Mr. Ellsworth, is very bad manners indeed."

"So it is, sir," agreed Tyrone hastily, "but—"

Again the reverend doctor raised his finger. "I am especially disappointed in your cousins' participation. They are older than you; if you should have known better, how much more should they have! I do not know if New College can continue to pay graduate fellowships to such sorts."

Tyrone gasped and once more sprang up. "Dr. Gauntlett, I beg of you—my cousins Benjamin and Austin are not wealthy men. They *need* those stipends! Nor were they the originators of the idea. It was at my request that they 'put the word out' among their friends and acquaintances—"

"But they shared in the proceeds?" interrupted the warden darkly. "In the ill-gotten gains?"

"Only because I insisted, sir." Tyrone took a deep breath, his jaw set. "If you must punish anyone, sir, it had better be me and only me."

The warden was silent a moment, seeing victory swing into view and not wanting to rush his fences.

"Were you hoping to stay on as a graduate fellow, Mr. Ellsworth?"

"I—was," Tyrone admitted. "If only because my cousins were here, and several other friends intend to stay on."

Yes, thought the warden, and that was precisely the problem. Too many undergraduates unwilling to leave the green pastures of New College for the wilds of the greater world. Well, this was one undergraduate Heaven had afforded him the means to expel from paradise!

He rapped his knuckles on the desk with emphasis. "Then I am sorry to inform you that, if you insist on taking the entirety of the punishment upon yourself—the punishment owing to your cousins as well as to you for this mischief—you leave me no choice but to revoke your qualifications for a graduate fellowship."

"Dr. Gauntlett!" breathed Tyrone, staggered. "Sir—could you not simply rusticate me for a few weeks?"

"I'm afraid not. You would hardly be back before term ended. I could reconsider, however, if you would like your cousins to bear their share of the blame. In which case I might rusticate you and withhold half of each of their fellowships…"

Half!

"No," said Tyrone. He knew how much bread his cousins' butter must be made to cover. "No, then. Very well. I will relinquish my claim to the fellowship."

"And you will cease to produce this…material?" Dr. Gauntlett insisted. "This tissue of pretense and falsehood?"

Tyrone thought the warden was laying it on rather thick, but he nodded slowly. "Yes, sir."

The warden rapped the desk again, this time with barely disguised satisfaction. "All right, then. You will leave Oxford when Trinity Term ends, and your space will be opened on the rolls. The fellows of Winchester College arrive in a fortnight, and I will give them the final numbers then." As he spoke, he carefully tore Tyrone's pages into fragments, which he then gathered together and carried to the fireplace. "You may go, Ellsworth."

It was a chastened young man who returned to his chambers and threw himself across his bed.

"Have you got my limerick?" demanded Ginger Peaches, thrusting his head in a half-hour later. His given name was Gerard Pinchbeck, but he had such violently orange hair that he had gone by the other from an early age.

"Gauntlett ripped it up and burned it."

"What on earth? What was Gauntlett doing with my limerick? I paid good money for that."

"It was the money I was raking in that alerted him. He thought my cousins and I must be selling intoxicants or smuggling in young ladies of doubtful reputation, so I thought it best to confess what we were actually engaged in. I thought he would see it as a mere peccadillo, but he took it most seriously."

"Rats," said Ginger.

Tyrone rolled onto his stomach and propped his head on his hand. "I am forbidden from taking on more work, Peaches, but since you already paid…" He proceeded to recite the verse, his schoolmate snatching at a pencil and paper to record it.

Word spread quickly, and in Hall his cousins Benjamin and Austin descended to sit on either side of him. Both of medium height with pale complexions, Benjamin was dark of hair and eye as his French mother, while Austin was reddish-blond with a wide, humorous mouth.

"What's this I hear, Ty?" Benjamin asked. "Gauntlett aims to kill our gainsome, profitful venture?"

"Not 'aims to.' He has killed it."

"That's nonsense," said Austin. "We'll go on as usual. Winthorp wants a sonnet to a Miss Hinkle. I told him you would produce not just any sonnet, but one in alexandrines because her Christian name is Alexandra. And be sure to mention her light brown hair and green eyes."

Tyrone's own eyes brightened at the challenge, and he tapped out the meter on the table. "Brown-tressed Alexandra with her eyes of green—no. Stop. Tell Winthorp I won't do it."

"What do you mean, you won't do it?"

Tyrone was not about to admit that he was afraid Gauntlett would deprive his cousins of some or all of their stipends. Benjamin and Austin might be relatively poor, but they were also spirited and perhaps heedless, and he knew they would urge him to fly in the face of the warden, let the consequences be what they might.

He shrugged therefore. "It was fun for a time, but with less than half a term left, I must apply myself to my studies."

"What stuff," said Austin. "When have you ever had to apply yourself to your studies?"

"And what do you mean you have only got half a term left?" asked Benjamin.

"I've decided to go back to Winchester," he explained. "I don't want to become a clergyman, nor have I got any ambition to tutor the younger fellows. Besides, there are so many senior fellows here that they outnumber every new, puling Winchester stripling five to one."

"But what would you do in Winchester?"

"Write a book, perhaps. Teach my younger brother or my nephews."

"You just said you didn't want to teach!"

"I said I didn't want to tutor Winchester scrubs."

"What are Willie and Peter and Edward but future Winchester scrubs?"

"And my father would like me to learn the rudiments of estate management."

"Whatever for?" Benjamin dismissed this. "Hollowgate goes to Florence when William Ellsworth is no more."

"My stepmother has a life interest," Tyrone reminded them. "And I don't think she's vastly older than Flossie. If I were never to marry, I might live at Hollowgate all my days, managing it first for my stepmother and then for Floss. Her husband is no squire."

Their argument continued in the same vein, off and on, for several days, and they were at it again over another dinner in Hall when a trencher slapped down opposite them. The three Ellsworths looked up to find a long and pale young man with dark brown hair and mournful grey eyes.

"Boulton," they greeted him. He was, strictly speaking a "commoner," and custom dictated he sit with his ilk at a lower table, but such was the top-heaviness at New College in that era that the gentlemen-commoners' high table was overstuffed, and the Ellsworths as often as not sat lower down in mixed company.

"Ellsworths. I would like a note. One signed, 'An Admirer.' For I must have something ready if I meet a golden vision."

"Have you not heard? I've retired," said Tyrone. "Gauntlett insisted."

"Then unretire, for time presses."

"What paragon is this whom you are so eager to prepare for?" asked Austin.

"Can't be Winthorp's Miss Hinkle because she has brown hair," said his brother Benjamin.

"Or Peaches' Miss Browne, because she's a ginger like he is."

"I don't know the actual color of the young lady's hair," admitted Boulton. "Whether it be yellow, brown or green hardly matters. When I called her 'golden' I referred more particularly to the other golden aspect of her: her fortune."

"You hope to meet an heiress in Oxford?" asked Tyrone politely.

"If Fortune favors me. Because I hear King has come. You know—Philip King, one of the Winchester fellows, to meet with the electors, I suspect. And he has brought his family, including his unmarried sister-in-law. Therefore, if I could arrange to meet her—"

"You can't mean Aggie is here." Tyrone stared. "That is—Miss Weeks?"

"You know her?" demanded Boulton.

"Of course I know her. She is my twin sister's dearest friend."

"Then tell me—Gauntlett said King married into a rich family. Is Miss Weeks really dripping with glorious wealth?"

Tyrone's mouth twisted in derision. "She is. But trust me, Boulton: you haven't got a chance."

"Why not? Are you certain you won't write me a note?"

"I can't *now*, as I have already explained. I have given Gauntlett my word. But that isn't all. I don't think she has got marriage in mind."

Boulton's mournful eyes held Tyrone's a long moment, as if he considered arguing the point. But then he shrugged. "I suspect you have got ambitions of your own. As if you had not already got money enough. You would not understand what these chances mean to someone in my position. But please yourself." He swung his legs out from the bench, picked up his trencher again, and marched away.

Austin gave a low whistle. "Too bad about your premature retirement, Ty. If anyone stands in need of your help it would be Boulton."

"Boulton would need more than a charming note," muttered Tyrone, digging into his food.

"Too true," said Benjamin. "He might be better served employing a mask maker. For Miss Weeks will take one look at his doleful face and run for her life."

But it would be neither Boulton's lack of eloquence nor his perpetually long face which would repel her, Tyrone suspected. It would be the heartbreak she endured years earlier. The man who stole her heart then had hardly been worth it, but there it was. And since that unfortunate time, she had never again shown signs of caring for another. Tyrone's sister Araminta had expected Aggie's recovery to be slow ("Because her heart is so true!"), but as one year gave way to the next, even optimistic Minta began to fear Aggie might never, never be heart-whole again. And while Tyrone had not dwelt on the matter in the interim as his twin had, he generally put faith in Minta's observations and opinions, which time lent increasing weight.

Because four years had gone by. And if Aggie hadn't found someone more to her liking than the scoundrel Francis Taplin in those four long years, she must not be the clever girl he once thought.

Chapter 2

As to the colonels, and the ensigns, and that young Oxford student, they won't at all do; officers are commonly worth nothing; and scholars...are the dullest men in the world.
— Fanny Burney, *Camilla* (1796)

It was her third proposal of marriage which drove Miss Agatha Weeks from Winchester.

"I don't see why you must go," said Araminta, when Aggie consulted her. Minta was in the family way and less able to romp, so she had taken to experimenting in the small laboratory of her doctor husband. While Aggie perched on a stool, Minta frowned over a new compound she was trying.

"Because I want the gentlemen of Winchester to light upon other victims. Listen to this one, Minta," Aggie said, unfolding the latest missive. "'My dear Miss Weeks, if I might be so bold to address you thus, from the moment you did me the honor of standing up with me at the assembly, I have thought ceaselessly of you.' At least I think he means 'ceaselessly.' He spells it s-e-a-s-l-e-s-l-y."

"Perhaps he means to say he thought of you always on dry land, with no sea nearby," suggested Minta, giving the ingredients in her mortar a good pound. "He *is* a colonel in the army, after all."

"Or he thought of me in Sicily. Or...uneasily."

Minta held her work out for Aggie's inspection. "Would you call that small crumbs? Nicholas says to bash it into small crumbs."

"I'd like to bash Colonel Wood into small crumbs," Aggie sighed. "The whole time he danced with me, he complimented everything he could think of—my eyes, my hair, my dress, my dancing, my conversation—as if he were the bailiff, come to take an inventory."

"In his defense, all those things about you are quite satisfactory, and other girls wouldn't mind it so much."

"But he left out what he liked best of all, Minta—my fortune. And for that dishonesty, I cannot forgive him."

"That's just nonsense," her friend replied stoutly. "If he had dared to mention your fortune as something he admired, you would have rejected him with twice the vehemence. And how can a man not admire your fortune? He would not be human if he did not admire your fortune."

"Mr. Carlisle did not consider *your* fortune to be your most sterling quality," grumbled Aggie.

"Yes, well—that was different," Minta hedged. "But *every other man* would be unnatural if he did not like your fortune. The truth is, Agatha Weeks, you are 'once bit, twice shy.' And it makes me and everyone who loves you so sad." (She would have expressed in much stronger terms her anger toward and dislike of the man who had broken Aggie's heart years earlier, but she knew Aggie wouldn't like it and would feel obligated to defend him, and that would accomplish nothing.)

"At any rate," Aggie resumed, "I won't have Colonel Wood. And if you love me, Minta, you will not ask me to. Let me go away for a little. See new things, new people."

"But why Oxford with your sister Phronsie, rather than London with Frederica? There would be far more new things and new people in town than in Oxford."

"Because Frederica's husband Mr. Chester is a tiresome old stick. So is Phronsie's husband Mr. King, but Mr. King at least does not pull a face if I bounce the children, and Mr. King does not say to his wife and grown stepdaughter how grateful he is that *they* are quiet and ladylike because *such* is not always the case."

Minta laughed. "I see your point, though perhaps Mr. King would be equally guilty of saying such things if he had any daughters. Very well. Go with the Kings to Oxford. I will miss you, but you can give Tyrone our best love and a packet of Wilcomb's shortbread."

It was this packet Aggie carried in the pocket of her pelisse as she trailed after Warden Gauntlett and Mr. and Mrs. King through New College Chapel, her older nephew James by the hand.

23

"The tall windows to the north and south date from William of Wykeham's own time," intoned the warden, gesturing. "You see Adam delving and Eve spinning. But perhaps the more remarkable specimens are the most recent, these of the Nativity of our Lord and the Adoration of the Shepherds, after a design by the great Sir Joshua Reynolds himself. Note that the glass is actually painted, and not stained..."

"Anaggie," whispered little James, tugging on her, "go out?"

She could not blame him. The tour had already lasted an hour, and the three-year-old boy had been extremely good. She knew exactly where he wanted to go: into the college's spacious gardens, which were bounded to the north and east by the old city wall. With a conspiratorial nod and a whisper to her sister Sophronia, the two made their escape, giggling to each other as they raced back through the front and garden quads, out the iron gates to the lawn.

"What will it be, Jimmy? Races?"

"Races!"

Aunt and nephew dashed back and forth across the damp grass, laughing and dodging gowned students and getting more than a little muddy. Aggie took care to let James win several times but also to beat him—by a hair—other times. When they were breathless, she would have liked to rest on a bench, but she knew better than to suggest it. "Hide and seek now?" she asked.

"Hide and seek!" he crowed. "Count to ten—no—twenty."

Obediently Aggie placed her gloved hands over her eyes and began to count, loudly and slowly. She could hear her nephew shriek with glee. Hear his rapid footsteps flying away. She waited until both sounds faded before saying, "…Nineteen…Twenty! Here I come."

Aggie suspected James would be in the niche of the city wall; therefore she headed slowly in that direction, following the line of shrubbery and flower-borders still bare of blossoms. "Where can he be?" she sang. "Where can that clever little mischief James King be? Is he in…here?" She parted the nearest greenery with her arms. "No? Hmm…where then? Here! Ah, alas—no Jimmy. Why, then, he must be…here!" She dashed around the tree trunk nearest the niche, expecting her little nephew to pop out, screaming with delight at her discovery, but instead she found an undergraduate leaning against it, a long and pale young man with dark brown hair and mournful grey eyes.

"I beg your pardon," he murmured, sweeping off his square, tassel-less cap.

"Oh, no, sir. I beg yours. I am sorry to disturb you."

"It's no disturbance," he said somberly. "Though we do not often see young ladies on the grounds."

"Mm," was Aggie's vague response. She began to back away, not eager for Phronsie to catch her speaking with someone to whom she had not been introduced. But before she took more than two steps, she knocked into little James, who had stolen up behind her.

"Got oo!" he cried. "Found oo!"

"But Jimothy, I was supposed to be seeking *you*."

"Your brother's name is Jimothy?" asked the young man. "Most unusual."

"James!" barked James.

"It's James," admitted Aggie. "And he's my nephew. Come, my fine fellow. Shall we go back to your Mama and Pa?"

But James' Mama and Pa had come to them.

"You missed the Cardinal Virtues, Agatha, also by Reynolds," her brother-in-law Mr. King informed her, leaning to pick up his son, only to draw back when he noticed the muddy condition of his boots. "But I see you have formed a new acquaintance."

"Indeed I have not," protested Aggie, seeing Phronsie's lips purse in disapproval.

"We have not been introduced," said the long, pale young man, sweeping off the cap once more. "And if the warden has been showing you the chapel, I am sorry he is not here to vouch for me. I am Mr. Gareth Boulton of Headbourne Worthy, where I will take up the curacy of St. Swithun's Church upon receiving my degree when term ends."

"Why, Headbourne Worthy is not far from Winchester, where we live," said Mrs. King, pleased to learn the strange gentleman her youngest sister had been standing too near was at least an incipient clergyman. She had been alarmed by his sleeveless black stuff gown, which bespoke his status as a commoner at the college. Depend upon it, he was poor, but at least he could be called a gentleman.

Mr. King, too, relented. With a bow he said, "Philip King, fellow of Winchester College. My wife Mrs. King. My sister-in-law Miss Weeks. My older son James."

His words sparked something in Mr. Boulton, his formerly languid air giving place to alertness. "What an honor and a pleasure, sir. Madam. Miss. The warden did announce in Hall that you would be paying New College a visit. I hope you find everything to your liking." This, then, was she! The wealthy young lady of whom he had heard! Warden Gauntlett had called Mr. King one of Winchester's greatest benefactors, even more so after his marriage into the noted Weeks silk-manufacturing family. And while the warden imagined a possible endowment for New College, future curate Gareth Boulton heard instead the siren song of personal benefit. But even as that song lulled him, this golden young lady began to withdraw. Not physically, to be sure—she did not move a step—but she withdrew from the conversation, leaving it to her elders. And she withdrew her attention, gazing off toward the city wall.

For Aggie had noted the change in the young man's manner and suspected the reason for it. He either liked Mr. King's importance or knew of Mr. King's wealth (or both) and therefore meant to fawn upon him. Bah! It might be the way of the world, but she need not be happy about it.

Mr. King and her sister did not seem to mind at all, however. Indeed, they accepted Mr. Boulton's desire to please as their due and graciously allowed him to point out some of the historical and aesthetic features of the grounds while Aggie and James trailed behind. She feared her brother-in-law might go so far as to invite Mr. Boulton for coffee with them at the Angel, but this at least she was spared.

Eventually they took their leave of the young man and made their way through the back gate, Aggie fingering the packet of shortbread in her pocket. Having never visited Oxford before, she had no idea what sort of place it was and imagined she might see Tyrone Ellsworth on the tour of the college, sitting somewhere reading a book, but luck had been against her. She would have to leave the shortbread with the porter. Or perhaps send a note from the inn.

Upon consideration, she decided on the porter. Aggie would be sorry not to see her friend's brother, that she might write Minta about it, but she could hardly summon him to the Angel.

Still, she thought wistfully, it would have been lovely to see a familiar face. As much as she had longed to be away from Winchester, Oxford was peopled entirely by strangers, and she was almost cowed by the great flocks of black gowns in the High Street. Flocks composed of sometimes drunken and often roisterous young men, spilling from the taverns, singing and shouting and shoving. If there was much study happening in this university town, it must take place hidden away, in the libraries and cloisters.

She borrowed pencil and paper from the New College porter.

Dear Tyrone, she scratched, *(I hope I may call you that). The Kings and I are in Oxford on a visit to your college. Minta sends this shortbread. Mr. King will be all day with the warden tomorrow, so Phronsie and I will play tourist. If I do not see you, I wish you very well. – Aggie.*

Chapter 3

What was he to think, what to hope
from this unforeseen rendezvous?
— Jean-François Marmontel, *Moral Tales* (1764)

Winthorp found Tyrone in the cloisters, tucked on a bench, book in one hand and apple in the other. "You must help me, Ellsworth, or I am lost!"

"Help you what?" Tyrone asked, hardly glancing at his classmate because he was at a terribly exciting point in the story. "If this is about Miss Hinkle of the light brown hair, I have already said I can no longer be of assistance."

"I know, I know. Ginger Peaches told me. He said you couldn't write anything. That you had given your word."

"Then this is not about Miss Hinkle?"

Winthorp dragged his bony hands through his overlong locks. "No, it is. But it's not about writing. It's about speaking. Or whispering, rather."

Intrigued, Tyrone shut his volume with a snap. "Let's have it, then."

"I took it upon myself to compose my own note to Miss Hinkle, asking her to walk with her maid in the Physic Garden, where I would chance to meet her at the glasshouse—the one with the pineapples. You know there are benches there and always people, no matter the weather."

"I know it. Well, what do you need me for? It sounds like you've managed quite admirably on your own."

"I can't speak to her, Ellsworth!" cried Winthorp, now wringing his silk gown in his hands. "Her beauty will tie my tongue. I know it. You must come and feed me lines. It would be easy enough. You might hide behind a large pot and buzz at me."

"That's ridiculous," Tyrone answered with a grin. "Suppose Miss Hinkle or her maid takes me for an overlarge bumblebee and swats at me?"

"I will pay you generously for your pains. Do come, Ellsworth. A mere hour of your time for, say, a crown."

The opportunity for amusement was too great a temptation for Tyrone. After all, the warden had outlawed Tyrone's written efforts in the service of Cupid, but nothing had been said against the oral variety.

"Mr. Ellsworth, sir," cried the porter Farrent as the young men passed. "A parcel and note for you."

"Parcel!" Eagerly Tyrone seized it, his eyebrows lifting when he saw the wrapper's translucent stains. He gave it a sniff. "Shortbread, by my life!"

"Come along, Ellsworth," urged Winthorp, impatient of mundane matters.

The Physic Garden lay a ten-minute stroll from New College, its imposing Danby Gate standing opposite Magdalen Tower along the High Street. Tyrone had been there many times, as had every resident of Oxford, and though not large, the garden's overgrown state, two glasshouses and alleys made it a popular setting for both exercise and rendezvous. On this cloudy and damp day, the glasshouses were particularly thronged, and Tyrone thought everyone in town must have been seized by the same inspiration as his college mate.

At Winthorp's behest, Tyrone preceded him into the conservatory which housed Oxford's pineapples. He perched upon the back edge of the largest pot convenient to a bench and opened his book again, as if he had merely chosen to read in the artificial tropics, rather than in a crowded coffeehouse or his college library.

Winthorp shambled up soon enough, taking his seat upon the bench with his back to Tyrone.

"I'm here," he hissed from the side of his mouth. "Say something and let me see if I can hear you."

"'I see a voice: now will I to the chink, to spy an I can hear my Thisby's face,'" recited Tyrone.

Alarmed, Winthorp spun all the way around to peer at him through the long green pineapple-plant leaves. "What was that? You had better move closer, or I won't be able to make you out!"

"If I move closer I will be perching on your shoulder, which would look quite odd," argued Tyrone. "We will just have to give it a try, and I will do my best to enunciate. That was *A Midsummer Night's Dream*, so perhaps too ambitious for a rehearsal."

"No Shakespeare!" insisted Winthorp, returning his gaze forward. "Speak *English*. Here she comes!"

Tyrone stole one sidewise glance at Miss Hinkle of the light brown hair and green eyes. She shared the Amazonian build of his twin sister Araminta, and he felt an unexpected pang for his sibling. At least an enforced return to Winchester would allow him to see her and all his family more regularly, he supposed.

"Miss H-Hinkle," blurted Winthorp, his bow like a tower toppling over.

"Mr. Winthorp." (Miss Hinkle's voice certainly did not remind Tyrone of Minta, for Miss Hinkle was loud as a gong.) "Go along, Sockfoot," Miss Hinkle boomed at her maid, "and come back in a half-hour. I will come to no harm here."

Indeed, with her stature and that bellow, Tyrone thought Miss Hinkle well able to defend herself against all comers. Not that she was unattractive, only his personal taste ran to less *amplified* young ladies. Perhaps Winthorp's plan would work. Miss Hinkle was not a person constructed to detect whispers.

"Won't you have a seat, then, Miss Hinkle?" asked Winthorp.

Her gracious acceptance of this offer was communicated to Tyrone by a *whoof* of fabric that rattled the pineapple plant leaves. But these sounds, however promising, were soon followed by uncomfortable silence. Or, at least, Winthorp was uncomfortable. Tyrone could *feel* it, even at the distance of two feet.

"What did you want to say to me, then?" hollered Miss Hinkle at last.

"I—er—I—that is—"

"I thought of you when I suggested the glasshouses," hissed Tyrone. "Such bright colors and life, no matter the season."

"You remind me of a glasshouse," bumbled Winthorp. "Bright and—bright and—"

"Full—of—color—and—life!" Tyrone amended.

"Full of the color of life."

Close enough.

Miss Hinkle blew out a satisfied gust. "Why, what a pleasant thing to say, Mr. Winthorp! You flatterer, you. My father warned me not to listen to anything you undergraduates say. He says you'll pay compliments to any girl, to get one to keep company with you."

It occurred to Tyrone that he had neglected to ask Winthorp his intentions toward the robust creature. With a Christian name like Alexandra and a maid to accompany her, however, she was clearly no shopkeeper's daughter, therefore caution and courtliness were in order.

"I wish I were better at compliments," whispered Tyrone, "for then I could write you a sonnet, one in Alexandrines."

"If I could write you a sonnet, I'd be better at compliments, Alexandra," declared Winthorp.

Fortunately Miss Hinkle's mock-indignant shriek masked Tyrone's groan. "I did not say you could call me Alexandra!" she reprimanded her would-be swain, accompanying it with a sock to Winthorp's arm that drew a muffled whimper.

"Pardon me—I am not my own master in your presence," suggested Tyrone.

"Sorry," said Winthorp.

"Go on then," she pressed. "Have a go at it. I do love a good sonnet."

In his panic, Winthorp almost turned his head to look at his helper, and Tyrone was forced to drop his book to the ground, that he might bend to retrieve it.

"I said I would if I *could*," protested Winthorp, improvising.

"Even a bad one is better than none," his lady insisted. "It's not every day a girl hears a sonnet to her."

"Brown-tressed Alexandra with her eyes of green," Tyrone uttered *sotto voce*.

"Brown dress Alexandra with her eyes of green…"

"Silly man, my dress is white! And isn't that too many syllables?"

"It's in Alexandrines, in your honor," Tyrone said impatiently.

"It's Alexandra, on my honor!"

"What?"

"What?"

Tyrone shut his eyes. This was hopeless. "Tell her you will write one later," he urged. Winthorp could always copy something from Spenser's *Amoretti*, and Miss Hinkle would be none the wiser.

"Oh, please," begged Miss Hinkle. "Never mind about my dress being white. And I'll forgive you the 'Alexandra' and getting the syllables wrong. Only do try again."

Tyrone pulled a face. "I certainly can't compose with your eyes upon me."

"I certainly can't be composed with your eyes on me," said Winthorp, and Tyrone gave him points that time for improving upon the original.

"La, Mr. Winthorp, what delightful things you say! I must know, then—in prose, if need be—which features first drew your attention?"

Now the one glance Tyrone had ventured was hardly sufficient to supply a detailed inventory, but perhaps generic praise would serve.

It did, and Winthorp proved far more proficient at repeating short, hackneyed phrases than complete sentences. Tyrone could reel them off without hesitation: emerald eyes, ruby lips, apple cheeks, the carriage of a goddess, etc.

"Gracious—it *is* you, Tyrone. What dreadful book are you reading?"

Wild-eyed, his head jerked up, and he found himself face to face with Miss Agatha Weeks. At least, he thought it was her. Though the Weekses were neighbors to the Ellsworths in Winchester, with Tyrone's sister married and no longer resident at Hollowgate, sightings of Aggie had been reduced to the occasional glimpse in church during vacations.

He had never paid much attention to her. She was merely his sister's comrade—someone with whom Minta had grown up, attended school, and played all manner of sports. He remembered Aggie's flyaway white-blonde hair and smaller stature. He knew she was rich. He knew she had wasted much time moping over a worthless fortune hunter who had broken her heart. But he had not remembered her being pretty, and he had not remembered ever being conscious of a—start—and a…glow upon seeing her. Perhaps because she was a face from home.

Her hair had darkened somewhat as she grew older, until it was now flaxen, and the blue silk of her pelisse made her blue eyes all the brighter. They were watching him, amused but also uncertain.

He rose hastily. "Good afternoon, Aggie. Though perhaps in this setting I had better call you Miss Weeks. I heard you and some of your family were visiting. What a pleasure."

Her uncertain expression deepened at his formality, but she answered, "Yes, I am here with the Kings—my older sister's family. Mr. King is a fellow of Winchester College and visiting with the New College warden. I'll call you Mr. Ellsworth, then, if you think it better. Did your porter not give you the shortbread and my note?"

He thought guiltily of the note, still unread in his pocket, but he pulled out the parcel of biscuits to show her. "He did. Thank you."

"But you haven't even opened it! Minta was so sure you would tear into it at once."

"Oh. Yes. I was in a bit of a rush to get here just now."

Puzzlement furrowed her brow. "Were you afraid someone might steal your favorite reading spot, the lip of a pineapple pot?"

"Well, as a matter of fact, one of my favorite spots was already taken." He nodded toward Winthorp and Miss Hinkle's bench, only to see the two of them had abandoned it and were now sauntering away, Miss Hinkle's gloved hand on Winthorp's sleeve! Success!

"Do you know them? You look quite pleased."

"Pleased to have them off my bench." He glanced about. "Surely you aren't here by yourself."

She shook her head. "Phronsie is yonder, by the rubber plant. My nephew James wanted to pluck a leaf and roll it up and see if it bounced."

"What a capital idea! I don't suppose Mrs. King let him." He gestured behind him. "Would you like to try the comfort of my coveted seat? Not to mention Wilcomb's shortbread. Whoever your cook is at The Acres, the shortbread produced there could never compete with Wilcomb's for tender, buttery crumb."

"I've had Wilcomb's many a time, thank you," replied Aggie, accepting his invitation, "and I agree with you whole-heartedly."

The parcel was soon unwrapped, and Aggie had just tugged off her glove to accept a rich, buttery wedge when James and Phronsie pounced on her.

"What is it, Anaggie?" demanded James, dragging her hand toward his nose, just as Phronsie scolded, "Agatha, how *can* you?"

"How can I what?" asked Aggie, breaking off a chunk for her nephew.

"Eat something so messy? And in public?"

"I'm afraid it's my fault, Mrs. King," said Tyrone, standing up to make his bow. And, when no light of recognition dawned in her paler blue eyes, he added, "I'm Araminta Ellsworth's brother Tyrone. Agg—Miss

Weeks and I met by chance here, but Minta had given her some shortbread to deliver to me. Won't you have some?"

Mrs. King shuddered as if he had offered her sheep's trotters, but she was too wise a woman to object to the acquaintance. Why, everyone in Winchester knew the Ellsworths to be one of the first families, despite their patriarch's many marriages and resulting ill-assorted offspring. Araminta and Tyrone's mother, for instance, had been governess to the first two children, had she not? (Another shudder.) Yet what a handsome young man Mr. Tyrone Ellsworth had become! Somehow Sophronia had imagined him a masculine version of harum-scarum Araminta—all activity and perspiration and a tendency toward scrapes. But no. He shared his sister's height and health, but neither he nor his black academic gown appeared at all out of order. And the regular features which made his twin vaguely-attractive-to-sometimes-pretty were on him finely cut and altogether winning. Yes, indeed. He was an acquaintance the Kings could safely cultivate and even be proud of. If only Aggie would sit up straight! And what did she mean, getting her fingers greasy with biscuit? Not to mention getting Jimmy greasy with biscuit, for one taste of the shortbread and he was crowding at his aunt's knees for more.

Despite her vexation Mrs. King pinned what she imagined was a convincing smile on her face, revealing her prominent front teeth. "Of course I remember you, Mr. Ellsworth. What a delight to find you here. Let me see…surely you can't be taking your degree already this June?"

"I am." He offered his handkerchief to James, who was wiping his fingers on his trousers.

"Will you stay on, as your cousin Benjamin has and as Minta says Austin will do?" asked Aggie.

Tyrone twitched. "No, I think not. I mean, Ben and Austin will stay, tutoring until heaven affords them curacies or some such somewhere, but I intend to return to Winchester. I have not yet told my family, so if you wouldn't mind keeping that to yourselves until I've had a chance to write…"

They gave him their assurances, though Aggie clapped her gloved and ungloved hands. "Minta will be so glad to hear it."

"And we too are glad to hear it," rejoined Mrs. King, with another flash of her front teeth. "Think, Aggie, another gentleman to dance with at assemblies, *not* that you have lacked for partners."

Aggie's pale complexion flamed, and she stood abruptly, snatching Tyrone's handkerchief from her nephew to clean her own fingers before pulling her glove back on. "Hm. Well. Let us not bore Mr.

Ellsworth with such trivialities. We had better be going. I have got shops I intend to look into."

"We are staying at the Angel Inn," Phronsie went on, ignoring her sister's turnabout. "And I am certain Mr. King would be glad to host a dinner for you and your cousins. And any other friends you care to bring. It would be a nice change for you from always dining in Hall, I imagine. Tomorrow, perhaps? For I do believe my husband will be dining at the college with the warden and all of you this evening."

It was plain to Tyrone that Aggie resented the invitation being given, but it was also plain to him that she did so from no personal dislike of him. Not that he would have refused in any event, for college men never passed up a chance to eat at another's expense. Therefore he bowed once more to Mrs. King. "Thank you for your kind invitation. I know I speak for my cousins when I say we accept with alacrity."

"Good-bye, then," said Aggie, her lips thin. She took hold of her nephew's hand. "Thank the gentleman and come along, Jimmy."

She waited until they had walked as far as The Queen's College and little James was distracted by the bawling of a coachman. Then she seized her sister's elbow and hissed, "Phronsie, I won't let you do it!"

"Do what, silly creature?"

"I'm not a child anymore, and I know very well you are thinking of matchmaking again, and I will have none of it."

Sophronia pulled her arm free calmly and resumed walking, tugging on her curious son as the coachman's language grew stronger. "Be sensible, Aggie. Why should we not invite our longtime acquaintances to dine with us?"

"Longtime acquaintances, indeed. You would not know Mr. Benjamin or Mr. Austin Ellsworth to pass them in the street, much less any stray friends Mr. Tyrone Ellsworth might bring. You mean to force one of them on me, just as you and Frederica have thrust every eligible man in Winchester at me for the past four years."

"I would hardly call Mr. Benjamin or Mr. Austin Ellsworth eligible," was her sister's retort.

"Don't dodge me, Phronsie. You know what I mean, and you know it's true."

"And what if it is? It's ridiculous, how long you have pined for that worthless man! Frederica and I have talked of it—"

"That's just what I won't have," interrupted Aggie. "I won't have everyone talking of it. I won't have everyone interesting themselves in whether I marry or do not marry. What is it to them or to you? Papa has fortune enough, as we know. I will never be a burden on anybody. Nay, when I am unmarried, I am free to travel with you and help with the children, so what complaint can you have, that you should always be trying to marry me off?"

Mrs. King sighed the sigh of all married women who are anxious to marry off the world entire. "I would not have thought you the sort of girl who would not marry simply because others want you to. I thought you far more sensible than that."

This caught Aggie up short, and some of her belligerence deserted her. "I don't mean to be unreasonable about it, Phronsie. I simply wish everyone would believe me when I say I no longer pine for Mr.—for that man. You can't think how trying it is, to have people think such things and say, ah, that is why she doesn't marry, when the truth is, no one I've met since has tempted me."

A wiser woman than Mrs. King would have kissed her sister and said, "Very well, we will leave these things to time and chance and enjoy you all to ourselves as long as we can." Had she done so, odds were Aggie might have accepted the very next unexceptionable man who asked, but Sophronia had never been unduly burdened with wisdom.

"You won't let yourself be tempted," Mrs. King accused. "So how can you say you no longer pine for that person? If you didn't, what was so wrong with Mr. Wood? Mr. Archer? Mr. Clements, that you should refuse them?"

Little James stared with round eyes at his mother and aunt as they bickered in undertones.

"Mr. Wood was a blockhead," snapped Aggie. "Mr. Archer hadn't a word to say for himself, and Mr. Clements was *thirty* years older than I am, with daughters our age! How can you, Phronsie?"

"All right—never mind Mr. Clements. I didn't mean him." Mrs. King waved the ancient widower off. "But Philip said Mr. Wood had a good head on his shoulders—"

"A good *block*head," Aggie muttered.

"And, as for Mr. Archer, most men haven't much to say. There are days when I cannot get twenty words out of Philip. I thought you would prefer a man of action—"

"Action?" Aggie's voice rose, and her sister glared at her and beckoned her onward. "What action can be attributed to Mr. Archer except the trouble of standing up to dance with me twice or thrice and putting a pen to paper to make his indifferent offer?"

With another wave, Mrs. King dismissed the other suitors as well. "It is too late to persuade each other in any case. You have refused those gentlemen, and they have taken themselves off. You must start over with those whom heaven chooses to send. Take Mr. Tyrone Ellsworth, for instance—"

James gave a squeak as his aunt's hand fairly wrung his. "Do forgive me, Jimmy," she uttered hastily before releasing him to point a reproachful finger at his mother. "I knew it! You must stop, Phronsie. If you insist on pushing anyone at me, I will not cooperate. I will take dinner in my room."

"Now, now, Aggie, don't take on so. You needn't marry Mr. Tyrone Ellsworth, but surely you will admit he is neither a blockhead, nor wordless, nor thirty years older than you."

"It doesn't matter! I will not have anyone forced upon me. Not Tyrone Ellsworth, not the king himself!"

Here Mrs. King finally realized she had overplayed her hand, and she tried too late to retract, giving an uneasy laugh. "As you will, dear termagant. Of course I will not force anyone upon you, so there is no need to take dinner in your room. Let us simply do the polite thing and have the young men to dine, and then I doubt we will ever have to bother with them again."

But the damage was done, and Aggie was determined not to give her relations any encouragement in their interference. It would be too, too humiliating for the young men to think her paraded out for their consideration.

"I will be at the accursed dinner," she counseled herself, "but in body only."

Chapter 4

It were grete shame, sayd Robyn,
A knyght alone to ryde,
Without squyer, yeman or page,
To walke by hys syde.
— Traditional Ballad, *A Lytell Geste of Robyn Hode*
(c. early 1500s)

Tyrone no sooner sauntered past the porter's gate than Mr. Boulton seized him by the button. "What's this I hear about Winthrop walking with Miss Hinkle? Ginger Peaches said you had something to do with it."

"Dear heaven, the speed of New College gossip," Tyrone sad. "And do lower your voice, you halfwit." With a lift of his eyebrows, he indicated the warden's quarters directly overhead.

"You said you were retired," Boulton bit out, more quietly.

"I retired from epistolary lovemaking. Winthrop's job was purely oral."

"You fiend! Why didn't you offer the same bargain to me, then?"

"Perhaps because you do things like call me a fiend."

"You called me a halfwit." Boulton's sloping shoulders sloped further, and his habitual mournful expression returned. "I apologize for the 'fiend.' I am beside myself. I had the good fortune to meet your acquaintance Miss Weeks yesterday in the gardens, but now I do not know how I can proceed."

Tyrone shrugged heartlessly. "Why don't you write her your own note, Boulton? If you've already been introduced, the work is half done."

"But you said she hasn't got marriage in mind."

"And so she hasn't. My writing a note for you wouldn't change that."

"Your recommendation of me might," insisted Boulton. "Suppose you were to write a note in your own name and say, 'Have you met my good friend Boulton? You would like him.'"

"Such an idiotic note would likely have the effect of alienating Miss Weeks from both you *and* me. But I say, Boulton. Let me do you a good turn, since you call me unhelpful and think I have wronged you. It so happens that the Kings have invited my cousins and me to dinner tomorrow at the Angel. Yes—I ran into them in the Physic Garden, and I daresay they couldn't avoid the acquaintance. Nevertheless we are invited, and Mrs. King said I might include any 'friends' I choose."

"Ellsworth," gasped Boulton, his grey eyes lighting with hope. "I will give you anything! I haven't much money, of course, but—but—I can spare the half-crown. Or, if you prefer, I will do the imposition

Hastings assigned you for missing Prayers, if you have not done it already."

"I have not," Tyrone replied, delighted. He held out a hand to shake. "'A translation of one of Pindar's victory odes into sound English.' Mind you do me credit, and consider yourself invited."

It was a cheerful foursome which made its way along Queen's Lane to the High Street the following evening, or, at least, the Ellsworths were cheerful, joking and whistling, while Boulton marched as one to his doom.

"What does she like?" he asked. "Poetry? Music?"

"My dear man, I can only speak for what she liked when she was younger and would get into all manner of scrapes with my sister."

"Well, did she like poetry then?"

"She liked—*they* liked—sport. You know—archery, cricket, tennis, pall mall. Anything which involved being out of doors and rumpling themselves."

This did not hearten the young man. With his long, clumsy limbs, Boulton had never been one for sport, and he dearly hoped the young lady had outgrown the tendencies of her earlier years.

The Angel Inn occupied a wide frontage along the High Street just past the Corinthian pilasters of All Saints' Church and the covered market. As every coach rumbling into Oxford stopped there, the young men were long familiar with it, but that did not keep them from tidying their attire and standing straighter before they headed within.

"Gentlemen." Bald-headed Mr. King came forward to greet them, when the innkeeper pointed them to the sitting room. "How glad I am you could join us in a less formal setting than Hall. Ah, and Mr. Boulton, our new friend!"

Such an address nonplussed poor Boulton, and he could hardly bear to glance at Miss Weeks to see what she made of it. When he did work up the courage, however, he saw that she had made her general curtsey and retreated, hands folded quietly. Her pretty hair was curled and dressed, and she wore white muslin, and Boulton was alarmed to note what a fine figure the girl had, when not swathed in her looser pelisse. All the young men favored Miss Weeks with admiring looks, in fact, but she repaid their admiration with silence and stiffness. Both Tyrone and Boulton thought she had been much friendlier on the previous occasions when they met, respectively, with her little nephew near, but the boy was nowhere to be seen this evening, their hostess mentioning the nursemaid having charge of James and his infant brother.

To balance Miss Weeks' silence, Mr. King subjected the young men to a daunting inquisition which encompassed their progress at university, their opinions of New College and the state of intercollegiate relations, their future plans, their continued ties to Winchester, and sundry details about each of their families.

"Perhaps he'd like to inspect our teeth presently," muttered Tyrone to Austin.

"I will spare him the trouble of asking, then," replied Austin, with a flash of his ivories. "But if he asks to see the contents of our pockets, would you loan me a quid?"

"I am the son of a clergyman and one of six children," Boulton was just then being made to confess.

"Gracious," breathed Mrs. King, a hand fluttering to her chest. "Brothers or sisters?"

"Five sisters." And then, guessing her next question he added, "all unmarried."

"What a dreadful burden unmarried sisters are," spoke up Aggie. "Please accept our sympathy."

Tyrone chuckled, but intercepting the dark look Mrs. King gave her sister, he hastily smothered it.

"Not *all* my sisters are burdensome," Boulton replied earnestly, picturing his stock sinking rapidly on the marriage 'Change. "Anne—Miss Boulton, rather—the oldest—contrives to teach my father's Sunday school. And we have got high hopes that Charity, the sister next in age to me, will make a good match."

"Charity is the beauty of the family, I suppose," suggested Aggie.

"Yes. Or, so some have said."

Miss Weeks might joke, but even Benjamin and Austin Ellsworth knew the existence of Boulton's many sisters did him no favors and might even neutralize the virtue of his curacy in the Kings' eyes. Not that they aspired to Miss Weeks themselves. Indeed, both cousins were worldly enough to know that neither they nor Boulton had any sort of chance, should Tyrone stir a finger that direction. But odd things were happening. Because Tyrone did not stir, seeming content merely to observe and enjoy the company, and, for her part, Miss Weeks showed no inclination to win him. Quite the contrary. Inasmuch as one could do so in a room that held only seven people, she ignored him.

When the waiters began to bring in the food, the young men held back, waiting for Mrs. King to indicate where they should be seated. But before she could do more than raise a hand and open her mouth, Aggie was at the table. "I'll sit at your right hand, Mr. King," she told her brother-in-law. "And—Mr. Boulton, why don't you sit on my other side?"

"But *I* particularly wanted to speak with Mr. Boulton," insisted Mrs. King, not to be outmaneuvered. "As well as Mr. Austin Ellsworth. Therefore, Mr. Tyrone Ellsworth, why don't you sit on Aggie's other side, and Mr. Benjamin Ellsworth opposite her?"

Aggie did not miss the alarmed glance the cousins shared, and she would gladly have tossed her soup spoon at Phronsie, who began at once to quiz Mr. Boulton about St. Swithun's in Headbourne Worthy, while Mr. King turned to occupy Benjamin Ellsworth. A conspiracy!

I will not say a word to Tyrone, she vowed. *They will not get around me that easily.*

But it was Tyrone who said a word to *her*, after some minutes and almost inaudibly, between sips of soup: "I am to be the chosen one, it appears."

The note of amusement softened her, and she found herself breaking her vow at once. "I am sorry," she whispered. "It is so embarrassing."

"Surely you and I, who have known each other so long, need not suffer embarrassment."

"But people *will* be so horrid about it— matchmaking, I mean. I promise I haven't got any designs on you. Nor ambitions at present to marry."

"I did not think you guilty of either. Therefore, if I promise not to offer for you, no matter the pressure of your relations, why not be friendly? It will please your brother and sister and make the evening more pleasant all 'round."

Aggie bit her lip, stifling an urge to giggle. "All right, then. But you promise?"

On the pretense of adjusting his napkin, Tyrone pressed his hand briefly to his heart. "Promise. I here swear on pain of death, you could not induce an offer from me for love or money."

Then she did laugh, her blue eyes lifting to his, while the Kings looked on approvingly. Mrs. King at once lost all interest in Headbourne Worthy and Mr. Boulton's future housekeeping plans, calling down the table, "We did not hear earlier, Mr. Tyrone Ellsworth, what you will do when Trinity Term has ended."

"If you did not hear, madam, it is only because my plans are rather vague."

"Will you stay on at New College?" asked Mr. King, already knowing the answer because Warden Gauntlett had boasted of opening additional spaces for Winchester boys.

"I think not. I will return to Hollowgate. Perhaps study estate management with my father."

"You, Tyrone?" wondered Aggie. "A farmer? I always picture you with your head in a book."

"Farmers read. Think of Virgil's *Georgics*."

"I can't think of them," she replied, "for old Turcotte never taught us anything that wasn't in French or English or Italian, and really not nearly enough of that."

"Agatha!" Mrs. King reprimanded. "*Mrs.* Turcotte, please." She smiled at the guests. "Hers is the finest seminary for young ladies in Hampshire, I declare. We were fortunate to attend."

"And even more fortunate when our school days ended," Aggie replied. "At least, Minta and I felt that way."

Mrs. King gave an uneasy titter, and Aggie suspected she would have received a kick to the ankle, had her sister not been at the foot of the table, but Tyrone only said, "That's too bad. My youngest sister Beatrice rather likes Turcotte's, and she never thought she would. She was taught at home by my oldest sister and then by my stepmother until she was twelve, you know."

"Yes, I do know. Minta and I have marveled more than once at Bea's liking for Turcotte's. But really it makes sense. Beatrice has always been neat and well-mannered and composed, unlike Minta or me. She will end in being head girl, you mark my words."

"Bea is indeed an angel," Tyrone agreed, "compared to you two." Another grin cracked his handsome face. "Why, do you remember that one time—it must have been the summer after my first year at Winchester because everyone was reading Ritson's *Robin Hood*. Mr. Gregory came to call—he was still at the rectory then, and my stepmother, the third Mrs. Ellsworth, called you and Minta in from the lawn—"

But Aggie was already laughing. "Of course I remember—and how ill-mannered of you to mention it!" Her gaze swept the whole table, inviting them to join in. "Minta and I were wild for Robin Hood that summer. We played it constantly. It's what made us first take up our sad attempts at archery. Minta was always Robin Hood, of course, and I was Will Scarlet or Little John or Alan-a-Dale, as the mood took us. And that day—which Mr. Tyrone Ellsworth so discourteously mentions—we set upon little Beatrice to be Sir Guy of Gisborne—"

"When my stepmother called them in," continued Tyrone, "in marches Minta, looking a fright as always, and Aggie with ropes about her—"

"—Because I was Little John, and he was tied to the tree—"

'—But Beatrice! Oh, heavens! What had they done to Beatrice?"

Aggie forgot herself at this point, slapping a hand upon the board in her mirth. "Minta had found the second Mrs. Ellsworth's sable tippet, and we wound it around Bea because, if you recall, the ballad said Sir Guy was 'clad in his capull hyde, topp and tayll and mayne.' Well, sable fur isn't a horse hide, but it was close enough. How Beatrice's mother shrieked when she saw her! I have always felt guilty and thought the decline in her health dated from that day, but surely that can't be true."

"It isn't, it isn't," Tyrone assured her, with a motion of his fingers before her. "*Ego te absolvo a peccatis tuis.*"

56

"What a—charming story," said Boulton from his end of the table, though he sounded anything but charmed. "How sorry I am not to have known you, Miss Weeks, in your frolicsome childhood."

"You will have to settle for knowing her in her frolicsome young-ladyhood," Tyrone told him. "For I hope you haven't given up all frolics, Aggie."

That was twice he had called her not only by her Christian name, but even by her nickname, and Mrs. King hardly knew whether the dinner were going well or ill. Surely Mr. Tyrone Ellsworth seemed to like Aggie, but if he did not intend anything beyond friendly joshing, these tales of Aggie's wild ways and this overfamiliarity with her would do more harm than good.

Mr. King must have come to the same conclusion, for he turned on their most illustrious guest and began doggedly to speak of farms and harvests and crops and country living. Tyrone took the hint, as did Aggie, and the remainder of the meal passed off harmlessly, if dully. Aggie lapsed into what passed for demureness but was in fact only vacancy, and there was only one flash of her true self when the young men were taking their leave.

"Miss Weeks, I have greatly enjoyed this opportunity to further my acquaintance with you," Boulton labored, bowing over her hand.

"Have you?" popped out of her before she could think, but she didn't need Phronsie to clear her throat to amend this to a bland "thank you."

"Till June then," was Tyrone's farewell.

"Yes, June," she replied.

But when the others were exchanging polite words, he leaned toward her again. "Give Minta my love. And that wasn't too 'horrid,' was it?"

She had to agree—it had not been horrid at all. Indeed, it had been jolly fun until the Kings decided decorum must be upheld. After Aggie returned to Winchester, it would surprise her how fondly she thought on the evening.

Tyrone's enjoyment, on the other hand, ended almost the moment they departed the Angel Inn. For, no sooner did the young men cut up Turl Lane than Boulton turned on him.

"I saw what you were at, Ellsworth," he accused, actually lunging at him to seize fists of his gown in either hand. "*This* is why you wouldn't help me, though you fobbed me off with talk of the warden forbidding you." Boulton followed this charge with his best good shake, his limited strength largely dissipated, however, through distribution over his ungainly height.

"What on earth are you talking about, you fool?" It was Benjamin Ellsworth who thrust himself between them, quickly joined by his red-headed younger brother, while a startled Tyrone calmly worked his gown free of Boulton's grasp.

To the young man's credit, believing right on his side, he was not intimidated by this show of family strength. "You know very well what I'm talking about. I asked Tyrone here to ingratiate me with Miss Weeks, but he claimed he could no longer write notes and such. He then invited me to this dinner on false pretenses, asking me to write his imposition for Hastings in exchange, but I find he means to win Miss Weeks for himself!"

"Keep your voice down," said Tyrone coolly. "There's no call to trumpet her name in the streets. I assure you, I have no intention of winning Miss Weeks for myself. It's not my fault if her relations have got their own ideas, and it will comfort you to know she does not share them. In fact, to set her at ease tonight, I made her the distinct promise that I would *not* offer for her. You wouldn't have me go back on my word now, would you?"

Boulton's gloomy features crumpled and worked as he considered this. Tyrone Ellsworth bore a reputation for quickness, cleverness. That was obvious, or he would not be in such demand to pen poems and notes and proposals for others. But these qualities also made him difficult to read at times, and Gareth Boulton was not the first New College man afraid he was being gulled.

"You—don't intend to offer for her?" he asked cautiously.

"I do not."

"Then all that talk of Robin Hood and childhood frolics…?"

"Simply making conversation, my lugubrious lobcock."

Boulton straightened. Smoothed his stuff gown. "Very well, then. I apologize for my conduct just now. You will understand this is serious business to me. We are not all rich as Croesus with the leisure and freedom to do or not do as we please."

"Hear, hear," said Benjamin, giving the streamers dangling from the yoke of Boulton's commoner gown a playful flap.

"And while you might have thought me mercenary at first, I would never pursue a young lady whom I did not also find a respectable and worthy creature," Boulton declared. "Which Miss Weeks most certainly is."

"Most certainly," soothed Tyrone, his mouth twitching.

"And pretty, to boot."

Tyrone bowed.

"Therefore, having assured myself of your absence of intention toward her," he concluded, "I will call upon her tomorrow."

While Tyrone might be altogether skeptical of Boulton's chances for success, harmony had been restored, and the foursome continued on their way, now with nothing more troublesome in mind than perhaps harassing any Brasenose or Exeter collegians who might happen in their way.

Chapter 5

Zounds he makes Love like an Oxford Scholar.
— Daniel Bellamy, *The Perjur'd Devotee* (1740)

"Your sister has a cold," Mr. Philip King greeted Aggie when she descended to the breakfast room the following morning. "I had hoped we were done with ailments, now that the weather is turning warmer."

In most ways Mr. King was an exemplary husband and father, not given to the commonplace vices which so often prove the downfall of mankind. He neither drank immoderately, ate immoderately, gambled, beat his wife or children, or troubled the female servants of the household. But perfection is impossible, and if there were ever times Mr. King's conduct tried men's souls, it was when illness struck. While Mr. King could treat his own maladies with unparalleled tenderness, illness in others was another matter altogether.

"I am sorry to hear it," answered Aggie. "Would she like me to go up to her?"

"You had better stay away," he advised. "I have already instructed the nursemaid to keep the boys isolated, lest they succumb, and I will be taking a separate room for the remainder of our stay."

"Oh, dear," Aggie said, determining she would visit Phronsie as soon as Mr. King was gone. Which was soon enough. After sitting at the farthest possible distance from her, erecting a week-old newspaper as a barrier, and bolting his tea and toast, he escaped without another word, as if she herself were a source of infectious miasmas.

Phronsie's nose was red and eyes watery, but she was sitting up and even mending the infant's gown as she sniffled.

"Dear Phronsie. How are you feeling? Shall I fetch you anything?"

"*He's* gone, I suppose."

"He has. I could ring for tea."

"I've rung, thank you. But you might read to me a while and keep me company, Aggie, and perhaps take James out for a walk, if Mr. King does not prevent you."

Dutifully Aggie removed to the window seat overlooking the courtyard and took up the first volume of *A Summer at Brighton*. She hammered at this for a good half hour, not particularly interested in the tribulations of Sir Osborne Woodland's daughters or their estranged half-brother, though she did wonder if Tyrone had read the novel. In any event, the entrance of the chambermaid relieved her.

"A Mr. Boulton to see Mr. King," she announced with a bob. "But I told him Mr. King was out, and then he asked for you, madam, and I said you were abed—"

"Abed!" shrieked Phronsie, mortified.

"—And then he asked if the young lady was about, so I put him in the small sitting room—"

With a groan, Phronsie fell back against her pillows. "Go, Aggie. He wants to thank us for the dinner, I suppose. Very mannerly of him, but you will do to receive his thanks as well as any of us. I would be obliged if you explained that it is illness, rather than idleness which prevents me receiving him. And don't bother returning straight away, Aggie, for I am going to rest."

As the chambermaid promised, when Aggie entered the small sitting room off the central passage, she found the long and lugubrious Mr. Boulton warming himself by the fire. He sprang forward at once, torn between bowing and approaching, and ended in half tumbling toward her.

"Miss Weeks! What a pleasure."

Biting her lip so that she would not laugh, she made her curtsey and chose a chair, wishing she might prop her feet on the fender. "Mr. Boulton, I am sorry my sister could not receive you. She is ailing this morning."

"I am grieved to hear it," he replied politely, "and hope she will recover soon. I wanted to express my thanks for the invitation last night."

With a bow of her head, Aggie murmured the expected responses.

The niceties satisfied, a little silence took hold. She could hear the rumble of voices and clink of dishes from the adjoining coffee room and thought how warm and bustling and friendly it must be for young men to gather in such places. How she would love to sit among them and debate the best boxer of the day or the merits and demerits of horses training for the upcoming racing season. But about Mr. Boulton or his promised curacy she could not think of a single question, and she began to pick at a dangling thread of the chair upholstery.

He cleared his throat. "I hope *you* are well, Miss Weeks."

"Oh, certainly, thank you. I am rarely unwell."

"How marvelous. You look very…healthy indeed. As Bacon remarks in his essays, 'Tender and delicate persons have so many things to trouble them; which more robust natures have little sense of.'"

"Ah…true," said Aggie uncertainly. He thought to impress her with his education, she supposed, though being called "robust" brought to mind livestock and horse-breakers and Gargantua.

Mr. Boulton drummed his long fingers on his bony knee. "Do you enjoy Bacon?"

"I imagine you refer to the man, and not the meat." It was a feeble little joke, but she could not resist poking at his earnestness.

He was startled. "Oh! Yes, the man. Though—if it comes to it—I like *both*, rather. And—you, Miss Weeks?"

She sighed, her eyes drifting to the clock. "I haven't got much idea of Bacon the man, so I had better just say the meat." Heavens, how minutes could crawl by! And how inane conversation could be. If only Mr. Boulton had been accompanied by one of the Ellsworths—any of them. In an instant, thought became speech. "Did none of the Ellsworths want to come along with you today?"

Boulton straightened his long frame, like a worker placing a scaffold against a tower to support it. "I'm afraid I didn't ask them," he admitted. "For I most particularly wanted to come alone."

"Have you got something you wished to ask my brother?"

"No, Miss Weeks. Though I respect your brother and sister greatly, it was in truth you I hoped to see."

Her?

Comprehension broke over her like the time Minta cracked an egg on her head, and the yolk and white ran down, viscous and unpleasant. Aggie was tempted to fly the room, and had she still been fifteen, she would have.

Her companion was staring at his hands as Aggie fought back this urge, so he knew nothing of it.

"Ahem. Yes. It was you I hoped to see," he resumed, balling his hands into fists so tight the knuckles whitened. "Miss Weeks, when I first had the good fortune to meet you—"

"Two days ago," she interrupted. "You met me two days ago."

"Yes. Since I first had the good fortune to meet you two days ago, I have thought to myself that I have never met a young lady like you."

"Well, give it time, Mr. Boulton," she answered. "Two days is not very long to meet *any* young ladies, much less one significantly like another, and Oxford is not overrun with young ladies to begin with." She glanced once more at the clock. It had only been ten minutes. Perhaps in another five she could rise and thank him again and make her escape, but five minutes was five minutes too long!

She could talk. She could take charge of the conversation and lead it away from danger. She could deliver a monologue on Phronsie's symptoms and Mr. King's fears thereof. Yes—

But before she could begin, she heard the crackling of a paper. Looking over, she saw that Mr. Boulton had unclenched his hands and was clutching and consulting a crumpled note.

"Miss Weeks, I may only have known you two days, but I already find much to appreciate about you. Firstly, your family's residence in Winchester, as I too hail from Hampshire." He raised his head in the middle of his sentence to fix his gaze on her, much as a minister might single out a guilty sheep in his flock when railing against a particular sin.

His head dropping again, he squinted at his paper. "Secondly, the respectability of your family and connections—"

"Pardon me, Mr. Boulton," broke in Aggie, stretching a hand toward him. "Are you reading from a memorandum? Is this a course in philosophy?"

He crumpled the note self-consciously, but then, with valor, conquered his embarrassment and smoothed it out once more. "I am indeed reading, if you will forgive me, Miss Weeks. This was too important a matter to trust to impulse and memory." Adjusting his seat on his chair, he uncrossed his ankles and re-crossed them with the other leg on top. "As I was saying, connections and so forth—yes. And thirdly, you are a young lady of pleasing person—"

"Mr. Boulton," her voice rose, half in exasperation and half in alarm. "I will stop you there, if you please. I believe I know which way your—notes— tend, and I will simply say that we had better not pursue the subject."

"Not pursue it?" he echoed blankly.

"That's right." She rose at this point, deeming it near enough to five minutes gone that she might be excused. Boulton scrambled up in turn, his memorandum fluttering to the carpet, sending him diving after it.

Aggie covered her mouth with her fingers until she could be sure of her expression. "I thank you for your compliments, but there is no need to share any more of them."

"But Miss Weeks!" Now he waved the little paper at her, as if to imply that its very existence demanded it be read. "You do not know what all I have got to say."

"I do not, but I suspect I know enough."

"I should have begun with your pleasing person, I suppose—"

"No!" She fought a childish desire to plug her ears with her fingers. "No thank you, Mr. Boulton. If you will excuse me, I had better go. I will pass on your regards to the Kings, and I wish you a very good day."

"But can you give me any encouragement?" he called, bewildered, to the door as it shut behind her.

Either she did not hear him, or she affected not to hear him, or she did not deign to make a reply.

In any case, the door did not open again.

It was a gloomier than usual Gareth Boulton who made his way back to New College, and his spirits were not much recovered by the time he was dining in Hall, some hours later.

"Who died, Boulton?" Benjamin Ellsworth accosted him, as he and his brother and cousin took their places on the benches beside and across from him.

"Or is it too steep a descent from the culinary delights of the Angel Inn to the humbler offerings of Hall?" mocked Austin, eyeing the abundance of gravy and scarcity of meat in the bowl before him.

At the mention of the Angel Inn, Boulton shuddered, and Tyrone was too quick for him. "Don't tell me—you called there today."

"I did," confessed Boulton, flushing an uneven crimson.

"Are you mad?" demanded Austin. "You just met the girl, and you declared yourself?"

"I didn't declare myself!" Boulton cried. But then, seeing their skepticism, he added, "She didn't let me. She stopped me before I was halfway through my notes."

Benjamin nearly snorted out his ale. "Halfway through your notes? You not only attempted to make love to a young lady of whose existence you were ignorant last week, but you did so with notes in hand?"

"Well—if Tyrone wouldn't help me," growled the frustrated young man.

Tyrone laughed. "I will not be blamed for this. If you had told me what you had in mind, Boulton, I would have advised you to spare yourself, for the sake of all involved. I told you she isn't too keen on marrying, and did you think you could sway her after so brief a time?"

"I thought the game worth the candle."

"The game *is* worth the candle," Tyrone rejoined. "I do not disagree with you there. Miss Weeks is a fine and fair and sensible person. Which is precisely why you should have strategized and bided your time and not snatched at her like an impatient schoolboy."

Boulton huffed. "It's all very well for you to speak of strategizing and biding your time. I suppose if you had run at Miss Weeks, she would not have fled the room before you could finish speaking."

"Nonsense," said Tyrone roundly. "If I had 'run at' Miss Weeks this morning, she would indeed have fled, but not before scolding me soundly."

"Scolding you?"

"For doing it in spite of knowing better," he explained.

Boulton said nothing more of the matter, bearing the teasing and raillery until the table talk drifted to other subjects, but when they were dismissed and Tyrone swung his leg over the bench to go, he put a hand on his sleeve.

"I say, knowing Miss Weeks as you say you do, do you think I've ruined my chances forever?"

"Good heavens, man! I cannot believe you have formed so strong an inclination in so short a period. There are hundreds of other possible curate's wives out there, of whom many might come more easily to hand. Why not put her out of your mind and start afresh with another, when you have had time to absorb this day's lessons?"

"Just tell me then," Boulton insisted, "—you said she isn't keen on marrying. I thought every young lady was! What then makes her different?"

Tyrone grimaced and cast a glance either direction to ensure they were not overheard. "Suffice to say, she once loved a fortune-hunting rogue, who behaved as fortune-hunting rogues do, and now she is more cautious."

The blotchy color came and went on Boulton's face again. "Well, of course her fortune cannot be overlooked. It would be naïve to think it could."

His companion's deprecating gesture only made him more defensive.

"'Fortune hunter' is so crass a phrase!" Boulton complained. "As if it were not more than could be asked of human nature, to be indifferent to fortune."

"Perhaps it is," agreed Tyrone, eager to be done with the matter. "But you might sympathize with Miss Weeks as well. For is it not also more than could be asked of any young lady, that she not resent admiration aroused by something so wholly extrinsic to herself?"

Boulton's only response was a wordless grunt.

"That's right," said Tyrone, cuffing him bracingly on the shoulder. "'And thus I seal my truth, and bid adieu.'"

That Gareth Boulton did not there and then renounce any hopes of Miss Agatha Weeks was not due to any particular folly or obstinacy on his part. Indeed, he was no more unwise or stubborn than other young men his age. While he did admire her sizeable portion (being human), it was also true that, had she possessed no other virtues, extrinsic or intrinsic, beyond that portion, he would soon have persuaded himself that she would not do. Nay—on that little handwritten list Aggie and his fellow collegians scorned, he had catalogued her wealth in a modest fourth position, after her personal charms and before her amiable affection for her young nephew. Was not this proof of his relative indifference to money?

He thought so, certainly.

And if he had believed, before the day's rejection, that Fortune favored the bold, he was willing to account himself wrong. If Tyrone Ellsworth declared strategy and patience would take the prize, Gareth Boulton was willing to try them. After all, the church in Headbourne Worthy was a mere two-mile walk from Winchester.

No, indeed, he congratulated himself. Miss Weeks had not seen the last of him.

Chapter 6

Full many a wanderer to the paths of peace
Ere now hath made return.
— John Wilson, *The isle of palms, and other poems* (1812)

While they were not often separated, when they were, Aggie and her friend Araminta rarely corresponded. They were much more the sort who would get together instantly upon the traveling party's return and continue as if they had never been apart.

Therefore, when the maid at the Angel Inn presented Aggie with a letter from Minta, her first response was trepidation, rather than delight. "Oh, please—let nothing have happened to her or the baby," she prayed. She glanced down the table to her brother-in-law Mr. King. Both the boys and the nursemaid had now fallen victim to Mrs. King's cold, which meant that Mr. King could barely be called upon to exchange pleasantries with Aggie for fear her persistent visits to both sister and nephews made her the next to fall.

Under ordinary circumstances, Aggie would have attempted to be gentler, but in her haste she blurted, "I'm going for a walk. It is a fine morning. I can take Phronsie's maid."

And under ordinary circumstances Philip King would have asked questions and consulted proprieties, but this morning he only gave a shiver at her loudness and the quantity of possibly virulent air she directed at him. "As you wish," he muttered.

Phronsie's maid Sperling was not sorry to escape the confines of the inn, and she had the added virtue of being a quick walker. Within minutes the two women had turned into St. Mary's Passage and emerged in Radcliffe Square. There, leaving Sperling to admire the Camera, Aggie slipped a finger under the wax seal and unfolded Minta's letter.

> *68 Canon Street*
> *Winchester*
>
> *30 May 1808*
>
> *Aggs—*
>
> *All are well and in good health here, so that isn't the reason I'm writing to you. It's something else altogether, and I thought I had better warn you. Nicholas was so fidgety the past few days I insisted on knowing what troubled him. Brace yourself, dear Aggie—it has to do with Francis Taplin.*

Aggie drew a sharp breath, crushing the letter to her breast as if she feared someone might read it over her shoulder. Francis Taplin? Because those who loved her avoided all mention of the man who had nearly broken her heart four years earlier, she had never known what happened to him in any detail. He had vanished from Winchester, and his half-brother Nicholas Carlisle—Minta's husband—had put it about that Taplin had become a gambler in London, to the family's shame. As Aggie's own father Frederick Weeks held the mortgages to most of the ancestral Taplin estate, the prodigal son's return must surely indicate he had completed the ruin of his family at last.

> *For the first time since he last saw him four years ago, Nicholas has heard from his brother. I have never told you what I knew of the man (because Nicholas swore me to secrecy), but he did not merely run away to London to live as a gambler. In truth, Mr. Taplin had resumed his dealings with a woman there, and Nicholas said this person was at one and the same time also mistress to a peer of the realm! A marquess, no less!*
>
> *Mr. Taplin now writes to Nicholas to say this woman bore her noble lover an illegitimate son, wherefore all manner of gifts were showered upon her, in increasing amounts as the years passed, because the bastard child was healthy and cheerful and winning. On the strength of these riches, Mr. Taplin and this woman married in secret.*

Well, that tale would be shocking enough, but if it were all, I would not have caused you pain by sharing it. No, it is that Mr. Taplin's fortunes have now taken an even more astonishing turn. Because in January, Mrs. Taplin died of the measles! The marquess then came for the child, at which time he discovered the existence of his inamorata's secret marriage. It is more thrilling than a play, Aggie, because Mr. Taplin declares the nobleman offered him a generous sum of money to turn over the boy! The marquess made two conditions: (1) that Mr. Taplin henceforward relinquish all claim to the child, and (2) that he leave England, never to be seen or heard from again. Aggie, Mr. Taplin has accepted that offer. Therefore he states his intention to emigrate to America, and good riddance, say I. But the rub is that he threatens to come to Beaumond again before he departs, in order to say good-bye to his father and Nicholas.

Oh, Aggie, Nicholas says he hopes Mr. Taplin will not be in Winchester longer than a few weeks, but I suppose you will return from Oxford before he is safely gone, and I thought you should be warned.

*Much, much love,
Minta*

For a very long time after she read this letter, Aggie stood stock still, her unseeing eyes fixed on the curving shape of the Radcliffe Camera. She and Sperling were nearly alone in the Square.

Francis Taplin to be in Winchester again! She could scarcely credit it. With time he had taken on the indistinctness of a dream, and the revelation of his shocking adventures did not make him any more real.

It was not that Aggie feared seeing him again, though she did, a little. She could tell herself over and over that there was no danger there, but the proof of the pudding must be in the eating, of course. But greater than the dread of seeing him again was the dread of everyone *knowing* she would see him again. Everyone would watch her, whether from concern or from a desire to gossip, and she must bear it. Oh, if only she and the Kings might draw out their time in Oxford and miss him altogether! But Mr. King was anxious to return, as soon as his family's health permitted.

Could she herself pretend illness? Heaven knew if there were any threat of infection, her brother-in-law would not want to be closed in a carriage with her for the time it took to travel. But feigned sickness would require her to lie in bed in an overheated room for at least two days, doing nothing and consuming only gruel and tea, and Aggie did not think her active spirit could bear it.

For a moment she thought ruefully that she should have heard Mr. Boulton out. To return to Winchester betrothed would have made Mr. Taplin's reappearance irrelevant. Or at least only mildly interesting to their neighbors. They might then have said Miss Weeks was wise to choose a humble curate, rather than a hardened gambler.

But engaging herself to Mr. Boulton was nonsense too. To go to such lengths simply to avoid the discomfort of scrutiny?

No, she must brace herself, as Minta advised. It was better and more courageous to face it out. There would be one burst of staring and whispering behind hands and condescending expressions of pity, and then it would be done. She would ignore it all, she determined. She would pretend it did not exist. Pretend *he* did not exist.

The maid Sperling made an impatient movement, recalling Aggie to her surroundings. Indeed, who knew how long she had been standing there, lost in thought. The Square had grown busier. Undergraduates and fellows, dons and duns passed to and fro, some of them turning curiously to regard the pretty young lady. With a lift of her chin, Aggie pretended not to notice. It would be good practice.

But she was aware of a tremble in her midsection. This world of men—who truly understood it? Aggie had grown up with only her two older sisters and

Araminta Ellsworth for company. Apart from their enforced attendance at Mrs. Turcotte's Seminary for Young Ladies, she and Minta had romped and skylarked and done as they pleased until the summer Aggie fell in love with Mr. Taplin and Minta with Mr. Carlisle. Minta married her Nicholas, but though Aggie refused Mr. Taplin, she found the old days were gone. It was not that Minta no longer enjoyed sport, but she had less time for it after marriage, even if she and Mr. Carlisle had not taken up lodgings in Canon Street, a good twenty-minute walk from The Acres.

And that left Aggie.

Sperling stifled a snort of amusement, and Aggie looked over to see a doctor of divinity, clearly intoxicated, leaning against the rotunda for support as he stumbled along, apparently hoping to reach Brasenose. But as the Radcliffe Camera was circular in shape, the drunken scholar made no forward progress by following the wall. He rounded the building once, puzzled, and then a second time, before a friend rescued him and led him onward.

There was more to see.

"—But Miss Hinkle—" protested a young man in a gentleman commoner's silk gown, hurrying after a strapping young woman who strode ahead of him and her maid. Her velvet pelisse brushed Aggie's boot, and she paused to make an apologetic face before halting and pointing a gloved finger at the young man.

"Don't you Miss Hinkle me," she boomed at her pursuer. "You told me you would write me a sonnet, and you've done nothing of the kind. I'm tired of your silly compliments to my emerald eyes and cherry lips. Haven't you got any new ideas? Or did you only mean to trifle with me?"

"Miss *Hinkle*," he pleaded. (Aggie and Sperling retreated decently, but Aggie thought they might have gone all the way to the Angel Inn and still heard Miss Hinkle.) "Miss Hinkle, I *will* write you the sonnet. But I told you I had trouble composing—"

"You told me you had trouble composing when I was looking at you. I haven't been looking at you continuously, so you evidently found something of higher priority to do with your time."

"I can't write in Hall during dinner," he pointed out, "and then a friend of mine—Peaches—had a dessert in his rooms which took up the rest of the evening. I felt my head barely touched my pillow before the bell was going for chapel and the scout beating on my door to get me up again—"

"You were up all night drinking, I suppose, as you college men do."

The young man gave a deprecatory shrug. "I had just a little sherry, my angel."

"I am *not* your angel."

"I thought, when we went for our walk the other day—"

Miss Hinkle struck across this. "I only walked with you, Mr. Winthorp, because you promised me a sonnet. Come now," she wheedled, as much as a girl of her proportions and loudness could be said to do so, "say something pretty to me. You might use it in your composition later."

"I—er—"

"Sockfoot," Miss Hinkle commanded her maid, "you take it down. I want to be able to remember it." From her reticule she extracted a tiny notebook and pencil and thrust it at her attendant.

"I—I—" Winthorp panicked, and Aggie rather pitied him. He was turning alternately scarlet and ashen. "'Shall I compare thee to a summer's day?'" he gasped.

"Something *original*," huffed Miss Hinkle, arms akimbo.

"Dear Miss Hinkle," Mr. Winthorp began to wheedle for his own part, attempting to slip an arm about her waist. The shove this met with nearly overset him, and he stumbled backward, tripping over his own feet to land in a billowing heap of black silk, tufts and tassels, his square cap sliding off the back of his head.

By this point Aggie and Sperling were not the only onlookers staring, and the humiliation of it all threatened to overcome the poor suitor.

"I had help!" he wailed, struggling to rise and put himself to rights. "All right? I confess it. I had help."

"What can you mean?"

"I mean a friend who supplied me with some initial compliments to pay you. Because you were so—glorious—and overwhelming. And I wanted him to help me with a sonnet to you because he's better at that sort of thing, but he refused, and so I have been hoping you would forget about it."

In another moment Aggie thought he might begin to cry, and Miss Hinkle must have thought so too because she unexpectedly unbent.

"There now," she said, brushing dust from his shoulders and sleeves and straightening his cap. "Why didn't you just say the truth, instead of leading me to think you were the poetic sort?"

"Because you never would have walked with me," protested Mr. Winthorp.

"Maybe, maybe not," she replied. "But you should have more confidence in yourself. What was that you were saying just now—that I was 'glorious and overwhelming'? Did your friend come up with that too, or was it you by yourself?"

"That was—me, by myself, Miss Hinkle." His voice lifted a few degrees in hope.

"Well, it's a start." She bestowed a smile on him and wound her arm along his. "And for that start, we'll take a walk now, shall we?"

In a minute they were gone, leaving Aggie to shake her head in bewilderment. Maybe it was not only the world of men she did not understand. Maybe it was the world of men and women together.

Chapter 7

Sigh no more, ladies, sigh no more,
Men were deceivers ever,
One foot in sea and one on shore,
To one thing constant never.
— Shakespeare, *Much Ado About Nothing*,
II.iii.882 (c.1598)

"Aggie, dear," breathed her mother, the pale Mrs. Weeks, pressing a kiss to either cheek when her youngest daughter descended from the carriage. "How lonely we were without you."

"I could have walked from the George," said Aggie. "You didn't need to send the carriage." She submitted to a scratchy kiss from her bald and bearded papa and looped her arm through his as they entered the house.

"You could not walk alone from the inn," Mr. Weeks remonstrated, "and it would have been just as much trouble to send Banniker to fetch you. You know how easily that maid of yours is distracted."

"It's just as well she was not in Oxford with me, then, because there was so very much to distract. Men of every age, shop windows, coffee shops, bells tolling the hour at different times! I very much enjoyed myself, apart from Phronsie and the boys catching cold and Mr. King being so tiresome about it."

"We are pleased the trip was a success," her mother said, sounding distracted as she herded her daughter into the front parlor. "But there is another reason we wanted to whisk you home from the George."

Mr. Weeks followed and ominously shut the door behind them. "We wanted to be the first to caution you."

"I think I know what it is, then," Aggie said, turning to face them and folding her hands over each other. "And you are not the first to caution me. Do you mean to tell me that *he* is here?"

Mrs. Weeks gave a little gasp, and Mr. Weeks' brow darkened. "Has that blackguard dared to write to you?"

"Papa! He has not!" she cried. "But even if he had, do you suspect that, after four years' time, I would be in any danger from it?"

Her mother hastened to embrace her. "You mustn't be angry with us for fretting over it, dearest girl. If we did not know how true a heart beat within you—"

"How could we help but fear there might be danger?" her father interrupted. "In those same four years you have never attached yourself to another, though you have had several offers from, dare I say, worthier men—"

Aggie groaned. "Simply because I refused these so-called worthier men, it does not follow therefore that I have been wasting away for Mr. Francis Taplin. Yes! I am not afraid to say his name, and you should not shrink from hearing it. Mama just said you both were lonely without me—are you so eager to marry me off, then?"

"We would not have you heartbroken," pleaded Mrs. Weeks.

"I am not heartbroken!" She looked like a little bull, with her nostrils flaring in indignation. "I am not heartbroken. And I resent everyone assuming I am. Perhaps if we put an advertisement in the *Chronicle* or pasted up a shop-bill: 'Miss Weeks of The Acres, Winchester, kindly informs the Public that, while she has not yet accepted an Offer of Marriage, she is entirely, unequivocally heart-whole.'"

Her mother gave her stiffened form another squeeze. "If you say so, darling, nothing would make us happier."

"If you are as heart-whole as you say," persisted Mr. Weeks, "how is it that you already know of his—of Taplin's—arrival?"

"Because Minta *told* me! Yes—Minta actually put pen to paper and sent me a note. And if you don't believe me, you may ask her."

"Of course we believe you," Mrs. Weeks declared. Her husband did not echo her, and she shot him a reproving look.

"So we are not the only ones concerned," he observed.

A defeated sigh. "You are not." Untangling herself from her mother's arms, Aggie sank in an unladylike sprawl on the chaise. "Let me have the worst of it then. When did he arrive, and how long will he be at Beaumond?"

In a wink her parents flanked her, forcing her to sit upright, that they might all fit.

"It was Orton who saw him descending from the London coach yesterday," Mrs. Weeks told her breathlessly, referring to the family butler. "And though Mr. Francis Taplin was always a handsome young man" –this with an apologetic smile at her husband— "Orton reports that he is positively *glorious* now—"

"Sophy," grated Mr. Weeks.

"Frederick, it is no use pretending otherwise," she retorted. "—Glorious because of his attire. I know Mr. Carlisle his brother put it about that Mr. Taplin had been gambling in London, but clearly he has been not only gambling, but *winning*. Most gamblers I have had the misfortune to know were the ruins of their family, so I cannot think how Mr. Francis Taplin has succeeded where so many have not."

"He did not get it by gambling," Aggie said shortly. "Minta says he has been paid off by some peer of the realm to avoid a scandal and to go away. I had better not say more, but Minta says he will only be in the neighborhood temporarily because he plans to emigrate to America."

Such a bursting budget of news silenced her parents as it had Aggie the first time she learned it, but she was heartened by her father's evident relief. She also saw the dozens of questions rising to their lips and hastened to add, "I don't know much more than that. I don't even know the name of the nobleman, but he must be very rich, if he could afford to lavish money on sending such a person away."

"It would have been ideal if the Kings had remained in Oxford another week," sighed her mother, when she gathered her thoughts. "Then you might have missed him altogether. Nevertheless, I am grateful beyond measure that he likely will not be in Winchester long, and you might avoid him by remaining at home until he does go."

At this Aggie fired up. "It's not as if I want to see the man, but why should I be obliged to hide at home, when I have done nothing deserving disgrace? That is—I admit to being foolish when I was not yet nineteen, but surely not even the most hardened or wishful gossips in Hampshire can expect me to behave as I did then."

Her father gave a wordless grunt. Which was not precisely agreement, and Aggie felt another rush of indignation.

"If only you were engaged," Mrs. Weeks mourned, wringing her hands.

"Or safely married," said her father.

"Well, I am neither. And I have no intention of changing my state merely to silence neighborhood chatter. Nor do I intend to hide at home. Suppose he is here longer than a week? Will it not give people more to talk about, if they think I fear seeing him again and will not venture beyond the bounds of The Acres? Not only will they say I must still care for him, but they will tell each other that *you* do not trust me out of your sight, Papa."

Another grunt, but Aggie could tell she was turning the scale in her favor. Even if her mother had not cast helpless looks between daughter and husband.

Frederick Weeks slapped his knees with firm palms, the regard he turned on his youngest fierce and searching. "I *may* trust you, I suppose. There will be no secret notes, no climbing out of windows, no nighttime escapades?"

"You won't run away with him to America?" her mother beseeched her.

Aggie's bosom rose and fell, but she managed not to roar her impatience. She was two and twenty now, after all. Almost three and twenty. Instead she raised her own hand, as if taking an oath. "There will be no secret notes, no climbing out of windows, no nighttime escapades, and no elopements to America with Mr. Francis Taplin. There. May I do as I please? Are you satisfied?"

What choice had the Weekses?

They must needs be satisfied. And surely Francis Taplin would be the one to hide at home?

Despite her show of bravado, Aggie was not as confident as she pretended, and it was as much as she could do in the days following not to peer furtively over her shoulder or duck into doorways or alleys if she saw any figure remotely resembling Mr. Taplin. When Sunday came, the small congregation of St. Eadburgh's marveled at the bonnet Miss Weeks wore, its brim so enormous a small family could have sheltered beneath it. The measure was hardly necessary, as the Taplins of Beaumond belonged to a different parish, but Aggie was happy to be spared curious stares.

When a week had gone by, the swell of gossip caused by Mr. Taplin's return metamorphosed into umbrage that he refused to show himself. Was he even still in Hampshire, or had he fled again under cover of night? But Aggie felt the knot in her midsection begin to loosen. So much so that she agreed to accompany the Kings to the assembly in Upper Brook Street. It would be a small one, peopled by local gentry, as the race season had not yet begun. And as most of the gentlemen who might attend had already proposed to her and been refused, it seemed a safe enough venture.

To her delight, the first young man she saw when she entered with the Kings was Tyrone Ellsworth. She did not know how she picked him out so quickly, having no expectation of seeing him again until after Trinity Term ended the following week, but there he was, tall and golden as his twin sister. Without his academic gown, she could see how his evening coat stretched across his broad shoulders to a nicety, and though his build was slender, there was nothing starved or meager about him. It was only the memory of how eagerly the Kings had pushed her and Tyrone at each other that stayed Aggie's impulse to seek him out and tell him frankly that he should ask her to dance.

But maybe he sensed her keenness, for he turned from talking to his brother-in-law Mr. Fairchild, his eyes sweeping the assembly room and lighting on her. At once a cheery grin lit his features, and his hand rose from his side in greeting, only to halt just past his waist as his entire person froze.

Aggie, who had drawn a breath in preparation of smiling and waving in return, checked her own movement. Had he mistaken her for someone else? Only see how his hand dropped back to his side and his smile vanished! But he was not alone in his inexplicable change. To either side of Tyrone, heads turned toward her; lips parted; arms were touched; fans were raised; a murmur of voices rose.

What on earth? Have I got something stuck to my face? Have I turned purple?

"Come along, dearest. And do hurry," whispered her sister Mrs. King, hitching an arm under hers and fairly tugging.

And then Aggie understood. *He* must have entered behind them.

In spite of herself, her breath quickened and her limbs seemed blocks of wood. She almost stumbled when Phronsie pulled on her. "I feel…faint," her older sister said. "Yes. Faint. Why don't we go into the coffee room and sit awhile? Or perhaps even—perhaps this wasn't a good idea to come tonight. I've been weak after my cold—"

"Stop it, Phronsie," Aggie hissed. "I know what you're doing. And I know you're perfectly well."

"Then *come*." Through gritted teeth and barely parted lips. Another jerk on her arm. "The cheek of that man! Showing up here, where you might be present, after all Winchester remembers how you threw yourself at him!"

All Winchester might remember her heedless conduct at eighteen, but Aggie did not intend all Winchester now to remark how Miss Weeks hid from the man who had broken her young heart. She gave a pull of her own, trying to work her arm free from her sister's grip. "He is merely another of my rejected suitors, and I am not going to run away." She might feel like throwing up, and her face might be hot with self-consciousness, but this must be faced.

"Ah, Miss Weeks. And Mrs…King, was it not?"

She had forgotten the smoothness and charm of his voice.

There was no alternative but to turn. Even Phronsie could not cut him, when he dared to address them directly. The two sisters dropped into their curtseys, and then Aggie raised brave eyes.

In a flash she took him in. Not just his appearance but the man in total. From his perfectly dressed hair and fine tailoring to the twist of his handsome mouth and the gleam in his eyes.

And he was a revelation. But not in the way she feared he might be, after all these years. No. She did not see Mr. Francis Taplin again and feel past wounds tear open. She saw him, and as with Saint Paul under different circumstances, immediately there fell from her eyes as it had been scales.

Aggie at nearly three and twenty years of age saw plainly that he was a dissipated man. The overwhelming handsomeness of his youth was now giving ground to the years spent in self-indulgence. He was hardened in attitude yet softening in person, particularly about his middle. And she saw for the first time his potential for cruelty. Not a cruel cruelty, if that made any sense, but rather a disposition to think firstly, and always, of himself.

There was no possible danger to her now. Only a pang, a regret of her own blindness and the time wasted mourning so unworthy a person.

"Will you do me the honor of dancing with me, Miss Weeks, if only for the sake of our long acquaintance?"

It was the last thing she wanted to do, but if she refused him, she could not dance the entire evening, and Aggie had no intention of sacrificing any more pleasures on the altar of this fallen idol. Ignoring Mrs. King's indrawn breath, Aggie laid a light gloved hand on his arm and let him lead her to the floor.

It was some minutes before they spoke. For her part, she was determined not to and hardly paid him the courtesy of eye contact, preferring to regard his right ear. She suspected, from the way he began to bob his head around, that he was trying to make her look at him, and this only increased her stubbornness.

"Miss Weeks, allow me first to say that you have fulfilled the early promise of your beauty," said Mr. Taplin at last, when they had been thrice through the figures.

"Hm," Aggie murmured.

"I was quite crushed by your refusal of me," he went on. "It was one of the reasons I have been so long from Winchester."

"Oh?" Honestly, what would the man tell her next? She could not resist saying, "What were some of the other reasons?"

Instead of appearing abashed, Taplin only gave a sigh. "Who can say what drives a young man to do what he does? I am a restless soul, Miss Weeks. I must wander. In fact, I have decided my wanderings will take me next to America."

"It's well that I refused you, then," Aggie said stoutly. "For I have no desire to go so far from home."

"Haven't you?" In taking her hand to lead her up the set, he tickled his fingers along her gloved palm, and Aggie avenged herself by flicking him as hard as she could with her own thumb and middle finger. Sadly, between their two layers of glove she could not cause him pain and had to content herself with his start of surprise.

Something of her indignation must have shown, for her eye caught Tyrone Ellsworth's down the line, and he raised a humorous eyebrow. Aggie's mouth quirked, and she felt her mood lift. It *was* ridiculous, after all. Did Mr. Taplin think her such a booby that he could recommence his assault as if no time had passed?

It seemed he did.

"How lightly you dance, Miss Weeks."

"Thank you."

"It is as if I were accompanied by a faerie on an enchanted midsummer eve."

Oh, for heaven's sake. That one received only a smirk from her. It did amaze her, however, to see a share of young ladies peeping at her partner with what could only be called admiration. The damsels to either side of Aggie were among these, and when the dance called for them to join hands in circle, Aggie thought the one to her right would faint, she went so crimson and clumsy.

"So," she rejoined, "what makes you want to go to America next?"

"With the country at war, there are few other places where I might satisfy my desire for travel."

"There's Bath," she suggested. "Or Cornwall. Or Scotland, say." She wondered if she could force him to admit he had no choice in the matter.

"Have you been to any of those places, Miss Weeks?"

"Not a one. Have you?"

"Not a one."

"Then why run all the way to America?"

"Are you hoping to persuade me to stay?" he smiled.

"I wouldn't presume." In a mildly belligerent tone she added, "You might go to the moon, if it pleases you."

"It might please me," he answered, ignoring her rudeness. "So much of one's enjoyment of any place depends on one's company."

That might have been the first true word he spoke all evening. Aggie's attention drifted to Tyrone again, and she saw him talking to his partner, a willowy creature with piles of chestnut hair. How much more fun it would be to dance with Tyrone than Mr. Taplin! But would Tyrone ask her? Surely he would.

"You like the young man?" inquired Taplin, following her gaze. "There's something familiar about him, although his features are so commonplace people must often think that."

"Have you forgotten him? He is the twin brother of my friend, the former Miss Ellsworth. Had she accepted your offer, he would have been your brother."

"Miss Ellsworth...oh—haha! My brother Nicholas's wife. Is it not marvelous how things work out? She who would have been my wife is now my sister, and he who would have been my brother is now my brother's brother. Which would make him my second brother, if there were such a thing. Ah, family."

"Will you miss your family, when you are so far away?" she asked politely. They had reached the top of the set and would only have to repeat the pattern once more, by Aggie's estimation.

"I will." He said this with a sudden return to seriousness—or flirtatiousness. That is, he squeezed her hand most unmercifully and leveled half-closed eyes at her in a killing fashion. "Therefore I thought I might bring family with me."

"The Carlisles will never go," she told him shortly, flexing her fingers when they were free again and scowling at him.

"Oh, I did not refer to Nicholas and his wife. I meant I hope to bring along a wife of my own."

Her incredulous snort was drowned by the closing strains of the music. Thanks be to God. A wife of his own, indeed! If Mr. Taplin thought she would greet his hint with joy, he would be sadly disappointed. But here was a whole roomful of poor simpletons with whom he might try his luck, and Aggie did not doubt he could succeed.

But whichever foolish young lady jumped at the chance to be Mr. Francis Taplin's chosen companion in exile, it would not be Agatha Weeks.

Chapter 8

No scholar…shall…be allowed to have Dogs, Guns, or Nets, for the destroying of Game, to the Injury of others, and the loss of their own Time.

—Oxford University, *Statutem de reprimendis sumptibus non Academicis* (1772)

From the serene expression on Aggie's face as Mr. Taplin returned her to her sister's side, few would have guessed at her inner confusion, but Mrs. King did not need to guess.

"What did he say to you?" she demanded, the moment Mr. Taplin moved away. "What could he possibly have had to say to you?"

"He wanted to flirt," admitted Aggie. "He wanted to behave as if nothing had happened and no time had passed."

"Oh, Aggie," her sister moaned. "What shall we do? Are you in danger again?"

"Of course not. Don't be ridiculous, Phronsie," she frowned.

"If you had only seen how everyone here was watching you, to see if you would faint or weep or whisper or—"

"And I did none of those things."

"But did you *want* to?" Mrs. King pressed.

Aggie was spared answering by the approach of Tyrone Ellsworth, but the little fillip of excitement which shot through her was quashed at once by her sister's satisfaction. "See here, Aggie—Mr. Ellsworth would make you a far better match, if you would only consider him! He is everything worthy: handsome, rich, good family—eek!" Aggie's ruthless pinch abbreviated Phronsie's list.

The sisters made their curtseys.

"Mr. Ellsworth, what a pleasure to see you again," Mrs. King purred. "We did not expect to, so soon. Has Trinity Term already ended?"

"It has not, Mrs. King. I'm afraid I've been sent down."

Aggie stared, and her sister choked in surprise. "S-sent down? Ahem—ahem. Excuse me. Oh, dear. But I thought you were about to receive your degree."

He grinned. "I was. And I am relieved to say it is not in jeopardy. Warden Gauntlett and I were able to come to an understanding—I would leave New College a little earlier than planned, and he would hurl my diploma after my unworthy head."

"But Tyrone—I mean—Mr. Ellsworth," cried Aggie, "whatever did you do to disgrace yourself?"

"Agatha!" hissed Mrs. King reprovingly. She imagined all manner of offenses common to young men, none of which could be mentioned in public. But even as she did so, she decided that, if necessary, they could and would be overlooked.

"Dance with me, and I'll tell you about it," he replied.

And while Aggie would have liked to thwart her sister's obvious desire to pair them, she did want very much to hear Tyrone's explanation. Moreover, dancing with Tyrone would demonstrate to the entire assembly that she did not intend to stand against the wall all evening, gazing besotted at Francis Taplin.

They took their places in the set, Aggie's eyes widening to note the admiring and jealous glances she drew from the other young ladies and their mamas. It was plain they thought she had already been favored by the two most desirable men present. If only the mamas knew the half about Mr. Taplin! Then they might gather their chicks closer and cease to resent her. Whatever Tyrone had done to get himself sent down from Oxford, Aggie was certain it could not compare to Mr. Taplin's misadventures.

"What did you do, then?" she asked, hardly waiting for the music to begin.

"When was the last time you were at Hollowgate, Aggie?—But perhaps I really ought to acquire the habit of calling you Miss Weeks."

"But if you call me Miss Weeks, I will be obliged to call you Mr. Ellsworth, and I don't know if I can manage it."

"Of course you can. In any event, we had better make the attempt, or we will be constantly blundering."

"Very well," she sighed. "To answer your question, Mr. Ellsworth, I haven't been at Hollowgate for months, at least. Though I see Minta in town constantly, and she comes often to The Acres."

"Well, you will have to start calling at Hollowgate again, if you hope to know why I was sent down," he replied mysteriously, with that humorous lift of his brow which made Aggie laugh.

"Oh, please tell me! I will still come, but you must tell me. You said you would, if I danced with you." She remembered Mr. King telling her sister of the undergraduates' "disgraceful" capers and pranks, most involving women and endless drink, but surely Tyrone had not brought back either of those to Hollowgate, she imagined.

"Would you not have partnered me without that lure?" he asked as they armed left and then right.

"I would have, but a promise is a promise."

"All right, then. There were multiple reasons I was sent down."

She held her breath. *Multiple*? Good gracious—it was the women and the drink, then.

Tyrone burst out in a laugh that made heads turn. "You should see your face! I think you've already got me down for—what is it?—smuggling, disturbing the peace, and fathering four children?"

"You!" She gave him a smack on the upper arm and heard a mama or two suck their breath in through their front teeth. Or maybe that was Phronsie, from clear across the room. Aggie was relieved, nonetheless. She would have hated to think Tyrone as degenerate as Mr. Taplin.

"If you come to Hollowgate," he resumed, "you will *meet* the multiple reasons for my premature expulsion. Or two of them, at least. The others I gave away. Because it's puppies, my dear Miss Weeks. I concealed a litter of them in my rooms at New College. Six altogether. And while Oxford might grudgingly overlook a single dog, if it be kept with a measure of decorum, a full litter of unruly puppies was deemed beyond the pale."

She had so many questions she could hardly begin. "One really is allowed to keep a dog at Oxford?"

"Not *allowed*, Miss Weeks. In fact, it has always been frowned upon and was expressly forbidden by statute earlier in the last century. Nevertheless, a number of dogs continue to be kept, even by the fellows."

"Is that how you came by these puppies? You kept a forbidden dog, which then produced them?"

He completed the figure-eight before responding. "No, it was precisely because I had no dog that my friend Ginger Peaches thought I would be the best one to saddle with them."

"Ginger Peaches?" echoed Aggie, picturing rosy summer fruit.

"Gerard Pinchbeck," he explained shortly. "The puppies had been given him by his sweetheart, who said her father intended to drown them if they were not got rid of. She appealed to Ginger Peaches, and he appealed to me. He told me to keep them for a week or a fortnight, at the uttermost, during which time he intended to sell them throughout the university population. But before his enterprise could be carried out, I was exposed and expunged."

"Alas," breathed Aggie. "But who exposed you, Tyr—Mr. Ellsworth? Was it the scout who cleaned your rooms?"

"No, no. Roark and I were on good terms."

"A hostile classmate, then? Or a tutor?"

He gave her a measuring look, and Aggie suspected he was determining what was fit for a young lady's ears, even if that young lady had been his harum-scarum twin's boon companion. "No…it was…another who peached. It doesn't matter who. Suffice to say, Gauntlett—the warden—was not well pleased. But *you* will be, Miss Weeks, when you see the cunning little creatures. I chose the stoutest, sleekest, roly-polyest pair for home. You remember how sad my sister Beatrice was when our terrier Snap finally departed this world? Well, she is much comforted by Scamp and Pickles. They're alike as two peas, brown and white, except Scamp has a black patch over one eye."

Aggie clapped her hands in delight. "I'll come as soon as I may to see them. What does Mrs. Ellsworth think?"

"Oh, they have charmed the entire household. I even caught Bobbin the footman petting them, and you will recall how he loathed Snap. But Scamp and Pickles confine their nipping and chewing to the inanimate and leave ankles in peace."

"Has Minta seen them yet? Perhaps Bea and I could walk them to Canon Street."

"She has, but you would be welcome to try. You and Bea would have to carry them, however. I'm afraid they haven't got much patience with the leash as yet."

"Were your friends very sorry to have you leave Oxford before term ended?" was her next question, and a grin fleeted across his face before giving place to something harder to interpret. Here was another secret, apparently, and as with the name of the puppy snitch, it was another one he intended to keep to himself.

"They bore it remarkably well," he answered at last. "And, since they are all alumni of Winchester College, I will see them every Election Week at least, when old Wykehamists gather. We quite have the advantage of you Turcotte's alumnae there."

Aggie gave an expressive shudder. "Minta and I could not wait to get quit of most of our schoolmates and the headmistress, and I suspect the feeling was mutual. I know Beatrice likes it at the school, but Bea has always been so neat and proper and *good*. With Minta and me, all that went against the grain, you know."

Instead of smiling as she expected, Tyrone looked thoughtful. Twice his lips parted to speak, and twice he closed them again. Aggie gave him one full time through the pattern of figures before losing patience.

"What is it? What are you afraid to say?"

He took a deep breath, as if to brace himself, but she saw a mixture of alarm and humor in his eye.

"What you say is true, Miss Weeks. You and Minta were always apt to get yourselves in scrapes. Therefore—I wonder—" He gave a helpless shrug. "You will think me impertinent now, but I must claim the rights of an almost-brother."

"Gracious! What insult are you about to offer me? If it's a very bad one, I will claim my own rights as your almost-sister and cuff you again." Had someone from Turcotte's Seminary spoken ill of her? As she cast outward, she glanced down the line of dancers to where Tyrone's earlier partner, the willowy creature with piles of chestnut hair, was doing the same. That one, for instance—was she a Turcotte's girl? She reminded Aggie of someone, but she could not put her finger on it at present.

"We are agreed, then, Miss Weeks," resumed Tyrone, when the figures brought them back together.

"And I will risk it, though it's as much as I'm worth to ask."

"Let's have it," she urged.

"It's this: I did not expect ever to see Francis Taplin again in my life, but here he is. And when I saw you dancing with him—" That was as far as he got before the fire in Aggie's eyes silenced him.

"Go on. You saw me dancing with him. And what impertinent question did that give rise to?"

A deprecating gesture with his palms. "You are angry. But I would have you recall that I was present, that time you climbed out of your bedroom window to seek him."

She might have been made of stone, her carriage was so stiff when they armed left and right again. "I recall. But on *that* occasion, sir, I had a message to deliver."

"A message which could not wait until morning, nor be delivered by a servant?"

"What is your point? Why do you throw in my face the foolish actions of years ago?"

"Do you consider them foolish now?"

"Would I call them the 'foolish actions of years ago' if I now thought them wise?" she snapped. "For the last time, sir, what is your question?"

Tyrone regarded her a moment longer, appreciating the sparks in her normally mild blue eyes.

He had always thought of her as Araminta's lieutenant, but now he realized that, too, was years ago.

"My question is, as Taplin finds himself again in Winchester and still single, have you got any lingering desire to attach him?"

A seething stew of embarrassment and indignation bubbled over within her. He might be her almost-brother, but his question was more than impertinent. It was *none of his business.* And if he thought—as the whole world seemed to think—she wanted to attach Mr. Taplin again, he was as benighted as the rest of them!

Aggie was no actress, and Tyrone could see she was furious. Well—it was worth it, to put her on her guard.

"Because I suspect he would be willing to consider the matter again," he went on slowly, "judging not only from his asking you to dance but also from the number of times he has looked this way."

The only response was a wrathful flare of her nostrils.

"And I would warn you, *Aggie*, that there have been whispers he was up to no good while he was away in London. I would not wish your heart broken again."

If she had not been so vexed, she would have thought it amusing to hear herself leap to Mr. Taplin's defense, despite being in complete agreement with Tyrone's opinion of the man. "I think you are all dreadful," she hissed, "with your whispers and your gossip and your well-meaning interference. Can you not leave a person in peace? Can a person not be allowed to have grown and changed? And if this is what you mean by being 'almost' my brother, I gladly excuse you from the role. Do not presume again to advise me in this affair."

He took a step back from the line of dancers, once more turning his palms upward: *I have said what I wanted to say.*

This seeming capitulation only made her more cross. Oh, he was willing to retreat now, was he, after he had already struck home with the dagger!

Their next pass through the pattern of the dance was wordless, Aggie hardly willing even to look at him. He ventured a remark about seeing a greater crowd gathered to dance once the Winchester races began, but her only reply was an unladylike grunt.

Tyrone clicked his tongue, half entertained and half chagrined. "Aggie, Aggie…"

"It's 'Miss Weeks,' I thought, Mr. Ellsworth," she said coolly.

"Are you not going to speak to me for the remainder of the dance, Miss Weeks?"

"Not if we are going to discuss what need not concern you." But she tossed her head and decided to carry the battle into his territory. "Why do we not talk about *your* dance partners, Mr. Ellsworth? Who was the unfortunate young lady you lately stood up with? I don't believe I recognize her."

"That may be because she is younger than you and Minta," he teased. "Because her mother told me when we were introduced that Miss Caraway has just emerged from Mrs. Turcotte's Seminary for Young Ladies, where she covered herself in glory as head girl."

"Miss *Caraway*?" whisper-screeched Aggie, her head jerking to regard Miss Piles-of-Chestnut-Hair with new eyes. "Her name is Miss Caraway? Can it be possible *that* is Clumpy Caraway?"

Tyrone bent with smothered laughter. "Good heavens. If by 'Clumpy' you mean 'Clementine,' I'm afraid it is. I never thought you and Minta guilty of cruel nicknames, having always believed it the particular province of young men."

"Minta and I didn't make the name up," she said, still marveling at the revelation. "It's what her cruel older sister—the original Miss Caraway and also a head girl—called her. She—Clementine—was rather round and squat back then. The first Miss Caraway ruled over the seminary, and Clumpy must have grown to follow in her footsteps."

"I can at least reassure you that the younger Miss Caraway does not strike me as cruel," Tyrone answered. "Dashing and witty, yes, but that need not shade into cruelty. Though, now you mention it, I have lit on who she reminds me of. It's Wyatt's poem about

Anne Boleyn—'Brunet that set my wealth in such a roar.' Did you read that one at Turcotte's? No? Too bad. It was originally 'Her that did set our country in a roar,' but Wyatt deemed that too dangerous to say. Let us hope Miss Caraway sets neither my wealth nor the nation in a roar. Thankfully, she seems lively good humor itself."

Aggie bit back a scoff. "I'm not surprised," she said dryly. "She was dancing with an eligible young man."

Again he clicked his tongue, his expression innocent. "Oh, Miss Weeks—are you so hasty to think ill of her? Can a person not be allowed to have grown and changed?"

He should not have said it, he thought later. Not when he had succeeded in getting her to speak again. But this reference to her earlier defense of Taplin silenced her at once, and the sparks returned to her eyes. Yes, Miss Caraway might not set things in a roar, but clearly Tyrone knew how it could be done with Miss Weeks!

They were delivered from their discomfiture soon enough by the musicians' closing strains, and Tyrone returned her to her sister's side. But, try as Mrs. King might, for the remainder of the evening she could not draw from Aggie another word about either Tyrone Ellsworth or Francis Taplin.

Chapter 9

He seemed desirous enough of recommencing courtier.
—Samuel Johnson, *Prefaces, biographical and critical, to the works of the English poets* (1781)

Despite the late hour of the assembly, Tyrone appeared in the breakfast room of Hollowgate only a few minutes later than usual, pressing back a yawn with his hand.

"There he is," declared his father William Ellsworth, beaming to have added one of his children back to the fold. They were sadly dwindled in number now, with three daughters married, and Tyrone was a welcome sight beside fourteen-year-old Beatrice and seven-year-old Willie. "Our Oxford graduate."

"A sort of one, at any rate," murmured Beatrice, giving Scamp another kiss and setting him back on the floor. (Tyrone had been dismayed to find his baby sister grown not only more womanly in his most recent absence, but also more satirical.)

Mr. Ellsworth ignored her slighting remark, as he did all unpleasant things. "And your mother and I were just observing how you are already missed by your friends." He indicated the stack of letters beside Tyrone's plate.

"I had no idea young men were such devoted correspondents," said Mrs. Ellsworth with her gentle smile.

"Everyone loves our Tyrone," his father pronounced. "Mrs. Ellsworth, we have been so blessed."

Tyrone, however, did not share his family's surprise at his pen-averse schoolmates troubling to write. Flipping quickly through his post, he plucked out his cousin Benjamin's letter first. The scrawl was brief but satisfying: "Ty—You were right. Now that you are no longer answerable to Gauntlett, the recommencement of our little business has met with great joy. I will collect funds, to be paid out monthly with a draft on the banker but told customers to write to you directly. Made a uniform list of Qs for new applicants. Do keep a tally so we can reconcile. – B."

No sooner had the puppy verdict gone against him at university, than Tyrone realized his expulsion ended his subjection to Oxford's statutes and strictures. Which meant he and his cousins might resume their profitable venture, providing interest and amusement to Tyrone and heaven-sent income to Ben and Austin. His cousins leapt at the news, and here was the result.

"With so many letters to answer, will you not be able to ride out with Falk and me today?" asked Mr. Ellsworth, referring to his steward.

"No, of course I will," replied his son, pushing the stack aside and attacking his breakfast. "These can be answered at my leisure, and I am eager to start my apprenticeship."

"You will have a little time, in any event. Falk does not expect us until eleven."

"How was the assembly last night?" asked Mrs. Ellsworth, shaking her head at little William when he slipped Pickles a crust beneath the table. "Were there familiar faces to welcome you home?"

"I saw Aggie," said Tyrone around a mouthful of toast. "With the Kings. And that Francis Taplin was there."

His parents exchanged glances, and Willie continued to eat steadily, but Beatrice sat bolt upright in her chair and dropped her spoon with a clatter. "That horrid rascal? I hope you cut him, Tyrone!"

"Now, Beatrice," soothed her stepmother. "You never cared for him when he was pursuing our Araminta, but that was all long ago."

"That may be," rejoined Bea, "but if you heard the talk at Turcotte's, you would know that all the older girls whisper about his return, and the rumors of how he spent the last four years only add to the glamour he casts over them. You wait and see—he'll try to marry someone respectable yet."

"I didn't cut him," Tyrone took up her earlier remark, "because we didn't speak. He did dance with Aggie, however, as well as with—"

"Aggie danced with him?" interrupted his youngest sister. "Oh, dear. Minta will be beside herself when she hears."

"Then Minta shouldn't hear," Mrs. Ellsworth said firmly. "There is her health to think of."

Tyrone pulled a face. "If it's any comfort to you all, I sounded Aggie on the matter when I danced with her, in order to warn her."

"And how did she respond?" asked Beatrice.

"With ire. But she is not an unreasonable girl. Even if she still thinks of him, I don't expect she will do anything rash after so much time. Moreover, surely Taplin will not renew his offer. Remember how Mr. Weeks threatened to cut her off without a penny if she married such a person? I'm certain the threat would still pertain."

"Only, Taplin isn't penniless anymore," Beatrice pointed out. "Or at least he doesn't dress like a penniless person."

"He never did. In any event, even were Taplin richer than he used to be, I still believe Mr. Weeks would object to the match on principle." His family's nattering on the subject made him cross, he discovered, as if their anxiety validated his own concern. But Tyrone Ellsworth had ever boasted an imperturbable disposition, and he did not mean to lose his composure now. He reached for the top letter in his pile and opened it.

"It's Aggie's heart I'm more concerned with," recommenced Mrs. Ellsworth, ignoring his hint that they should move on. "After so many years, I hoped she would forget her fondness for him, but she hasn't. Or at least not enough to choose another. Suppose Mr. Taplin's reappearance plays havoc with her affections again?"

"If he breaks her heart a second time, she might never marry," sighed Beatrice. "And I do so like Aggie."

"A delightful girl," Mr. Ellsworth proclaimed from his end of the table. "But as we know too well, 'Full many a flower is born to blush unseen and waste its—'"

"Yes, my dear sir," interrupted his fourth wife, "but as I myself was very nearly one of those unseen flowers wasting her sweetness on the desert air, I think it not too much to ask that those who *do* see the flower blushing might put forth a little effort on her behalf."

This was too metaphorical for her husband to follow—was Mrs. Ellsworth commending him for plucking her from anonymous spinsterhood, or was she expressing resentment for the community's earlier indifference to that spinsterhood?—so he made no response other than to smile.

"How might we put forth some effort, Mama?" Beatrice prompted, understanding better.

But Mrs. Ellsworth only shook her head helplessly. She knew Aggie's mother and sisters had suggested various young men at various times, to no avail. What could the Ellsworths possibly accomplish, beyond expressing their approbation if ever another eligible young man came along?

It was Tyrone who surprised them with a suggestion. "Though I know little of traditional matchmaking strategies, coming so recently from New College I do have personal acquaintance with a number of promising young men." He held up the letter he had just read. "This one, for instance. Gareth Boulton may not possess the charm of a Francis Taplin, but he is a respectable fellow who will shortly assume the living of St. Swithun's in Headbourne Worthy."

"You propose distracting Aggie with a not-as-charming clergyman?" Beatrice asked doubtfully. "Is he handsome?"

"Er—Boulton is not *un*handsome."

"Meaning he is unhandsome. I suppose he is dull as well?"

"Beatrice," chided her stepmother.

Tyrone thought of Boulton's long, mournful features. If Boulton was not dull, precisely, neither was he interesting. But he could *be* interesting, with a little help. And it was Tyrone's help Boulton requested.

"She need not marry him," he muttered, more to himself than his family. He thought the power to make Aggie love one such as Boulton lay outside the ability of any pen, but if Boulton could be made attractive enough to divert her until the danger passed—that is, until Taplin were gone again—would that not be enough? What a gamble Boulton was taking, asking Tyrone to undertake a sustained verbal assault on the young lady! He must be pinning his faith on success, or how could he afford a half-crown per effort?

I will give him a discount, for Aggie's sake.

"She need not marry Boulton," he said again, his gaze sweeping the breakfast table. "But another suitor—a worthier one—might prevent her from dwelling too much on Taplin."

"But how do you propose to bring him to her attention?" Mrs. Ellsworth wondered. "Headbourne Worthy is not distant, but I don't suppose Aggie ever ventures there, so it would entirely depend on encountering Mr. Boulton at random in Winchester."

"He could come for dinner," suggested Beatrice, "though Aggie might think it odd if we invite her as well."

"Not if we invite Minta and Carlisle," Tyrone said.

Mrs. Ellsworth did not need to look to her husband to know he loved a full house and welcomed any occasion to lure back those birds who had flown the nest. "A very good idea. As you are the only one acquainted with Mr. Boulton, Tyrone, you had better be the one to arrange it. Shall we say in three weeks' time? Or a month? Your birthday, even. That would give him time to finish at New College and settle in his new parsonage. Only give Wilcomb a day's notice, that she and I might set the menu."

An hour later, Tyrone rode alongside his father and the steward Falk as they looked over the Hollowgate acreage. There were crops to inspect, tenant farmers to confer with, a culvert in need of repair. Tyrone looked, listened, managed to ask an intelligent question or two, but to tell the bare truth, his mind was elsewhere.

He was composing Boulton's first letter to Aggie.

In his letter to Tyrone, Boulton had been candid about his failed first assay at the fortress of Miss Weeks' singleness, perhaps because Tyrone already knew the worst of it.

As I told you and your cousins, I came prepared to offer for Miss Weeks after the dinner at the Angel. I had a sheet of notepaper, on which I catalogued the benefits of such a match, but before I managed to give them full expression, she forbade me to speak further. She said she guessed which way it all tended and didn't need to hear the entirety. I cannot help but feel that she might have given me a different answer, had she only done me the courtesy of hearing me out.

In the event you would like to draw upon any of the points in my memorandum, they were as follows:

1. *Our common upbringing in Hampshire.*
2. *The respectability of her family and connections.*
3. *Her personal charms. (Here I would have enumerated her pleasing features, fine figure, affability, etc.)*
4. *The size of her portion. It would make possible a comfortable married life and allow me to rise higher in my profession.*
5. *Her pleasing affection for her nephew, which might be included above in number 3.*

Because I was not permitted to list her specific charms, might this be a good place for you to begin? I leave it to your judgment. I ignored your advice not to address her so soon, Ellsworth, and suffered the consequences. I am now prepared to give you due credit. Your cousin B promises you will now be able to resume your services, and I would like to hire you for a sustained campaign, with the first letter smoothing over the difficulties of my last meeting with Miss Weeks and preparing the ground to meet her again in Winchester.

Please forward your draft with all haste. I will do my utmost to submit to your strategy, copying your words verbatim or writing to you again before I send anything onward.

It would not be right to take Boulton's limited monies if he were not willing to make a good-faith effort to win Aggie for the fellow, and Tyrone determined he must therefore do his best, even if he still suspected any effort would be fruitless in the end. At the very least Aggie would be able to compare the addresses of a respectable man to those of a scoundrel, and if she persisted in preferring the scoundrel's, she must be abandoned to her fate.

"Boulton's" letter to Aggie had better begin with an apology, at any rate, because she most likely would not be eager to hear from him again. Tyrone was debating the level of obsequiousness the apology required when he saw at some distance the lady herself, also on horseback, alongside her father.

"Weeks!" cried Mr. Ellsworth cheerfully, waving his riding crop. "Halloa there, Weeks!"

Mr. Weeks lifted a hand in return, and the two parties closed the distance until they faced each other across the brook dividing the two estates.

"My son Tyrone is returned for good from Oxford," announced Mr. Ellsworth, his chest expanding. "Falk and I begin to teach him the management of Hollowgate."

The sonless Mr. Weeks bowed in acknowledgement. The eye the former silk manufacturer ran over Tyrone was measuring. "You will be a welcome addition to the county," he said politely. "I cannot say I have ever seen you on horseback before."

"I hardly blame you," replied Tyrone, "for I have rarely been on horseback, to this point. Greaves our chief groom chose our most broken nag for me this morning, for my own safety."

Mr. Weeks frowned at this, but Tyrone saw Aggie hide a smile.

"For my own part," Tyrone continued, "I'm not certain I have ever seen Miss Weeks ride either."

Here her father sighed and shook his head. "Because she and your sister were ever wont to run about the countryside like gypsies."

"If we had been allowed to ride astride like the gentlemen, I imagine we would have ridden more often," his daughter rejoined.

"I don't know if it was the riding aside that troubled Minta," said Tyrone, whipping his gaze up from the trim little ankle which peeped from her habit. "I'm afraid we Ellsworths aren't much for riding in any fashion, apart from Pa here."

But the older gentlemen were more interested in business, and they soon were rehearsing the same topics Mr. Ellsworth had just discussed with Falk.

Tyrone nudged his "broken nag" gently across the muddy brook. "Good morning, Miss Weeks. Does this mean you are speaking to me again?" The cool June day brought the roses to her cheeks, and the wary look she gave him made him mischievous.

"I was rude last night, wasn't I?" Aggie admitted. "But you were impertinent, Mr. Ellsworth, truly you were. We will try again and hope to do better. But should you insist on touching upon that one particular subject, I will ride off, trusting you could not follow because of your inferior seat."

"How ungracious of you to assume it would be my inferior seat, Miss Weeks. If I were to lose my seat, could it not equally be the fault of the sad creature Greaves assigned me?"

"I am no expert, but I don't see a thing wrong with that horse."

"Ah, but you do with its rider?"

"Come, Mr. Ellsworth. Let us not bicker." Aggie stroked the mane of her own glossy mare. "I am surprised to see you this morning accompanying your father."

"I know, I know. Because you always picture me with my head in a book."

"No. That is—yes, I do, but this morning in particular I am surprised because I thought—you might call on Miss Caraway."

His eyes widened. "Anne Boleyn? Do you suppose she expects me to?"

"She might. Gentlemen do sometimes call on the young ladies they danced with." Color washed over her face, and she prayed he wouldn't ask what she was doing, then, riding after her father, instead of sitting in the parlor at The Acres. She did not *think* Mr. Taplin would call that morning. The presence of Mr. Weeks alone should be sufficient to keep him away, but better safe than sorry was Aggie's opinion.

"Another helpful lesson," Tyrone nodded. "The morning is full of them. In my defense, I danced with several young ladies, including you. If I am reproached for my failure to appear, I could say I called on you first. I do not see how a man can be expected to visit eight to ten ladies in the course of a morning."

"It's that you asked Miss Caraway first," she persisted, not knowing why she did not let the matter rest. What was it to her, if Tyrone Ellsworth chose to dance with Clumpy Caraway? And she should shut her mouth, rather than plant ideas in his mind.

His brow creased in thought, Tyrone stared into the distance. He had hardly been able to avoid asking Miss Caraway to dance. The girl had collided with him almost as soon as he entered the assembly room, and then there was her mother, making apologies and rapping her daughter with her fan before crying, "But aren't you Mr. Tyrone Ellsworth? I believe two of your sisters were schoolmates of my two daughters, Caroline Caraway (now Lady Downing) and Clementine here. Miss Caraway, rather." Tyrone had paid little attention to his sisters' talk of schoolmates, but Miss Caraway was pretty enough, and he was willing to make his sisters' acquaintances his own. Therefore he had asked her to dance, and that had been that. Her dash and sparkle had come as a pleasant surprise, as much a surprise as learning this morning that his sisters, in fact, disliked the Caraways.

"Very well," he resumed after a minute, "if I must call on her at some point, I will. I don't suppose you have got any idea where the Caraways live?"

"None," Aggie replied shortly.

The sun was higher now, and the horses growing restless. The older men concluded their talk.

"Off we go, Aggie," Mr. Weeks called, beckoning to his daughter. "You said you wanted exercise. Let us see how well you manage to stay on if Sable trots. Good day to you, Ellsworths, Falk."

She turned Sable at once and followed, without once looking back. Not that Tyrone expected her to, only he found himself waiting to make sure of it. Then he clicked his tongue and urged his mild nag back to the Ellsworth side of the brook, his thoughts returning to Boulton's letter.

Chapter 10

*The wrongs that you have seene In me,
my future vertues shall redeeme.*
—Anonymous, *No-body and Some-body:
with the true chronicle historie of Elydure* (1606)

Before another day went by, Aggie walked to Canon Street to call on Araminta, taking her route through town. And by the time she arrived there, she had even more to tell her.

"Minta," she announced breathlessly, "Banniker and I have just come from Mme Blanchet the dressmaker, and you will never guess who was there! What's more, I had just seen her yesterday coming out of the draper's."

"Oh, heavens, how can I guess? But if it was at the dressmaker, and if it was a 'her,' at least it cannot have been Francis Taplin." Minta waved Aggie through the plain but comfortable cottage to the backyard. The Carlisles had chosen their home particularly for its backyard, as Mr. Carlisle thought it would be sad if his active young bride had no room to romp unless she walked back to Hollowgate. Within the walls of her yard Minta did not bother with a garden. Apart from a small paved terrace, large enough for two benches and a table, there was only grass and a few shade trees.

"Ought you to be doing that, Minta?" she asked, when the latter took up a racket to swat a ball in her direction. "You're so enormous now you might capsize." Aggie caught the ball after it ricocheted off the fence, however, and tossed it back. "It was indeed not Francis Taplin," she continued, "though he asked me to dance at the assembly."

Minta froze, and the ball hit her ankles. "Mr. Taplin was at the assembly, and you danced with him?"

Aggie fought a surge of impatience. Must *everyone* respond with alarm? Did *everyone* in the entire world fear Mr. Taplin need only whistle, and she would come running?

But Araminta Ellsworth was her oldest friend, and if anyone deserved a full explanation, it was she. She set her shoulders. "Yes, I saw him and he asked me."

"And—how was it?"

"It was…an anti-climax. Oh, Minta! I came away disappointed with myself. Disappointed that I had cared for him in the first place. It was not that he was older and less handsome than I remembered, though he was indeed those things. (He was still good-looking enough that all the young ladies admired him.) It was that he was no longer my *beau ideal*. No. He only struck me as—I don't know—soft and selfish and weak from self-indulgence. I rather resented him asking me to dance. Because I think he did it for amusement, to see if it would cause me pain. And it did cause me pain, only not in the way he imagined. It hurt me because I thought I should never have wasted an instant thinking of him."

Minta drew a long breath, taking Aggie by both hands to give her a searching look. After a moment it was clear she believed her because a smile overspread her candid features. "Ah."

"Yes," said Aggie glumly. "You were right from the beginning, and I was wrong, so you needn't triumph over me."

"Shame on you, if you think I would feel triumph over this," scolded Minta. "Any triumph I feel is over Mr. Taplin. Let's rent a gig and drive to Beaumond. I should dearly like to throw a few plums at him, if not run him down altogether. Nicholas thinks I shouldn't walk farther than Hollowgate in my condition, so it had better be a gig, but we should act fast, or Mr. Taplin will be off to America before I can gloat over him."

"I have no intention of going anywhere near Beaumond," Aggie declared. "And with our history of driving misadventures, don't let Mr. Carlisle hear you talk of renting a gig. It would be just like you to tumble out and do yourself or the baby an injury."

Minta ignored this. "I suppose Mr. Taplin did not dare to call at The Acres after the assembly, knowing how your father dislikes him."

"I took care to be out of the house, but he did not call."

"The coward! I am not a bit surprised. Never mind the man. You were saying, you saw someone at Mme Blanchet's. Was it my aunt Jeanne? She dearly loves to look in at the dressmaker's, just to have a good talk in French."

Glad to have done with Mr. Taplin, Aggie leaped to catch Minta's next whack of the ball and then bowled it underhand back to her friend. "It was not Mrs. Charles Ellsworth. I told you you wouldn't be able to guess. Minta, it was Clumpy Caraway. You remember her? Caroline Caraway's younger sister."

Araminta shuddered. "Bah! I certainly remember Caroline Caraway and her court of sycophants, lording it over us at Turcotte's when we were pupils. Caraway is Lady Downing now, isn't she? But Clumpy? …Hmm…she was the quiet little creeping girl, wasn't she? I don't recall her very clearly, but I remember pitying her. It must be hard to have Caroline Caraway for an elder sister, especially after the grand marriage she made."

"But that's just it, Minta. Clumpy no longer creeps. She's no longer pitiable! She has grown into *Clementine* Caraway, tall and graceful. And her hair, which used to be no definite color, has darkened to a shining chestnut. Not only that, but Tyrone says Clumpy herself was promoted to head girl as her sister had been!"

"Tyrone says?" Taken up short, Minta stared. "What would he know about it?"

"He danced with her at the assembly. And told me she was 'dashing' and 'witty.'"

"*Clumpy Caraway*? My brother Tyrone praised her thus and danced with her?"

"Yes and yes. It was the first dance. Whilst I was encumbered with Mr. Taplin."

Minta whistled. "Astonishing. Oh, Tyrone. What can it possibly mean? Not what I fear it might mean, I hope. 'Dashing' and 'witty'! Aggie, tell me—did he look like a mooncalf while he danced with her?"

"I wouldn't know. They were away down the line."

"Because it would be simply wretched if he liked her," said Minta. "Imagine having Lady Downing in the family!" Another shudder.

"Well, it was just one dance," Aggie observed, feeling an inexplicable sinking in her midsection. She did not like how seriously Araminta considered the matter. "You did not think my one dance with Mr. Taplin the high road to ruin."

"No, but Mr. Taplin asked *you*, rather than the other way around. And Mr. Taplin is a flirt, and Tyrone is not. And he does not lightly throw out compliments to young ladies. In fact, I cannot remember ever hearing him apply such words to any of them! Who else did my brother partner?"

"I didn't watch him the whole evening, Araminta," protested Aggie. "Nor did I know all the young ladies there. All I can say is, Clementine Caraway was certainly the prettiest of his partners. He danced with me the once, of course, later, when he told me these things."

"That's the least he could do," Minta said roundly. "For my sake he ought to have asked you twice."

"Don't be silly. Knowing me should not be a duty."

"Who said anything about duty?" Minta shook troubled fists. "Oh, I don't like to think of Tyrone marrying. He's so bookish and odd and quibbling. He will be taken in by the first girl who sets her cap for him, I know it! And who wants a wily, ambitious girl for a sister?"

"In fairness, we don't know Clementine Caraway is wily and ambitious," Aggie said.

"Her sister certainly was, and how can a 'dashing' and 'witty' girl be anything but?"

"But Clementine Caraway is not *Caroline* Caraway, at any rate. Or, not altogether." Aggie frowned over this, for it was undeniably true in their experience that head girls at Mrs. Turcotte's followed a certain pattern: tall, queenly, superior, beautiful, ruthless to the less admired.

That Minta guessed her thoughts was clear in her reply. "Name one single head girl at Turcotte's who didn't glory in having the whip hand over everyone else."

Aggie could not win this. She shrugged. "Fair enough. But maybe Clementine won't set her cap for him."

"She would be foolish not to," muttered Minta. "He's handsome and clever and rich. Tyrone may not boast a title like Lord Downing, but he has got everything else. Even if she does not choose to marry him, she will certainly choose to *collect* him."

"Oh!" breathed Aggie, not liking that picture at all.

Minta threw her friend a sharp look. "I don't suppose you'd like to marry him yourself? It would save me a deal of trouble."

Aggie rolled her eyes. "You're not the only one with that idea." Briefly she told her about the Kings' maneuvers in Oxford. "But I won't have it! I admit I chose poorly where to bestow my affections the first time, but I refuse to let people dictate where I ought to bestow them now. It's shameful how unmarried girls are treated! As if we were the pox, to be got rid of as quickly as possible."

"All right, all right. You needn't burst your buttons. It was only an idea. I'd far prefer you as a sister to Clementine Caraway."

"You don't need me as a sister because we are already as good as sisters."

"True. But—oh, Aggie—if *I* want you to marry in general, it's only because I think marriage is delightful."

"Well, there are plenty of gentlemen with whom marriage would be anything but delightful," Aggie retorted. "And if you are truly my friend, you will not push people at me or push me at them."

"I am truly your friend and better than a sister." Minta assured her. She raised a solemn hand. "I do hereby promise you, Agatha Weeks, I will neither push people at you, nor push you at them. I will in no way interfere with where you choose to bestow your affections."

"Thank you." Aggie couldn't help but be reminded of Tyrone's promise at the Angel. The twins were great ones for swearing mighty oaths where she was concerned, it seemed.

"I will make only one exception," Minta added. "Because if you settle on another person as dreadful as Francis Taplin, I cannot, cannot promise not to interfere."

Here Aggie punched her in the arm, and Minta burst out laughing.

The housemaid, a stout woman of four-and-forty years, appeared in the doorway. "Mrs. Carlisle, will you be wanting Miss Weeks to take any refreshment, or do you intend to send her away thirsty and hungry as you did Mrs. Kenner when last she called?"

"We had better have lemonade, Terry, thank you," replied Minta solemnly. But when the door shut behind her, she and Aggie smothered giggles. "Isn't she alarming? A perfect dragon. It's so very hard to get good servants, however, and Terry does everything marvelously. It's only that she dotes on Nicholas and thinks the good doctor deserves a more ladylike wife. Nicholas said we could dismiss her, but why would we? She makes me laugh a hundred times a day."

After the beverage was duly offered and partaken of, Aggie took her leave, Minta just squeezing her hand before she went. "You must be my eyes and ears, Aggie."

"What eyes and ears? Be your own eyes and ears."

"Eyes and ears on Clementine Caraway, of course. I don't mind walking around town and such, but I might not have your knack for running into her at random, and I likely won't go to the Race Ball and such things. So you must be my eyes and ears."

Aggie gave an expressive sigh. "Very well, though I'm sure your housemaid Terry would tell you it isn't very genteel to set your friend spying on other young ladies."

"Which is why Terry need never know a thing about it. Good-bye."

When Aggie and her maid returned to The Acres, Mrs. Weeks met them in the entry, nodding a dismissal at Banniker and assisting Aggie to remove her bonnet. "My dear love, you have received a letter. From *Oxford*. Who could be writing to you from there?"

Aggie turned it over in her hand. "G.B.," she mused. Quickly enough her color came. "Oh. I think I know. It's that gentleman, Mama. You remember when Phronsie and Mr. King invited the Ellsworth young men to the Angel? They brought along this Mr. Boulton, a classmate and shortly to be the new curate of St. Swithun's in Headbourne Worthy."

Mrs. Weeks put the back of her hand to her lips. "And you told him he might write to you?"

"Of course I did not, Mama."

"Do you think it is—an offer?"

Aggie sighed. "I hope not. Let me read it, and I will tell you about it afterward."

Without waiting for her mother's response, Aggie slipped away, bounding up the stairway to her room. Banniker did not blink an eye to see her young mistress kick off her shoes and leap atop her bed. She only shook her head and laid out Miss Weeks' hairbrush because it would clearly be required again.

Mr. Boulton had an unexpectedly smooth and flowing hand; there was not a single blot on the page, and Aggie thought surely this fair specimen must be a copy of his original composition.

10 June 1808
New College, Oxford

Dear Miss Weeks,

Please pardon me for writing to you and for the nature of our last meeting. My attempt to pay my addresses to you was foolish, I now recognize, given the brief nature of our acquaintance. More foolish yet was bringing notes with me, as if I were presenting myself for examination! Will you accept my embarrassed apology and have the goodness to blot my actions from your remembrance?

When I return to Hampshire shortly to take up my living, I aspire to be on good terms with not only my parish but the larger community. A community, Miss Weeks, which I pray might count you in its numbers.

Your most obedient servant,
Gareth Boulton

She was undoubtedly surprised. When her mother asked her if the letter contained an offer, Aggie would have dared to bet it did. She assumed that, after having been forbidden to speak in person, Mr. Boulton elected to have his full say on paper, where he could be neither interrupted nor denied the opportunity.

And yet, here was this note! Brief. Rueful, yet...manly in its honesty. She liked the way he confirmed her earlier reproof. He did not pretend it never happened. He did not try to defend himself. He simply acknowledged it and asked her pardon. He paid no silly compliments; he asked nothing but that she accept this olive branch.

She had thought Mr. Boulton a clumsy, callow young man with an eye for nothing but her fortune, but now she felt a stirring of respect. He was capable of learning from his mistakes, it appeared. And eager as Aggie was for that quality to be recognized in herself, how could she deny it to others?

She would gladly forgive him, she decided, folding the letter up and sliding off the bed. If he was no longer going to behave nonsensically and had decided to treat her as a rational creature, she was more than willing to change her opinion of him.

Humming a little to herself, she went in search of her mother.

Aggie could have no way of knowing, of course, Mr. Boulton's agonies over this note. He had deposited his half-crown with Benjamin Ellsworth and received this draft from Tyrone the following day, a draft which provoked a fit of indignation and half-formed fancies to demand his money back.

Apologize? And so abjectly? He had done nothing wrong! *She* had been discourteous in refusing to hear him out! And what possible objection could she have to his list of her virtues? And, as if these shortcomings were not short enough, why did Ellsworth not put something complimentary in there? Why did he not begin to rebuild, as it were?

For some hours Boulton paced and fumed. One moment he told himself he would not copy it. The next he thought he would copy some of it but improve it.

But Ellsworth must have suspected the effect his draft would have, for, at the bottom of it he had written, "Verbatim, Boulton, or on your own head be it. – T.E."

And T. E. prevailed.

With a sigh and a grumble and more than one ruined sheet of paper, Gareth Boulton did at last succeed in producing the clean copy which so impressed Aggie.

Chapter 11

Lead in your Ladies ev'ry one: Sweet Partner,
I must not yet forsake you.
—Shakespeare and Fletcher, *Henry VIII,* I.iv.107 (1623)

Between the beginning of the races, the quarter sessions and Assizes, and Winchester College's Election Week, the town and its environs were full to bursting.

"I hoped to convince my parents to pay a fortnight's visit to Hollowgate," Benjamin told his cousin Tyrone, "that they might let their house. I told Pa he could likely make as much in that time as Winchester paid him for a term."

"What came of it, then?" asked Tyrone, signaling for another ale. It was the annual gathering of former Wykehamists at the George Inn, and more than a few alumni were heavily in their cups, keeping the proprietor and barmaids well-occupied.

"Mama rejected the idea," answered Austin, thumping down his own tankard. In his mother Jeanne Ellsworth's French accent he mimicked, "*Il y a assez de barbares ici, sans en inviter d'autres.* Imagine calling Ben and me barbarians, much less our Oxford friends!"

"My aunt's insults aside, aren't we squeezing enough money from those same friends?" Tyrone said. "I've been suffering cramps of the hand, I've written so much, and my stepmother grows suspicious of the sheer number of my devoted correspondents."

"Don't say you're tired of it, Ty," Benjamin coaxed. "You can't imagine how glorious it is to be flush! You do this for amusement, but to Austin and me, it is our very livelihood. We intend to expand our sales efforts into the Queen's College and Hertford next term."

"You must recruit a second writer, then, to share the work."

"But everyone will want you, Tyrone—your rate of success cannot be equaled! For someone with no sweetheart of his own, you have managed to secure sweethearts for everyone who applies to you."

"Not everyone," he frowned thoughtfully. "Or not yet. Boulton is the outlier."

"Boulton aimed higher than one's typical Oxford toast," Benjamin pointed out.

"True," agreed Austin. "No ambitious shopkeeper's daughter or penniless provost's niece for him. He wanted a wealthy bride. And he took matters in his own clumsy hands. Which meant you began in a hole, cousin."

"I think I have got him out of the hole, at least. I wrote him an apology, and he said he received two lines in return from Miss Weeks, saying she pardoned him and wished him well."

"But now that he's taking up residence in Headbourne Worthy, how do you intend to prevent him blundering into the metaphorical ditch again?"

The Wykehamists around them struck up another round of the Election grace, and Tyrone was obliged to raise his voice and lean in. "I told him on no condition was he to pursue her or call on her. He was to trust that he would see her at the Race Ball or some other festivity, in which case he might ask her to dance. And on that occasion, wherever and whenever it might take place, in between discussing impersonal trivialities, he was to utter the line, 'I'm afraid I always express myself better in writing.' That will lay the groundwork for future attempts."

"How did Boulton like your advice?" Austin pressed.

"He didn't. But he grudgingly accepted it because he had to admit my apology had opened the door for him again."

"Have you changed your mind, then?" asked Benjamin. "Do you now think, with his obedience to you and plenty of time and effort, he might win her?"

A whoop went up as one of the former prefects let a coin ring on the bar and called for more drinks all around.

"If she is willing to be won," Tyrone replied, "Boulton will have as good a chance as any. And I begin to think she might be willing. Minta tells me so, and she would know."

His sister had called a few days prior at Hollowgate to see the puppies, and Tyrone seized the chance to quiz her on the subject, waiting until Minta was lying flat on her back on the parlor carpet, Pickles climbing on her and Scamp licking her face.

"I invited Aggie to meet the puppies," he ventured, "but she has not yet come."

"Yes. She said she danced with you at the assembly in Upper Brook Street." Laughing, she pushed Scamp away, and he tumbled onto his back.

"After she danced with that scoundrel Taplin. What does Carlisle say? How long does his brother intend to be at Beaumond?"

"As long as he possibly can, I suspect. His father says he speaks of waiting until autumn, so that he may book passage on a ship following a northerly route."

"Autumn! That leaves plenty of time for mischief."

"Yes," sighed Minta, "but at least he's been off fishing somewhere since the assembly, so Aggie has been spared additional awkward encounters."

"Spared—or has she regretted his absence?"

His twin sat up as abruptly as her unwieldy figure would permit. "When I say 'spared,' I mean 'spared,' Tyrone. I have sounded Aggie on the matter, and I am convinced she speaks honestly. No—the greater danger is that she will never marry at all, now.—What? Why do you look at me like that?"

"Like what?" he returned, wiping his countenance clean.

"Like you know something I don't."

"At this point, I know nothing that you don't."

"Hmm. I don't know if I believe that. Do you intend to ask Aggie yourself?" Minta said baldly.

"Me?" His voice was mild. "How could I, when I've sworn to her I would not? It was the only way I could get her to talk to me in Oxford. She seems to think everyone is trying to marry her."

His sister regarded him through narrowed eyes. "Frankly, nearly everyone is. And if you aren't, that's your blockheadedness, because Aggie is a *trump*. One could go farther and fare worse. Much worse."

"I don't doubt it," was his soothing reply.

There was no sign of Boulton until the Tuesday of Election Week, when Tyrone and his brother-in-law Robert Fairchild were crowded in School at the college to hear the Medal speaking. While Fairchild's nephew Paul had not made the New College roll (there being too few spaces), he had got the gold medal for English verse and would attend Christ Church as a commoner.

Paul Tillwood was just finishing his speech when a shuffling and a murmuring at the back announced the entrance of long and lugubrious Gareth Boulton, squeezing into the row. His drooping eyes widened when he caught sight of Tyrone, and he commenced a series of pointing and gestures to indicate he would speak with him. To these Tyrone gave one nod and returned his attention to the Latin verse medalist.

"Ellsworth!" Boulton cried, seizing him by the shoulder when the speeches were done and everyone emerged to mill about under the plane trees. "Here you are."

"Boulton. Have you settled in at—where *does* the curate of St. Swithun's, Headbourne Worthy, live, anyhow?"

"In the vicarage. A spacious but deteriorating house, truth be told, but my sister Anne contrives to make it comfortable. Useful creature, Anne. My father was sorry to lose her services, teaching the Sunday school, but Anne wanted a change of scene."

"Perhaps your next sister can take the Sunday school over—Charity, was it?"

Boulton shrugged this away. "Not likely. Charity is spoilt by being the beauty and not much good for anything. My mama and next sister Margaret will have to take it up, I suppose."

"Well, I am glad you have got Miss Boulton to keep you company for the time being. As someone with many sisters, however, I can vouch they have a most inconvenient penchant for marrying and running off to live their own lives, so don't be surprised if Miss Boulton does not grace your hearth overlong."

"Oh, Anne won't marry. She's already quite old—thirty or thereabouts, I imagine. From my father's first marriage. And hasn't a penny, no more than the rest of us. I say, Ellsworth—she'll likely come to the Race Ball with me. Do me a favor and ask her for a dance, will you?"

Most young men would have quailed at such a request, but Tyrone was amused. "All right, then. Only you must warn her that I am a lazy idler and not the marrying kind."

But Boulton had already devoted more concern than usual to his elder sister. "What if Miss Weeks does not attend the Race Ball? I walked up and down the High Street yesterday in hopes of seeing her but was not so fortunate. Do you think she will watch the races themselves? Not that it matters. I thought of going, but Anne said we haven't got the money to rent a carriage and that it wouldn't do for the new curate, just read in, to be seen there."

"I haven't got the least idea if Miss Weeks will be at the ball or not," replied Tyrone. "But if she is not, I will write you some excuse to call at Hollowgate, depend upon it. If she *is* at St. John's Rooms, however—"

"I know, I know," said Boulton hastily. "Then I am to speak on nothing of importance but must be certain to say I express myself better in writing. I won't forget."

Aggie paused under the portrait of bewigged Colonel Brydges as she entered the assembly room at St. John's, accompanied by her second sister Mrs. Linus Chester. Unknown to Aggie, Sophronia and Frederica had put their heads together and agreed that *on no condition* could Agatha be left to encounter Mr. Francis Taplin again without one of them nearby. It was all well and good for Araminta's older sister Mrs. Simon Kenner to offer chaperonage, but *circumstances were such* that family must be present.

But it was not Mr. Taplin who first drew Aggie's eye. That honor lay with Clementine Caraway. And, though she was lovely, Miss Caraway probably would not have been of such immediate interest were Mr. Tyrone Ellsworth not just then bending over her hand. Probably asking her for the first dance again. Or for the supper dance. Or both.

"G-Good evening, Miss Weeks."

Aggie and Frederica turned, and Aggie's smile was genuine, if muted. "Mr. Boulton! How goes it with you? May I introduce you to my sister Mrs. Linus Chester? Frederica, this is Mr. Boulton, whom Phronsie and I met in Oxford. He was a classmate of Mr. Tyrone Ellsworth."

Frederica already knew all about Mr. Gareth Boulton (from that same conversation with Sophronia), but as there were only two categories of young men at the moment—Mr. Taplin and Not Mr. Taplin—she curtseyed and beamed upon him. "What a pleasure, Mr. Boulton. My sister Mrs. King tells me you are the new curate of St. Swithun's in Headbourne Worthy."

"I am." He flushed with pleasure to think himself sufficiently important to be discussed among the Weekses. "I was read in on Sunday. And, if I may…" Turning, he looked over his shoulder and beckoned an equally long and lugubrious young woman of uncertain years. "This is my sister, Miss Boulton. Anne, here are Mrs. Linus Chester and her sister Miss Weeks."

They curtseyed again and made dogged conversation about the Boultons' new home and duties while the musicians began tuning their instruments. Then Boulton bowed again to Aggie. "Miss Weeks, if you would do me the honor of dancing with me…"

She was just nodding her acquiescence when she spied Mr. Taplin weaving his way across the ballroom in their general direction. No longer away fishing then, nor yet bound for America? "Which dance?" Aggie asked abruptly.

He gulped. "Er—the first? If you are not yet engaged."

"I am not engaged."

Wanting to hoard his supply of trivial comments, he bowed again and walked away with his sister, saying he would help Miss Boulton find a chair beside one of their parishioners. Aggie in turn clutched at Mrs. Chester to lead her in the opposite direction from the approaching Taplin, only to see him smoothly alter course and intercept them.

"Mrs. Chester! Miss Weeks! How delightful. I hope I might have the pleasure of dancing with each of you this evening."

Mrs. Chester gave an uneasy titter, and Aggie could feel her sister's pulse speed. "Oh. Mr. Taplin. How long it has been. Good evening. I'm afraid—I'm afraid I do not intend to dance. I am an old married woman now."

"How sad for me. Perhaps I might draw up a chair beside you for a long chat a little later. And what of you, Miss Weeks? Do you intend to dance?"

"Yes," Aggie said unwillingly. "But Mr. Boulton has claimed the first."

"Admirable of him. Then if you would grant me the second…?"

There was no alternative. She curtseyed—hardly more than a jerk of a movement and then cried, "Oh, look, Frederica—there is Mrs. Kenner. We had better greet her. Excuse us, Mr. Taplin."

"Oh, oh, oh," moaned Mrs. Chester. "I *promised* Phronsie I would keep an eye on you, and now here you are—promised to Mr. Taplin for the second dance."

"It doesn't matter," huffed Aggie. "I keep telling everyone it doesn't matter. I don't want to dance with the man, but I am perfectly capable of keeping an eye on myself. The more fuss you make, the worse it is, Freddie."

But Mrs. Chester continued to bite her lip and fidget, and Aggie was relieved when the musicians were at last ready and Mr. Boulton came to fetch her.

The ball began with a longways dance, that other couples might join the lines as they were able, and no sooner did Aggie take her place than who should be deposited beside her but Clementine Caraway? Her partner was Tyrone Ellsworth, of course, who acknowledged Aggie with a quirk of his finely cut mouth. So that was how it was, was it?

When the dancing master instructed them to "take hands-four from the top," Aggie found Tyrone and his partner would make up their two-couple set. Therefore she turned to Miss Caraway. As Aggie was four years her senior, it was only appropriate that she be the first to recognize their prior acquaintance. "Good evening, Miss Caraway," she said quietly. "I don't know if you remember me, but I was a pupil at Mrs. Turcotte's seminary some years ago."

"Indeed?" was Miss Caraway's unexpected response as the dancers dropped hands again.

If she was flattered by Aggie's condescension, she hid it well, but Aggie forged on. "Yes. My dear friend Araminta Ellsworth and I were some years younger than your sister Lady Downing."

"Ah," the willowy young lady said. "I see. Older girls. I will have to ask Caro if she remembers you." With that she returned her attention to Tyrone Ellsworth, favoring him with a warm smile.

The dance began, with puzzled Aggie lurching into it a beat late. Did Miss Caraway truly not remember her or Minta? It seemed unlikely, since they had not changed nearly as much in appearance as she had. Perhaps she was vexed to be reminded of her earlier, awkward years, or she feared being remembered by her former uncomplimentary nickname. Or perhaps she and Lady Downing did not get on, and Miss Caraway resented references to her.

"Or perhaps," Minta would say later, when Aggie recounted the evening, "however different they used to be, Clumpy Caraway and Caroline Caraway are now as like as two peas."

It was not that the thought did not occur to Aggie, but she dismissed it to pay attention to the figures.

"Miss Weeks," began Mr. Boulton forcefully, "you shine this evening."

"Thank you."

"Yes. You shine." He gathered volume with his courage. "I would even say you shine like a—like a—like an icic—*deuce* a bit!" This last bit burst from him, as he suddenly hunched over, hopping and limping.

"Gracious!" exclaimed Tyrone. "Pardon my clumsiness, Boulton. Inexcusable. Laming you for life would be no *trivial matter. Not enough can be said* on the subject."

"Oh, my," giggled Miss Caraway. "I had better beware of you, Mr. Ellsworth, if I don't want to be lamed for life."

"Miss Caraway, it would be impossible for me to step on *your* feet, dainty as they are," Tyrone answered. "Just as it's impossible to avoid those pedestals supporting Boulton."

"What can you possibly mean?" Aggie frowned at him, seeing how poor Mr. Boulton had gone red as a tulip. "The size of Mr. Boulton's feet is in no way extraordinary."

"You don't think? Take care, Miss Weeks, lest he break your shins with those rafters."

"Miss Weeks," rejoined Boulton faintly, when the dance led them up the room and away from the other two. "I beg your pardon for my swearing. Inexcusable in a lady's presence."

"I have heard worse, Mr. Boulton. Think no more of it. And Mr. Ellsworth did stamp on you with inexcusable vigor. There is no rigadoon in this pattern."

He bowed in answer, but said nothing, though at several points she thought he would speak again. When they had worked their way to the top of the room and stood staring at each other, Aggie decided he was so mortified she had better say something, or he would be writing her another apology.

"How was your reading-in, Mr. Boulton? Do you think you will like St. Swithun's?"

"It was…as it should be, Miss Weeks. And I think St. Swithun's will be…all that I expect."

She blinked at his vagueness. "Did you always want to be a clergyman? I think it is a taxing profession, no matter whether the congregation be large or small. Our curate Mr. Hepple is kept very busy, though the parish is modest in size. There are the services, of course, on Sundays, and the sermon to write during the week, but also the sick to visit and people to counsel and others needing marrying and burying."

"Has—Mr. Hepple got a helpmate?"

It was her turn for hesitation, and when she answered her eyes were wary. "Do you mean—a wife? Er—yes. He does. He has Mrs. Hepple."

But Mr. Boulton must have realized he had drawn too near the verge because he tugged at his neckcloth and threw a fearful glance down the line of dancers.

"Do you feel well, Mr. Boulton?"

"Perfectly well."

He was a very deliberate dancer, Aggie noticed. More apt to step and march than to glide and hop. But perhaps Tyrone had made him feel bad about the size of his feet, and he was afraid of injuring her. Impulsively she said, "Was Mr. Ellsworth one of your particular friends at New College? If he was, you know he can be quite whimsical at times. My friend Mrs. Carlisle—his sister—says his brains are addled from all the books he has read."

Instead of putting Mr. Boulton at his ease, Aggie's remark brought on another tug to the neckcloth and another glance down the room. "Yes. Quite the reader, Ellsworth. And yes—he can be odd at times. I would not say he was a *particular* friend—only his cousins might be called his *particular* friends at New College— but his terms were good. That is—he gave me good terms. I mean—we *are* on good terms."

"I rejoice to hear it," said Aggie, bemused.

She gave up on conversation and contented herself with looking about at the other couples as they began to make their way back down the room. Tyrone and Miss Caraway circled back into view, making their own way up the lines, she tossing her head and throwing remarks at him, and he smiling.

"Hasn't the weather been pleasant?" blurted Mr. Boulton, recalling Aggie's attention. "Pleasant weather. Good for the races."

"I did not attend the races," Aggie replied dutifully, "but my friend Mrs. Carlisle said Worthy Down was rather muddy because of the recent rain. She said the wheels of her carriage almost stuck fast."

"Oh, well, yes. It did rain a little. Nor did I attend the races myself."

Once more through the figures. Tyrone and Miss Caraway drew nearer. Aggie wondered if the musicians would wind to a close before or after their original foursome was reunited. Her question was soon answered when they were within one couple of the other two. The music began to slow, and Mr. Boulton made his bow and extended an arm for her.

"I—apologize—if I have been distracted," her partner said with (she thought) unnecessary loudness. "I have always—er—expressed myself more fluidly in writing."

"What's this?" Tyrone was suddenly beside them, Miss Caraway on his arm. "Boulton, have you been boring Miss Weeks?"

"I'm afraid so. With nothings and trifles."

"That's not so," protested Aggie, unwilling to see Tyrone find another thing to criticize in his poor schoolmate. "We spoke of his new curacy and a clergyman's many responsibilities and the value of helpmates."

"Helpmates!" Tyrone's brows lifted a fraction.

"*She* talked of helpmates!" Boulton insisted.

"Why, Miss Weeks," teased Miss Caraway, "you do not waste time, do you, in beating about the bush."

"Waste time?" echoed Aggie. Miss Caraway was smiling, but Aggie felt indignation swell her bosom. She dared to imply Aggie was setting her cap for Mr. Boulton? Her lips pressed together to hold in what would too certainly be a sharp reply, only to have their interchange interrupted.

"Pardon me," a silky voice broke in. "Miss Weeks, I believe I have the honor…"

Aggie forgot everything else in her dismay.

The second dance was upon her, and come to claim his due was the bowing, smirking, smooth Mr. Francis Taplin.

Chapter 12

What on earth can be, So lovely as Sweet constancy.
—Anonymous, *Almira* (1762)

Before Aggie and Mr. Taplin had even taken their places in the set, she decided this would be the very last time. She refused to spend another ball or another instant in dread of him. Discourteous or not, she would tell him she no longer wished for his company. What would be the worst which could happen? He might remark to his other partners on Miss Weeks' obduracy, on her inability to let bygones be bygones, and those young ladies might shake their heads, unaware of their own danger. But it was not Aggie's duty to look out for them. That responsibility fell to their own mamas and chaperones. Her more pressing difficulty was how to begin the subject.

A minute or two passed, Aggie going through the steps by rote and gazing somewhere over his shoulder, before Taplin took matters in his own hands. "Miss Weeks, it seems that while I have been away fishing, you yourself have become a fisher of men."

"Mm," said Aggie. Whether this opening was about her being a faithful member of the parish of St. Eadburh's or (more likely) an allusion to her dancing with Mr. Boulton, she refused to show curiosity.

Instead, she tried to deflect him: "Did you catch any fish?"

"Some. But I must say, none so sleek and shining and prized as what I hope to capture in future."

"Oh." Honestly. How ridiculous, his smoothness. Especially coming on the heels of poor Mr. Boulton's hesitancy.

She wondered if he pressed *every* partner's hand whenever the dance permitted. If he did, it was a most trying habit. And if he only pressed her own hand, that must stop at once. After a particularly lingering squeeze, Aggie vowed she would be ready for him on the next occasion. Why, she would even take a leaf from Tyrone's book!

The opportunity came at the very next hands-across. When Aggie extended both her hands, stiff as two boards, Mr. Taplin reached for them caressingly, drawing his fingers along their length, from wrist to fingertips. Sparks flew from her eyes. Veering abruptly from her designated path, she rammed the corner of her pump heel down upon his shoe.

Mr. Taplin gave a yelp which must have been heard in neighboring towns, for it carried above the music and caused heads to turn.

"Oh, dear me," said Aggie, her eyes hard. "Mr. Taplin, do pardon my blundering."

"Make no m-mention," he coughed, his eyes watering. He tried to put weight on the injured foot, but his features screwed up with the effort. "Miss Weeks—if you will forgive me—" Reaching for her hand, with no nonsense this time about fondling it, he limped from the line of dancers, taking her with him.

Their departure caused confusion, as the three couples below them were forced to scramble and change positions, and every other couple in the line watching them go suffered missteps and misdirections. Aggie failed to notice—this would be her chance to deliver her Final Speech to Mr. Taplin, and she was determined not to miss it.

Hobbling past the portraits of the Earl of Wiltshire and Sir Paulet St. John, Taplin led her to the coffee room. So near to the beginning of the ball the smaller space was deserted, apart from a few servants, and Aggie jerked free from him as soon as they were alone.

"Mr. Taplin." Her chin lifted as she fixed him with a beady eye.

"Lemonade, Miss Weeks?" He took a cup the waiter poured and handed it to her.

"Thank you, no." She set it back upon the table. Taking a deep breath, she clasped her gloved hands together and looked at him directly for the first time that evening. "Mr. Taplin, I do beg your pardon again for stepping on you—"

"Heh heh," he chuckled, "as if something so featherlight as your dainty foot could harm me."

"Yes, well, in any event, I am sorry for the passing discomfort I caused—"

"If you did me any wrong," he replied, "I insist on your company as my recompense." He leaned toward her, with the help of a hand placed on the refreshment table, and she backed away a step.

Had he always been such a hardened flirt? She was more and more embarrassed to think of all the time—all the years—she had wasted sighing over him.

"Mr. Taplin, *listen,*" she urged. "We may only have a moment to ourselves, because I am certain my sister Mrs. Chester saw us leave the ballroom—"

"Yes," he interrupted, narrowing the space between them again. "You are right, Miss Weeks. We must take what opportunities we are afforded."

"Exactly. Therefore, Mr. Taplin, let us waste no more time. And this is indeed a waste of time. Your time and my time. I entreat you, sir, as you are a gentleman—"

"As a gentleman!" he exulted, seizing her that instant in his arms and smashing his lips to hers.

Aggie gave a muffled shriek, writhing and trying to shove him away, but with him clutching her by the shoulders she could not do more than wriggle. His grip tightened, constricting her arms to her sides and her chest to his, but rage inspired her. Managing to work her knee upward between them, she rammed her heel downward once more on the same toes she had struck before.

Magically, both her mouth and her person were released, as Mr. Taplin roared his pain and began to hop about on his good foot, cradling his wounded one.

(The waiter at the beverage table pretended blindness and began wiping the cup in his hand furiously.)

"If you would permit me to finish my sentence," hissed Aggie, wiping her lips roughly with the back of her glove, "I ask you to leave me in peace. Do not ask me to dance again. Do not force your company on me. Do not speak to me, if it can politely be avoided. And never, never, never kiss me again."

"Cruel mistress!" he moaned, tumbling down onto a chair. "What harm was there in attempting to revive a pleasant memory?"

"There was no such memory, sirrah," retorted Aggie magnificently. "These are my final words to you, and if you will not obey me, I will let my father know of this insult. Farewell. Do not follow me."

"I couldn't if I wanted to," sniffed Mr. Taplin, wincing as he tried to wiggle his toes.

But Aggie did not deign to acknowledge this last. She whipped away, intending to sweep from the room, only to halt a few steps onward, arrested by the motion of figures retreating from the coffee-room doorway. Blast! *Who—?*

Her blood was up, however, from her confrontation, and before another second passed, she was hastening forward—almost running—to catch the identities of the witnesses. Let them try and gossip about her—she would tell them a piece of her mind!

"Good gracious," murmured Tyrone Ellsworth, when Agatha Weeks charged out of the coffee room and straight into him. "Do be careful, Miss Weeks."

"Did you—? What were you—?" she sputtered, her defiance abandoning her when she saw behind him Mr. Boulton and her sister Frederica.

"Miss Weeks!" bellowed Boulton, surging forward. "Has something happened?"

But Tyrone raised a cautioning hand, and even Mrs. Chester pleaded, "Mr. Boulton, do hush."

"But—but—" Boulton rose on his toes, trying to peer around Tyrone, who now blocked the entrance to the coffee room. Other heads were turning again, to see what the fuss was.

"But nothing," Aggie rejoined, trying to steady her breath. She hoped her mouth was not too bruised or her dress rumpled. "I was so unlucky as to step on Mr. Taplin's foot as we were dancing, and he has gone to sit in the coffee room until he is recovered." She raised challenging eyebrows at Tyrone, and he bowed and retreated to let her pass.

"But were you not—did he *trouble* you, Aggie?" whispered her sister, coming to clutch at her. "I thought I saw—but Mr. Ellsworth was in the way—"

"Ellsworth deliberately *obstructed* us," insisted Mr. Boulton.

"I plead one of those unfortunate moments when everyone tries to be in the same place at the same time," said Tyrone deprecatingly. "Much as when you were dancing with Taplin." He was watching her rather closely, an unreadable gleam in his eye, and Aggie felt her face warm. Had they all seen what happened, or only Tyrone, or none of them?

"There was no trouble that anyone need bother about, Frederica," she answered as evenly as she could.

"Miss Weeks," Mr. Boulton began again, his chest swelling, "permit me to say that, *if* you had any trouble, I would be—"

"—Boulton would be happy to light candles for you at St. Swithun's," finished Tyrone.

"Light candles?" echoed Aggie and her sister.

"And say prayers," continued Tyrone. "Isn't that right, Boulton? And maybe you would even write a sermon about God being a very present help in trouble."

"That might be very well-intended of him, but I don't think my sister should be mentioned in any sermons," Mrs. Chester objected, drawing herself up.

"Oh, certainly not," agreed Tyrone at once. "Absolutely not. I only meant, Mrs. Chester, that Boulton has always expressed himself remarkably well in writing. Wouldn't you say, Boulton? That, to your mind, for you there is no parallel to the *written word*?"

"Er—yes," said Boulton, at last remembering himself and the instructions he had received. "Yes. I would say that. I express myself most ably in writing, when I can give a deal of thought to it." His face lost some of its animation and settled back into its customary mournful lines. Then he could not play the hero now and amaze Miss Weeks with his zeal on her behalf?

He sighed. "Perhaps you might dance with me again, Miss Weeks?"

"You must give others a chance before you claim a second one," interposed Tyrone. "Therefore you'd better dance with me, Ag—Miss Weeks, rather—if you feel equal to it."

"Why wouldn't I feel equal to it?" she countered warily.

"Oh—no reason at all. Though, after the adventures you have already had this evening, one wouldn't want you to be…overtaxed."

'Adventures'? 'Overtaxed'? Then he *had* seen what took place in the coffee room!

"I will dance with you," she said. "I am perfectly well."

It was a repeat of the assembly a fortnight earlier, with Aggie drawing envious and admiring looks, having been asked to partner the two most dashing men present (as well as poor Mr. Boulton). More than one mama observed to another behind her fan that she certainly hoped Miss Weeks would not crush the foot of *this* partner, as she had the last. "My Griselda may not be as wealthy or in demand as Miss Weeks," said one, "but I trust she can conduct herself in a ballroom without maiming those around her."

Eventful as the ball had been thus far, a different kind of flutter assailed Aggie as she made her curtsey to Tyrone. Because Mr. Taplin's looks had been spoiled for her by a truer knowledge of his character, she now thought Tyrone alone bore the palm for handsomeness, from his golden-brown crop of hair to his good-humored features to his upright figure in its fine tailoring. Indeed, had she not known him nearly all her life, Aggie thought she might be in some danger.

But there could be no possibility of danger dancing with Tyrone Ellsworth. There was not the least flirtation in his gaze or words. He did not fiddle and grapple with her fingers when he grasped them. He did not pull her unduly close when they linked arms to exchange positions. So why did Aggie feel a little breathless?

"I commend you on your nimbleness, Miss Weeks," he said during the promenade.

"After my performance with Mr. Taplin, I suppose you were fearful for your feet."

"I might say the same to you," he answered lightly. "Though my clumsiness with Boulton earlier was child's play, compared to what befell Taplin. Nevertheless, I am not afraid. I have seen you dance—and danced with you myself—enough to know your feet are perfectly in your control. If you trod upon Mr. Taplin, I venture you had very good reason to do so."

She thought about denying it, but what was the need? Tyrone could be trusted.

"I was determined he should know I am no longer the girl I used to be," Aggie replied, her voice pitched only for his ears. "The one who imagined all sorts of perfections in him."

"I honor your sentiment, Miss Weeks."

"Thank you. Mr. Taplin was…not as receptive as I could have wished; therefore I was obligated to be somewhat stiff in urging my point."

"Given this lack of receptiveness, however, dare I say it might have been unwise of you to follow him to the coffee room alone?"

She frowned at him. "Perhaps. But you understand I was resolved to make an end of it."

"To deliver the message, by any means necessary, I suppose?"

"Yes."

"Even if it risked him taking advantage of your isolation and insulting you?"

Her heart was going quite fast, all of a sudden, and something flashed in his eyes, vanishing before she could be certain. Had it been condemnation? Anger? Was he telling her he blamed her for what had happened, or did he not even know what happened?

Aggie only knew that she had no more patience for misunderstandings. She did not intend to clarify matters with Mr. Taplin, only to muddy them elsewhere.

Therefore she returned fire for fire. "Mr. Ellsworth, I ask you straight: what did you see in the coffee-room?"

He answered with equal directness. "I saw you kissing Taplin."

"Correction," Aggie rejoined. "You saw Mr. Taplin kissing *me*. There is a vast difference between the two, I will point out. And if you saw *that*, you also saw I was an unwilling participant who took care to show my unwillingness."

"You did. My own toes ached in sympathy."

With that little joke, he punctured her indignation, and Aggie almost laughed.

"Forgive me, Aggie—Miss Weeks, rather. If I am flippant, it is because it is the only avenue available to me."

"What do you mean?"

"I mean, I believe he behaved abominably and—as your friend—I wish I had the right to tell him so."

"Oh." She was briefly nonplussed. They had come to the promenade again, and she lay her hand in his absently, staring straight ahead. But when they reached the top of the room and separated to either side, she had time to think it through.

"As my friend, then," she resumed, when the figures brought them together again, "I ask you to do nothing. You have already done much, in preventing Mr. Boulton and Frederica from getting a clear view of what went on, and I thank you for that."

He sighed. "I thought you might say as much. But really—if you derived any satisfaction from mashing Taplin's foot beneath your emphatic heel, you must understand that your friends would heartily enjoy a share in that sport."

Then Aggie did giggle. "I understand. And I thank you for your friendship. Wait till Minta hears! She already wanted to throw plums at the man. But no one else must know, do you hear me? I threatened to tell my father, but truly I would hate to, not only because Papa would be so furious, but also because he would surely call in the Beaumond mortgages in revenge, and whom would that punish but poor Mr. John Taplin, the villain's father? So say nothing. Promise me."

His mouth twisted wryly. "Another promise? How many does that make?"

"This is only the second. Promise me you will not accost Mr. Francis Taplin about what you saw and that you will tell no one."

"It seems one should only be allowed to exact one promise at a time from others," Tyrone said with a rueful shake of his head. "If I make this one now, may I break the first?"

Her gaze sharpened. Surely that could not be—he could not be guilty of a flirtatious remark!

"I'm afraid not," was her light response.

"At least remind me what my first promise was, lest I break it out of sheer forgetfulness."

Ah. Not flirtation, then. But only what Minta called her brother's oddness and quibbling.

"You promised, on pain of death, that you would not offer for me. Not for love or money," she prompted him softly. "A promise that should be easily enough kept."

"Ah, yes. To be sure. A trifle, that one. I wonder I bothered to swear."

He was teasing again, but Aggie could not help but be aware of a little pall cast over the remainder of the dance. A pall that was not lifted when, later in the evening, she saw Tyrone escorting Miss Caraway into the coffee-room for the supper.

Chapter 13

Esteem is the commencement of affection.
—Thomas Cogan, *A philosophical treatise on the passions*
(1800)

10 July 1808
Headbourne Worthy

Dear Miss Weeks,

I thank you for the pleasure of our dance at the Race Ball and trust you are recovered from your exertions there. I thank you as well for your forbearance and patience in letting me express my thoughts more clearly on paper. Miss Weeks, you might have noticed my concern when you emerged from the coffee room, but I assure you, those concerns sprung solely from distrust of such a character as Francis Taplin. I have no doubt a young lady as sensible as yourself knows precisely what she was about. I ask no questions. Suffice to say, I hope to win the honor of being your friend, and should you ever require my services in any capacity, you have only to call upon them.

Miss Weeks, while we were dancing, you were kind enough to ask if I had always wanted to be a clergyman. I will tell you the truth and say that it was a profession I viewed at first with uncertainty.

For exactly the reasons you described when you spoke of the exemplary Mr. Hepple. That is, I recognized the office of curate requires sincere dedication of time and effort to one's flock. While the Church has received its share of criticism for supplying rich livings to those who do little to earn them, I believe such cases are vastly outnumbered by curacies which are too often the opposite: heavy work for minimal (earthly) renumeration. I am fortunate in that St. Swithun's is a small parish, and the modest income afforded me by the holder of the living is thus more equitable than others I know of. My sister Miss Boulton and I hope to supplement this income, at any rate, by boarding a pupil or two.

Anne and I hope you will do us the honor of calling, if you are ever in Headbourne Worthy.

> *Your obedient servant,*
> *Gareth Boulton*

This letter, like the note of apology Tyrone had written in his name, Boulton also argued point by point.

"Why do you not ask questions of what happened in the coffee room?" he demanded of his former schoolmate.

"Because she will not thank you for doing so," answered Tyrone. He had brought his composition in person to the rambling, dilapidated parsonage in Headbourne Worthy and perched on a threadbare chair in the parlor. "I asked about the coffee room myself when I danced with her, and she was not pleased, though I've known her for years. How much more displeased would she be by questions from you, who know her not at all?"

"But—but—then what did she say happened with Taplin?"

"She didn't." Tyrone was splitting hairs here. *He* had told Aggie what had happened, and not the other way around, but there was no need for Boulton to know this. "But she did tell me that, whatever he might have said to her, and however unwelcome or inappropriate it might have been, it is at an end," Tyrone continued, "because she told him in no uncertain terms never to address her again."

"I know you told me he was a scoundrel and a fortune hunter," said Boulton, "but I saw how the other ladies admired him. Handsome and well-tailored and all that."

Tyrone shrugged. "That may be, but Miss Weeks does not share their admiration, and that is all that matters here."

"Still and all, I would like to know what happened."

"Then ask her yourself, after she has agreed to marry you."

"You think she might marry me, then, Ellsworth?"

"I would calculate your odds at twenty per cent."

"Only twenty per cent! What am I paying you for?"

"You are paying me a fraction of my usual charge," Tyrone reminded him, "and if you do not like your odds, you are welcome to dismiss me and have a go on your own."

"No. No. Not yet. I may question you, but there is no harm in following your strategy a little longer," Boulton conceded with a sigh. "But I wish you might say something stronger than that she can call upon my friendship and my services."

Tyrone only gave another shrug. The Boultons' maid-of-all-work entered with a bang of the door and a tray of clattering tea things, and Boulton looked more mournful than ever. Could not Anne have served them herself? She at least could be trusted to be quiet and not break anything. His one servant's inadequacies brought Boulton to his second complaint.

"I don't see what good it does at any rate to harp upon my poverty," he grumbled. "Even if you tried to dress it up in nobler language."

"Nobler language—stuff," returned Tyrone. "She would be suspicious if you tried to hide your poverty.

She knows you're poor—you're a curate! She knows you're poor as surely as she knows she is rich, and you're a fool if you think otherwise. This way she sees both your manly resignation as well as your ambition to better your situation."

"But I don't want to take on pupils!" protested Boulton. "Wherever would I put them? Only half the rooms in this place are habitable."

"If you have more than one, they needn't all live in the parsonage. Are there no village boys whose parents aspire to send to Winchester?"

"Oh—I don't know. There may be. I had not thought of it."

"There you are, then. You might even be able to afford a second servant, a competent one."

Boulton's resignation might not have been manly at that point, but it was, at least, resignation. He blew out a long breath. "Fine. Give it to me, and I will copy it."

Aggie folded the letter from Mr. Boulton and gazed meditatively upon the abbey ruins, her slippered foot brushing through the grass beneath to keep the swing in motion. When she and Minta were children, they delighted in exploring the grounds of the Weeks' estate, but now one was more likely to see sheep grazing beneath the crumbling walls of the former convent. This afternoon, however, Frederica and her two stepchildren were come to visit, and the boys were climbing over the rubble, leaping and whooping.

Mr. Boulton continued to surprise her, Aggie thought.

It was true that he was dismayingly inarticulate in her presence, but he admitted as much, and Aggie could only assume it stemmed from shyness of her. And if so, his fluency could only increase as his acquaintance with her increased. Were she to judge him from his letters alone, the two specimens she received were enough to convince her that he was a sensible, manly, honest, even *thoughtful* young man.

She liked very much that he did not ask any questions about the coffee-room contretemps—even Tyrone had not been able to help himself there. Mr. Boulton's refraining demonstrated a trust in her judgment and her character which soothed Aggie, after everyone else's anxiety and gossip and fuss. Of course, Mr. Boulton had no idea how silly she had once been about Mr. Taplin, but it comforted her to think he deemed her sensible now. Why, even Minta, who knew her best—even Minta had not been easy in her mind when Mr. Taplin returned!

"Of course Mr. Boulton still hopes to marry me," Aggie said aloud to the birds and grasses. She gave herself another push with her toe. "Otherwise why should he speak of friendship and asking me to call?"

But even as she spoke, it sounded conceited to her ears, and she blushed. She was not ordinarily the sort of young lady who thought everyone in love with her, and though the last few years had given rise to a mistrust of others' motives, they had not yet made her cynical. Or not so very cynical. She did not yet think all the world made up of fortune hunters.

"It could be," she added to any of nature which cared to listen, "that Mr. Boulton once wished to marry me, though he hardly knew me, but he has since learned from his mistake. He is ashamed of himself, perhaps. Especially now that he has taken orders. So he sets henceforth a humbler goal: he seeks a patroness of sorts."

Her face brightened. That was it! He was not going to beleaguer her with proposals of marriage. Instead he hinted courteously that she might suggest him as somebody's tutor.

"And I can," announced Aggie, hopping up from the swing. "I'll speak to Frederica directly."

With her husband absent in London, Mrs. Linus Chester *née* Miss Frederica Weeks had resumed her favorite post in the morning room of The Acres, with its scrolled wallpaper and walnut Hepplewhite furniture. When Aggie burst in and flung herself on the sofa, Mrs. Chester looked up from the desk where she was writing letters. "Goodness, Agatha. At your advanced age, must I still say to you, 'Decorum'?"

"No, you needn't bother. Freddie, what would you say to getting a tutor for little Linus and Miles? Linus only has one more year to prepare for Winchester's entrance examination, you know, and you were just saying that Mr. Hiram could hardly recall his own name, he is so old."

Mrs. Chester's brow knit. "Yes, Mr. Hiram is most inadequate. I retain him out of pity, you know. If we did not pay him, heaven knows what would become of the man, and he was my own Linus's tutor when he was a boy."

"A hundred years ago," muttered Aggie. "Why not pay Hiram a little annuity then?" she pursued. "And let him retire? Because pity will not prepare little Linus and Miles for school."

Mrs. Chester gave her characteristic *hm-hmm-hm* chuckle, waving her pen at her sister. "How full of advice you are. Why do I suspect you want to nominate a new tutor for the boys?"

"I do, as a matter of fact. But you will lose nothing by it. This one is young and learned and eager for employment."

"Eager for employment?" repeated Mrs. Chester. "I cannot imagine Tyrone Ellsworth being eager for anything."

"Who said anything about Tyrone Ellsworth?" demanded Aggie. "I am speaking of Mr. Gareth Boulton of Headbourne Worthy."

At once her sister rose to her feet. "Mr. Boulton? Why should you wish to help him?"

"Why shouldn't I? He's a poor curate who must make both ends meet, and having a pupil or two would be just the thing."

"Oh, Aggie, what are we to do with you?"

"What do you mean?" she felt her color rising.

"I mean, have you chosen another entirely inappropriate person to give your heart to? First that Taplin rascal, and now a penniless curate?"

Had Aggie been ten years younger, she would have stamped her foot and thrown something at Frederica, and the temptation was still strong. As it was, she had to content herself with slapping her open palms against the seat cushions. "For mercy's sake, I never want to hear Francis Taplin's name again in the whole course of my existence! I was an idiot about him, I freely confess, but I am an idiot about him no longer. Therefore if you love me, banish his name from this house!"

Mrs. Chester shrank as if under bombardment, holding up her own palms in surrender. "Gracious, Agatha. You're simply a savage. Though I must say I am relieved by your declaration."

With a groan, Aggie fell face forward on the sofa. "I *am* a savage. Forgive me, Frederica. Just the name of that man is enough to make me fly into a temper."

"Very well," her sister took a seat beside her and patted her back gingerly. "I will not mention him again if I can help it. But—is your heart given now to Mr. Boulton, dear? He's so terribly poor."

"Nor is my heart given to Mr. Boulton," Aggie mumbled into the cushions. But she was still vexed enough to add, "Though, if it were, what would be the harm? My portion is large enough, and Mr. Boulton at least has no mountain of debt to be cleared."

To her amazement Frederica said, "True. Moreover he and his sister Miss Boulton are respectable and genteel. It is no easy thing to find a great catch, such as Phronsie and I did."

Aggie sat up and stared at her sister to see if she was in earnest. Bald, hypochondriac Mr. King a catch? Widowed Mr. Linus Chester with his several children a catch?

"*Hm-hmm-hm,*" chuckled Frederica, seeing she had succeeded in riling her. "Made you look. But if you are not already attached to Mr. Boulton, might I make a suggestion?"

Frederica would make it whether Aggie permitted it or not, so she pressed her lips together and gave one short nod.

"Now, Aggie, Phronsie told me how unaccommodating you were at Oxford, when she invited Mr. Tyrone Ellsworth to the Angel for dinner."

"Oh—Freddie…"

"Oh, *Aggie*," mimicked her sister, "listen to me. Why not Tyrone Ellsworth? Think how you love Araminta."

"Tyrone is not Araminta."

"Tyrone is not *not* Araminta."

"What?"

"But if we want Tyrone, we must act quickly. No—hush—hear me, Aggie. I already observed at the Race Ball that Miss Caraway has her eye on him. I could not determine whether his own affections were yet engaged, so we must do a little friendly prying and call upon her."

"Frederica! What nonsense are you talking?" protested Aggie. "Firstly, I don't want to call upon Miss Caraway. She was quite off-putting toward me at the ball, and I don't think she would welcome us. Secondly, it is no concern of ours whom Tyrone Ellsworth marries, and if he chooses her, it's his own misfortune."

"Oh, Aggie, how can you be so trying? I thought you enjoyed competition."

"When there is a prize I am desirous of winning!"

Mrs. Linus Chester sucked on her upper teeth thoughtfully. Phronsie had told her it was no use trying to convince Aggie of anything. "I had hoped she had outgrown her headstrong tendencies, Frederica, but it appears she is bull-headed as ever, only she is more circumspect about it." After the events of the Race Ball, Mrs. Chester was not so certain about her younger sister's supposed circumspection, but she agreed with her older sister that Aggie had not left behind her stubborn recklessness. Therefore she must play her cards carefully, and how fortunate if Aggie herself had dealt her a trump!

Folding her hands neatly in her lap, Mrs. Chester composed her features and her voice. "My dear girl, it is immaterial to me whether you marry Tyrone Ellsworth or another eligible gentleman. As I said, catches come in a great variety of forms. But Phronsie has got a bee in her brains about Tyrone Ellsworth in particular and has talked of him as a match for you until I am weary of it."

"Then tell her to mind her own business and never mention it again to you!"

"You think I have not done so?" Mrs. Chester retorted. "No, dear girl, this is where we must outsmart her. We will go through the motions of considering Tyrone Ellsworth, and then, when he does not offer for you, we will sigh and say we did our best."

Aggie was scowling in suspicion before her sister was half done with her sentence. It was not the usual course of things for her and Frederica to scheme against Phronsie. No—too often, if not always, it had been the two elder against the younger.

"No…thank you," she said. "I am sorry if Phronsie is exasperating you, but I do not see why I should have to do anything about it."

"Won't you help me, Aggie?" coaxed Mrs. Chester, sliding an arm about her sister's waist. "You know how Phronsie can be. Only do come and call on Miss Caraway with me—I will do all the talking, if you like—and, in return, I will call on Mr. Boulton with you and consider him for the boys."

For a second, judging by how Aggie stiffened, Mrs. Chester thought she would reject the offer outright. But gradually, gradually, Aggie's person softened into flesh and blood again.

Then Mrs. Chester had only to hide her triumph.

"All right," uttered Aggie at last. "But will we bring the boys along to the Caraways', if we go to Headbourne Worthy directly after?"

"Of course not, you goose. How can I ask Miss Caraway anything, if I must keep the boys in order? Linus and Miles will do just fine at Hollowgate, but let us order the carriage at once."

"But we don't know where the Caraways live!"

"You think Phronsie did not tell me? Come."

Chapter 14

Be ignorance thy choice, where knowlege leads to wo.
—James Beattie, *"The Minstrel; or, the Progress of Genius,
Book II"* (1775)

Tyrone had not left Hollowgate that day with the intention of calling upon Miss Caraway. Indeed, it was only when his youngest sister Beatrice had driven them out of town along the Weeke Road and they trotted into the village of Sparsholt that he tipped the brim of his hat back and glanced around keenly. "I say, if we've come this far, what would you say to paying a call, Bea?"

Beatrice, precise as she was in all things, kept her eyes on the road and the reins of the cart steady. "If you like. I would welcome the practice. You must give me warning of the turns, though. Whom do you propose to call upon?"

"The Caraways at Caraway House."

She inhaled sharply, "Oh, Tyrone, no!"

"Why, no? It will be a quarter-hour of your time, precious Beatrice. I ought to have called sooner because I've twice now led off a ball with Miss Caraway, and Aggie tells me that's what's expected. I didn't know where the Caraways lived, so I excused myself the first time, but Miss Caraway made mention of it at the Race Ball. She said some of the limes were being replaced in the avenue leading from Woodman

Lane, which branches east from Sparsholt. So you see, she was very specific in her hint, and now there is no avoiding it."

Unhappily, Beatrice pulled down on the right rein, and Silver turned obediently into Woodman Lane. "But when Miss Caraway was head girl at Turcotte's, Tyrone, she never particularly showed any liking for me."

"All the more reason to make the call short."

"Did you agree to drive with me this morning, just so you might lure me into this?"

"No, indeed," he replied. "I came driving with you because I wanted to come driving with you. Had you taken us toward Romsey, I would never have remembered my duty to Miss Caraway."

When she was much younger, Beatrice had been prone to cry over every last little thing, but it was not her tears which Tyrone feared now. It was her critical adolescent tongue he would avoid if he could. He was spared, however, by the enormity of the crisis in her mind. Oh!—suppose he were to fall in love with Miss Caraway! she fretted. How very unpleasant that would be, to have a head girl for a sister-in-law. Bea wished and wished an older sister were present. If Lily were with them, her beauty and guile would put Miss Caraway in her place. And if it were Minta, Minta would not hesitate to warn Tyrone against foolishness.

Too soon they spotted Caraway House's vaunted avenue of limes, running at a southeastward angle to intersect Woodman Lane.

Her delicate features screwed in apprehension, Beatrice pulled gently downward to slow Silver, and then she lifted up on the left rein for the sharp turn. The avenue of limes was indeed long; it felt as if they would drive halfway back to Sparsholt. But at last, with her quiet, "Whoa," they drew up before the grand, three-storey 17th-century brick house with its perfect symmetry, numerous mullioned windows, and white trim.

"I think we are not the only visitors," she murmured, gesturing toward the pretty gig standing further along the circular drive, its horse held by a liveried servant. Another groom came forward to take the reins from her and assist her down.

Beatrice was right.

When the footman led them to the drawing room of Caraway House, a high-ceilinged chamber with paneled walls, it was not only Miss Caraway standing before the bay window to greet them. Across from her stood two other callers.

"Speak of the devil, and he'll appear," said Miss Caraway joyously, sweeping him a curtsey. "Mr. Ellsworth, what a surprise and pleasure. And you have brought your sister with you. I believe you are already well acquainted with Mrs. Linus Chester and Miss Weeks."

"We are." Dismay flashed through him, that this visit should coincide with theirs. Well, let her think what she would—Aggie was the one who told him to come. "If you were speaking of me, I can leave again to allow you to finish."

"Never," cried Miss Caraway. "You must take a seat and hear what we have to say of you." She waved him toward a Sheraton chair with silkwood marquetry before patting the place beside her on the sofa. "And Beatrice—may I call you Beatrice? It's so difficult to break school habits!—please do join me."

Beatrice could not recall a single occasion in which Miss Caraway spoke to her unbidden at Turcotte's, much less addressed her by her Christian name. Younger girls had been beneath the head girl's notice, unless to reprimand them, something never necessary with Beatrice. Miss Caraway's unusual affability increased her misgivings, but she took the seat indicated.

A tiny silence fell. Miss Caraway took up her needlework. The Ellsworths' appearance had interrupted an intricate dance, in which Mrs. Chester attempted to probe Miss Caraway regarding Tyrone's feelings, and Miss Caraway with equal determination attempted to probe the Weekses' intimacy with him. A conversation which could hardly be resumed. Or could it? A little imp inside her made Aggie say, "Miss Caraway, I believe you were saying how fine-looking Mr. Ellsworth is."

Miss Caraway blushed—actually *blushed*—and gave an uneasy laugh, and Aggie at once knew she had been unsportsmanlike. The game was between her older sister and Miss Caraway, after all, and it had not been her place to interfere. If Miss Caraway were genuinely taken with Tyrone Ellsworth's charms, and he with hers, matters would play out quickly enough.

"Miss Weeks," murmured Miss Caraway, "are you always this forthright? We girls must keep our secrets."

"She is," struck in Tyrone, "but I will affect deafness, if you like. Should I also pretend I did not hear you call me a devil?"

A giggle met this, but it was not a spontaneous one, and Aggie could see their hostess was recovering. "I beg your pardon. It's merely an old saying. Though I daresay you have got mischief enough in you."

"Do I? What say you, Miss Weeks?" he surprised her with this direct address. "Am I a devil? You've known me longest."

"Nonsense. Bea has known you longest."

"Yes, but I protest asking a sister's opinion," he returned. "Not least because Beatrice is at an age when those around her must expect to have their vanity punctured with some frequency."

"Ooh," breathed Miss Caraway eagerly, turning to accost the young girl beside her, "do tell us some stories, Beatrice. I am inclined to trust the testimony of a sister more than a—friend. Sisters see behind the public face, you know. What sort of brother is Mr. Ellsworth?"

Aggravated anew by Miss Caraway's assumption of familiarity between them, Beatrice only replied, "With only one brother I have got no one with whom to compare him."

"Don't you? Aren't several of your sisters married? My brother Lord Downing is a very stern sort. He would not know a joke to meet it in the street and thinks me frivolous, I'm afraid. There is no devil in him, but his goodness is such that it verges on devilish."

Aggie thought it clever (if tiresome) how Miss Caraway succeeded in reminding them she was connected by marriage to an actual baron, when she probably knew very well that Beatrice's brothers-in-law counted merely an attorney, a clergyman, and a humble doctor.

"Very well," said Beatrice, "if we include those sorts of brothers, I would say Tyrone is not so well-looking as my brother Mr. Fairchild, nor so clever as my brother Mr. Kenner, and not nearly as kind as my brother Mr. Carlisle. I do not think him a devil, but that might only be because he is too lazy for true devilment."

"What did I tell you?" Tyrone asked with mock ruefulness. "Punctured vanity."

Miss Caraway gave a merry laugh, and Aggie pressed back a smile, but Beatrice glared, having intended to be wounding rather than witty. The touchy fourteen-year-old crossed her arms over her middle and vowed inwardly that she would not speak another word for their amusement.

"And you, Miss Weeks?" Miss Caraway pressed. "As the one who has known Mr. Ellsworth the second longest, we turn to you now. Is he a devil? I would prefer to hear a variety of opinions before forming my own."

Aggie could not prevent a note of impatience in her own voice. "He is a devil indeed if he will suffer us to speak of nothing but him."

"Too right," he agreed at once. "Though in my defense I will plead, Miss Weeks, that *you* were the one to introduce me as a subject. Nevertheless, change is in order. Miss Caraway, my sister and I called particularly this morning to see how you fared after the exertions of the Race Ball."

"How kind of you, Mr. Ellsworth."

"I'm no Mr. Carlisle, but I do what I can."

A purring chuckle greeted this sally. "Yes. As you see, I am perfectly well." That he might judge for himself, she extended her graceful arms wide (one in front of Beatrice, who looked like she would love to bat it away).

"I do see." He bowed his head in acknowledgement, and Miss Caraway ducked her own coyly, while Aggie drummed her fingers on her knee and consulted the longcase clock. If possible, she would prefer not to play audience to their courtship performance. Her eyes slid to her sister's face, but Mrs. Chester failed to notice because she was studying the flirting couple through speculative eyes.

Perhaps the incipient wooing could be hurried along, Aggie considered. Then her middle sister could inform their older sister, and Aggie would be left in peace. "Phronsie, it is fruitless to hope Tyrone and Aggie will marry," she pictured Frederica saying, "because he is positively *besotted* with Clementine Caraway." And Phronsie would sigh and say, "Too bad. But at least Aggie says she does not care, and her heart will not be broken again."

But was that the bald truth—that she did not care? Ever since she deceived herself so thoroughly regarding Francis Taplin four years earlier, Aggie resolved to go through the remainder of life with her eyes open and her self-estimation ruthlessly factual. Which meant—she must admit it niggled her, the thought of Tyrone and Miss Caraway making a match of it. It did not overpower, but it niggled.

But because it niggled, that was all the more reason not to be guilty of injustice toward them. In Aggie's opinion, girls were far too quick to turn on each other, in their desire to attract husbands, and while Miss Caraway was no particular friend of hers, it would be mean and small to begrudge her.

Still, Tyrone and Miss Caraway could manage the matter unsupervised.

"What a lovely day for a drive," Miss Caraway was declaring.

"So it is," Tyrone agreed. "Warm, but not oppressive. And by taking the Weeke Road and not Race Way, we avoided much of the traffic."

"I adore a drive on a summer's day," she said, beaming.

"Mm, yes," smiled Tyrone. "Delightful."

A heavy pause followed. *Ask her to accompany you, you dolt!* Aggie's foot twitched, but he was too far away to kick.

Valiantly, Miss Caraway tried again. "You said while we were dancing that you are not much for the races, Mr. Ellsworth, but I am glad your indifference to horses does not preclude you driving them."

"Oh, but I'm afraid it does, Miss Caraway, or nearly. I didn't drive here today. Beatrice took the reins."

"Beatrice!" She turned round eyes on the girl.

With a grimace, Beatrice broke her vow of silence. "I was in a carriage accident some years ago. Therefore it is important to me to learn to drive." And then, since the deed was done, she added, "Nor can we invite you for a ride today because we took the cart. It isn't big enough."

"Are you certain? Miss Caraway would be so slender a passenger," suggested Aggie mischievously.

She almost laughed when Beatrice turned a reproachful scowl upon her. "Perhaps *you* and Mrs. Chester could drive her, in that case."

"It's an idea," said Aggie. "Miss Caraway, Frederica and I drove the gig, but I daresay the squeeze would not be any tighter than the Ellsworth's cart. We go next to Headbourne Worthy to call on the new curate Mr. Boulton and his sister Miss Boulton. Would you care to join us?"

"Off to see Boulton!" exclaimed Tyrone, right over the top of Miss Caraway's demurral. "Whatever for?"

"Is it so astonishing?" returned Aggie. "Why should you be the only one to call upon dance partners?"

"Because I'm the gentleman. It would hardly do for young ladies to go chasing gentlemen about the county."

"'Chasing gentlemen'! Good heavens, is that what I'm doing?"

"It is more usual, Miss Weeks, for us to wait at home to receive our callers," Miss Caraway pointed out, "rather than flushing them from their coverts."

Aggie resented both Tyrone and Miss Caraway assuming she was hunting Mr. Boulton, but she could not help but admire the latter's skill with metaphor. Bookish as Tyrone was, Miss Caraway's wit must please him mightily.

If he was delighted, however, he hid it well, for he was regarding Aggie with a furrowed brow.

The sight of it vexed her. Was he not just teasing her? Did he honestly believe she was "chasing" Mr. Boulton? Ridiculous! Apparently Tyrone would never forget she had once climbed out of her bedroom window to seek Mr. Taplin. That occasion could indeed be deemed "chasing," but not this.

Never mind. Aggie and her sister had spent the requisite amount of time in the Caraway drawing room and could now be on their way. While Aggie might be above flinging obstacles in the path of Tyrone and Miss Caraway's budding courtship, she hardly needed to sit there and be upbraided by them.

Spying the tightening of her sister's lips, Mrs. Chester intervened. "It's my fault Aggie and I are calling upon the Boultons. Really, you two must not suspect her of anything so *forward*. You see, I require a tutor for my young boys, and Mr. Boulton declared he was willing to take some on. Therefore you find us in the gig today."

"Killing two birds with one stone," said Aggie. "To put it in the hunting parlance you both favor."

"He begged such a favor of you while you were dancing?" asked Miss Caraway. "How peculiar! I am glad I had not the honor of being his partner, then."

"He did not ask while we were dancing, no," Aggie returned, goaded by the hit at Mr. Boulton. But as soon as she spoke, she colored, not eager to mention that Mr. Boulton was writing to her.

"He did *not* ask you when you were dancing?" Now Mrs. Chester's curiosity was aroused.

"He must have asked when he called afterward, then," amended Miss Caraway. She tossed her head at Tyrone. "My word. I hope *you* haven't come to issue demands today, Mr. Ellsworth, in guise of a friendly visit."

"Heavens, I hope not," he replied. "For if I have, I've forgotten what I planned to burden you with."

"Did Mr. Boulton call at The Acres?" Mrs. Chester pursued.

Aggie's heart sped. Why did anyone care? "He—didn't. I—don't remember when he mentioned wanting pupils," Aggie lied. "What does it matter? One talks of so many things, all the time."

"Perhaps you read it somewhere?" Tyrone prompted. His level, penetrating gaze made Aggie begin to sweat.

"An advertisement in the newspaper!" Miss Caraway clapped her hands.

"He wrote to me!" bellowed Aggie. "I—er—remember now. A note. To thank me for dancing with him."

"Not a particularly memorable note, it seems," Tyrone murmured. "Your recollection required a considerable jog."

"Not everyone can turn a phrase like Shakespeare," she replied curtly. She could be rude to him, if not to Miss Caraway. "But it was a perfectly adequate note. Manly and to the point. You needn't be a snob just because you consider yourself a literary genius."

"Ooh," Tyrone gave a mock groan, putting a hand to his ribs. "Another wound to my vanity. And this one the more painful, for being unexpected. *E tu, Brute?*"

"Are you indeed a literary genius, Mr. Ellsworth?" questioned Miss Caraway, admiration lighting her eyes.

But he shook his head. "Ah—that's a trap I won't fall into. If I say yes, I am an immodest devil. And if I deny it, Miss Weeks will say I do so only in hopes of someone giving me the lie."

"Come, come," Miss Caraway coaxed. "Do not put me off. What do you write, sir?"

"He writes letters to his friends," spoke up Beatrice again. "Dozens of letters to dozens of friends."

It was Tyrone's turn to appear uncomfortable. "It's no proof of genius, in any event."

"Proof, rather, of a loyal and affectionate heart," Miss Caraway praised. "La, Mr. Ellsworth, how everything merely serves to enlarge your fame. I would love to hear some of your writing read aloud. I simply adore a good letter-writer."

This would have been the perfect time for Tyrone to produce some masterpiece from a waistcoat pocket for her perusal, but he made no move to, and Aggie had to assume he either had no convenient sample upon him, or he was too obtuse to go about this courtship properly. She raised significant eyebrows at him. The dunce! He could at least recite some poetry, or something.

Tyrone's eyebrows rose in return, his expression bright and vacant.

Aggie gave up. On his own head be it. Whatever the case, she longed to be gone.

"Come, Freddie." Aggie seized her sister's elbow and drew her to her feet. "We should be on our way."

Beatrice looked at her brother hopefully as the Weeks sisters rose, but Miss Caraway must have read her mind because she sprung forward, extending a hand toward Tyrone, who was also getting politely to his feet. "Oh, dear—I do hope you and Beatrice will stay another few minutes, Mr. Ellsworth, for I believe they were preparing lemonade and sandwiches for the haymakers, and I must ply you with them, for work of the drawing room is strenuous in its own fashion. And you may stay and partake as well, of course," she added to Aggie and Mrs. Chester.

The Ellsworths must perforce remain, but the two sisters made their excuses and were soon enough outside Caraway House, being assisted to climb once more into the gig.

Aggie waited until they had passed down the endless avenue of limes and turned again into Woodman Lane before saying, "I think you may safely tell Phronsie it is hopeless. It was plain as daylight that Miss Caraway has set her cap for Tyrone and plain as well that he has no objection. He is a little stupid about it, to be sure, but if she perseveres the prize will be hers."

"I don't know about that," answered Mrs. Chester, to Aggie's surprise. "Mr. Tyrone Ellsworth strikes me as having the convenient ability to ignore what he does not feel like facing."

"Oh!" breathed Aggie, not sure if she liked this description of him. "It's odd you should say such a thing. Minta always complains that if her father Mr.

William Ellsworth does not want to see something, he refuses to see it. But I don't think Tyrone is much like old Mr. Ellsworth."

Mrs. Chester only shrugged. "Who can say? All I mean is that, Miss Caraway may try to catch him, but if he does not feel like being caught, I suspect Mr. Tyrone Ellsworth will prove slippery enough."

The part of Aggie which had niggled earlier found satisfaction here. And then she was embarrassed by her dog-in-the-manger attitude.

"Well," she rejoined, "your lesson would be a good one for Phronsie to learn, too. If you think Miss Caraway must make him willing before she can catch him, the same would have to be said in my case. Tyrone could slip out of my clutches—should I choose to clutch at him—with equal ease."

"Mm," said Mrs. Chester, slowing Silver as they came up behind a cart heaped with hay.

Aggie thought her sister would continue the subject when they turned onto the Stockbridge Road and the hay cart continued toward Weeke, but she said nothing.

"You *will* tell Phronsie our findings, won't you?" she prodded. "So she will leave me alone?"

"I will tell Phronsie," agreed Mrs. Chester.

Aggie felt a weight lift off her. It was all she asked—to be left to marry or not marry, as she pleased. In her happiness she untied her bonnet and pulled it off, to let the sun play on her face. Mrs. Chester did not even reprimand her for this.

It was a lovely day, a lovely summer day.

Only when they rattled into Headbourne Worthy did her sister speak again, picking up the thread of their conversation as if it had not been dropped.

"I will tell Phronsie you and Tyrone Ellsworth will never be a match," Mrs. Chester began anew. "But will anyone tell Tyrone Ellsworth?"

Chapter 15

I follow him not
By any token of presumptuous suit.
—Shakespeare, *All's Well That Ends Well* (c.1598)

When the sisters drew up to the Boultons' rambling parsonage in Headbourne Worthy, the front door flew open, and a maid goggled at them. She was a creature of uncertain years with wispy hair straggling from under her cap and long, prominent teeth which reminded Aggie of a rabbit.

"Are you here to see the curate?" she demanded.

"We are," answered Mrs. Chester quellingly, affronted by the servant's manner. "Is there anyone to take the horse?"

"No one."

"Is Mr. Boulton at home, then?"

"He's at the church. But I can call Miss Boulton." Before they could reply, she retreated a step, half shutting the door and roaring, "*Miss Boulton! Visitors in a gig!*"

In an instant the long and lugubrious Miss Boulton swept out, muttering a terse word to the maid as she passed, which dismayed the woman not at all. Miss Boulton was then compelled, after making her curtsey to the gig occupants, to turn once more. "Hackitt, run to the church and fetch Mr. Boulton.

And if you see a likely boy, tell him we will give him tuppence to come and hold the horse."

Hackitt must have been younger than she looked because, with another goggle at the callers, she galloped away, one hand to her cap and taking the boxwood hedge at a leap.

Miss Boulton shut her eyes briefly. "I apologize for receiving you out here, Mrs. Chester, Miss Weeks."

"Say nothing of it, Miss Boulton," answered Mrs. Chester graciously, inwardly thanking Providence for placing her in a higher station in life. "Have you and your brother settled in your new residence?"

"We have, thank you. The previous tenant left a great many things behind, but I have managed to dispose of much of it among the poorer members of our flock, with the happy result that Gareth has made a study from the room overlooking the churchyard, and I myself have got a morning room of sorts. If Hackitt succeeds in finding a boy, I would be glad to show you."

"A study!" Aggie noted brightly. She nudged Mrs. Chester with an elbow. "Frederica, why don't I sit here, and Miss Boulton can give you a tour? I don't mind a bit."

If Miss Boulton was startled by Aggie taking her polite remark so literally, she gave no sign. And as Mrs. Chester certainly would not be easy sending her boys to study in a home she had not seen, she climbed down willingly enough.

Good. Aggie wanted to be alone. She removed her bonnet again and lounged back in the corner of the gig, that she might prop one leg across the seat. What had Frederica meant, saying that Tyrone Ellsworth ought to be told he and Aggie would never be a match? Aggie had not dared pursue the subject. She needed to think and think.

It was plain Miss Caraway encouraged Tyrone's attentions. Plain that, if he chose to pursue her, he would not be rebuffed. Not that anyone would be likely to rebuff him. He was eminently eligible.

Even Aggie's discourtesy toward him, at the Oxford dinner or on other occasions, was not a rebuff, in that a rebuff required Tyrone to put himself forward, and Tyrone never put himself forward. No—quite the opposite. He never need lift a finger because anyone and everyone did all the work for him. With his looks and wealth, he might marry a duchess, if he pleased, but Aggie would bet the duchess would still be the one putting forth the effort.

Was Frederica implying that, if Aggie put forth effort, Tyrone would be willing to be ensnared by her? That, if he was not subject to any grand passion (a condition impossible to picture him in), he liked her well enough to be caught?

She imagined herself flirting lavishly with him. Making teasing comments, praising him, hinting, giggling at his slightest humorous remark. Unflagging exertion, day after day, ball after ball, call after call, for who knew how long, in order to have him shrug his shoulders at last and declare it might as well be her as anyone else.

She had been the pursuer before—with Mr. Taplin—and see where it had got her. The man had offered for her in the end, but now she thanked heaven fasting that she had not accepted him.

No, Aggie thought. She could not do it again.

She would not.

She could not bring herself to pursue and persuade. Was it too much to ask, that, if she ever considered marriage again, her prospective spouse be the pursuer? That he consider the prize of her heart one worth laboring for?

It just might be. But having already tried, painfully, the kind of love which gave all, to receive little in return, she now refused to hold herself so cheaply again. No, she resolved, she would not. If no one ever entered her life who was willing to give all, in order to receive all, well—it was not really so bad never to marry.

No sooner did she reach this conclusion than she heard the clopping of hooves and the rattle of a carriage in the lane. Hastily Aggie sat up, shaking out her skirts and glancing over to see the very object of her thoughts approaching, driven handily by his younger sister Beatrice. Twice in one day? Aggie replaced her bonnet and was tying the ribbons when they drew up next to her.

"What is this?" Tyrone asked lazily. "Were you refused entrance?"

"There was no boy to hold the horse," Aggie explained, "so I am doing it while Miss Boulton shows Frederica the parsonage. But what are you doing here? Headbourne Worthy lay out of your way."

"We come to deliver an invitation," he replied. "A little birthday party at Hollowgate for Minta and me."

"Why, Minta said nothing to me of it, and I saw her only yesterday."

He blinked in mock alarm. "Oh—forgive me. I meant to say I am here to deliver an invitation to Boulton."

"Oh!" Aggie's lips parted, and then she clamped them shut again. Then it was a family party, and she herself was not invited?

But Beatrice leaned past her brother. "And *I* am here to invite *you*," she said crossly. "Because of course you are wanted. Minta didn't ask you because she doesn't even know of it yet. We are thinking Friday. Say you'll come! Greaves will fetch the Carlisles because of Minta's condition, and he can easily fetch you as well."

"That would be lovely," agreed Aggie, smothering her own stab of annoyance to see how Tyrone hid a smile. It was proof that she was right. He might tease her because he liked her, but it was the indolent teasing of a brother.

Pooh. Let other moths fly at that flame.

"Ellsworth! Miss Weeks! Miss Ellsworth." The parsonage door flew open again, and there was Mr. Boulton on the step. His breath was short, so he must have come at a trot from the church, but Aggie thought it gave him much-needed color. "I do beg your pardon that I wasn't here to receive you, and that I haven't anyone to hold your horses, but perhaps—" He glanced hither and yon, as if intending to enlist any convenient passerby.

"Never mind it, Boulton," Tyrone interrupted. "Beatrice and I aren't stopping."

"Not stopping?"

"Afraid not." In a moment the dinner invitation was given and accepted, the curate's politeness metamorphosing into eagerness when he learned Aggie too would be present.

"Miss Weeks!" He rounded on her with enthusiasm. "I cannot thank you enough for suggesting me as a tutor to your young nephews—I met Anne and Mrs. Chester as I passed through the house. I only hope I will prove satisfactory in the role when we begin in September."

"Then you are agreed upon it? Mr. Boulton, I am delighted!" After the day's trials, Aggie's success on this point lifted her spirits markedly. "But it was your own suggestion, so I cannot take all the credit."

"But you must," he said earnestly. "I made mention of it with no idea that you would take it upon yourself—indeed, had I known you would, I would have said nothing in the first place, lest you think I was begging a favor."

"Oh, nonsense," she replied. "Neighbors must help each other, and I did nothing but match your wishes to my sister's need, with this happy result."

Still he thanked her repeatedly, and then repeated his repeated thanks when Mrs. Chester and his sister emerged from the parsonage, and then Miss Boulton must add her own thanks to the pile. All told, it was some minutes before Aggie and Mrs. Chester could get away. Aggie wondered at the Ellsworths' lingering throughout this, as did Beatrice, who even prodded her brother once, but he had removed one of his gloves to pick at his fingernail and paid no heed.

Only when Mr. Boulton assisted Mrs. Chester back into the gig, still expressing his gratitude, and the good woman took the reins from Aggie did Tyrone replace his glove and lift his hand in careless farewell. "Have you heard enough, Beatrice? Why do we not get under way, unless you are tired from all your driving?"

"I was waiting for you to say we should go," she hissed in protest, before giving a shake of her head and deciding to save her breath. With a nod to the others she bid the horse walk on.

"We will see you Friday, then, Miss Weeks," said Mr. Boulton. When Mrs. Chester raised an eyebrow at this, he added quickly, "Hollowgate hosts a small dinner to mark the birthday of Ellsworth and his sister Mrs. Carlisle."

The realization that Mrs. Chester was likely not included among the guests made him flush at his own awkwardness, and Aggie took pity on him. "A small dinner indeed, Freddie. Beatrice didn't even say whether Minta's sisters' families or her cousins would be there, and I forgot to ask. In any event, after the Ellsworth carriage picks up the Carlisles, it will come for me."

From Frederica's raised eyebrows, Aggie knew she considered this additional evidence of Tyrone Ellsworth's interest, but Aggie had no intention of canvassing the matter further. As they drove back to The Acres, therefore, she plied her sister with questions about the parsonage, Miss Boulton, Mr. Boulton, the boys' planned tutelage, and what Mr. Chester would make of it all, until Mrs. Chester herself was completely distracted by the consuming interests of her family.

The gratitude Mr. Boulton lavished on Aggie and her sister was not confined to them alone. The following day, having come upon Tyrone in one of the coffee-houses in the High Street reading the newspaper, Boulton dropped into a chair at once and gave the back of the sheet a tap.

Probably fewer than a man in a thousand could bear such an interruption without annoyance, and Tyrone was not among these paragons of patience. Lowering the newspaper, he frowned upon his former schoolmate, but the latter was already signaling the waiter and failed to notice.

"Ellsworth," he began, when his coffee was ordered, "what luck to meet with you. With Miss Weeks present yesterday I had not the opportunity to say all that was in my mind."

"It must be urgent, if you insist on saying it now."

"Now, now. Don't be surly, Ellsworth. I wanted to tell you that you were right and I was wrong. For the tutoring idea was a stroke of genius! I cannot express how it has heartened me, to see with what alacrity and affability Miss Weeks snatched at the suggestion."

"Yes," said Tyrone quietly, "it surprised me as well."

"And the dinner invitation to Hollowgate! My cup overflows. You have proved more than a paid amanuensis to me—you have shown yourself to be a true friend."

Crisply Tyrone folded the newspaper and slapped it on the table. "Firstly, Boulton, an amanuensis is one who takes dictation or who copies out a text already written, neither of which describes what I have done for you. And secondly, I assure you that you have got nothing to thank me for. Had you not requested my help and paid for my services, I would not have lifted a finger."

Instead of appearing abashed by this reproof, Boulton's long features curved upward in a witless smile—well, perhaps 'witless' was harsh, but Tyrone's sudden irritability made him unkind.

"Some people do not like to be thanked," Boulton soothed, palms uplifted in deprecation. "I will say no more of it. In fact, Ellsworth, I daresay my need for your assistance will soon draw to a close."

"What do you mean?" The question emerged more curtly than Tyrone intended, and he suppressed a grimace.

The waiter placed a murky saucer of coffee before Boulton, which he then swirled and sugared and stirred and tentatively sipped. (Fortunately he found it to his satisfaction, or Tyrone might have dashed it to the table in his impatience.) Setting the cup down precisely, he replied, "I mean only to say that I take such encouragement from my rapid progress with Miss Weeks—"

"*What* progress? She recommended you as a tutor to her nephews. What more can you possibly be referring to?"

"Ah." Boulton raised a finger. "Not only did Miss Weeks recommend me for her nephews—which she most certainly would never have done had she felt an aversion to me—but she *raced* over to Headbourne Worthy almost as soon as she received my note."

"'Raced'? Nonsense."

"Raced," persisted Boulton. "Therefore, Ellsworth, at the dinner to which you have so graciously invited both me and the young lady, I think I may safely be trusted now to speak with her on matters additional to sport, weather and wallpaper patterns. That is, I may now expand upon the trifles you insisted were my only safe topics for conversation."

"I did not realize you had kept to them," Tyrone ground out. "Was there not some mention made of 'helpmates' at the ball? Hardly a trifle, when spoken of between unmarried people. But leave that for now. See here, Boulton—you have sent the girl one apology and one longer note, danced with her once or twice, and been hired to teach her young nephews, and now you believe yourself nearly at your goal?"

His companion's chest swelled with stubbornness. "I do. And at Hollowgate on Friday, I intend to see which way the land lies. If she continues amiable and encouraging toward me, I plan to offer for her again."

Boulton threw his head back, his eyes distant, as if picturing that golden scene. "Therefore," he resumed after another moment, oblivious to Tyrone's frown, "I have got one final commission for you."

He waited, the witless smile flickering again over his long features, but Tyrone would not give him the satisfaction of asking him to elaborate.

Boulton cleared his throat and took another gulp of his coffee. "I mean to say," he continued, a little flustered now, "I am asking you to write me a proposal. Not a letter one, you understand, but a—a set of speeches. Like a scene from a play. Lines to deliver in person. I will do my best to commit them to memory, of course, since Miss Weeks did not approve of me consulting my memorandum on the previous occasion, but I confess it would give me courage to have something in hand to refer to."

Still Tyrone said nothing.

Boulton seized his coffee cup and downed another swallow. He eyed Tyrone over the brim. When the latter merely held his gaze, Boulton took another sip, one so generous it ended in him choking on it. Erupting in coughs, he fumbled the nearly-empty cup back in its saucer with a clatter.

"I—ahem!—hope that would be amenable to you. I know you wrote the last two things for a pittance, Ellsworth, but for a proposal of marriage—ahem! ahem!—I want your best work and am willing to pay the entire half-crown fee. Nay—in order to have it before Friday, I would double that! I would pay you a full crown."

At last his companion replied. "You will pay me nothing because I am not going to write it."

Still coughing in abbreviated bursts, Boulton went an uneven pink. He picked up his cup again and then replaced it once more. He dug for his handkerchief and coughed a few more times into it.

"But—ahem!—What do you mean? Do you mean you haven't got the time to write it?"

Tyrone shook his head. "I mean I haven't got the inclination. To be perfectly frank. Moreover, it's too soon, I tell you, Boulton."

The curate straightened, stiff and offended. "I know you gave me slender odds some time ago—"

"More like some *days* ago," muttered Tyrone.

"—And apparently you do not credit my progress. Tell me the truth: do you doubt my chances because of that scoundrel at the Race Ball? The one who broke her heart—and then dared to—to—You saw what went on in there, in the coffee-room at St. John's House! I could not. You were in the way. But did he—did he dare to—"

"Keep—your—voice—down, Boulton," Tyrone bit out, fire in his eye.

"But—but—"

Tyrone gave another, fierce shake of his head. "Miss Weeks assured me nothing occurred in the coffee-room that anyone need address. I advise you, therefore, to forget about that other person and never mention him in connection with her again."

Briefly, Tyrone shut his eyes. What was *wrong* with him? Temper, temper.

"Look here," he resumed, when he had himself in hand. "I will write your proposal speeches—wait—hear me out—but I would like it noted that I think it too soon. Nor will I answer for how they are received."

From Boulton's creased brow, Tyrone judged he wanted to pursue the subject of Taplin and Aggie in the coffee-room further, but Tyrone's abrupt capitulation distracted him.

"You *will* write it then? And—and—it goes without saying—you will do a good job of it?"

Tyrone met this with silence.

"Of course you will," Boulton added hastily. "Pardon the implication, Ellsworth. Courtship tears a man's nerves to shreds, you understand. Makes him say all manner of nonsense. Of course you will do a good job of it. But—will I have it before Friday?"

"You will," replied Tyrone. He took up the newspaper again and unfolded it. "But, again—if you are so stupid as to use it prematurely, you will have only yourself to blame."

"Certainly, certainly," Boulton assured him, the provoking smile once more in evidence. "I will choose my moment."

With that, he set a coin down beside his saucer and rose, leaving Tyrone in possession of the table and free to erect the paper once more as a barrier between himself and the world.

Chapter 16

A man that flattereth his neighbour
spreadeth a net for his feet.
—Proverbs 29:5, *The Authorized Version* (1611)

Madame Blanchet, the most select and stylish modiste in Winchester, occupied a sparkling shop with bow window in Great Minster Street, facing upon the cemetery of the great cathedral. Aggie not being terribly interested in clothing, whenever a fitting required her to visit, she usually combined the errand with another. On this occasion she dropped in at the toymaker's in the Square, where she found a bright blue paper kite with a violet tail for her nephews Linus and Miles. It being a fragile creation, Aggie did not trust her maid Banniker to carry it, and thus it was Aggie who witnessed its destruction when the door to the dressmaker's shot open and a willowy young lady sailed out to collide with her.

"Dear me," said Miss Clementine Caraway, "do watch where you're going. Oh! Is it you, Miss Weeks? What sort of bauble have you got there? A fan?"

"It was a kite," said Aggie. "But now it is kindling."

Miss Caraway's laugh trilled. "How droll you are! I do like that shade of blue—so rich and bright. It would match my eyes. Too bad Mme Blanchet hadn't any muslin that color. You can't imagine how difficult it is, having *dark* blue eyes, rather than a commoner shade like yours or Miss Beatrice Ellsworth's."

Aggie couldn't think how poor Beatrice came in for a share of the insult, but she had no desire to prolong the encounter by asking. Miss Caraway seemed in no hurry to go, however, and remained blocking the entrance, her maid over her shoulder waiting as if there were nothing she would rather do than stand behind her mistress, clutching an armful of parcels.

"So kind of you and your sister to call on me at Caraway House. It can feel remote. How I wish my dear sister Lady Downing lived nearer to hand, but she and Lord Downing spend most of their time in London, unless they are in Kent at his family seat."

"I hope she is a good correspondent, then," replied Aggie with a nod. But Miss Caraway did not step aside.

"This is the second time I've seen you here. Has Mme Blanchet been making you a new gowns as well?" was her next question. "Only a few alterations? However will you manage? I love this season occasion after occasion after occasion—only, one can't show up wearing the same thing over and over without exciting comment. And I daresay the difficulty must increase as the years pass. Have you found it so?"

"You make it sound as if I were two-and-forty, rather than two-and-twenty," remarked Aggie, a tinge of crossness discernible in spite of herself.

Another trilling laugh. "Oh! La! Do pardon me, Miss Weeks. I suppose you remember when you were eighteen—how vastly older everyone else seemed."

Aggie had taken hold of herself again and said wryly, "I'm afraid it's so long ago I can't recall."

"Well, I assure you it is so. In any event, I have got another dress ready—" She indicated her parcel-laden maid "—for Saturday's concert, and then my ivory-striped silk is newly trimmed for the next ball. Still, I pray the gentlemen are less observant of such matters than the ladies."

"Indeed," said Aggie. "Though if they did notice, it would hardly be courteous of them to mention it."

"How providential they are required to be courteous! Would it not be dreadful if someone like Mr. Ellsworth noted that you wore your white silk with the net lace twice?"

Aggie's lips twitched. "Not so very dreadful. I've known Mr. Ellsworth long enough that if he remarked on such a thing, I could threaten to box his ears for impertinence."

"Box his ears!" echoed Miss Caraway in exaggerated amazement, her laugh rolling out again over the quiet cathedral yard. "You would make a dangerous enemy, Miss Weeks."

"How fortunate then that I consider no one my enemy," returned Aggie. "Now, if you would pardon me, Miss Caraway, I do not wish to be late for my appointment."

At last the girl yielded her place, striding away up Great Minster and trailed by her burdened maid. With a wrench, Aggie tore her eyes from her. Had she just told a lie, claiming she had no enemies? Probably. For what was Mr. Taplin, if not an enemy? And what did Miss Caraway consider herself, judging by the pains she took to insist on her superior connections and youth? Plainly the girl viewed Aggie as a rival for Tyrone's affections, preposterous as that sounded. What indication had Aggie ever given, that Miss Caraway should take on so?

Perhaps it would save everyone a great deal of trouble, Aggie thought, *if I simply explained to her Tyrone is hers for the taking, and she may leave me in peace.*

Putting aside these ruminations, Aggie entered the modiste's neat establishment, with its numerous looking glasses and pink brocade furniture. Mme Blanchet was engaged in measuring a slender young lady half hidden by a screen, but an older woman rose to greet her. "Aggie, *mais quel plaisir!* Beatrice, *regarde.*"

"Good afternoon, Mrs. Ellsworth, Mme Blanchet, Beatrice."

At her aunt's bidding, Beatrice Ellsworth poked her head around the screen. "Is she gone?" she whispered.

"I suppose you mean Miss Caraway? Yes, she's gone."

The rest of Bea followed, swathed in blue-sprigged muslin and bristling with pins. "Oh, Aggie, it was horrible to have her come in when I was getting fitted. She complimented Mme Blanchet on being able to dress such a variety of girls, 'even those who have yet to blossom'!"

Her aunt Jeanne dismissed this with Gallic practicality. "The blossom will come. There is no need for the hurt feelings."

"But Aunt Jeanne, that is easy for you to say, when Uncle Charles always says he was nearly blinded by your beauty the first time he got a good look at you. You have got no idea what it is like to be unbeautiful."

Jeanne clicked her tongue. "You think I do not know? I know. And one day I will tell you the story. But for today, you must *fais-moi confiance*. You must trust me."

But with fourteen-year-old gloom, Bea sighed. "It was still discourteous of her. I *know* I haven't blossomed, except to get tall and stick-like. There was no need for her to say so."

The rest of them rallied to cheer her up, admiring the simple and flattering lines Mme Blanchet arranged for her. Beatrice's virtue lay in her everlasting neatness. No one looked more trim and fresh in white, and the modiste never feared her creations would be stained or torn when Beatrice wore them.

Aggie (and Beatrice's older sister Araminta, for that matter) had been another story entirely, though depredations to their clothing were rarer as they grew older and opportunities for sport dwindled. Still, if Aggie planned to visit Minta, she wisely wore her older gowns.

When both young ladies finished with their fittings, Beatrice agreed to walk back to Hollowgate with Aggie and her maid, so that Mrs. Ellsworth might return directly home. And no sooner had they parted ways with the latter at St. Thomas Street than Beatrice looped an arm through Aggie's and pulled her ahead of Banniker.

"Aggie, how glad I am of a chance to speak with you apart," Bea said. "I couldn't, with Aunt Jeanne there—she is so interested in love affairs, you know. I knew if I mentioned anything, she would be sure to bring it up again later and get me in hot water."

"Good heavens, Bea," teased Aggie, poking her, "don't tell me you are involved in a love affair!"

"Of course I don't mean me! I'm speaking of Tyrone."

Aggie's playfulness shut off like a spigot. "Tyrone? Is he concerned in a love affair?"

"He will be if he doesn't beware," answered Beatrice ominously.

"I suppose you mean with Miss Caraway?"

The young girl gasped. "Then it's so, already? He's said nothing, of course, to any of us. What do you know, Aggie?"

"I don't know a thing. I only guessed Miss Caraway because we just saw her. Did she say something before I came in? Besides you not blossoming yet, I mean."

Beatrice waited until they had passed the Black Swan Inn, less crowded with lawyers and journalists now that the Assizes were concluded.

"It was not anything in particular she said, Aggie—it was her manner as a whole. When we were together at school, and she was head girl, and I was a nobody, I would not have taken for granted that she even knew my name! But you saw how it was when we called at Caraway House—and it was the same today— anyone would have thought we were bosom friends at Turcotte's!"

Aggie made a wry face. "Dear Beatrice, you may find that Miss Caraway is not alone in wishing to befriend you now."

"What do you mean?"

"I mean that you have got a very eligible brother, and until he marries, I would not be a bit surprised if Miss Caraway and plenty of other young ladies do what they can to make a favorable impression. If they butter you up a little, it does not necessarily follow that they will not come to care genuinely for you, as you become better acquainted. At any rate, you had better resign yourself to the process because Tyrone will be much pursued, I suspect."

Troubled, Beatrice absorbed this unwelcome news in silence, not even glancing up when they passed through the West Gate.

"Of course he will marry," she said at last. "And of course I would rather have a new sister who is pleasant to me than one who is not, even if it is self-serving on her part at first. But—Aggie—what if I never come to like her?"

Aggie well remembered how she and Minta disliked their own head girl, when they were Beatrice's age. But was Clementine Caraway as insufferable as her older sister Lady Downing, née Caroline Caraway, had been?

She paused to put her arm about the girl's bony shoulders. "Oh, Beatrice. You have been especially fortunate in being so fond of all the new additions to your family. Such a good troop of brothers-in-law! But such is hardly the case with everyone."

"Do you not like Mr. Chester or Mr. King, then?" asked Beatrice, dropping her voice.

"They are just fine," Aggie replied firmly. "Absolutely fine. Good husbands to my sisters and—fine. So I also consider myself fortunate in my connections."

It was faint praise, to be sure, and Beatrice's face indicated she found it less than persuasive. But there was nothing more to be said. So, pressing her lips together, she gave a heavy nod, and they walked on.

On the afternoon of the dinner, the Ellsworth carriage rolled up to the open courtyard of Hollowgate, a square, two-storey Jacobean house faced in red brick, and Greaves assisted the Carlisles and Aggie to alight. Aggie wore again her white silk with the net lace, if only to prove two things to herself: that she was not trying to impress Tyrone Ellsworth, and that she would not let Miss Caraway's smiling taunts cow her.

But when she followed the Carlisles and Bobbins the footman into the drawing room, it was not this defiance which brought the color to her cheeks and glow to her eyes. It was the news the Carlisles had given her in the carriage.

"Aggie, guess what—Taplin is gone!" crowed Minta, heaving her bulk to Aggie's side of the vehicle to squeeze her eagerly.

"He said nothing to us, but my father found a note this morning," Nicholas Carlisle explained, in answer to Aggie's astonished look.

"But Minta," gasped Aggie, "you told me he would not go until autumn."

"So I did, because so he said. But then his note to Mr. John Taplin declared he could wait no longer and had booked his passage on the *Sparrow* out of Bristol! He said Mr. Taplin might write to him at the Ship and Castle in Wine Street until 25 July, but after that he must wait for Mr. Francis to write to him again from Philadelphia when he was safely arrived!"

"I am speechless." Aggie shook her head in amazement. "And do you really believe he has gone?"

Carlisle's mouth twisted ruefully. "The best proof we might offer is that several banknotes were missing from my father's drawer, with which he intended to pay the quarterly interest owed to your father."

"Oh, dear," blushed Aggie. The fact that Beaumond was heavily mortgaged to her father was one of the reasons Mr. Weeks so opposed Mr. Taplin years ago. "I am so sorry."

"There is no need for apologies when one has done nothing wrong," Carlisle assured her sincerely. "Especially when it is your own father my brother has robbed."

But Aggie didn't care about a hundred pounds more or less owed to her father's account—he would scarcely notice its absence. Indeed, her papa would deem the money well lost if Mr. Taplin were truly gone.

It was beginning to register in her mind.

Mr. Taplin, gone.

Whether it had been her own actions which hastened his departure she would never know. All she knew was that—for a very, very long time or even for ever and ever—she was free of him. Free from his shadow over her life. Free from the fear of encountering him wherever she went. Free from the well-meaning and ill-meaning eyes of Winchester studying her to see how she bore his return.

Free, free, free—thanks be to God.

Hence the radiance that lit her from within as she reached Hollowgate, a radiance plain for all to see.

Boulton saw it and hardened in his resolve to win her. Her fortune might still be her chief glory, but she was a pretty little thing, which always helped, and with Heaven's help he would make her a good husband.

Tyrone saw it and wondered, something stirring uneasily within him. Could blundering Boulton be right? Was she warming to the man? Was this sparkle for *him*?

Boulton fingered his waistcoat pocket, where Tyrone would bet a hundred guineas the blasted proposal speeches were stowed. For Tyrone had kept his word and written the things. Written them well. His own sense of honor would not permit him to produce anything second rate, though the urge to do so had been there. He had been disturbed, in fact, to realize how earnestly he wanted to see Boulton fail.

"Welcome, all," beamed Mr. William Ellsworth, arms spread wide. "How I love to have family about me. And Mr. Boulton, our new friend. I tell you, Mr. Boulton, the grief of losing successive children to marriage is counterbalanced by new sons" (with a nod at Carlisle) "and the appearance of grandchildren." He viewed Minta's ungainly size with delight and no doubt would have pointed it out, had Mrs. Ellsworth not taken hold of his right arm. "And as for Aggie, she has been so often at Hollowgate from her childhood years that she is practically another daughter. Are you all acquainted with Tyrone's school friend Mr. Boulton? Yes? No? Allow me to introduce you…"

Mrs. Ellsworth having counseled her husband that Mr. Boulton and lovelorn Aggie must become better acquainted, Mr. Ellsworth made much of the long-featured curate, seating him at his right hand at the dinner and placing Aggie directly across. Still buoyed by the good news of Taplin's departure, Aggie was happily oblivious and willing enough to humor Mr. Ellsworth.

"Aggie, Mr. Boulton says he is a tremendous walker," Mr. Ellsworth pronounced. "You must pardon me, Mr. Boulton, but I seldom venture from Hollowgate and even then am often on horseback. But Aggie, *you* will have some favorite walks to suggest, won't you? You and Minta were always wandering the countryside."

"As he is an alumnus of Winchester College, sir, I am certain he must already know the same walks I do," she demurred.

"Ah, but Miss Weeks, you cannot be certain of that," replied Boulton in his mournful tones. "When we inferiors were relieved from our studies by a holiday, we were only allowed to roam about on our own if a friend invited us for a visit. Otherwise we were turned out *en masse* on St. Catherine's Hill before breakfast for Morning Hills and again in the afternoon for Middle Hills. So you see, most of my walking was confined to such occasions with my schoolfellows."

"What a shame, when walking the downs is such a treat," said Aggie. "And there is Oram's Arbour, along the footpath from Weeke, where they hold the sheep fair in October, and the view from St. Giles' Hill, of course."

Mr. Boulton fairly lunged at her suggestions, leaning so far forward his neckcloth was in danger of touching his soup, and saying intently, "I thank you for those proposals, Miss Weeks! Perhaps you might guide my sister Miss Boulton and me to them one afternoon."

Even then Aggie did not see in his eagerness what everyone else at the table saw. Having cast herself as his patroness, she replied benevolently, "I would be glad to. And you know Mrs. Carlisle and I believe firmly in the healthfulness of being often out of doors.

228

So when my nephews Linus and Miles are in your care, I do hope you will encourage them in walking and sport."

"Of course, of course."

"Aggie," called Tyrone. He was seated along the same side of the table as she, so she had to lean forward to see him. "You've never been so generous as to show me these marvelous walks."

"Because you're a lazy, indoor sort of person," she replied. "Besides, if you were genuinely curious about them, you might have asked Minta all these years."

"But suppose the curiosity has come over me now," he pursued, "as well as a desire to be in the open air? One can't sit and read books all one's life."

Boulton frowned at Tyrone and said heavily, "Still—you might read them just a little while longer. And you have got Miss Ellsworth here to show you good walks."

"You can't mean Bea," wondered Tyrone. "My dear Boulton, if you were better acquainted with my younger sister, you would know she never has a speck on her nor a ribbon out of place because she is as much an indoor sort of person as I am purported to be."

"I do prefer to walk on pavement," admitted Bea.

"There. You see? So Aggie, when you are leading these cross-country tramps, I hope you might include me."

"Well, I suppose so. But it will make everything so complicated. The Boultons will send me a note, and I will have to send *you* a note. Though I suppose I could simply say, 'The Boultons and I are going to meet at the Obelisk at eleven to walk the downs. If you want to come, come.'"

He whistled. "That *is* complicated. I don't blame you for hesitating."

Aggie laughed, but Boulton added crossly, "We won't wait long for you." Then, remembering himself, he favored the company with a forced smile. "That is, the rest of us will be anxious to make the most of the time."

"That's settled, then," spoke up Minta, giving a rap on the table with her knuckles. "But shouldn't we talk about my birthday now? Or mine and Tyrone's? I have thought of a gift you all might give me after dinner."

"Whatever you like," declared Mr. Ellsworth.

"'Unto the half of my kingdom,'" quoted Tyrone. "Careful, sir, with rash vows like that."

"Oh, I don't want anything so very bad," Minta said. "Only, may we dance after dinner, Mama? I haven't bothered Nicholas to take me to a ball this summer because I'm so enormous, and who wants just to stand there and watch? But no one will see me here. Please!"

"Of course, my dear, if our guests have no objection."

There were none, and it would be difficult to say who greeted the news with greater satisfaction: Aggie, who loved to dance, or Mr. Boulton, who foresaw another opportunity to ingratiate himself with her.

Chapter 17

To be sure I an't now a little at a loss to know whether I've made a good hand of this, or whether I've put my foot in it.

—George Brewer, *Bannian Day* (1796)

Duly after dinner, while the gentlemen indulged in some of Mr. Ellsworth's passable port, the ladies prepared the drawing room for dancing, Aggie and Minta collapsing in laughter when Minta tried to help roll the carpet and toppled over to her hands and knees.

"Gracious, Araminta," chided Mrs. Ellsworth as she took her seat at the pianoforte, "do be careful. What would Mr. Carlisle say?"

"Nicholas would not say a thing because he has seen it all before," returned her stepdaughter, struggling up. "Now who will be my first partner? Will it be you, Willsie Will?" She seized her younger brother's hands, and Aggie took Beatrice's, while Mrs. Ellsworth plunged into Sellenger's Round.

They had got through it twice before the gentlemen joined them, and Mr. Boulton approached Aggie at once to beg the honor of her hand.

"Certainly, but you needn't be so formal here, Mr. Boulton." They were joined by the Carlisles and Tyrone with Beatrice, Tyrone calling out, "If Minta chose dancing for her birthday, I choose the first dance. Madam, may we have White Wheat?"

"And somewhat slowly, for my sake," laughed Minta.

With only three couples, one danced as much with the others as with one's own partner, and exclusive conversation was impossible. So when Mr. Boulton asked Aggie if Monday would be a good day to walk the downs, Tyrone responded before she could. "Monday would be agreeable. Oh—or should I pretend not to know about it until Aggie tells me?"

"You should indeed," Aggie said in mock reproof. "For I do not believe anybody was addressing you, sir, so don't be surprised if I completely forget to tell you about it."

"Well, then, if we maintain this pretense of not hearing each other's private conversations," resumed Tyrone, "I will take this opportunity to tell Beatrice that I tremble lest Miss Weeks tread upon my foot, for I have seen the damage she can inflict."

"Mr. Boulton and I might say the same of you," Aggie replied, "if we had heard you."

"Miss Weeks is so light of foot that one would as soon fear injury from a butterfly!" exclaimed Boulton.

"Zounds!" hissed Tyrone to a giggling Beatrice. "We are overheard!"

"You would do better to fear *my* clumsiness," returned Minta, "for I am now the size of a walrus."

"Surely not! I have never seen a walrus, but surely not. Perhaps a baby walrus. One no older than two at the uttermost."

Then a laughing Minta tried to slap her brother as they circled, only to lose her balance again and require her husband's arm to catch and steady her.

It was only Mr. Boulton who did not seem to catch the joke, for he continued to address Aggie alone.

"My sister Miss Boulton was very pleased to make your acquaintance and the acquaintance of Mrs. Chester," he began again.

"What about *my* acquaintance?" mourned Tyrone. "For I met her on the same occasion."

"Or mine?" piped Beatrice, entering into the spirit of things.

"Or mine, though I have not yet had the good fortune to meet Miss Boulton," Minta said. "Nicholas likely will first, unless she enjoys relentless good health."

Boulton met these sallies with a mixture of confusion and indignation, and Aggie took pity on him. "You mustn't mind us, Mr. Boulton. Teasing comes naturally to those who have known each other a good long time."

"'Buzz, buzz!'" said Tyrone. "Did you hear something, Bea?"

"Only a buzzing bee," replied his twin because Beatrice was giggling.

"I don't know what there is to tease about," grumbled Boulton, stalking across to meet Beatrice at his long first corner.

When Aggie took Minta's and Tyrone's hands to turn in their star, she raised her eyebrows and widened her eyes speakingly. At once Minta gave a nod—she would stop—but Tyrone only feigned blank innocence. Not wanting to be overheard, Aggie resorted to crushing his fingers (and Minta's, since the three of them had joined hands in the star). Ever loyal, Minta united with her at once in the effort.

Tyrone gave a piteous whimper, as the new puppies did when they got underfoot and suffered the consequences.

"Dear me," said Minta. "Did I tread on you at last?"

"No, dear sister," he replied. "It was my own mistake. But I had thought blood thicker than water."

"Not this water," said Aggie.

She had her way. Mr. Boulton was allowed to make the remainder of his vapid comments in peace, while the rest of them pretended deafness.

White Wheat was followed by Strawberries and Cream and then Greensleeves and Yellow Lace, after which Minta declared herself spent and took Mrs. Ellsworth's place at the instrument. Tyrone was prevailed upon to accompany her on his fiddle, and so

Aggie found herself on the sofa with Mr. Boulton beside her.

By this point, awareness could not but dawn on Aggie, reluctant as she was to acknowledge it. Mr. Boulton's attentions would not allow her to do otherwise. Had she been an older woman or a married woman, she might yet have persuaded herself that his assiduity was that of a supplicant to his patroness, but she was neither of those things. Therefore it could only be that the earnest curate once again aspired to her affections.

And I share the blame this time, she accused herself. *Had I been persistently cool toward him, he would not have resurrected his hopes.* But alas, she had believed what she wanted—that there was no longer any danger—and he had mistaken her kindliness for something more.

If Aggie had any lingering doubt, it was dispelled when Mr. Boulton leaned closer and said, "Do you play, Miss Weeks? If so, I beg you to favor us with a performance."

Now, Aggie had endured the usual instruction at Mrs. Turcotte's seminary without demonstrating any remarkable talent, and neither the Ellsworths nor her Weeks relations ever pestered her about it. So it wasn't really a lie to answer, "No, I'm afraid. I don't play or sing."

"What a shame," he murmured. "You have got small fingers."

With difficulty Aggie managed not to pull a face, but she did clutch her "small fingers" together in her lap. She assumed he meant it as a compliment, but the man was clearly no poet.

The lively piece Minta and Tyrone played had toes tapping and Mr. Ellsworth humming by this point, and Aggie did her best to appear enthralled by the music, angling herself slightly away from her companion.

For the second time in a week, she pondered the idea of marrying someone. She had rejected Tyrone Ellsworth as a potential suitor because he was too indolent, inclined to leave all the work of pursuit and falling in love to her. But was it any better for a man to be too active? Mr. Boulton certainly proved willing enough to pursue, but he skipped over the love business altogether!

No, she concluded soon enough. She might never marry, but if she did, there would have to be love. Love felt as urgently by her lover as by herself.

Nevertheless, if Mr. Boulton were truly going to offer for her a second time, she had better hear him to the end, that her refusal could be understood as final.

"*I* sing," blurted Mr. Boulton, suddenly hovering about her ear.

Aggie could not repress a start. "We will have to hear you, then," she replied. It would be one way to dislodge him from her side. Glancing around the drawing room to see if anyone had noticed his boldness, her eye caught Tyrone's, and she felt her face heat. Tyrone gave a slow smirk, his gaze keen and knowing, which only made Aggie turn redder. She slid an inch away from Mr. Boulton and began plying her fan vigorously, so he could not draw so close again without being rapped by it.

Abruptly, Tyrone made a figure of eight with his violin, skipping ahead to the closing bars and catching his sister off guard, so that he concluded while she was still mid-measure and frowning at him.

"*Bravi!*" crowed Mr. Ellsworth, leading the company in applause. "Splendid," he added, right over the top of Beatrice protesting, "That isn't how it goes."

"What marvelous talent our children possess," Mr. Ellsworth told his wife.

"If not the ability to read music," muttered Araminta. "I do believe you ran right over the *Da Capo*, Tyrone, and went straight for the *Fine*."

"Did I? Inexcusable. But perhaps Aggie would like to perform now," suggested Tyrone.

This out-of-the-way proposal met with universal surprise, and no one responded for a moment. Then Aggie saw Minta's mouth pop open, and she hastened to speak.

"No, thank you," Aggie said firmly. "I never do play, you know. But Mr. Boulton here tells me he is a proficient singer. Perhaps we might prevail upon him…?"

They did. After the curate made the requisite modest demurral, he sprang up to leaf through the Ellsworths' sheet music, conferring with Minta on his choices. Meanwhile, Tyrone replaced his fiddle in its case and sauntered over to take Boulton's place on the sofa beside Aggie.

Her heart gave an uncomfortable flutter, as if he had jumped out at her, but she thought it was half in response to his nearness and half in exasperation.

He said nothing, and she could think of nothing to say either. The room grew warmer, however, or *she* grew warmer, so she began to ply her fan again.

In the meantime, Mr. Boulton and Minta came to agreement and set the music in order. While Minta straightened to play the opening bars of "The Soldier's Adieu," he composed himself solemnly, his eyes boring into Aggie.

She raised her fan an inch higher as a shield and flapped it vigorously.

"Gracious, what powerful gusts," complained Tyrone, once Boulton clasped his hands beseechingly and launched into his "Adieu, adieu, my only life, my duty calls me from thee."

"There are other seats you might choose," she answered shortly.

"But none so comfortable."

Aggie snapped her fan shut. She studied its carved sticks so she need not raise her eyes to the performer.

If Mr. Boulton chose to address his song to her, he could do it to the top of her head. "Is that better?"

"Better," Tyrone answered through barely-parted lips. "I might even say now things are perfect. Though, don't you want to watch? All his valiant looks and 'thund'ring cannon's rattle' are quite wasted on me."

She ignored this provocation. "Whyever did you ask me to play just now?" she demanded, still examining her fan sticks. "You know I never do."

"I know. And I thank you for answering me when you did because it was on the tip of Minta's tongue to call me a forgetful blockhead. But, you see, I did particularly want to speak with you."

The flutter rippled through her again, and she tightened her midsection to repress it. "How then would you have spoken to me if I were playing?"

From the corner of her eye she saw his shrug. "If you had agreed, I would have stayed up there with you to accompany you or to sing, and I would have managed to say my piece at some point, having overcome the chief difficulty of prying that limpet Boulton from your side."

Aggie bit back a smile at this description. "Well, then?" she prompted. "Here is your chance to speak."

"Very well." He leaned forward himself, his elbows on his knees, his chin on one hand, for all the world as if Boulton's performance held him rapt. "The

Soldier's Adieu" finished, Boulton had moved on to "Susan."

"You would think he was all that stood between us and Napoleon, from these songs he has chosen," Tyrone mused. "First he was a soldier, now a sailor."

"In his defense, I don't suppose there are many songs written for lovesick curates."

"There *ought* to be," he replied, "for I suppose a curate may be as lovesick as the next man."

She said nothing to this, but when she ventured a glance at Mr. Boulton, he was indeed directing the warbling sentiments of 'lovely dear' and 'falling tear' at her head, and she lowered her gaze again.

"That could work," Tyrone resumed, half to himself. He hummed ahead of the tune, tapping the meter on his knee. "Say perhaps…" —and he began to sing, very low, in her ear, as near her as Boulton had been, his warm breath stirring her hair— 'The pulpit calls me from thine arms. Let not my pretty Aggie mourn. The deacons roar, yet safe from harm, Gareth shall to his dear return.'"

"Hush!" Turning her head, she fixed him with a glare only he could see, clenching her fan to resist whacking him with it. "It's wrong to pain people, even if you are clever about it."

"But he can't hear me," said Tyrone reasonably. "Unless you mean my jokes pain *you*."

"I will not stay to hear such nonsense, at any rate. If you have got something sensible to say, say it, or I will sit somewhere else."

He quailed in mock alarm. "'Rebuke me not in thine anger, Miss Weeks,'" he affected to plead. "You will beat your breast in remorse when I tell you I only wished, as your friend, to caution you."

"Against what, pray?"

He winced briefly, aware he was making a muddle of things. "Perhaps 'caution' is too strong a word. What I intended to say was that I believe Boulton intends to propose to you—" (Tyrone almost added "again" but remembered just in time that she did not know he knew of that failed attempt.)

"And why must I be forewarned of that?" Her eyes glittered danger at him.

"Forgive me—I thought you—That is, I thought it would not be welcome news to you," he fumbled.

"Whether the news be welcome or not, it concerns only me, Mr. Ellsworth, and I would ask you, please, not to interfere in something so manifestly *not your business*."

He bowed. What else could he do? And his jaw tightened, but Aggie did not see it, for she had defiantly returned her attention to the singer, her pulse hammering. Who did he think he was? Who had asked for his opinion? As if she could not make up her own mind! She, who had already refused Mr. Boulton once, without Tyrone Ellsworth's assistance! She was sick—sick to death—of everyone and anyone thrusting his nose in her private concerns. For the last time, she was no longer a silly girl of eighteen, and they would all do well to remember it. She had already decided, completely on her own judgment, that she would refuse him. Kindly, decisively, and finally. So there.

Rather than interfering between Aggie and Mr. Boulton, Tyrone Ellsworth would do far better to see to his own affairs. After all, it was not *she* who was tumbling unawares into a cunningly-placed marital net! Indeed. Let him remove the beam from his own eye before he sought to remove the mote from hers!

"'Lest precious tears should drop from Susan's eye!'"

Mr. Boulton ended his song with his chest outthrust and head thrown back, reminding Aggie of a spaniel pointing out the game, but she burst into applause. "Bravo, Mr. Boulton! Bravo! May we beg yet one more song of you?"

His long features lifted, transforming from a Greek tragedy mask into its comedic counterpart. "Thank you. Thank you, Miss Weeks. All of you. I would be—delighted to sing one more song."

Minta stared at her friend in frank puzzlement, but Aggie recommenced fanning herself. "Delightful," she said loudly, to drown out little Willie's protests to his mother. "Capital."

It was, Aggie decided later, an example of cutting off one's nose to be revenged of one's face. For she did not honestly want to hear another song from the curate, and now he felt justified in directing the entirety of it toward her, leaving her with no alternative but to sit there and take it. Nor did she have the satisfaction of putting Tyrone Ellsworth in his place, for, instead of retreating in vanquished silence at this show of favor toward Mr. Boulton, he made use of the additional cover it provided.

"Again, I beg your pardon," he murmured, barely audible even to her. He addressed her shoulder, as she did not deign to turn and acknowledge him. "If I have interfered, it was kindly meant. If you...care for him, and he for you..."

Aggie held up a finger to hush him, but her indignation was receding and her sense of humor returning in force because Mr. Boulton *would* make the dreadfullest mooncalf faces at her. Did he imagine this the surest way to woo?

Mr. Boulton here waggled his head and struck another pose. It was too much for Aggie. She shut her eyes and fingered the fan in her lap, trying to stifle her laugh.

Tyrone's low voice came again. "Do you think he loves you?"

He deserved no response to this impertinent question, but she did not have enough practice in being angry at Tyrone. She gave the slightest shrug, whispering back, "How can he? He still hardly knows me."

"Ah, but perhaps he will tell you he only awaits your permission to unleash the full force of his affection. I daresay, he will even borrow Shakespeare and tell you, 'Say thou art mine, and ever. My love as it begins shall so persever.'"

Her breath caught. Her flutter returned. The sudden roar of blood in her veins muffled even Mr. Boulton's ballad. Without realizing, Aggie shook her head slowly. Because what was happening? What did it all mean? Was he flirting with her—encouraging her to pursue him? Or did he overstep the bounds of friendship from brotherly interest, meaning simply to alert her to Mr. Boulton's intentions?

She would have no answers that evening.

The song ended; the tea things were brought in; conversation became general. Minta booted her brother from the sofa and claimed his spot, and Aggie did not know whether to be grateful that Mr. Boulton could not sit there or resentful that Minta drove Tyrone away.

When she lay in bed that night, a yawning Banniker having undressed her and braided her hair, she tossed and turned till the early hours, going over and over the same questions. It was not until the clock in the entry hall struck two that she finally drifted off. But a last thought darted like a silvery fish through the deeps of her consciousness: *If I had been Clumpy Caraway, I bet I could have brought Tyrone to the point tonight, whether he wanted to be there or not.*

Chapter 18

What a damned Piece of Work have I made on't!—I..shall lose my Match, and as to Harriot, why, the Odds are that I lose my Match there too.

—George Colman, *The Jealous Wife* (1761)

*I*t's wrong to pain people, even if you are clever about it.

Aggie was not the only one whose sleep had been disturbed. Tyrone lay awake equally long, feeling sick.

So that was what she thought of him. That he was the sort of overclever person who wanted everyone to acknowledge his superiority while he laughed at them behind his hand. An unkind—conceited—braying ass.

Well, why *had* he inserted himself into Boulton's bunglings, rather than leaving the man to be hoist with his own petard? Or, at least, hoist with the petard he had purchased from Tyrone.

He had inserted himself because, from the moment Boulton came into the coffee-house, gloating over how Aggie "raced" to Headbourne Worthy to satisfy Boulton's hint about taking on pupils, Tyrone had not enjoyed a moment's peace.

Had Aggie begun to care for the man? For long, lugubrious, solemn, impoverished Gareth Boulton? A person whose first interest in her had been for her fortune? In all the years Tyrone had known Boulton, they had never become close, nor would they ever, chalk having nothing to do with cheese. Could *this* be the person Aggie would choose to spend her life with? Tyrone could not picture it. Why, Minta wouldn't like Boulton any better than Tyrone did! The girls would grow apart. The families would grow apart. With Aggie's fortune to bolster him, Boulton might not moulder perpetually in Headbourne Worthy as the curate of St. Swithun's, but even if he were granted a prosperous living in Winchester, how often would his heavy company be wanted at Hollowgate?

Moreover, all this estrangement Tyrone envisioned was his own fault. He admitted as much to the puppies Scamp and Pickles as he sat on the bench in his sister Florence's walled garden. "I suggested him as a distraction from Taplin," he told them, "but he has proven only the lesser of two evils. Much the lesser, perhaps, but still an evil you understand."

They did not find the master's confessions unduly absorbing, and Tyrone had to keep tossing them a stick to hold their attention.

But these things were not all.

He had been haunted by these anxieties, yes, but there was more. There was his anxiety *over* those anxieties.

That is, there was more to it than the fear of losing a family friend or having played a part in it.

Because, would he have felt any better had Aggie been in danger of marrying another person, whom Tyrone had not aided with his own pen? Would Tyrone have rejoiced if she chose some wealthy lordling whom all and sundry spoke well of, one with wit and charm enough to speak for himself?

"It would be worse," he confessed to the puppies, nudging the nearer one with his foot. "In Boulton's case, at least, I flatter myself that some modicum of her affection for him is misplaced and actually intended for me. Won by me." But no sooner did he speak the words aloud than he groaned and put a hand to his eyes. There he went again, with the conceited braying.

He tried again, taking a deep breath.

Truth.

He would speak the whole truth, if only to the pair of dogs rolling at his feet in the gravel. It would be the equivalent of Midas' barber whispering the king's terrible secret into the hole in the ground.

"Scamp, Pickles," said Tyrone.

They stopped their rolling at once, Scamp rising on his hind legs to sniff at the stick now out of reach on the bench.

"In due time," promised Tyrone.

"Scamp, Pickles, I need to tell you something. It won't take long. It's this: I think I have begun to care for Agatha Weeks, enough that I do not want her to marry anybody but me."

Pickles hunched over to chew on his haunch, and Scamp began batting at his brother's tail.

"You are taking this more calmly than I expected," Tyrone continued. "I admit I was troubled by the revelation. I've known Aggie forever, you realize. And for the life of me, I cannot put my finger on when the change began. Somewhat recently, I suspect. In the Physic Garden at Oxford, maybe? In any case, having now become aware of my...affections for her, I curse myself for having gone about everything hind end foremost."

He moved restlessly, and the stick rolled off the bench, setting off a frenzied tug-of-war between the pups.

"No—stop—Boys—listen to me," commanded Tyrone. "The question is whether I go to The Acres this very morning and make a clean breast of it, or if I am bound by honor to let Boulton have the first go." When neither puppy proved inclined to answer, Tyrone snatched the stick from them and waved it above his head. "All right, then. If you won't answer me, we'll do it this way, as when the priests cast lots in the Bible. Here are the rules: I will throw this for you, and if Scamp gets it first and brings it back, I'll go to The Acres directly; but if Pickles prevails, I'll give Boulton one week of grace."

It was not, strictly speaking, a fair field. Scamp had proven himself the faster dog, but Tyrone persuaded himself that odds must be given him, as Boulton already held the lead by so large a margin.

Giving a short whistle, he swung the stick in a circle above him and let it fly. Off raced the puppies, Scamp in front and Pickles lolloping behind. Things looked promising for Tyrone until Scamp crashed into the gardener's basket, oversetting it and sending a ball of twine unrolling across the path. Instantly the stick was forgotten, and Scamp pounced on the ball, worrying it between his jaws. Pickles missed this exciting development, having caught sight of a butterfly, at which he leapt and snapped. The butterfly flitted away unharmed, and when Pickles came down again, he trotted along to retrieve the stick.

"Dash it, Scamp," growled Tyrone, when Pickles dropped the stick at his feet. Stalking over, he wrested the twine from the distracted puppy, wound it again into a ball, replaced it in the basket, and removed the basket to the safety of the bench. "Should have cleared the course. We will say best two out of three, then."

Away flew the stick once more, and away flew the puppies. This time Scamp reached it first. Lionel cheered, but then the garden door opened. All thoughts of fetching ceased on the instant. The stick fell from Scamp's jaws, as he and Pickles hastened to greet the visitor with barks and scrabbling.

"Heyday! You remember me, then, fine fellows?"

"Ben!" Tyrone greeted his cousin, striding toward him. "I did not know you had come back again."

"Not only am I back again," answered Benjamin Ellsworth, "but I come bearing gifts." Straightening, he reached in his pocket and drew out a small, chinking bag.

"Money?" wondered Tyrone.

"Of course, money. Are you so rich you've forgotten you are paid for our venture?"

"But I thought you were paying me with a bank draft."

"Money always seems more real when it makes a sound. Besides, Austin and I bought our mother a trifle with our earnings and wanted to deliver it ourselves. I tell you, Ty, our little business has changed everything for us."

His dark eyes flashed with excitement, and Tyrone felt his stomach sink, even before something poked him in the leg and he looked down to see a proud Pickles again presenting the stick to him. *Blast.*

"Look, Ben—about the business—"

"Things are quiet at Oxford during the long vac," Benjamin interrupted, "but word has spread from the gownsmen to the townsmen, and we may pick up a job or two there."

"Ben," Tyrone began again. "I am retiring. For good this time."

His cousin stared. "Whatever for? You can't mean it."

"I do mean it. I'm getting out."

"But *why?*"

"I want to do other things now."

"Like what?" Benjamin held up his palms, indicating the empty garden they stood in. "Like thinking? Like sitting? Like reading? You cannot tell me our enterprise has left you no time for anything else."

"Well—suppose I wanted to write a book? If I am expending all my creative energy on these pitiful scraps of poems and pedantic proposals, what would remain to give to my own works?"

But Benjamin only crossed his arms over his chest and regarded him fixedly. "Far be it from me to squander your visits from the Muse, cousin. What would you write, if you were no longer burdened with requests for pitiful scraps?"

"I—I don't know," admitted Tyrone.

"Exactly. Therefore, what would you say to continuing our efforts until you light upon a project?"

"But this is so—reprehensible!" Tyrone protested. "We make money from deception and lies! How do you expect ever to become a clergyman, if you can't see the wrong in it?"

"What wrong? If, as the song goes, 'tis love, 'tis love, 'tis love that makes the world go round,' we do no harm by increasing that love."

"But suppose some of the people our work brings together should never be united in the first place?" he persevered. "Suppose they are mismatches, but a poem here and a *billet doux* there and an affecting proposal yonder make the young lady think the gentleman someone he is not?"

Benjamin frowned at this. "I suppose you mean to say we are not expediting the inevitable, but rather deceiving the young ladies, to a greater or lesser extent."

Tyrone nodded vehement agreement, relieved to be understood without having to go into his personal case in point.

"And I suppose you are saying the deceived young ladies are won over by *your* charms, in place of our customer's," Benjamin continued. "A monstrous conceited thought, but likely true in the main." Ruminatively, he took a seat on the marble bench, bending to rub Scamp's head.

Tyrone dropped down beside him, firm in his decision but feeling guilty all the same for his cousins' sake. "I hope you and Austin haven't spent all your earnings already. What did you buy Aunt Jeanne?"

"A new bonnet and silk petticoat. The best Oxford had to offer." He sighed. "But we weren't fools. Of course we've saved the rest. Not for Austin and me the fanfaronade and flutter. Things are too dear."

"You and Austin might continue the work yourself," suggested Tyrone.

A skeptical look. "Right. I think not. He and I are no heroes of the pen."

"You might copy things out of books."

Benjamin held quite still. "We…might. It's an idea. It's an idea! Yes—Tyrone, what would you say to collecting and compiling the work you have done up to now, and publishing it in a book? You know—think of Richardson's letter-writing manual! People still consult that thing, though it's so old-fashioned now. A new one would be welcome, I think, but this one tailored to courtship situations. You have already written to young ladies of different backgrounds, so it would boast broad appeal. And what deception would be involved in this case? We could say in the preface that the examples given within are intended to be adapted and improved upon, not copied slavishly, etc. etc. Yes! Yes! You gather up and order the bits and title them and expunge any details which anyone would recognize. Just address them to 'Miss A' and 'Miss B' and so forth. And then Austin and I will take charge of finding a publisher for the manuscript. We may divide any earnings in the usual fashion."

"But—"

"It can be published anonymously, if you prefer. Though if it be successful, we will happily reveal your authorship to the publisher when you are ready to present him with another work. And if no one accepts it for publication, nothing is lost. Our business is still at an end, and Austin and I will manage as we always have."

"But—"

"But nothing, cousin. This answers all your objections. No more new customers, no more deception, no more frittering away of your time and efforts. If a young lady consents to be courted by a young man who has used our handbook, the victory is his own."

"Provided he really does 'adapt and improve upon,' what he finds there," Tyrone pointed out.

"If he does not," replied Benjamin, sensing victory, "on his own head be it. The book will be a public affair, and should he simply copy from it verbatim, he risks exposure and ignominy." He grinned. "Nay, if there is a Muse of moneymaking, she has visited me today. This proposed handbook provides a tidy conclusion to the whole matter, while still offering hope for Austin and me to salvage one last windfall. Come—shake hands and be sworn."

Tyrone grinned in return, ruefully. "I will, but on one condition."

"Name it."

"The earnings, if any, from the book be entirely yours and Austin's. Then I need not hear another word about your poverty, much less pity you for it. Something tells me, coz, that you will end your days twice as wealthy as I."

Even as Tyrone brought to a close a chapter of his life he would prefer Agatha Weeks know nothing about, the die had already been cast. For that same morning when Aggie finally woke, heavy-headed and bleary, she found her maid Banniker waiting beside a tray on the dressing table.

"Good morning," yawned Aggie. "Is it so late?"

"You missed breakfast all right," said Banniker. "And even the tea and toast I've brought you are likely stone cold by now. But—there's a note for you."

The girl's manner made Aggie sit up, rubbing the sleep from her eyes. "Did it arrive in the post?"

"No, miss. A boy left it with Orton, who passed it to me. And the disapproving look he gave me! As if I told you to pass secret messages with anyone. Only think if your pa finds out."

Aggie's first thought was that Tyrone had written to her. An apology for his interference. She threw off the covers and reached for the note, adding, to the maid's disappointment, "Thank you, Banniker. I'll dress myself this morning. You may go."

It was not from Tyrone, however.

2 August 1808
Headbourne Worthy

My dearest Miss Weeks,

Pardon my daring in writing to you, but I have been able to think of little else since you first gazed upon me in the gardens of New College. In that blessed moment when our eyes met, yours "shone sweetly lambent with celestial day," and my heart has never since been my own.

"That's laying it on with a trowel," muttered Aggie, aware of the swoop of anticlimax in her gut.

Not Tyrone then. Mr. Boulton.

"And I am most decidedly not his 'dearest' Miss Weeks." If she were not resolved to hear him out this time, she would have tossed his note aside until she had eaten some breakfast. Drivel was hard to bear on an empty stomach.

Therefore I take pen in hand, for though I have not got your permission to write to you, "Heav'n first taught letters for some wretch's aid," Miss Weeks, and the letters "live, they speak, they breathe what love inspires."

"I dread to think what love inspires," said Aggie. "But let's have it, sir, with no more beating about the bush." As if he read her thoughts, she turned the sheet over and read:

1. *We share a common upbringing in Hampshire.*
2. *I admire the utter respectability of your family and connections.*
3. *You possess uncommon charms in the way of pleasing features, fine figure, affable nature, and so forth.*
4. *And lastly, your portion will make possible a comfortable married life and allow me to rise higher in my profession.*

O, divine Miss Weeks, I confess that,
   When from the censer clouds of fragrance roll,
   And swelling organs lift the rising soul,
   One thought of thee puts all the pomp to flight,
   Priests, tapers, temples, swim before my sight.

If I cannot speak my love to you, how will my soul ever again know peace? Please say you will meet me this afternoon at four by the Obelisk you mentioned.

Yours breathlessly,
Gareth Boulton

"What ails the man?" Aggie marveled. "One minute he spouts flowers and flourishes, and the next he sounds as if he were reading the parish roll."

She had seen three samples of his writing now and had to say she preferred the earlier two. Had he possibly asked for his sister's help in composing this one? While Aggie had no intention of marrying him in any case, if an opportunity presented itself when she refused him, she would tell him gently to trust his own instincts in future.

Thankfully Mr. Boulton could not bring his sister along while he did his proposing, so Aggie prayed his offer would be delivered sensibly, with a minimum of this gushing.

Shaking her head, Aggie tossed the note aside and took a bite of her cold toast, followed by a swallow of tea.

At least Banniker's curiosity would be satisfied, for she must accompany her mistress to the Obelisk. The maid would guess what passed, even at a polite distance, which meant the news would be widely known by nightfall.

Only think of it! To be rid of Mr. Taplin one day and Mr. Boulton the next! Two men in two days. At this rate she could send every unmarried gentleman in Winchester about his business by Michaelmas.

The looking glass was the sole witness to the blush that came and went across her cheeks. There was one man alone who would be spared her unceremonious dismissal.

The one who disdained even to enter the lists.

With a sigh, Aggie seated herself at her dressing table to finish her breakfast and prepare for the day.

Chapter 19

At the end of this lane stands an Obelisk, erected in 1759, to commemorate the dreadful visitation of the plague, which in 1666 almost reduced the city to a heap of solitary ruins.

—Charles Ball, *An Historical Account of Winchester with Descriptive Walks* (1818)

Because Aggie balked at telling her maid she was going to meet Mr. Boulton, she was compelled to make a mystery of it. The two of them walked into town therefore to the circulating library beside the White Hart Inn, Aggie half hidden by her wide-brimmed bonnet and her plainest gown.

A bell on the door jingled as they entered, and despite her attempt to be nondescript, Aggie heard her name called before her eyes adjusted to the shady interior.

"Miss Weeks, good afternoon!" sang a familiar voice. "Do come and join Mr. Ellsworth and me as we debate whether *Sir Charles Grandison* or *Clarissa* be the better Richardson book."

With a sinking heart Aggie complied, pasting a smile on her face and marching through the shop to the bookcase before which Miss Caraway and Tyrone stood. Feeling decidedly *de trop,* her gaze swept over and past him, noting he appeared as discomposed as she by the unexpected meeting. Miss Caraway, on the other hand, glowed with delight.

"I have it for *Sir Charles Grandison*," said Miss Caraway, "but Mr. Ellsworth was just saying to me that he finds Sir Charles 'insufferable'! Can you credit it, Miss Weeks?"

Aggie gave a vague smile. "I'm sure he has his reasons."

"Just the one: I despise him because he's thoroughly noble and virtuous," said Tyrone.

"But that's just why I admire him!" cried Miss Caraway. "I assure you it has nothing whatever to do with the character in the book named Signorina Clementina."

She gave an enchanting titter, but Tyrone overlooked this opportunity to flatter her. "It isn't natural to be so faultless," he insisted. "And asking the reader to endure hundreds of pages of such a creature is criminal."

"What book will you be getting then?" asked Aggie mildly. "If not the odious *Sir Charles*?"

"Oh—another Richardson," he said, tucking the volume firmly under his arm. She could only suppose, by its slimness, that it was *Pamela*. "And you? What are you here for? Miss Caraway wanted the second volume of *Tankerville Family*, but—"

"But some wretched person has it already," his admirer finished. "It isn't you, by chance, Miss Weeks?"

"No, sorry," said Aggie, conscious of the Guildhall clock chiming outside.

"Too bad. But Mr. Ellsworth says he will recommend me a book." She lifted her chin at Aggie in a challenging manner. "I suppose you would like a suggestion from him as well?"

"Not at all," answered Aggie, backing away. They might finish their rendezvous with her blessing! "I was just here for…" Reaching behind her, she snatched a book from the closest table.

Tyrone raised skeptical brows. "You were here for *New Foundations of Political Economy*?"

"Yes," lied Aggie stoutly. "Papa asked me to pick it up for him. I only hope he doesn't ask me to read it aloud after dinner."

"Where are you going in such haste?" he asked, as she retreated another step.

"Away. Off. I have—another errand—and I don't want to be late. If you would excuse me—"

Before they could reply, she turned and hurried to the counter. The clerk's eyes widened at the book she handed him. "Such a title for such a pretty young lady," he hemmed. Aggie attempted another polite smile with little success and was greatly relieved to escape to the High Street.

"Where to next, miss?" asked Banniker, accepting the book from her mistress without comment.

"Homeward. Though—perhaps we might cut through Oram's Arbour." Her voice was thick from a suspicious tightness in her throat. What was it to her, if Miss Caraway and Tyrone chose to spend the afternoon together? Or if Miss Caraway was so patently willing to do all the pursuing and flirting and cooing which Aggie herself scorned?

Resolutely, she put them from her mind. She had more pressing cares at present.

Aggie could not say whether relief or dread held the greater sway when she and Banniker passed through the West Gate and spied Mr. Boulton leaning against the platform beneath the Obelisk, fanning himself with his hat and studying a paper in his hand.

"Oh, look. There's Mr. Boulton," she said, her voice sounding higher than usual. "I'll just step over and greet him."

Her pretense of surprise was immediately exposed, however, for the gentleman caught sight of her and rushed forward (nearly stumbling into the road), hollering, "Miss Weeks! How punctual you are. What would you say to a walk in the Arbour?"

"Very well," she submitted, affecting not to hear her maid's hitched breath. "You've dropped your paper, Mr. Boulton." She bent to retrieve it and nearly knocked heads with him as he scrambled to snatch it up.

"I've got it, I've got it," he said, coloring. But in bending down, another letter slipped from his pocket unnoticed, and it was Banniker who caught this one and held it out for the young man. "Heavens," he muttered, whisking it from the maid's fingertips before she or Aggie could see the direction. "Thank you." Cramming his correspondence back in his pocket, he extended an arm for Aggie and led her across the street.

When Aggie and Minta were younger, Oram's Arbour provided a vast area for their activities where they could practice archery or play cricket or catch-ball or run races without the eyes of family or servants upon them, and Aggie thought she could never have imagined it would one day be the setting for occasions like this.

They had not gone a hundred yards down the footpath before Mr. Boulton began clearing his throat furiously. "Ahem. Ahem! Miss Weeks, if we might pause here a moment—thank you. You are not too warm? Good, good. Lovely day, if warm. Ahem." He adjusted his hat and then clasped his hands alternately, first with the left on the outside and then the right. With a heroic effort then, he made a rush at his next fence. "—Miss Weeks, it can be no great mystery to you why I asked you to meet me this afternoon. Not after—my note this morning."

"I had better hear what you have got to say at any rate, Mr. Boulton." She folded her own hands together, trying to appear calm, but ended in crossing her arms, that she might clasp her elbows for support.

More furious throat-clearing. "Thank you. Ahem. *Ahem!* Miss Weeks—" He threw back his head and gazed into the distance toward the ripe cornfields. "Miss Weeks, after such a letter as I have written, it can come as no surprise to you why I—"

"The style of your letter did surprise me, I confess," she broke in. "It was—more florid than your past communications."

"Oh?" was his unhelpful response. He attempted a smile, which emerged more of a grimace. "Indeed. Well. Where was I? Er—Miss Weeks, after such a letter as I have written, it can come as no surprise to you why I begged for the opportunity to speak with you."

How many times would he repeat himself? To assist him in coming to the point she said, "It did seem to require the courtesy of hearing you out, sir."

"Ah. I thank you. As I was saying, it can come as no surprise to you why I begged for the opportunity to speak with you—"

"After 'such a letter' as you wrote," she interrupted, a vibration of impatience now audible. "Yes, I believe that has been clearly established. Please continue, Mr. Boulton."

He removed his handkerchief from his pocket and swiped at his brow. "Of course. Yes. Pardon me. To the point." He shut his eyes for a moment, his lips moving silently, and Aggie began to wonder if the man suffered from overheating. Before she could ask, however, his eyes flew open again and he forged ahead.

"When I begged for an appointment with you in Oxford, Miss Weeks, I was premature. I was—foolish. I confess I was impetuous when I heard of your family's reputation and connections to Winchester and—and when I saw your manifold charms firsthand in the college gardens. I did not love you *yet,* but I saw that you were loveable, and therefore I overreached. You refused to hear me at the time and rejected me—rightly. I cannot recall the day without embarrassment and hope you will have the goodness to wipe it from your memory."

In spite of herself, Aggie was once more impressed. *This* was the Mr. Boulton she preferred. The manly one who admitted fault and took responsibility for his mistakes and spoke to the point. Not the one who uttered overblown nonsense about lambent eyes and rising souls. Nevertheless she still could not love him, even when he was being sensible. Not now, not ever. How could she? Not when she loved—

With her own gasp, Aggie began to cough.

"Miss Weeks! Are you all right?" Mr. Boulton fussed, waving Banniker over. "You there—come and thump your mistress on the back."

But Aggie shook her head, holding up a hand to stave off any thumping. "I—I am fine. Just—swallowed a bug or something. Pray continue, Mr. Boulton."

He swallowed, chewing his lip for a moment and frowning. "I was saying…"

Dear Lord, let him not begin at the very beginning again! To forestall this, she prompted, "You ask me to forget your attempted proposal in Oxford. I will do so. Let us never think on it again."

Relief washed over his long features. "Right. Thank you. Ahem. Well." He took a deep, deep breath. "This might not be the best timing or best way to go about it, but I have been encouraged by your kindliness in recommending your nephews to my tutelage."

Her eyes widened warily. Oh, dear. So she had indeed brought this second proposal on herself. He would think her capricious, then, for refusing him. He would think she toyed with him.

Mr. Boulton dropped to one knee in the grass and looked like he would like to take one of her hands in his, only she was gripping her elbows again. "Miss Weeks, my admiration for you only grows, the better I know you. I know I have got little to offer you beyond my good name and honorable profession, but if you would consent to be my wife, in my great good fortune I would number myself among the first men in the kingdom."

It was nicely put. She appreciated his delicate acknowledgement of the inequality of what each would bring to the marriage, and that he did not try to paper over it with showy declarations of love. It allowed her to reply with sincerity, "Mr. Boulton, your offer does you credit."

"Does it?" he brightened.

"It does. But I will be frank with you, even as I thank you for it, and tell you that I must refuse."

He wilted at once. "Refuse?"

"Yes. But I wish you every blessing in the future and feel certain that such honest and manful sentiments as you have expressed here today will soon bring you success."

"You refuse," he murmured.

"Yes. I'm sorry to cause you any pain. But I do. With finality."

"But—but—"

"Mr. Boulton, you had better rise. You will be seen."

He did rise and brush himself off, only to pace back and forth. "I knew I should have gone about it differently! I told h—I knew it!" Abruptly he halted in front of her, his ordinarily mournful eyes alight with vehemence. "I knew I should have spoken of love!"

"Indeed, no," protested Aggie, retreating a step before those eyes. "It would have made no difference. It might even have hurt your cause because—"

"How could it possibly have hurt my cause? You have refused me!"

"It might have hurt my respect for you," she retorted, "which you still enjoy, if you have not gained my affections."

"I should have mentioned it," he insisted. "I had a speech, if it seemed appropriate—"

"Mr. Boulton, please do not—"

But he had already dropped to his knee again, hand over heart. "A speech if she—if *you,* rather— doubted the sincerity of my esteem. Thus: 'Say thou art mine, and ever—my love as it begins shall so persever!'"

Aggie stared, her mouth falling open. "What?"

"It means I will love you more and more, all my days."

"I *understand* what it means," she almost snapped. "But why did you say it?"

With bruised dignity, he heaved himself to his feet again. "Because—it fit the occasion. It's Shakespeare."

"I don't care if it's the man in the moon!" said Aggie, still dumbfounded. "What did you mean about having a speech—*that* speech prepared?"

"Miss Weeks," he said stiffly, "being a young lady, you can have no idea how difficult it is to embolden oneself for the task. It is no easy thing to lay your heart and hand before someone who might—who *does*—reject them. If I have recourse to notes—if I practice and prepare speeches—I beg your sympathy."

It was the better version of Mr. Boulton again. The manly, honest one. The one Aggie would have liked, if she could. As a result, her sympathy came readily. "I do sympathize, sir. I never thought of it before. It does require a great deal of courage to—open oneself—to possible rejection. No wonder you wrote some notes! In case everything flew out of your head in the moment. I do see, Mr. Boulton, and I beg your pardon for discomfiting you. I would say only—and you in turn must understand that I mean it kindly—that you do best when you speak frankly and without art, as you did just now. That is—when you are simply yourself, without the Shakespeare or the poetry."

The young curate regarded her with astonishment. "Are you—in earnest, Miss Weeks?"

"Of course I am," she laughed. "Would I say such a personal thing if I were not?"

"Then I...thank you. It is perhaps the most heartening thing anyone has ever said to me."

The two young people gazed at each other with the first true coincidence of feeling in their acquaintance. Aggie felt altogether friendly toward him, and, for his part, a pang struck Boulton. An awareness that Miss Weeks might be a treasure worth the winning, entirely apart from her wealth.

"I thank you," he said again. "And I will heed your kind words. Miss Weeks—having learned now how better to please you, can you give me any hope that, if I chose to try again—"

"I'm afraid not," she broke in gently. "Forgive my bluntness, but I would like to return you honesty for honesty. However, I would be proud to call you my friend, Mr. Boulton. May we wish each other well?" She stuck out a hand, and he took it to shake, but then at the last moment turned it and gave it a courtly kiss.

Then, with a bow, he strode away in the direction of town.

"Goodness," sighed Aggie, sinking to the grass. Relief at being through her trial seemed to drain her of everything else. Pulling off her bonnet, she lay back and covered her face with it. "I just need a moment to recover. To think. Let me know if someone comes, Banniker."

Who knew proposals were such arduous things? If Aggie could have been magically transported to her bedchamber at The Acres in her current posture, she would have been asleep in a minute. Though maybe her exhaustion had as much to do with her wakefulness the previous night as with Mr. Boulton's addresses.

She might have dozed a little. Or not. Only some minutes passed because the next thing she was aware of was the tickle of a fly walking up her bare arm.

Shaking it off, Aggie struggled to a sitting position and looked around. Banniker had retreated to the shade where she sat reading something to herself, tracing the lines with her finger, her lips moving soundlessly.

"Did I sleep?" asked Aggie.

The maid gasped and the sheet sailed from her fingers. "Oh! What a fright you gave me, miss!" Scrambling up, she retrieved it and approached her mistress, holding out the note before her.

"Is it for me?" If it were, Aggie could not imagine Banniker would read it.

"No, miss," answered Banniker slowly. "Nor for me. It fell out of Mr. Boulton's pocket at some point, and I found it in the grass. I shouldn't have read it, I know. I didn't—for oh so long! But then curiosity got me, and I just peeped inside. I wasn't going to read it through. But then I saw the Ellsworth name in a flash, and I couldn't help myself. So then I just read the lines at the bottom, which said, 'May Ellsworth's magic words operate on your lady love as they did Miss Kemp.'"

"You probably shouldn't tell me anymore," Aggie said half-heartedly, eaten up with curiosity. "It isn't my correspondence."

But Banniker knew on which side her bread was buttered and hastened on. "But, miss, I ought to tell you because—because it will help you understand Mr. Boulton better. You see, the rest of the note—the main part—was in a different hand. It was to a Miss Kemp, and it was all flowers and poetry and seeing her in St. Cross Church and her lamb-like eyes—"

"St. Cross Church!" echoed Aggie. Why, she had gone with the Chesters to St. Cross Church when they were in Oxford! And "lamb-like eyes" could not be—

She gave in and snatched the note from her maid to read herself. Eagerly, Banniker perched at her shoulder, more to devour her mistress' expression than to re-read what was written there.

It was a love note. Florid, high-flown—and riddled with the very phrases Mr. Boulton had used in his missive to her that morning. There were the lambent eyes and censer clouds and rising souls. But what did it all mean? That Mr. Boulton had copied it was clear, but who had given it to him? And did the postscript mean what Aggie thought it meant—that this love note was written by Tyrone Ellsworth? Who, then, was Miss Kemp? Did Tyrone make a habit of letting his love notes fall into other hands, or had Miss Kemp been the careless one?

All this time Aggie had fretted over Miss Caraway, but Miss Caraway was not the first to attract Tyrone's eye. Here was proof. And he had succeeded with Miss

Kemp, judging by that same postscript. The words had "operated" on her.

With supreme distaste, Aggie wadded the note up in a ball. Then she remembered it must be returned to Mr. Boulton, now presumably with an explanation for its condition. Steadying herself, she carefully smoothed it again in her lap before handing it to Banniker.

"Put that in the book to carry home, will you? I will deal with it there."

She could hardly bear the thought of touching it again, but she would have to. Not straight off, perhaps. She need not fluster Mr. Boulton further, when he must appear in church the following day. She would send it back to him after church.

If only it didn't feel like her own heart was the thing crumpled and crushed, never to regain its original form again.

Chapter 20

There is nothing discovers the true Temper of a Person
so much as his Letters.
— Addison and Steele, *The Spectator, No. 284* (1712)

When the Ellsworths entered their pew at St. Eadburh's, Tyrone allowed his parents and siblings to precede him, that he might sit on the end. By dint of fiddling with the pew door to ensure it shut properly, he was able to peek over toward that of the Weekses, two rows back and across the aisle. To his disappointment, not only was Aggie seated at the farther end, beyond her parents and the Chesters, she was wearing that confounded bonnet with the enormous brim again. He could see nothing of her face and, between the bodies of other parishioners, only slivers of her lovely person. On his third frustrated glance, Mrs. Chester caught him and raised a questioning eyebrow, forcing Tyrone to slump back and admit defeat.

The service never seemed longer. But at last Mr. Hepple pronounced the benediction and Tyrone sprang up, determined to intercept Aggie. He could not possibly return to Hollowgate without learning whether Boulton had yet spoken.

In the churchyard he fed the brim of his beaver hat through and through his fingers, suppressing his fidgets and nodding and bowing like an automaton to any who addressed him. The Weekses emerged at last,

Mr. Weeks pausing in the doorway to say something to the vicar and blocking the egress of his wife and daughters.

Just when Tyrone thought he would join the party on the church step, Mr. Weeks concluded and moved along. Out spilled another share of the congregation, Aggie among them, and Tyrone hurried forward.

"Good morning, Aggie."

Her blue gaze was cool and calm. "Good morning." If she felt any agitation, he could not see it. Why, she was as neat and unruffled as his sister Beatrice this morning!

"May I have a word with you?"

"Certainly."

"How—er—did your other errands fare?"

There was the merest twitch of her mouth, but Tyrone saw it. He saw as well Aggie's sister Mrs. Chester watching them. With seeming nonchalance, he angled himself to block the woman's view.

"Fine," said Aggie. "Errands are successful if they are completed, are they not?"

There was no courteous way to thrust oneself into another's business, and Tyrone had been in suspense too long in any case. "I am glad to hear it. But, say, Aggie—you didn't happen to see Boulton yesterday, did you?"

Caught off guard, the truth slipped out. "I—did. That is—yes—on my way back home I did happen to see Mr. Boulton." She fumbled with her reticule briefly. "Good Mr. Boulton. I do believe he and I will become friends."

"But nothing more than that, eh, Aggie?" pressed Tyrone. "I mean—did he ask you to become more?"

Her bosom swelled. "I am certain that if he did, it would be none of your concern."

"How could it not be my concern? You being so long connected with my family."

"I mean to say, you would do better to let such a thing be *told* you, rather than inquiring."

"Then there *is* something to tell me? Something like an engagement? There cannot be."

She stared at him. "If there cannot be, why do you ask? I repeat, sir, you shouldn't presume on our long acquaintance to pry into private matters."

"Oh, Aggie, how can you 'sir' me and call such things private? If I were Minta you would tell me, wouldn't you?"

"But you are not Minta—Tyrone," she relented. "Therefore I need not put up with this. If you feel inquisitive, why do you not ask Mr. Boulton? Good day to you."

With a curtsey, she left him.

Tyrone swallowed an oath and replaced his hat, half in mind to go after her. Why did she not just answer the question? Boulton must have proposed, or she would not have taken on so. But if she had refused the man, would she not have said as much? By the same token, if she had accepted—unthinkable thought!—would she not have hinted at it, if coyly?

It was maddening not to know for certain, after he had waited.

Pickles having twice brought the stick back to him, Tyrone had submitted reluctantly to the will of the gods and yielded Boulton the first chance to speak. The man being in a nettle to do the deed, Tyrone thought an allowance of two days more than sufficient.

Aggie's unexpected appearance at the circulating library would have made shipwreck of Tyrone's good intentions, however, had Miss Caraway not been present. Cursed Miss Caraway, who had glimpsed him in the street and followed him in! (Truth be told, Tyrone had spied her as well, but he pretended sudden absorption in the coach passengers descending outside the White Hart. Not that his ruse had spared him, in the end.)

One thing he knew now: he could not rest until he had an answer. He would ride over to Headbourne Worthy at once and catch Boulton before his afternoon service. And he would bring a groom this time, to hold his horse while he chased the curate down.

The angular maid with straggling hair was sweeping the front step of the parsonage when Tyrone rode up.

"Good day to you," he called. "Is Mr. Boulton returned from morning service yet?"

Struck dumb by this apparition, her lips parted to reveal long teeth, and she nodded.

"Splendid. Will you announce me, then?" Swinging down, he handed the reins to Gotch.

The young man's approach roused her. With a gulp she turned to flee inside, only to collide with the closed door. Before Tyrone could do more than exclaim, Hackitt (for it was she) ripped the door open and vanished within. Stamping and banging and hollering followed, and then Boulton appeared in the doorway.

"Ellsworth! What are you doing here?"

"Good day to you as well," returned Tyrone. "May I have a word?"

Boulton blanched and looked like he would have made some excuse if he could, but then he nodded as dumbly as Hackitt and retreated to allow Tyrone passage.

"We had better use my study, rather than the parlor."

Thinking of Miss Boulton's presence and the clumsy maid's, Tyrone said, "Or we might take a little walk."

"No, better not," Boulton demurred. "Parishioners about, don't you know. No one will bother us here. Anne is still at the church, and that maid makes enough noise to cover a retreating army."

The curate's study lay at the back of the house, its window overlooking the churchyard. Boulton gestured toward an unsteady-looking chair before the fireplace, but Tyrone was too restless to sit.

"Thank you. No. I won't keep you long," he said abruptly. "See here—I've just come to ask if you used my proposal speeches yet. That is—if you have offered for Miss Weeks."

If possible, Boulton went even paler. "What a question!"

"I know it's impertinent and none of my business," admitted Tyrone shortly. "Though I do maintain a professional interest in my—works—as it were."

"Well, then—er—yes. I did. Make use of the speeches. And was summarily refused. As you predicted."

Tyrone expelled a slow breath as he turned away to the window, that Boulton might not see the grin spreading across his face. Then she was unattached and free! No more Taplin, no more Boulton. The field was clear, and Tyrone might in honor break a lance in the lists. Never mind that she had been frosty to him that morning at church—perhaps she had read his intentions and remembered finding him with Miss Caraway. No girl liked to think she was one of many. Well, he could explain that away easily enough.

As impatient as he had been to get the truth from Boulton, he was now as eager to be on his way.

A knock at the door was heard, however, and the door banged open before Boulton choked out an "Enter!"

"Note for you, sir, from The Acres, and the boy is waiting for your reply," Hackitt announced, her prominent eyes sliding back and forth between the curate and his caller.

Both Boulton's and Tyrone's hearts sped at the words "The Acres," Tyrone's then plummeting to his boots as he imagined Aggie had changed her mind.

"If you would excuse me," croaked Boulton, accepting the note.

"You go right ahead," said Tyrone magnanimously, claiming the chair which had been offered earlier. If Boulton thought he would leave the parsonage now, before he knew what that missive held, he was fated for disappointment. The maid would have to drag Tyrone captive in chains before he could be got rid of.

Boulton observed Tyrone's resolve, and his shoulders drooped. With a failed attempt at nonchalance, he seated himself at his desk and opened the note. A second, wrinkled sheet fell out, which

Boulton no sooner unfolded than he thrust in his coat pocket, going red as a poppy. He then read the enfolding sheet, another wave of color washing over his features.

"What reply should I give?" asked Hackitt, agog to see the effect she had.

Boulton looked down. Read the sheet again. Looked up. "The reply," he said faintly. "The reply is 'Yes, it was his.' And please close the door behind you, Hackitt."

Tyrone could not hold his tongue to save his life. "Good news? Bad news?"

Had Gareth Boulton been a different sort of man, more worldly-wise, confident and smooth, he would have turned the question aside or answered in a way which left Tyrone none the wiser, but poor Boulton was none of these things. He required preparation and practice in order to carry off singular discourses such as marriage proposals or lying to people under scrutiny.

As a result, he turned his lost gaze on Tyrone and then blurted, "Ellsworth, I'm afraid I have got a confession to make."

"Good heavens, man! What can it be that makes you look like that?"

A dozen thoughts careened through Tyrone's head simultaneously, colliding and tangling. She was going to marry Boulton after all! But Boulton looked like he would be sick. Then—then she had consented to elope with him, but now he had lost heart. Or—no—she had said she would willingly marry him, except that then her father threatened to cut her off without a shilling!

Boulton lowered his eyes again to the note. "You...have known Miss Weeks a very long time, you say."

"Years and years." Tyrone longed to shake the news out of the man. "And she is my twin sister's dearest friend."

Boulton nodded, his Adam's apple bobbing with his gulp. "The fact is, Ellsworth, I sent Miss Weeks a letter before I proposed to her. In order to butter her up, as it were."

This information distracted him. "One of your own authorship? Well, I needn't tell you I wouldn't have recommended it. But as you have already told me the end result of our efforts, why own to this part in it now?"

"Because the letter I sent her was largely cribbed from another—composition—of yours. Not one you wrote for me, but one you wrote for another. I—er—requested a copy because this person owed me a favor."

"Lord," said Tyrone, shaking his head. "Don't tell me it was the limerick I wrote for Ginger Peaches!"

"No, not that. It was—ah—the note to a Miss Kemp from Johnson."

At this Tyrone barked a laugh. "That rubbish? Ah, Boulton, that one would not be at all to Miss Weeks' taste and no doubt hindered your cause." Giving the chair he sat on a rock, he rose again, cheerfulness restored. "You are forgiven. I suspect I should have guessed these things might get passed around. A good reminder for my next literary endeavor: the warning and guidelines on usage must be very clear."

"Yes, well," muttered the curate, rising himself. "I am relieved you take this so easily, Ellsworth."

"So Miss Weeks not only refused you, but she returned your mawkish letter? I'm sorry for the blow to your feelings, but you would do better to toss that effort on the fire."

But Boulton got the greeny look again and clutched his heart over his inner pocket. "Ellsworth, I had better tell you that Miss Weeks did not return the letter I sent her. It—ah—it so happens that I was carrying the original note you wrote for Johnson to copy, and it fell from my pocket, I suppose, in Oram's Arbour, where Miss Weeks' maid discovered it."

It was Tyrone's turn to pale and falter. The need for his hand to remain hidden in others' love affairs went without saying, but Tyrone now found that, more than any other young lady on earth, he did not want Miss Agatha Weeks to know anything about it. He could not remember—had there been anything in

Johnson's note which connected it to him? There must have been, or why should Boulton be so uneasy?

When Tyrone could master his voice, he said, "What was Miss Weeks' question to you, if I might ask?"

Boulton licked his lips nervously. "After explaining how and where the maid came to possess the note, she asked, 'Did Mr. Ellsworth send you this?' And, as you heard, I answered, 'Yes, it was his.'"

As if impelled by invisible strings, Boulton retrieved it from his coat. "Here it is—what she found. What I dropped."

Tyrone took the wrinkled page and unfolded it. There, in Johnson's scrawl, was the flowery composition Tyrone had written for Miss Kemp. When the warden tore up Tyrone's copy, Johnson had begged him to dictate its lost contents, as he had for Ginger Peaches, and Tyrone had obliged. And there, also in Johnson's hand, was his addendum to Boulton: "May Ellsworth's magic words operate on your lady love as they did Miss Kemp."

The room felt suddenly hot. "Miss Weeks asked if *I* sent you this?"

"Ye-e-es." Warily.

"And you answered, 'Yes, it was his.'"

"As you heard."

"So I did. But in fact I did *not* send you this, nor is it truly mine, as we have learned from its fate after it left my hand. It was originally by my pen, yes, but the letter itself and the sentiments within belong to Johnson. Nor did I send it to you, Boulton. *Johnson* did."

"True. True in the main," agreed Boulton. "Perhaps I could have clarified that. But Miss Weeks will likely not split hairs about it."

"Miss Weeks is an intelligent girl," persisted Tyrone, "who will no doubt guess that, if you had such a letter from me on your person, it might not have been the first time I suggested—not the first time I put words in your mouth."

"Oh, I don't know about that, Ellsworth. She might not give it another thought." The curate looked smug as he remembered Miss Weeks telling him she liked him best as himself. Ellsworth might plume himself on his wit, but the next time Boulton tried his luck with a young lady, he would save his money and Ellsworth might go hang!

Bitterly, Tyrone folded Johnson's letter again and tossed it on the desk. Of course Aggie would give it another thought. Aggie would not have written to Boulton this morning and awaited a reply if she were not giving it another thought!

Which would be preferable? For Aggie to think Tyrone had been making up to some Miss Kemp person, treating that young lady's reputation lightly by sharing the progress of that flirtation with friends; or for Aggie to learn Tyrone had no relationship with Miss Kemp whatsoever, but provided such materials to whomever paid him? On balance, he thought the former. Better to say Miss Kemp had been a passing whim, a whim he regretted as much as he regretted mentioning her to others. It was a lie, but surely this small lie was less destructive than admitting to Aggie his participation in deceiving *numerous* young women, including herself!

He had better go at once and tell the small lie, before she put more of the pieces together and came to the truth herself.

But first he must ensure Boulton's silence.

"I say, Boulton, you may be right," he began. "Perhaps Miss Weeks has now received your reply and put the matter out of her mind. But you understand, because of the long intimacy between her and those of us at Hollowgate, I would rather Miss Weeks know as little as possible of my—ah—business at Oxford, and I daresay you would agree that she would best be kept in ignorance of my involvement in your own attempted courtship. It would reflect well on neither of us, I'm afraid."

"Oh, I don't know about that," was Boulton's most unexpected reply. "Although Miss Weeks did refuse me, it occurs to me that one day, perhaps in a year or two if I am still so inclined, I might try my chances with her again. Without your assistance, that is.

Because—Ellsworth—Miss Weeks was kind enough to say—after I bumbled out various sentiments, for which I had no preparation—extempore, as it were—that she preferred when I spoke for myself. When I *was* myself. Therefore it would actually be to my benefit to inform her that I trusted foolishly to the handiwork of others, rather than making my own case."

This time Tyrone sank to perch on a corner of Boulton's desk. Good heavens. Had Aggie really said such a thing? That she preferred the plain, unvarnished Boulton? If she had, Boulton would indeed have no call to keep the secret. Quite the opposite, as he pointed out.

"Boulton," he blurted, rising again. "Should you later find Miss Weeks yet unmarried and decide to address her again, I do see your reasons for making a clean breast of things *at that time*. I only request that you wait until that moment, if that moment ever comes, before you do so. It so happens I am winding up affairs. That is—I have already informed my cousin Benjamin that I will no longer take on such writing assignments because I have come to dislike their clandestine nature. Therefore, Boulton, if you would wait a year or more to expose me, it would make all the difference. By then I will be more respectably employed and such things may be ascribed to youthful folly and deemed safely in the past."

To Tyrone's vast, vast relief, after frowning over this proposal a minute, Boulton gave a firm nod. "I see your point. And, frankly, I suppose it will not matter who provided my inspiration, now that Miss Weeks knows my words were not solely mine. She might even prefer never to be reminded of it in future. *I* might prefer never to refer to it, as a matter of fact. Far better all around simply to present myself to her and to the world as I am, for better or for worse, henceforth."

"That's the spirit," Tyrone declared, clapping Boulton's shoulder. "Let us both learn to be wiser men. And you must pardon me as well, for not advising you from the very first to dispense with disguises of any sort, even verbal ones. Let us shake hands on it, sir, and then I will leave you to your afternoon service."

Chapter 21

And thus halfe truth shall come to light, and I,
Be wisely cleer'd by double villany.
—R. Gomersall, *Tragedie of Lodovick Sforza,* I.iv.22 (1628)

Tyrone's initial elation faded before he reached the joining of Race Way and the Weeke Road. Yes, honor was satisfied and Aggie was free, but how precisely should he mount his attack on her single state? Ought he to rush at her, casting himself at her feet and declaring whatever nonsense came into his head? Such had been Boulton's strategy, and only see how he fared! Certainly Aggie preferred him to Boulton, through long acquaintance and from love of Minta, but would it be enough to prevent a refusal? Liking was not love, of course, but could not so modest a spark with care be fanned into fire?

One thing was clear: he must speak to her.

And sooner, rather than later.

For even if he were able to keep a tight rein on impetuous desire, he must give her some explanation for what she had already discovered. Boulton's carelessness forced Tyrone's hand, and thus the little lie must be told. Let her think him guilty of folly with a certain Miss Kemp but let her not see his hand in Boulton's affairs! The curate had promised a year of silence, and perhaps by then Tyrone and Aggie might be safely married, in which case Tyrone himself would unfold the whole tale for her amusement and escape with no more than a teasing reprimand.

This last picture bolstered his courage. Yes, he would begin his campaign at once. But in order to do so, he must know something of Aggie's plans, and the best source of that information would be his sister Araminta. Clicking his tongue to Ebony, he nudged him in the direction of the Carlisles' home.

After depositing his horse at the stable in Southgate Street, Tyrone slapped the dust from himself and proceeded on foot toward Canon Street, where he hammered smartly on the door of the modest dwelling.

"Good afternoon, Terry. Is your mistress at home?"

The stout housemaid's stern expression melted at the sight of him. "Mr. Ellsworth, sir, she is indeed. You come right in." It was only when they were in the dim passage and the door shut behind him that she added, "I was just preparing some refreshment for her and Miss Weeks. Mrs. Carlisle did not request it—she never does remember—but it being so warm a day…"

"Miss Weeks is here?" croaked Tyrone, halting abruptly. But it was too late for retreat.

"Mr. Ellsworth to see you, Mrs. Carlisle," announced Terry, observing with patent disapproval her young mistress sprawled across the sofa, one hand on her swollen midsection and the other trailing to the floor.

"Tyrone!" cried Minta in a guilty tone. His sister and Aggie must have come in recently from the outdoors because they were pink from exertion and their hair rumpled. Tyrone thought Aggie had never looked prettier, she was so fresh and sprightly. Her bonnet and gloves had been tossed aside, but she was even now reaching for them.

"How lovely!" Minta said, glancing from one to the other. "Do sit down. Bea isn't with you?"

"No Bea," he answered, his own color high. "You aren't going—Miss Weeks—are you?"

"I am," Aggie replied shortly, tugging on the first glove. "I must get home."

"But Miss Weeks, you will overheat. I was just preparing a tray of currant wine and biscuits," Terry protested, even as Minta heaved herself upright and mourned, "Oh, Aggie."

"I will be perfectly well, thank you, Terry."

"Then I'll walk you back to The Acres," Tyrone suggested, springing up from the seat he had just occupied.

"There's no need, Mr. Ellsworth. My maid Banniker is here somewhere. In the kitchen perhaps."

"That she is," Terry remonstrated, "where I just left her, looking quite spent and recovering with her own cool drink. But if you aim to go now, miss, I will roust her. Such is the life of a servant."

Aggie pressed her lips together but was forced to yield, pulling off her glove once more.

"Thank you, Terry," said Araminta meekly, her lips twitching. "We will have the tray. That would be splendid. Tyrone, please sit. I'm sorry Nicholas isn't here to see you, but directly after church Mrs. Olstrop complained of heart palpitations, and off he went. Aggie and I have just come in from a walk ourselves."

Tyrone wondered if it added to his conceited, braying-assness to suspect the girls discussed him on their walk. Otherwise, what reason could there be for this awkwardness? Furtive looks exchanged between Araminta and Aggie; his own gaze studiously avoided; conversation confined to Mrs. Olstrop's health history and Mr. Hepple's sermon and the excellence of the currant wine and biscuits.

When the farce ended, Aggie rose again with determination. "Thank you, Minta, but now I really must go."

"And I," put in Tyrone, on his feet at once.

"Surely you did not drop in on your sister merely to talk over such commonplaces as we just have," observed Aggie.

"Of course I did," he lied valiantly. "And another time I will do the same with my sisters Florence and Lily. You cannot imagine how we miss these little nothings around the table at home, now that they are all married. How much of life is made up of the companionable sharing of commonplaces."

Minta sighed and tossed Aggie her remaining glove. "Tyrone is going to walk with you willy-nilly. Best not to duck these things."

Minutes later Tyrone and Aggie, trailed at a circumspect distance by Banniker, walked up Canon Street into Southgate Street, past the very stable where Ebony waited in vain his master's return.

But Tyrone hardly remembered he had ridden there. He was too addled. For a man of easy words, having finally got Aggie to himself, none offered themselves at this most momentous moment.

"Most momentous moment," he muttered.

"I beg your pardon?"

"Nothing."

But this would not do. *Well-begun is half done.* Then surely even a poor beginning was better than nothing. Therefore: "Aggie—Miss Weeks, I mean to say—the Carlisles' home was not the first place I called this afternoon."

"Fancy," returned Aggie. She was setting a whacking good pace, in his opinion, for one with limbs not nearly so long as his.

"You will not ask me where else I called, I see, so I will tell you. I come from Boulton's in Headbourne Worthy."

Then her speed did flag, briefly. But only briefly. Tyrone feared they would be at the foot of The Acres' drive before he managed to say a fraction of what was needed.

"Are you such good friends now?" asked Aggie. "Or was it a professional call?"

"Professional call?" Tyrone faltered. "I-I am no clergyman."

"Clergyman? Oh, dear me, no. I meant you might have called upon Mr. Boulton much as Mr. Carlisle has upon Mrs. Olstrop's heart palpitations. For, if I am not mistaken, Mr. Ellsworth, you also consider yourself an expert in matters of the heart."

Tyrone's stomach sank somewhere to the region of his ankles. A dreadful suspicion clawed at him. Was this more than a young lady's disappointment with a friend's character?

"What makes you say so?" he asked, his voice hollow.

She paused to cross Archery Lane. There was little traffic, it being Sunday afternoon, but it was near the hour, and various bells from various clocks began to make themselves heard, near and far, in staggered succession.

Aggie walked on but did not answer. In truth, she was considering how to proceed.

But Tyrone could not bear the suspense. "Miss Weeks—while I was with Boulton, your note arrived, and I—saw how it struck him, so I asked him the nature of it. He told me not only that he had proposed to you without success, but also that he had…looked for inspiration in a—in a note I had—er—written some time ago for—someone else."

She said nothing, and the cursed colossal brim of her bonnet shielded her from observation. They were nearly to the High Street.

In her silence, Tyrone found himself fighting the urge to babble. And somehow, the small lie he had intended to tell was forgotten in what he deemed a better one because it was half truth. "I have got a…book I am writing, you see. A handbook of sorts. I don't know if you are familiar with it, but Samuel Richardson, in addition to writing the novels for which he is so famous, began with publishing a letter-writing handbook. That's what I was in search of at the circulating library. It's full of examples. A father to a son on keeping good company. A mother to a son on enduring hardships. A-a-a-an offer of marriage from a young man to a young lady. Her response to the same. A recommendation for a servant, and so on. But Richardson's book is over sixty years old now, so I propose to write another. A newer."

Her strides slowed perceptibly, and not merely because they had turned into the High Street. The clangor of the bells had died away by this point, to be replaced by the rattle of wheels in the road and the steps and voices of passersby.

Drawing courage from the fact that Aggie did not scoff at his story, he plunged onward. "What Boulton dropped so carelessly, and which you kindly returned to him, was a specimen of the sorts of—er—sample correspondence my book will include. My cousin Benjamin Ellsworth proposes to act as my agent and find a publisher for it."

At last she stopped and looked at him. "I congratulate you on the idea, Mr. Ellsworth. I imagine many will find your 'specimens' useful, as Mr. Boulton did, and hope to learn from your hard-won experience."

Hard-won experience? This was the time, he supposed, when he should tell the little lie he originally planned. He should say that, ha ha ha, to be sure, his fleeting attachment to Miss Kemp at least yielded an abundance of material from which others might profit.

But the clear, measuring gaze she turned on him choked the words in his throat, and he felt telltale heat rise to his face.

"Will all the specimens in your book be drawn from your correspondence with Miss Kemp?" Aggie asked. "I do hope she has granted her permission. But perhaps that would be shutting the door after the steed be stolen."

"Shutting the door...?" he repeated blankly.

"Surely you are familiar with the expression, Mr. Ellsworth, writer that you are. I mean of course that it appears you have already shared this note with someone who had no business seeing it, and I daresay Mr. Boulton was not the only person with whom you shared it."

"I—I—"

"And I do hope the other—gentlemen—who might have seen your correspondence with Miss Kemp were more careful of the notes than Mr. Boulton, lest letters of such an intimate nature be dropped in fields from Oxford to Southampton."

"Aggie," he pleaded.

"*Miss Weeks*, please." Taking up her skirts, she swept into motion again, and, with a despairing gesture, he followed after.

"Agg—Miss Weeks, that is—I will make a confession: I have been a foolish and heedless person, and not careful as I ought to have been of various young ladies' names, perhaps—"

"Did you say 'various'?" marveled Aggie, halting again as they passed through the West Gate. "'*Various* young ladies'? Then Miss Kemp is not the only victim?"

"Oh!" Too late he realized this new blunder. "I—of course I needed a *variety* of sample letters, you understand."

"How fortunate then that you were able to draw upon a *variety* of letters you had written to young ladies," Aggie returned. "Dear me."

And then the thought that Aggie believed he had made love to countless maidens in Oxford forced another chunk of the truth from him. "I wrote such things, yes," he blurted, "to several young ladies in addition to Miss Kemp. But I swear to you I did not do so on my own behalf! I never did. It was not *I* who fancied Miss Kemp, Aggie—it was a Mr. Jerome Johnson! For a half-crown he gave me her name and the essence of what he wanted to say, and I wrote it for him. I am sorry he passed it along to Boulton. I would not willingly have any young woman's name bandied about. I should have thought of the possibility, but I did not."

The look she turned on him could only be described as disappointed, and it struck him to the heart. "Oh, Tyrone," she said, "if you have done this, there were so very many things you didn't think of. If I may ask, how *many* young ladies do you mean by 'several'?"

"How many young ladies did I assist other people in wooing?" He thought it could not be emphasized enough that, whatever number he gave her, the number of times his heart was involved would be nil.

"Yes."

"Well—I cannot be precise without—er—checking, but I believe perhaps a couple dozen?"

Her mouth dropped open. "A couple *dozen*? You mean to tell me there have been a couple *dozen* young ladies whose names might be 'bandied about' as Miss Kemp's has been, if other customers of yours have passed your work around as has Mr. Johnson?"

He flinched at the word "customer" but gave a reluctant nod. "But Aggie—if it mends matters any with you, I don't believe anyone made a practice of passing such things around, so perhaps Miss Kemp's note—shown to Boulton at his specific request, might be the first. Perhaps the only."

Shaking her head, Aggie gave a bitter sigh. They were in Cock Lane now and would soon reach the point where he must leave her. "Oh, Tyrone, you don't know that for certain, do you? Once something is written down, who knows what might become of it? You might ask every last customer to return to you what you wrote, but that would not thereby ensure it had not already been seen by another or by many others."

There was no possible answer to this because it was true. Everything she said was true. It was scarcely even a comfort to him that Aggie had slipped and used his Christian name again.

He could not see around the expansive brim of her bonnet, but Aggie's brow was troubled. She was making further deductions. Terrible ones.

"Not only do you not know what might have become of these—works—of yours," she resumed thoughtfully, "but I suppose there was some discussion in their creation. That is, you must have had a reputation for your...skill. Otherwise, how would the idea have occurred to anyone? It could not be that a couple dozen young men independently decided to approach you and ask for your assistance in furthering their affairs."

Tyrone was unhappily reminded of his interview with Warden Gauntlett. He had no desire to incriminate his cousins Benjamin and Austin, but the alternative was to let Aggie believe he had run all over New College boasting of his adeptness with pen and heart!

"There was some discussion," he admitted. "And one...success... would lead to other requests for help. But they sprang from good intentions," Tyrone added hopelessly. "These requests. Courtship is a difficult thing, and what can be more important than love? To ask for help is neither easy nor something one tends to boast about. I would never have agreed to write anything for dishonorable reasons—to seduce or to dally or to mock." Not that he had asked many questions about his customers' motives, he supposed.

Unwittingly he had helped his cause, however, because he touched the same sympathetic chord as had poor Mr. Boulton.

Yes, Aggie thought, it must indeed be difficult at times to be a man. In any other challenging situation, a man would not only be forgiven for availing himself of what resources he could, he would be encouraged to. Should love be the only exception? But, then again, this was *not* the same because helping oneself in this case required injuring others.

When she replied, she did so with the added intention of making firm her own resolve. "I do begin to understand how difficult it must be, to offer one's very self up for another's judgment and possible rejection," said Aggie. "When Mr. Boulton made his unfortunate proposal, he said as much, and I sympathized. I did. It did not change my answer to him, but I sympathized. Therefore, I truly do understand why these other young men might have come to you. But in doing so, they exposed the objects of their affection to levity and gossip and notoriety. That it was unintentional or done without malice aforethought does not change that fact."

They arrived at the brick-and-iron arch marking the entrance to Hollowgate's drive, but when Aggie slowed, Tyrone shook his head. "If you please, I will continue with you. There is more to say. You are entirely right, Aggie, in calling us—me—thoughtless.

Stupid, even. Young men will always talk of young ladies—to stop that altogether would be impossible—but what I did contributed to it. And, as you point out, what I did has left physical evidence which I can neither control nor destroy. I do not know if it makes any difference in your opinion, but I had already decided to shut up shop, as it were, so at least there will be no more stray letters to real people floating about. Any 'examples' I include in my proposed handbook would be for general situations and be addressed anonymously as 'to Miss A' and 'to Miss B' and such. Moreover, they would come prefaced with a warning that they were not intended to be used verbatim nor traced back to actual individuals."

"I wonder if such a warning made any difference to readers of Richardson's manual," mused Aggie. But more pressing questions loomed, and she lapsed once more into silence.

Some yards onward, just when an ember of hope kindled in Tyrone's breast that he might escape the worst consequences of discovery, she spoke again.

"There is something else I suspect you have not thought of."

He swallowed. "What is that?"

"That—what would happen, if any of the young ladies learned they had been deceived?"

"Oh—Aggie—surely not 'deceived'!"

She turned reproachful eyes on him. "Tyrone, what other word could be used for it?"

"If—if a man quotes poetry or-or-or presents a young lady with the gift of a book he did not write or flowers he did not grow, none of those things are considered deception."

"They would be if she did not know him to be quoting poetry, or if he declared he had written the book or grown the flowers!"

"Why should such an ass tag his every word with a footnote in the former case?" countered Tyrone. "Or feel the obligation to clarify who wrote which book or grew which flowers in the latter?"

"That is not the point! I say the point is the deception. I speak of an instance where she might have loved him for the poetry he spouted or the book she thought he wrote—"

"Or the flowers she thought he grew?" Tyrone interrupted. "You see it's all nonsense. Why would she care who grew the flowers?"

"All right. Perhaps the flowers were a silly example," conceded Aggie, "but it would be one thing for our hypothetical gentleman to quote Shakespeare undetected, and quite another for him to pay a living, breathing person to compose his speeches for him. Suppose she tells him she likes his words, and he is too shy or too fearful to tell her they were none of his own? Is that not deception? Is she not, in all truth, liking *your* words, Tyrone Ellsworth? Is she not, in some fashion, won over by *you*?"

It was no more than Tyrone had thought to himself in Florence's garden, when he asserted that any affection Boulton might win from Aggie was by right his own. But he could not let her tread this dangerous path.

"You will swell me with conceit," he tried to tease, "telling me a couple dozen young ladies are in love with me. Come, come. Suppose a letter of mine opened a door for a young man who might not otherwise have been given an opportunity to stand on his own feet? What of it? I cannot speak every word for him, for the rest of his life. And if a young lady accepts a young man for one piddling love note, when everything thereafter belies it or fails to please her, how can I be blamed?"

"Is that the most you ever did for each of them, then?" she asked. "One note, and only one?"

He hesitated. It was impossible that he should not.

"One small, initial deception would be less egregious than a continued one," she said, determined to be reasonable. "After all, I suppose there might often be some small deception in any beginning." She thought of Miss Caraway's sudden friendliness to Beatrice, as well as dear Minta's costume-related deceptions when trying to win Francis Taplin.

Tyrone found himself in a wretched quandary. If he told Aggie he wrote but one paltry note for each of his supplicants, she was prepared to overlook his past foolishness, and he might get on with trying to win her. But if he told the truth—! How had he come to be in this position, when he had fully intended to tell his one small lie and be done with it?

Supposing he told this new, somewhat larger lie? He had one year's grace promised from Boulton, and who knew how circumstances might have changed by then? Nor was there any guarantee Boulton would ever bother to reveal Tyrone's deception after the year was gone. The man might be happily wed to some other young lady by then, his attempt at Miss Weeks forgotten in his surpassing contentment.

But if he had *not* forgotten Aggie—if Boulton decided he would indeed try again to attach her—well, Tyrone would just have to pray it would all be irrelevant by then. That, in a year's time, Aggie would be either fully won by him, Tyrone, or already so hopelessly against him that it mattered little what additional reason she might have to reject him.

Taking a bracing breath, he answered her lightly. "Oh, yes. Reprehensible as it was, it was just a note here or there. I could hardly have corresponded with a dozen young ladies at a time! Suppose I had, and confused them? Miss Kemp for Miss So-and-So for

Miss Something-or-Other? That would have made short work of my business."

To his relief, she laughed. "I did not think of that. No, you are right. If it had been so, you would have needed a register of sorts to keep track of such things. Or a secretary."

"Ha ha ha! Indeed yes. But here we are at The Acres." Tyrone looked up the tree-lined drive to hide another stab of panic. He must remember to warn his cousins never, never, never to mention the business either, for he knew very well that Benjamin kept exactly such a register and occupied exactly such a secretarial role.

Aggie turned to hold out her gloved hand. "I am glad we had this opportunity to speak. I am sorry for Miss Kemp and any others who might suffer being talked of, but I trust in future no other young ladies will be placed in their unenviable position. Tyrone, I must confess now that I thought you guilty of worse."

"Worse?" he gulped.

"Yes." Her smile was rueful. "You must pardon me, but there were times when Mr. Boulton quite puzzled me—when he sounded most unlike himself. I could not seem to put the pieces of him together into one consistent person, and I wondered. All of which is to say, I fear the letter my maid found, which I returned to Mr. Boulton, was likely not the only example he has secured of your writing. You might want to ask him. Because I would not be surprised if he has amassed your entire collected works! What else could explain it?" She laughed and shook her head. With a glance to ensure her maid was out of earshot, she added in a lower voice, "When Banniker told me what your note to Miss Kemp said, Tyrone, I was certain I had hit on the solution to the mystery. I was certain that, if Mr. Boulton sounded like different men at different times, it must be because he cribbed from others, and here was one of the others! So confess: did you write his first note for him, or did he collect your writings behind your back?"

Chapter 22

A Man who can be worth a Lady's Acceptance, will never be ashamed or afraid to appear openly.
—Samuel Richardson, *Letters Written to and for Particular Friends* (1741)

A coach rumbled by on the Romsey road, followed by a dray loaded for the market, and the noise and dust and need for retreat these entailed purchased another moment of reprieve for Tyrone.

But when the diversion was past, Aggie turned back to him with her look of expectant amusement.

And he realized he could not do it.

One lie he had managed. The second had been pressed from him. A third was impossible.

But she was waiting, and so he said, "I did write Boulton's apology note for him."

"Ah ha!" cried Aggie, giving a triumphant little hop. "And is it going in your book? 'A young man to a young lady, on having offended her'?"

"I had not thought of it."

"I *knew* I was right," she declared. "Then tell me this: did any of your couple dozen customers ever request you write for them a proposal of marriage?"

"A few," choked Tyrone.

"And was there something in one of them from Shakespeare? Something about persevering love?"

"A common hack, I'm afraid."

"Is it? I would never have noticed the quote, had you yourself not repeated it to me at your birthday dinner."

"My range of ideas can be limited." He tugged on his cuffs.

"Are you feeling quite the thing, Tyrone? You have turned pale, yet you perspire."

"The blasted heat—pardon me."

"Forgive me for detaining you, then. I did not realize you were so warm. Would you care to call at The Acres? You might enjoy something to refresh you, and our groom could drive you back to Hollowgate."

"I rode," he muttered. "Ebony is at Serle's in town."

"Rode? Good gracious! Then whyever did you offer to walk with me? I had Banniker." She peered up at him with concern, for he looked more ill by the second. "Never mind that, at any rate. Long can drive you back to town for your horse, in that case."

"Aggie." His hand lifted but fell short of touching her sleeve. "I—have got more to say about Boulton. Would it be possible to send your maid along? You and I might walk a little way up the drive."

"Of course." The deed was soon done (Banniker's shoulders slumping to be sent away when there was so much of interest to learn), and Aggie led the way toward the abbey ruins, taking care to keep in the shade as much as possible. The uneasiness which their conversation had dispelled made its return known in the pit of her stomach. What could he tell her of Mr. Boulton that made him look like that?

She shut her eyes a moment, the dark shape of the abbey wall outlined red against her closed lids. Had Mr. Boulton been talking of her in this flurry of notes requested and sent? Had she herself become a 'Miss Kemp' among Tyrone's customers? Somewhere in Oxford, did a raw undergraduate bid Mr. Boulton, "Send a copy of Ellsworth's apology—perhaps my Miss Thus-and-Such will prove as forgiving as your Miss Weeks. I've enclosed my two shillings. Yours etc."

She could not bear it, she thought. Was it not bad enough to have been the talk of Winchester when she was eighteen and again these past several weeks? At least with the loathsome Mr. Taplin gone for good she hoped never to have his name again linked with hers. But now to learn she would once more be the object of gossip and jokes, glee and commiseration, and this time with no foot she could crush to finish the matter?

It would not be as bad, she tried to assure herself. She was merely someone Mr. Boulton apologized to but did not succeed with. There was nothing incriminating there. But, sensitive as she was to a repetition of her embarrassment, she dreaded further talk. This time she had no control over what would be whispered of her or who would do the whispering. Her name, passed back and forth, through the halls and chapels and streets of Oxford and beyond! Why, if she discovered Mr. Boulton had set this ball rolling, she would drive straight to Headbourne Worthy and—

"I wrote more than Boulton's apology letter for him," Tyrone uttered to her back. "I—I wrote the letter which set you and Mrs. Chester off to Headbourne Worthy to hire him as a tutor. I—counseled him more than once about you when he asked my advice. And, if he sought additional samples of—my work—from others—to make his second offer for you, they were—they were supplementary to a set of speeches I wrote for him."

Her imagination having traveled so far down its different path, Aggie could not immediately comprehend what Tyrone was telling her, and she turned to regard him blankly. It made it worse for him, actually, because he was forced to watch her rehearse his speech in her head; he was forced to watch understanding dawn on her.

Aggie sank onto a block of moss-covered masonry.

"Then—you mean to say you…contrived Mr. Boulton's courtship of me?"

"Contrived? No! That is to say, I did play a role in giving him some things to say, but 'contrived' implies artful scheming, whereas—"

"You do not consider giving Mr. Boulton things to say, in order that he might win favor from me, 'artful scheming?'" insisted Aggie.

"I mean only that such words make my actions sound malicious, when they were not, Aggie."

"Because you thought it would be a *good* thing, if I were to marry Mr. Boulton?"

"No, not that at all. In fact, I thought—and I told him so more than once—that he had little chance of winning you under any circumstances, and he would do better not to try. But he was determined to try, Aggie."

He did not even know if she heard him. She was staring at the abbey ruins, her lips slightly parted and arms hanging limply by her sides. Then it was not one tiny little apology letter out there in the world to get about? It was an entire *catalogue* of offerings! What had he said? An apology, a request for assistance, a *set of proposal speeches*?

Mercy.

"Why did you do it, Tyrone?" she asked hoarsely. "Make sport of me in such a fashion? Was my long friendship with Araminta and your family of so little weight? What claim had Mr. Boulton on your loyalty, that you should hold it superior to mine?"

"Aggie…" his voice was anguished. He tried to sit beside her on the masonry block, but she shifted away from him. There was no anger in the movement, only numb hurt, and he drew back at once.

"You had no need of money," she murmured. "How could you even accept Mr. Boulton's coin, poor as he is? Did you do it for amusement?"

"Neither for sport nor for money nor amusement," he vowed. "None of those reasons."

"Then why?" Her anger was beginning to catch up to her comprehension, and her breath quickened.

"When he first asked, at Oxford, I refused. Not for any virtuous reason, I am ashamed to say, but because the warden discovered my enterprise and insisted I cease and desist. I might have refused Boulton in any case because I—knew of your—past heartbreak—pardon me for mentioning it again—and I told him he would do better to choose someone else. Someone more…open to wooing."

Aggie's fists clenched in her lap. Every hint, every reminder, of the whole world thinking she never overcame her feelings for Mr. Taplin only made her angrier. Had no one anything else to think of? Did everyone believe her so hopeless and helpless that they must all form opinions and be in a fidget to interfere? Sometimes she thought she hated everyone, even those she loved most dearly, for these constant reminders of her folly.

"He ignored my advice," Tyrone went on, "and attempted to make his ill-fated offer for you after our dinner at the Angel Inn, as I am sure you recall."

"I do recall. And if I refused to hear him then, why on earth did you think you could help him succeed later?"

"Because Taplin was back!" cried Tyrone. "I thought—we all thought—it would be...good for you to have some sort of distraction, lest you be—be—"

She held up a peremptory hand. If she heard one more word, she might burst into flame. "*We all thought*"?

Suddenly Aggie wanted nothing more than to be alone. Forever, if possible. But if not, at least for a very long while.

Because, reasonable or not, she was angry at positively everyone.

At her parents and family for their fear-prompted matchmaking.

At Mr. Taplin for returning to vex her and to set her world in a pother.

At every gentleman who had offered for her in the last year.

Of these, at Mr. Boulton in particular. Had he taken her at her word the first time, she need never have been the object of Tyrone's perfidy.

At Minta. Because even Minta had feared Mr. Taplin's effect on Aggie and because Minta had dared to suggest Tyrone as a match for her.

And, of course, at Tyrone himself. At Tyrone especially.

At Tyrone *especially* especially. Tyrone, whom she had come to consider a friend in his own right. Tyrone, whom in her heart of hearts she acknowledged she now thought of as a great deal more than a friend.

But his friendship for her turned out to be a phantom. A creation born of her own fancy and his unspecific geniality. He thought no more of her—respected her no better than—the Miss Kemps of Oxford. Miss Weeks of The Acres was simply another credulous young lady to be gulled with fine words, and not even because he wished to win her! No—Tyrone Ellsworth wanted nothing from her—from any of the poor victims of his pen. He deceived and connived for nothing more than passing amusement and a few superfluous half-crowns.

And he claimed he had taken up Mr. Boulton's cause in order to "distract" her from Mr. Taplin?

Finally she spoke again, but her voice shook more than she would have liked. "Your defense, then, Mr. Ellsworth, is that you wove your tissue of lies in order to *protect* me, and you did it with the approval of 'all'?"

"What? No! I mean—yes, I meant to protect you in a manner, but my family knew nothing of my—efforts. My siblings and parents." This took him within half a breath of naming his cousins, and he hurried on. "Truly, Aggie—"

"Miss Weeks!"

"Truly, Miss Weeks, my interference was well-meant. A mere distraction. Had there been any danger of you coming to care for Boulton, I would have refused to have anything to do with it. And I never will again undertake such things, I promise."

Rising to her feet, she squared her shoulders. There was little dignity left to a girl who has been made a fool of, but Aggie was determined to salvage what she could. At eighteen she made a fool of herself over Francis Taplin, and now at two-and-twenty that early mistake had made her vulnerable once more. Vulnerable to disaster the more dangerous because hanging unseen under false colors of friendship.

Tyrone would not be the only one to make promises that day.

Never, never again, Aggie vowed inwardly. Never again would she assume any man was exactly what he seemed. Never again would she trust how a man presented himself on paper. Was it not treacherous enough to form an opinion based on the face a man presented to the world?

"Promise what you like," said Aggie. "I must be going."

"But Agg—Miss Weeks," Tyrone pleaded. He reached for her again, a movement she evaded as she marched away. "Miss Weeks, say you will forgive me, and we will be friends."

Aggie felt the heat of tears, and whether they sprung more from anger or from anguish she could not then say. She paused without turning back to look at him. "I intend to 'live peaceably with all men' as much as it lies with me, Mr. Ellsworth, but pray do not make such demands of me now."

She left him. Not to return to the house straightaway because she was not mistress enough of herself to face others. No—wretched occasions like the present called for solitude and invisibility, and it was fortunate Agatha Weeks knew every inch of her family's estate.

And now, in light of the day's painful revelations, she knew every inch of her heart as well. For was it not plain that, of all the people Aggie was angry with, she was most so with herself?

For being duped, yes. For being made to appear the fool again, certainly.

But, most of all, for allowing herself to love him.

Aggie did a great deal of thinking over the next few days, both in the privacy of her chamber and over long walks. She kept to the grounds of The Acres, that she might be spared even her maid's company or her family's. There was another ball, from which she excused herself, pleading headache. Headache as well, when Minta sent a note asking why she did not come again to Canon Street.

She carefully re-read the small collection of missives from Mr. Boulton and Tyrone, now seeing Tyrone's hand everywhere and wondering at her own stupidity. How could she have believed Mr. Boulton's feeble apologies for his lack of eloquence when he spoke to her face to face? Her only excuse was that she had not expected to be deceived, and so she easily was.

Her memories of Oxford now struck her as similarly suspect. Why had Tyrone invited Mr. Boulton to the Angel Inn, if they were not particular friends? And if Tyrone had dozens of customers, had they been all around her? Everywhere she looked? How many of the pairings and would-be pairings she had seen were his handiwork? What of the couple at the Radcliffe Camera, where the girl accused the young man of not writing the sonnet he promised? Was *he* a customer? And who were the wronged Miss Kemps, a sisterhood to which Aggie now belonged?

To think she had so recently wished Tyrone might notice her charms and pursue her! Did he even have a heart? Only someone who knew nothing of love could dash from one girl to the next and the next, spouting poems and promises with seeming sincerity.

No, let Miss Caraway have him, if she could get him. There was more heart in Aggie's little finger than in Tyrone's whole person, and though he had treated her with contempt, she would never again give him the opportunity to do so.

"I got over Mr. Taplin, unworthy as he was," Aggie meditated. "How much more easily, then, will I forget Tyrone Ellsworth? To do something for a second time can only be easier, the more so if I make every effort. I nursed my affection for Mr. Taplin longer than I need have—I see that now. But I will not make that mistake again. My eyes are opened, and I am an older and wiser woman. Yes, indeed. Tyrone Ellsworth will be ousted from my heart by Michaelmas, or my name isn't Agatha Weeks."

Or so she told herself.

Chapter 23

Come, sisters, cheer we up his sprites.
—Shakespeare, *Macbeth*, IV.i.1699 (c.1606)

Aggie might not have attended the next ball, but Tyrone did. He came in a daze of misery, hoping in spite of everything that she might be there and her temper softened. But she was not there. Both her older sisters were and both Tyrone's older sisters. Boulton was. The whole county was, it seemed. But not Aggie.

"Good evening, my dear brother," his sister Lily, Mrs. Simon Kenner, greeted him. "Will you dance with Florence first or me?"

"Either. Doesn't Simon want the first with you?"

"It wouldn't do to stand up with one's husband right off. I suppose I might dance with Florence's Robert and she with my Simon, but you look rather pale and pitiable." She angled her head to catch his eye. "Are you even listening to me, or is there someone you are waiting on?"

Lily glanced behind her at the arched entrance to Burchard's assembly room, just as a young woman with piles of chestnut hair appeared.

"Ooh…do you know that one? She's lovely. You must, because she's coming this way. Won't you introduce me?"

His eyes had skated right past the brunette Miss Caraway in search of Aggie's flaxen hair, but then with a start he found Miss Caraway directly before him. She was beaming. "Mr. Ellsworth! It's been an age. How goes it with you?"

"Well, thank you," he lied, making his bow. "May I have the pleasure of introducing my sister Mrs. Simon Kenner? And here comes another sister as well. Florence, may I acquaint you with Miss Caraway? Miss Caraway, Mrs. Robert Fairchild."

The Ellsworth sisters were as interested in Miss Caraway as she in them, and the three ladies chatted steadily until the musicians began to tune their instruments.

"Has Lily already claimed you for the first dance?" asked Florence mildly, turning to her brother. "If she has, I will go and sit with the other matrons."

"He hasn't, in so many words," replied Lily. "He said either one of us might do, as if he could hardly tell us apart."

"We had better yield, in that case, to Miss Caraway," Florence suggested. "You two go ahead, Tyrone, and Lily and I will *both* sit with the matrons."

"Speak for yourself," retorted Lily. "I want to dance, and if I can't have Tyrone, I will flutter at another beau."

Before he knew what he was about, Tyrone found Miss Caraway's hand on his arm, and he was leading her to the floor.

But despite her earlier declaration, Lily made no move from her sister's side. "Would you look at that!" she murmured. "That girl has most certainly set her cap for our dear boy."

"And why not?" returned Florence. "He is quite eligible. We might not even get our dances with him, if he chooses instead to partner all the unmarried young ladies. I suppose Miss Caraway is quite a catch herself, if she is the sister of Lady Downing."

"Yes. She took pains to let us know that."

"Now, Lily, we asked if her family had been long in Winchester. Therefore she was within her rights to name her admirable connections. Suppose he had met someone while at Oxford? He might have married and gone into altogether another part of the country, and we should only have seen him once or twice a year."

"True. Papa will be pleased if he marries so near Hollowgate."

"Papa will try to persuade them to live *at* Hollowgate," laughed Florence. "He may have even succeed. I think it would be easier for a daughter-in-law to live under another man's roof than a son-in-law, and Miss Caraway there looks like she would do anything Tyrone asked."

Even from that distance, they could see plainly Miss Caraway smiling and talking and tossing her head of thick hair.

"Pooh," said Lily. "Show and flirtation. *Not* that I don't think she likes him, but who doesn't like Tyrone? The question is, does Tyrone like Miss Caraway?"

Despite their scrutiny, neither sister could guess. Not when he danced with Miss Caraway, and not when he danced with other young ladies present. In every instance, he was courteous. He nodded; he smiled faintly; occasionally he spoke. But there was a listlessness to his carriage. A fatigue to his features, when his partner was not looking his way. Beloved as he was to his sisters, it did not escape their notice.

"That's it," said Lily. "I'm going to dance with him next."

"But suppose he's already asked someone?"

"Nonsense. Have you not seen? The girls have figured out that he chooses whoever stands nearest him when he returns his partner. Tyrone *does not care* who partners him. Something is wrong."

Just as she predicted, when Tyrone accompanied Miss Eagleton back to her mama's side, he made his bow and then drifted toward a squadron of hopeful looking misses, whose welcoming smiles changed to scowls when Lily inserted herself between them.

"My turn," she sang, weaving a hand through his arm. "Unless you have already promised someone."

"Promised?" he repeated vacantly.

"That is exactly how you used to sound if I spoke to you while you were reading. You're not hiding a book in your pocket, are you?"

To Lily's surprise, the sleepiness vanished from his eyes. "Hiding a book? I'm not hiding anything."

She raised delicate brows. "I'm glad to hear it. How have you found the adjustment, dear boy, from Oxford to home? Is Papa driving you mad?"

"Not a bit of it. He lets me do whatever I like."

"And what do you like?"

The figures separated them, but Lily was certain she saw a shadow fleet across his features as he took the hand of the woman diagonal.

"I ride with him and Falk," Tyrone resumed, when they came back together. "I read; I write; I go for walks or drives. From time to time I play my fiddle."

"And these are enough? They content you?"

"What do you mean?"

"What do you mean, what do I mean?" Lily retorted. She exchanged positions with the gentleman on her own diagonal and then exchanged back. "I mean, you would be happy enough to do these things for the rest of your life? Would you ever want to marry and bring someone to Hollowgate or find your own home together?"

His face did darken this time. "I don't know who I'd marry."

"Silly Tyrone—say the word, and it is done! Flossie and I were just remarking on how you might pick and choose among the girls here. Short of a title, you lack nothing to make you a prince among men, and they all appear eager enough to be chosen."

Tyrone's gaze took in the assembled company politely. "Thank you for your confidence in me."

"There's no hurry of course," she assured him. "Though do you prefer any one of them to any other?"

This drew a faint smile. "If I did I wouldn't tell you. Mind your own business, Lil. And tell Flossie to do the same."

But Lily told her older sister nothing of the kind. As soon as she rejoined her, the two sisters were claimed by their husbands, and there was no time for a word until they separated at the ball's end to walk home.

"Meet me at Minta's tomorrow afternoon," ordered Lily, patting a yawn away. "I'll send a note to Beatrice, too. This one requires all hands to the pump."

The appearance of Mrs. Fairchild, Mrs. Kenner, and Miss Ellsworth in Canon Street the following day sent the housemaid Terry into a fit, for which the only recourse was to dispatch her to the nearest pastry shop, that she might make up a tray worthy to offer the doctor's visitors.

"Gracious, what a convocation," said Minta, when enough chairs had been gathered and Terry sent off. "Don't you know better than to surprise me into playing hostess? I already live in fear Terry will give notice, and then I will have to borrow somebody from Hollowgate."

"Never mind that now," Lily dismissed this. "And when are you going to have that baby? You and Mr. Carlisle have got only the one sofa, and you occupy the whole of it."

"Nicholas estimates I have got at least another six weeks," Araminta protested, "and if you wanted more sofas, you should have called us all to Hollowgate. I can still get about, you know."

Lily huffed. "We could not meet at Hollowgate because then Tyrone would know and possibly overhear!"

"Oh!" breathed Minta. "Is this about Tyrone?"

"Lily and I saw him at the ball last night," Florence explained. "He was very popular."

"I had to strategize even to get a dance with him," declared Lily. "But I got it, and it was enough to allow me to draw some serious conclusions." Seeing she had her sisters' full attention, she leaned forward and looked at each of them in turn to draw out the moment.

"What already? Out with it," grumbled Minta.

"I believe our Tyrone is going to marry."

Uproar met this assertion, naturally. A shower of questions so intense that Lily held up her hands, laughing. "Hear me out, and I will tell you all. As I said, our brother was terribly popular and easily the most eligible man there, save Lord Maxwell, but as *he* is Papa's age if he's a day, Tyrone truly was without rival. He danced every dance—"

"The dreadful flirt." Minta made a face. "He remembered to dance with Aggie, I hope?"

"Aggie wasn't there," put in Florence.

"Not there? She must still be suffering from the headache. She hasn't come to see me in days, and when I called she was quiet and pale and cross."

"*In any event,*" rejoined Lily loudly, "he danced every dance and seemed as pleased to dance with one girl as the next. Therefore, it is plain to me that, left to himself, he will fall to whoever is most determined."

"Everyone knows that," spoke up Beatrice. "I just hope he doesn't choose a ninny."

"That's just it, girls," insisted Lily. "Don't you see? If Tyrone doesn't care, *we* ought to choose for him. Use the weight of our opinions to sway him toward a sister we would like."

"Tyrone, of all people, cannot be persuaded by mere words," Florence pointed out. "If we were to put someone forward, he would likely laugh us off and continue on his own way."

"Say we were to befriend the girl, then? He's not stupid, after all. He might not marry a girl simply because we like her, but he would surely consider it a point in her favor. Moreover, our friendship with her would afford her more opportunities to win him."

"True," agreed Florence. "But we hardly knew any of the young ladies there, Lily. They were all in the schoolroom when you and I reached marriageable age."

"Yes, but that is where Minta and Beatrice may assist us." She beamed upon her two younger sisters. "Girls, what do you think? I did a little poking and prying over the course of the evening, to learn what I could of the various young ladies' families and situations, and I have concluded that the best match for him would be Miss Caraway of the Caraways outside Sparsholt. Sister to Lady Downing."

Lily was not prepared for the reaction her suggestion received. Araminta gasped and then choked, and Beatrice emitted a screech, leaping to her feet.

"Not her! Anyone but her!"

"Mercy, Bea! What is wrong with you?"

"She was head girl at Turcotte's!"

"What's wrong with that?"

"You and Flossie had governesses," Minta rallied to her younger sister's aid, "so you have got no idea of the *tyranny* of which head girls are capable. Lady

Downing was a head girl herself, and the most self-satisfied, uppish, *insufferable*—"

"Well, I did not suggest he marry Lady Downing," interrupted Lily with a grimace of impatience.

"But her sister is cut from the same cloth," Bea insisted. "I might have been an insect at Turcotte's, for all the kindness she showed me, and it was the same with all the younger girls. We were not important enough to notice, unless it was to reprimand us. And then—and *then*, after she saw Tyrone this summer, she has become all grace and flattery and pretended friendship toward me!"

With a flick of her fingers, Lily dismissed this. "Oh, honestly, Bea. Of course she warmed to you when she learned you had an eligible brother. Any girl with her wits about her would do the same. I would be more concerned if her conduct toward you did not alter in the slightest. Be reasonable, you two. Miss Caraway has looks, respectable connections and fortune, not to mention clearly a head on her shoulders. We might do far worse."

"But I want Tyrone to marry Aggie," muttered Araminta.

"Oh, Aggie would be lovely," Florence said. "If she could ever be brought to marry anyone."

"I think she could. Now. She told me she no longer cares for that Mr. Taplin."

"How glad I am to hear it! Isn't that good news, Lily? After so many years?"

"Splendid news," said Lily shortly. "But there are two problems: firstly, if Tyrone has not noticed her yet, he likely never will; and secondly, if he is to be caught, he must be pursued. Do you think Aggie could be brought to pursue him?"

"No," Minta sighed. "I think she will never pursue anyone again."

"There, then." Lily dusted her hands of Aggie. "Miss Caraway it is. I daresay she will be at the music meeting at St. John's House? We might all attend, and Florence and I will engage her in conversation beforehand or at the interval. And then, at some point, I will impulsively say the family is gathering at my house for tea, and would she like to join us?"

"Won't that be suspicious?" asked Florence. "If she is the only non-family-member present?"

"Even if she notices, she won't mind a bit," answered Lily. "And she will make use of the time, if she knows what's what."

"But Minta and I don't *want* Miss Caraway to make use of the time!" young Beatrice objected again. "I don't like her, and Minta doesn't like her sister Lady Downing. That's two votes to two, so we ought to choose someone else to encourage."

"No, because Flossie and I are older than you, so we take precedence," argued Lily. "If you have got someone better to nominate, name her now. Someone *other* than Aggie Weeks because I have already told you why Aggie Weeks won't do."

Seeing her younger sisters swell with indignation, Florence laid a calming hand on Lily's arm. "Lily, darling, I'm afraid my vote has been counted prematurely. I am neither for nor against Miss Caraway until I know her better."

"Fine." Lily blew out an exasperated breath. "Let us proceed with the music meeting plan on the assumption that Miss Caraway is a *probationary* candidate. If Flossie approves of her, then you two must do your best to come round, but if Flossie does not, we will make no more attempts."

The discussion must be left at this unsatisfactory point, for Terry returned with the pastries, and then Flossie and Lily must get home to see to their children and households. But Beatrice lingered until the older two were gone. Then she pulled her chair closer to Araminta's sofa.

"How managing Lily is! You are Tyrone's twin, Minta. If anyone were to choose him a wife, it ought to be you."

"If anyone were to choose Tyrone a wife, it ought to be Tyrone," replied her sister. "If only he weren't so infernally devil-may-care!"

"Minta, what bad language," reproved the primmer Beatrice. But she was too anxious to maintain her disapproval. "Do you think if you were to tell him that Miss Caraway is not as agreeable as she seems, he would listen to you?"

"No. He would make a joke of it, and she would catch him all the same."

"What if you warned him she was trying to catch him?"

"He would think he couldn't be caught. Not because he thinks himself too clever, but rather because he doesn't think about it at all." Minta shook her head. "You'll see, Bea. She will play on his indifference, and he will shrug and decide she will do as well as any."

"I can never love her," vowed Beatrice.

"Of course you can. Eventually," Araminta told her. "After all, don't we manage to love Lily?"

Chapter 24

Love on her breast sits panting
And swells with soft desire;
No grace, no charm is wanting,
To set the heart on fire.
—John Gay, *Acis and Galatea* (1718)

Tyrone could be forgiven for mystifying his sisters. Their understanding of him was hampered by differences of sex, temperament, and time spent apart. Not only was he their sole brother, but his head had ever been buried in a book at home, when he had even been at home. Unlike his sisters, he had boarded away at school, first at Winchester College and then New College, Oxford, with the result that, of all the siblings, Tyrone had been the most absent, both in mind and body. When his sisters failed to discern that he was in love and—furthermore—heartbroken about it, it was from their lack of practice, not their lack of skill.

He agreed readily to attend the music meeting with the family. He was willing to go anywhere where Agatha Weeks might be found.

And Aggie was indeed present. Minta had seen to it. "Of course you'll come," she told her. "Headache or no headache. If I can sit through *Acis and Galatea*, and I am big as a house, you can ignore a trifling headache. Besides, Nicholas says he will make you a tincture if you do not improve."

It was the threat of the tincture which miraculously "cured" her headache. Aggie hated taking medicines. Nor could she hide at home forever. She had given four years to the worthless Mr. Taplin's memory; she would not give another four to Tyrone. He had deceived her and made her ridiculous, but he was an inevitable member of her world, and she must learn to tolerate the sight of him.

The annual Hampshire Music Meeting would be held over the course of two days in the ballroom of St. John's House and at the church of St. Maurice, and Lily decided they had better attend the "pastoral serenata" at St. John's because the audience would be larger and the space unobstructed, two points in its favor if they were to give Miss Caraway her chance without arousing Tyrone's suspicions.

The evening began smoothly. By dint of purchasing more tickets than their party required and coaxing her husband to arrive almost when the door opened, Lily laid claim to the foremost two rows of chairs nearest the entrance, so that every other concertgoer must needs pass them or be invited to join them.

"Flossie, Robert, you see I have saved you the seats in the second row by the aisle. I know your love of music. You will have an excellent view of the performers there. Good evening, Papa, Mama. Or course you must sit in the first row, in front of the Fairchilds, and you too, Beatrice. But Tyrone, I hope you will take this chair in front of Simon and me." Lily indicated one at the opposite end of the front row, where he and Miss Caraway could not miss each other if they tried.

But it was the Carlisles who came next up the stairs, accompanied by Aggie. Tyrone stood up so suddenly to make his bow that his chair knocked into the one beside it. "Good evening, Minta, Carlisle, Miss Weeks."

"Move a few places on, Tyrone," his twin bid him. "I will be fearfully uncomfortable if I must sit the whole time, so Nicholas and I had better be on the end, and of course Aggie must be by me."

With alacrity (and ignoring Lily's sputters of protest) he obeyed, his heart hammering to think of spending so much time bare inches from Aggie. And surely she would follow the Ellsworths afterward to the Kenners' home behind the cloisters? How lovely she looked in white silk with net lace! Had she ever worn that gown before? Its paleness accentuated the flush of rose across her cheeks and the glow of her skin.

Her chin lifted, and she murmured an unintelligible greeting. He waited for her to take her seat before doing the same, taking care to place himself on the rightmost edge chair, where the folds of her skirt just brushed against the length of his leg.

"Are you a great lover of Handel, Miss Weeks?"

The hush of his voice thrilled her, a sensation followed swiftly by shame that she should react so. Keeping her eyes trained on the program she answered quietly, "I have heard 'Love in her eyes sits playing,' of course." She blushed even as she said it, for John Gay's libretto was printed on the page, plain as the sun at noon-day about "love on her lips" and "love on her breast" and "soft desire." She might as well have thrown herself across his lap as to point out such things.

Indeed, he began to hum the melody, quiet and close. That is, Aggie doubted if anyone heard him but her, but that she did hear him every fiber and nerve of her person confirmed.

To her equal relief and disappointment, he broke off abruptly because his sister Mrs. Kenner reached between Aggie and Tyrone to tap her brother's sleeve. "Why, here is my new acquaintance Miss Caraway! The room has filled up so—Tyrone, do let her know we have got a seat for her and her friend."

The friend turned out to be none other than Miss Caraway's older sister, the famed Lady Downing, and it fell to the reluctant Araminta to perform introductions. Both Minta and Aggie well remembered Lady Downing from her days as their own head girl at Turcotte's—superior, elegant, supercilious—therefore it was with uneasiness and astonishment that they found themselves greeted with unwonted warmth.

"Mrs. Carlisle! Miss Weeks—it is still Miss Weeks, I believe? What a pleasure. How fondly I remember your liveliness in my seminary days. Such vivacity. My dear Clementine has told me of meeting you both all these years later. I have not been in Hampshire as much as I would have liked—Lord Downing's Parliamentary duties, you understand, so I delight in these opportunities to return to my home country. Empty seats? Those ones? Ah, you are too kind Mrs. Kenner. With the crush of traffic to reach here, I was afraid Clemmy and I would be relegated to the last row. Do excuse us—thank you, Mr. Ellsworth. Clementine, why don't you take the chair next to Mr. Ellsworth? You know I would prefer to be nearer the aisle."

Therefore, when the pastoral opera began, Tyrone sat between the girl others intended for him to marry and the one he himself intended to marry. Between the girl in full pursuit and the one whom he had driven away.

Miss Caraway did her utmost. She fanned herself and apologized if she was blowing him about. She rattled her program. She hummed. She tapped her foot. She gasped. She fluttered a hand to her bosom at affecting moments.

But Tyrone noticed none of this. For an hour and a half, every thought, every scrap of attention, was fixed on Agatha Weeks. He faced the performers, of course, straight as an arrow, but they might have spared their efforts. When Aggie smoothed her program on her knee, he saw it. When she raised a gloved hand to rub a tickling nose, he knew. When she leaned to murmur something to Araminta on her other side, Tyrone strained to hear.

Not that Aggie gave him much to observe. She was too paralyzed herself at his nearness. Too aware of him to behave naturally. What did he mean by it all? Sitting next to her—had he had a choice? Addressing her? Humming? Was it anything, or nothing? He wanted to be forgiven, she knew. He wanted to recover their friendly ease, as if nothing had happened. As if he had done nothing to hurt her. He sought lazy comfort, as a cat would seek a pool of sunshine to nap in. And she would oblige him eventually, she knew. It would be impossible to dislike Tyrone forever. He had been shallow and thoughtless, but not malicious.

But she knew as well that she could not give him what he wanted now. For her own peace of mind she could not. One day, when she no longer loved him—perhaps then.

Nor was this threesome alone in ignoring the serenata to watch the love scene closer at hand. Doubtless the performers of *Acis and Galatea* complained to each other afterward that never before had the two foremost rows been so inattentive, and didn't this just prove the Winchester music meeting was going to the dogs?

Beatrice Ellsworth, utterly vanquished by having Lady Downing beside her, nevertheless made note of the pains Miss Caraway on her other side took to captivate. If Bea had any doubt that Miss Caraway aimed to please Tyrone, she need only remark her sister Lily's complacent half-smile.

"It must not be," the girl whispered to herself, drawing a sidelong glance from Lady Downing. "I won't let it."

When the last notes had been played and the singers and musicians duly applauded, Lily turned at once to the Caraway sisters. "Ah, there is nothing like music!"

"Indeed," Lady Downing inclined her head. "What a pleasure when the London artists make their way to the provinces in the summer."

More important matters pressed than Lady Downing's condescension or opinions on the performance, however, and it was arranged quickly enough that the gathering would move to the Kenners' home behind the cloisters in the cathedral close.

Aggie had no choice in the matter, having come with the Carlisles, but in truth she wanted to see what came of Miss Caraway's assault as much as the rest of them. Nor would Beatrice submit to returning to Hollowgate with her parents. "Please let me go to

Lily's. Tyrone will be with me, and I do so much want to go. Please!"

Mr. Ellsworth swelled with familial pride. "Who am I to forbid my children doing what they love best— being together? Very well. Mrs. Ellsworth and I will betake our aged selves home and leave you young people to further enjoyment. Good night."

Never mind that the fourth Mrs. Ellsworth was closer in age to his children than to him. She placed her hand on his arm without protest and let him lead her away.

It was a balmy evening and the short stroll from St. John's House to the Kenners' made more delightful when the walkers slipped from the Causeway into Paternoster Row to escape the carriage traffic. The vast cathedral loomed solid in the soft, lamp-studded darkness, its ancientness muting their chatter and proving oddly comforting to both Aggie and Tyrone. It whispered of afflictions, which felt heavy in the moment, yielding as all did to the weight of time.

True, agreed Aggie to herself, *but that does not mean one gets to skip over any of the unpleasant bits.*

As a prebendary of the cathedral and grandson of the dean, Simon Kenner and his small family occupied a charming home behind the cloisters. Not overlarge but neat and elegantly furnished according to Lily's taste. Araminta's maid Terry would have wept to work in such a clockwork home with four servants, including a nanny who looked after the children. But even the orderly Wallis could not prevent her charges Edward and Katharine from hurtling down the stairs when they spied so many aunts and uncles, and for several minutes all was hubbub.

Tyrone tossed little Katharine in the air, drawing shrieks of laughter, though he nearly missed catching her when he saw it brought a smile to Aggie's face. Before he could catch her eye and share the moment of enjoyment, however, Miss Caraway's abundant hair obscured his view, and there were her gleaming teeth as she cried, "Who's this beautiful, bouncing girl?"

Katharine settled in her uncle's arms, sucking on two of her fingers and regarding the pretty young lady with wide eyes.

"My niece Katharine. Katy, this is Miss Caraway."

"So pweased to make youw acquaintaince, you dawwing poppet," Miss Caraway lisped at the child. "May Miss Cawaway howd you?" She extended her arms to take Katy, but the girl shook her head with all the discourtesy of childish frankness and buried her face in her uncle's neckcloth.

"Fie, Katy," reproved her mother, "where are your manners?"

"Not to mention you're slobbering all over your uncle," added Minta.

344

"Shall Wallis put you to bed now? I thought you would be asleep already."

Katy was detached from her uncle and handed over to the nanny, but not before Miss Caraway made one more attempt, cocking her head and blinking at the little girl, waving her fingers beside her left eye, like a sea-anemone in an invisible current.

"Night night, Katy. Can oo possibwy sweep wifout a wuwwaby?"

"There, there," Tyrone replied, with a flicker of impatience, "no need to give the child nightmares."

"Naughty man," cried Miss Caraway with mock offense and a rap of her fan.

"Clementine is a *marvel* with children," declared Lady Downing, accepting the seat indicated. "My own simply *adore* her, and I have told her more than once she is born to be a mother."

"It must be why she was chosen by Mrs. Turcotte as a head girl," Florence said kindly, handing her a cup of tea. "Would you like sugar, Lady Downing?"

"Thank you. Yes, two head girls in one family!" Lady Downing shook her head deprecatingly. "Mama told Mrs. Turcotte that perhaps it would be better not to select Clementine, after my *own* tenure as head girl, lest it incite jealousy in the other pupils, but Mrs. Turcotte insisted that Clementine earned it through her own worthiness. She insisted there was no one the younger girls admired and respected so well and even declared it was exactly as it had been in *my* day, when she chose me for the office."

Araminta muffled a snort with a clearing of her throat and then made a show of blowing on her tea to cool it, but her eye caught Aggie's, and they both had to look away quickly.

It was Beatrice who spoke up suddenly. "Miss Caraway, do you remember one Trishy Alcott?"

At any one time, Mrs. Turcotte's Seminary for Young Ladies enrolled perhaps fifty girls in total, but Miss Caraway tilted her luxuriant head and studied the ceiling, affecting to search her memory. "Trishy Alcott…?"

"Patricia Alcott," repeated Bea. "She is younger than I am. Perhaps nine or ten years old now. Madame Froissart is ruthless with her in French lessons because whenever Trishy tries to say something in French, out comes something in Spanish!"

Miss Caraway gave a tinkling laugh and looked around the room to invite others to join her. "Of course! The little Alcott girl. That was her name you say—Alcott? Not only did she *parle comme une vache espagnole,* but she actually *spoke* Spanish!"

"But why on earth would she speak Spanish, Bea?" asked Minta.

"Because her mother is from Spain. Her father is in the navy and met her mother at the very beginning of the war, when his ship was captured and he was put ashore on parole, and Mrs. Alcott and her mother sold the prisoners fresh fruits and things from their garden. It's quite a story of forbidden love. But Mrs. Alcott married Captain Alcott against her family's wishes and now she waits for him in Portsmouth while he sails all around, capturing prizes and getting richer and richer! So it is no wonder Trishy ends up speaking Spanish when she is not speaking English, for that is all her mother speaks to her."

"What a curious story!" Lady Downing said quellingly, noticing that her younger sister had gone rather greeny. "That is why it is so important for like to marry like. Another valuable lesson to be learned in school. But I must say—whatever is Mrs. Turcotte teaching her pupils now? Surely it is not to monopolize the conversation among your elders, Miss Ellsworth."

Here Lady Downing made a tactical error, for however freely the Ellsworth siblings might criticize or hush each other, and however much respect Lily Kenner would like to show so exalted a guest in her home, and however much Lily might push forward Miss Caraway as a candidate for Tyrone's wife, the Ellsworths bore it very ill for an outsider to take the office of family critic upon herself. Lily drew a sharp breath, and only her husband's grin and cautioning hand on her shoulder prevented a retort. Florence bit her lip, frowning, and Minta huffed and struggled into a more upright position, the better to engage the tiresome woman. But Mr. Carlisle clicked his tongue and took up his wife's wrist to test her pulse, drawing her indignation, as a metal rod fixed to the top of a building conveys the current harmlessly to the earth.

Only Tyrone was free to express his disapprobation, and, to his sisters' surprise, he did so. "Ah, Lady Downing, if you have any rebuke to deliver my sister, you had better apply it generally. For we have always been a family which encouraged the free sharing of thoughts." He turned deliberately to Bea. "Do tell us why you mention this fascinating Trishy Alcott. But be quick about it. We mustn't bore Lady Downing."

"Ha ha ha," interjected Miss Caraway. "Naughty man. You must have known Caroline was only teasing." She tried to whack him again with her fan but was seated an inch too far away, and the cushion beside him absorbed the flirtatious blow. "Ha ha ha. Mrs. Kenner, may I trouble you for another cup?"

But her attempted diversions were not enough because, as Lily obliged with the teapot, Tyrone prompted, "Well, Bea?"

Beatrice favored Miss Caraway with a long look, as if to say, *I could, you know, if I chose, tell what you do not want him to hear.* But then she folded her hands neatly in her lap and said only, "I am afraid Trishy's history was more interesting than what I had to say about her. Never mind."

"Hmm," was Lady Downing's response, her eyes narrowed. But the ground was too treacherous for her to continue, and she struck out on a new path. "I say, Miss Draper was in voice tonight, was she not? I'm afraid Mr. Goss was a trifle hoarse, but Miss Draper…"

Accepting the change of subject, the company took it up and the conversation moved on.

It was Minta who broke up the party an hour later, when she could no longer disguise the size and number of her yawns.

"We had better be going," her husband the doctor announced. "Though we live but five minutes away, if you fall asleep and I'm forced to carry you, it will feel like five leagues."

"Pooh," returned his wife. "I'm not half as big as Mrs. Boyer was when she had twins and you had to help Mr. Boyer carry her into the house."

"No, but as you point out, I had Mr. Boyer's assistance."

"And here you will have Aggie's. Aggie, you'll take hold of my feet, won't you?"

"At least one of them," said Aggie, "and perhaps your reticule, if Mr. Carlisle asks handsomely."

Reuniting each lady with her wrap and gentleman with his hat proved a to-do, but at last it was accomplished, and the groups set out their separate ways, Aggie managing not to look back over her shoulder as Tyrone and Bea escorted Lady Downing and Miss Caraway in the direction of the cathedral and High Street. But she and the Carlisles were no farther than the deanery when Minta groaned, "Oh, bother. This is Miss Caraway's fan. I got so hot in there I snatched it off the table. Run it back to her, will you Aggie?"

"No, Mr. Carlisle, I don't mind," Aggie assured him when he began to protest. "Minta would knock me over if she leaned on me as she does you, so this will be quicker. I'll be back in a flash."

Dashing back through the cloister, she rounded the front of the cathedral and stopped short.

For there, unmistakably, even in the dim light, was a couple in an embrace. A young woman with her head thrown back, the young man leaning over her, his arm wrapped about her.

"Oh, Mr. Ellsworth," breathed Miss Caraway. "Yes."

Chapter 25

Once warn'd is well bewar'd.
—John Dryden, *Fables ancient and modern* (1700)

Aggie backed away on tiptoe, the fan in her hand forgotten. When she was safely out of sight, hidden from view by the mighty cathedral itself, she ran a few steps before stopping to lean against the stone wall, her forehead pressed to its rough, cool surface. The fan fell to the walkway with a clatter.

It was no more than she expected, she reminded herself.

Miss Caraway made no secret of desiring Tyrone, and everyone knew he was too easygoing to take pains himself. He would be won by whoever set out in pursuit. And even before Aggie learned of his deception, she had decided not to join his pursuers. Should she not now feel doubly vindicated in her choice?

To see Miss Caraway succeed should have been no surprise. But it was.

Oh, it was.

"What does it matter, anyway, whom he marries?" she whispered. "He is a liar, of sorts." No, no—not a liar precisely. He was careless, heedless of the finer feelings. He had conspired to deceive *dozens* of young ladies and Aggie most of all. He was not worth a moment's distress.

Then why, oh why, did it hurt so much?

When Lady Downing's gig was readied at the stable in Buck Street Lane and the two ladies dispensed with, Tyrone and Beatrice proceeded along the Causeway toward the High Street and home. Anxious as she was to speak, Beatrice hardly knew how to begin and wished her brother would say something, but he seemed content to keep his own counsel, merely whistling one of the melodies they had heard that evening as they passed St. Maurice and the market house.

By the Buttercross she broke down. "It was too bad Miss Caraway could not find her fan."

"Mm? Yes, too bad."

"At least she succeeded in getting you alone with her."

Tyrone halted as if he had run into the side of a building. "What do you mean by that, Bea?"

She gulped. "Nothing. I mean—" and then it all tumbled out. "I mean, she likes you, clearly. And—oh—Tyrone, if you marry her, I will do my best to love her. Of course I will. But it will require effort, and we Ellsworths are not used to that, you know. Learning to love Flossie's Robert or Lily's Simon or Minta's Nicholas required no effort at all."

"What makes you think I am going to marry Miss Caraway?" They were walking again, and Beatrice could have sworn she caught a note of dark amusement in his voice.

"Well, aren't you? She wants you to."

"And here I thought it took two people to make a marriage."

"Then you aren't going to marry her?"

"Not that I'm aware of."

"Oh! I must say I am relieved. It's just that we were all so certain—"

She felt his arm stiffen beneath her hand. "We *who?*"

"Flossie and Lily and Minta and I! We all agreed you would likely marry whoever took the trouble to chase you. Lily and possibly Flossie were for Miss Caraway, while Minta and I were—we preferred *not* Miss Caraway," she concluded lamely.

"Sisters," he sighed. "So that's how it is. I do hope you wagered money on it, Bea, for it looks like you and Minta will win. I will certainly marry '*not* Miss Caraway.'"

"You had better tell Lily that."

"I will, if you don't tell her first," he answered wryly.

"But do be careful around Miss Caraway, Tyrone. Don't let her flirt with you and lead you off by yourself as you did tonight, or you will end in marrying her whether you like it or not."

"Mm. Thank you for the advice, my interfering adolescent."

"You're welcome," she replied ingenuously.

"And now that I have given you my word, may I ask again why you mentioned this Trishy Alcott person and why it made Miss Caraway uneasy?"

"I will tell you now, now that I know you won't marry her. You see, as I said, Trishy often made mistakes during French lessons, and Miss Caraway's French is so excellent (according to Madame Froissart) that she was often called upon to help in the younger girls' class. Whenever Trishy would blunder, Miss Caraway would correct her in front of everyone and make her write lines, and soon enough Trishy hardly dared to open her mouth. I don't board at the school, you know, but my friend Celia said that Trishy grew so distressed by the sight of Miss Caraway that she tried to avoid her as much as possible. And one night, when the younger girls were climbing the stairs to go to bed, Miss Caraway and some friends were descending. Miss Caraway pointed at poor Trishy and demanded she ask permission to pass in French, and Trishy couldn't manage a word. She tried to flee, but she slipped on the staircase and rolled to the bottom and broke one of her arms! What do you think of that, Tyrone?"

"I think it is a good thing Miss Caraway no longer attends Turcotte's, or she might resent you bringing up such an incident in company and have her revenge. Little fool! You say you would try to love her if I married her, but here you have stumbled at the threshold."

Beatrice sighed. "Yes, I suppose you're right. She probably thinks of me as an enemy now. I don't care though. Not if you don't."

It was quiet in Cock Lane. They nodded to the sentry as they passed the barracks but encountered no one else.

"Tyrone," she whispered, as they turned in at the arch marking the drive to Hollowgate, "if you don't plan on marrying Miss Caraway, then is it *not* true that you will marry just anyone who chases you?"

He kicked a stone in the gravel path. "It is not. I will *not* marry whoever happens to chase me. I don't know where you all got that idea."

"It's your indolence, I suppose. Your easygoing nature. We supposed you would do whatever was most comfortable for you, and it being so comfortable to be loved, why would you not marry the first pleasant young lady to do so?"

"Clearly you all thought I was not only easygoing, but also a halfwit, incapable of looking after myself."

"Oh, Tyrone. It's only that we love you, you know, so of course we are concerned."

They said no more, left to their own thoughts. Beatrice fought an urge to skip over the crunching gravel drive, now the weight of worry had lifted. She would not have Miss Caraway for a sister!

Tyrone's feelings, however, were more complicated.

When the valet had been dismissed and sleep proved elusive, he dragged an armchair to the window and threw himself in it. Moonlight pooled on the Hollowgate lawn and frosted the leaves poking above the walls of Florence's garden.

His sisters were right to be concerned. Not that Tyrone had any intention of marrying Miss Caraway, but that he must be on his guard. Ridiculous, really. Tyrone did not believe Miss Caraway was in love with him, any more than he was in love with her. But this was the world they lived in, the class they belonged to. They were expected to marry and marry a particular sort of person, and love might or might not enter in.

"Dear me," Miss Caraway had said, when they crossed through the cemetery and reached the Square. "Caro, I've left my fan at the Kenners, and it's my favorite."

"You had better go back and retrieve it, then," Lady Downing replied. "Mr. Ellsworth, if you would be so kind as to accompany my sister, Miss Ellsworth and I will wait for you here. Do not hurry. There is something magical about shop windows at night, is there not, Miss Ellsworth?"

In retrospect, the two Caraway sisters likely contrived the situation, but in the moment Tyrone agreed to it courteously. Miss Caraway took his arm, and he led her back through the yard of grass and ancient headstones toward the cathedral. The stone path seemed level enough, but when they were just before the great arch leading to the two center doors, she stumbled. Automatically, he threw out an arm to catch her, and she fell back heavily against it, almost oversetting them both.

"Pardon me," she breathed, her head lolling against his arm. "So clumsy of me—a touch of grfglglgl."

"What was that?" he bent his head nearer to hear more clearly. "Miss Caraway—are you all right?"

"Oh, Mr. Ellsworth," she said, tugging at his lapel to steady herself. "Yes."

It might have been his imagination, but her voice seemed to echo off the immense façade of the cathedral. She shut her eyes, head still hanging back, and torn between impatience and amusement, Tyrone could not resist giving her a little shake. Carrying the tiresome girl back to Lady Downing or onward to the Kenners' would only lead to questions, and he had rather she recover her own powers of locomotion.

When the little shake failed to rouse her, Tyrone wickedly pretended to let his supporting arm drop. Sure enough, Miss Caraway's eyes flew open, and she at once stuck out a leg to steady herself.

"Feeling better?"

Her fair brow puckered in a scowl before she could prevent it, but she wisely ducked her head to hide it and gave her skirts a businesslike brush and shake. "Much better, thank you. You know, Mr. Ellsworth—I am a trifle fatigued, I think. Never mind about my fan. I will see to it another time. Would you take me back to my sister?"

Tyrone laughed inwardly over the incident at the time, but now, in light of Beatrice's warning, he found nothing amusing in it. He had no intention of being entrapped, even by so attractive a person as Clementine Caraway. There was only one person in all the world he wanted to marry, and though that one person had no desire to marry him, it changed nothing. For her sake he would henceforth steer clear of any and all compromising situations, he decided. Because Agatha Weeks was not one to bear a grudge forever. She would unbend sooner or later, and then, if she did not set her heart on another, he could apply himself steadily and with calculated effort, to win her.

But he frowned over this last. Considering it had taken her four long years to forget Taplin, how long would it take her to forget Tyrone's deceitful actions and consider him anew?

"Supposing you were not yourself," he murmured aloud. "Not Tyrone Ellsworth, that is, but another person who came to Tyrone Ellsworth, seeking his advice. If I were not myself, would I not advise myself, as I did Boulton, to begin with an apology?"

He would.

Then the question arose, would a written apology be better or a spoken one? She might refuse any note from him—might shudder at the sight of it—but he could hardly find occasion to apologize in person at another ball or music meeting or tea at the Kenners. And if he called at The Acres, that would definitely look like he was courting her, and then Aggie would just as definitely tell him to go away.

Resting his temple against the glass, Tyrone gave a rueful chuckle. Perhaps it wasn't his own *modus operandi* he should consult—it was Boulton's. He could write out an apology to carry in his pocket and then haunt the grounds of Hollowgate along its border with The Acres, in hopes of meeting her, at which time, depending on how things proceeded, he would either give her the note or speak its contents.

Yes. And then, if he did not encounter her on the grounds, he would wear a groove between The Acres and Minta's home in Canon Street, in hopes of meeting with her there.

Launching himself from the armchair, he took up the tinder box from the mantel, composing his apology even as he struck the flint against the steel and blew on the spark. When both tapers in the candlestick were lit, he carried it to the desk, still muttering to himself.

An hour later he copied the final draft and lay down the pen, stretching wearily. Now he understood Boulton's tendency to argue over every sentence, for Tyrone had done the same with himself. Should he strike an obsequious note or a commonsensical? Did he sound remorseful for the pain he caused her or just weak? Did his love for her leak through every word, try as he might to prevent it?

When he awoke the next day the morning was all but gone. In answer to Tyrone's questions, the footman Bobbins reported that "Mr. Ellsworth and Mr. Falk have ridden out to oversee the remaining harvest, and Mrs. Ellsworth and the children gone to glean blackberries and nuts." This was splendid news, for it meant he might walk where he pleased on the estate without having to answer questions.

After finishing his breakfast, Tyrone tied leashes to Scamp and Pickles' collars. Making sure his painstaking apology letter was in his pocket, he set out with them in the direction of the brook, where he proceeded to walk up and down until he was hot and even the puppies began to drag and gnaw at the leather straps.

No Aggie.

For another hour he sat in the shade and threw a stick for the dogs, but it was all in vain. He should have tried the walk to Minta's instead, he berated himself. Surely she took herself there, eager to talk over the music meeting.

The following morning he wandered up and down St. James's Lane and Canon Street. After some time, he returned the dogs to Hollowgate and retraced the route a few more times alone. He then made a circle through town, in case she decided to do some shopping. He stopped in at the circulating library. He zigzagged down Southgate, up St. Thomas, down Little Minster, and up Great Minster. Finally he ended up in Canon Street again, only to be told by the maid Terry that the doctor was out seeing patients and Mrs. Carlisle had gone to visit her aunt Ellsworth.

So much for the vow he had taken to pursue her steadily, for however long it took. His apology letter burned in his pocket. It was one thing to picture years of patient perseverance but quite another to suffer another day to go by without a glimpse of her. Confound patient perseverance! Patient perseverance could begin the moment he started the ball rolling. Patient perseverance could begin when his apology was delivered and he had seen her face again.

By the third morning his resolution evaporated.

Let her think whatever she might.

Let her cast him from her presence.

Let her do what she would—he *must* see her.

Without a word to his family, he had Ebony saddled and rode over to The Acres. His appearance there sent an undergardener scrambling to summon a groom, but when the man appeared, Tyrone dismounted and marched up the steps, trying not to acknowledge the courage which leaked from him with every step. It was too late for retreat. Even if he fled now, the servants would all put their heads together to remark on young Mr. Ellsworth's bizarre behavior, and the Weeks family would know about it almost as soon.

An excuse, an excuse—he needed an excuse for his presence.

The butler Orton opened the door, his blank expression giving no indication that young Mr. Ellsworth's appearance was in any way odd.

"Good morning, sir."

"Good morning. It's Tyrone Ellsworth, here to call upon Mrs. Weeks and Miss Weeks." Even as he said it, he cursed himself for cowardice. What would being ushered into the presence of Aggie's mother do, except create the problem of how to get rid of her?

"Miss Weeks?" echoed the butler, as if he had never heard of such a person.

Tyrone's brow corrugated with annoyance. "Yes. Miss Weeks."

"But—oh—but—"

"But *what*, man?" he interrupted, his hands clenching. "Spit it out." Was Aggie closeted with someone else at present? Had that blasted Boulton come to try his luck again?

Orton took umbrage at someone of his dignity being urged to speak in such vulgar terms, and he therefore took pleasure in announcing, "Mr. Ellsworth, sir, I regret to say Miss Weeks is gone."

"Gone? You mean, out at present?"

Orton's lips thinned, and he shook his head with feigned regret. "Mr. Ellsworth, I'm afraid that, not only is Miss Weeks from home today, but she is from home for an indeterminate time. She is—*gone*."

Chapter 26

Worthing, distant fifty-nine miles from London, eleven westward of Brighton, possesses many attractions, which contribute to render it a desirable residence for those who really wish to enjoy the benefits of sea-bathing or air.
—John Feltham, *A guide to all the watering and sea-bathing places* (1803)

Aggie had never before seen the sea. Her father was far too occupied with the silk manufacturing business and then with estate management to indulge in holidays away, and though her mother spent weeks at Bognor with an aged aunt one summer, her descriptions of the quiet and the breezes and the treeless village and bare shingle hardly inspired. Mrs. Weeks was therefore surprised when Aggie expressed the unprecedented wish to accompany her sister Mrs. Chester to Worthing.

"But Aggie, Frederica won't be there longer than a fortnight. You know Mr. Chester is anxious not to miss his partridge shooting."

"But if I go with them, Mama, Freddie may stay longer because I will be with her," Aggie pointed out. "It's not as if she's dying to watch Mr. Chester shoot partridges. And if she and I frolic by the seaside, she will forget about missing her boys, now that they have gone to the parsonage in Headbourne Worthy."

Mrs. Weeks sighed, flapping her embroidery frame upon her lap. "Very well, Agatha. I haven't got any strong objections to this whim of yours, except that your father and I will miss you, and I cannot understand the suddenness of it."

To this Aggie could not respond, except to hug her.

Aggie had once called her brother-in-law Mr. Chester a "tiresome old stick," and two days with him and Frederica in a post-chaise did not alter her opinion, but she was so grateful to leave Winchester behind that she almost loved him for providing the means of her escape. And Worthing was lovely. Enclosed by the Sussex Downs like a jewel in its setting, it boasted an endless level stretch of fine, hard sand which the sea constantly bore away, leaving behind pebbly shingle. The house they had let was on the very edge of this beach, and as soon as they were settled and Mr. Chester gone to Stafford's to read the newspapers, the sisters rushed out to walk the inviting strand.

Frederica had plenty to say about the town amenities and what she longed to do in the coming days, to which Aggie absently agreed, willing enough to be carried along in another's wake and left to her own thoughts. Thoughts which never strayed far from Tyrone Ellsworth.

Had he and Miss Caraway announced their engagement yet? Would Minta bother to write to her about it? Before departing, Aggie sent a note to Canon Street, describing the Worthing trip as a fanciful notion and promising to return when the baby was born or soon thereafter. Minta replied as playfully, begging for a seashell, but neither of them mentioned Tyrone.

Perhaps she had made all the wrong choices, Aggie thought. If Tyrone was so easily won, perhaps she should have swallowed her pride and her wounds and made the attempt. A few dances, a little banter, a thwack or two with her fan, and he might have been hers. So what if he'd made her appear foolish with Mr. Boulton? How much more foolish was it that she had lost him to Clementine Caraway's wiles?

He might have been hers and she his. There would have been the rest of their lives to find something deeper and more lasting.

The wind tugged at her bonnet, and Aggie clapped a hand to the top of it.

But was Tyrone Ellsworth capable of anything deeper? Tyrone, the languorous house cat, sleeping in the sunshine. One might pet him and coo at him and claim him, but a cat would do what he pleased.

She wondered if, in the intimacy of engagement, Miss Caraway teased him about Aggie.

"When I first met you, I thought you certainly must be the property of Miss Weeks," Miss Caraway would jest as she leaned upon his arm, smiling up at him.

"Aggie?" he would laugh. "There's never been anything between us. She's my sister's old playfellow, is all. I did once encourage a schoolmate to woo her—even helped with suggestions and that sort of thing—but she refused him. Who knows if she'll ever marry."

"How kind of you to try to help! I think everybody ought to marry, if they can, though I don't suppose many of them will find the happiness we have found."

"How could they?" he would murmur, drawing her to him, his head bending to hers.

"Aggie!" Mrs. Chester repeated, poking her with the tip of her parasol. "Have you been attending? I said here is the new assembly room. I will tell Mr. Chester to make the acquaintance of the master of ceremonies. What do you say?" Giggling, she pressed a hand to her lips. "*Hm-hm-hmmm.* Because what could be more amusing than a seaside *affaire de cœur*?"

Aggie stifled an exasperated groan. She might flee Tyrone Ellsworth's triumphant love affair, but apparently there was no evading her sisters' attempts to marry her off. "Frederica, must we? Can't we simply bathe and dine and read and walk and ride? Why must we dance and meet people?"

"Because dancing and meeting people is delightful, my dear grumbler. And as you are here as a guest of the Chesters, you must do as the Chesters do. Besides, we want to know as many suitable people as possible before Linus abandons us for the partridges."

Given how seldom Aggie and Mr. Chester spoke more than ten words together, she suspected she would hardly notice his absence, but the following day he unwittingly used his small allowance to effect the maximum damage.

"So your childhood friend is soon to marry, I hear," he addressed her over dinner, signaling the waiter to refill his glass.

Aggie paused, spoon in mid-air. She set it down hastily. "Which—what have you heard, then?"

"Which friend?" demanded his wife.

"That Tyrone Ellsworth," he answered. Maddeningly he tasted his soup and then reached for the pepper mill to add a few grinds. "Ran into Cusworth at Wickes's today, who had just been in town with Downing."

"Downing?" echoed Mrs. Chester. "If you refer to Lord Downing, you can only mean you heard Tyrone Ellsworth is engaged to his wife's sister."

"That's right," he rumbled. "Name of Carrington."

"Caraway," said Aggie softly. It was one thing to imagine Tyrone engaged and another altogether to hear it spoken of impromptu.

"Caraway," he nodded. "That was it."

"Well! Imagine that," Frederica declared. "Tyrone Ellsworth to marry Miss Caraway! She made quick work of him, did she not, Aggie?"

"She did." The soup before her might have been cement, it felt so heavy and tasteless. "I—wonder Minta didn't write to me."

"She never does," her sister reminded her. "And likely she has other things on her mind, in her condition. It's nearly her time, you know."

"I know."

"Did Lord Downing tell Mr. Cusworth when the marriage would take place?" Frederica asked her husband.

Now Mr. Chester had to chew a chunk of bread before he could reply. Aggie wished she might hurl her own at him. But at last the lump was got down, chased by a sip of wine.

"No," he said shortly. "Not officially announced yet. Cusworth told it to me in strict confidence, so we will say nothing, if you please."

Aggie grimaced. "In strict confidence," foot! If it was such a secret, why did Lord Downing tell this gossipy Cusworth person, who he must have known would turn around and tell others? There was a pain in her chest, and she rubbed it absently, but it was not the sort which could be rubbed away.

"You're looking flushed, Aggie," her sister admonished. "And where has your appetite gone?"

Aggie managed a faint smile. "Nothing a good sea-bathe won't remedy. Thank heavens we are in the right place."

Sea-bathing did help, if only because the experience was so novel and the water so bracing it left Aggie gasping for breath. The first time her burly "dipper" shut her in the bathing-machine and disappeared to coax the horse into the surf, Aggie clung to the wooden bench and had second thoughts. This would be fun, if Minta were there, but alone Aggie wondered if her dipper hadn't the look of an undetected murderess.

The horse hadn't far to pull the cart—just until the water was as high as the machine floor. Then the murderess's red jowly face reappeared. "When ye've changed, I'll lower ye down. Will ye be wanting the rope around ye?"

As long as the rope was not intended for her neck, Aggie supposed she wanted it.

But when she was in her flannel shift, the rope about her waist and the meaty woman helping her down the steps, Aggie at once understood the popularity of bathing. Why, this was marvelous! Every inch of her tingled and almost stung; the power of the waves rocked her about like a rag doll; and for the time it lasted she forgot all about heartbreak and Tyrone Ellsworth.

This was the answer. She would announce that she was removing to Worthing for the next several years until the sea washed all memory away.

There were others willing to help her forget.

Another day onward, Aggie found herself in her familiar white silk with net lace, curtseying as she was introduced to Mr. Bagger. *If I marry this one,* she thought, *I will be Aggie Bagger. Agatha Bagger. Agatha Bagatha.* Poor Mr. Bagger had come to Worthing to improve his health, and his clothing did indeed hang bagging from his gaunt frame. His lined face reminded her somehow of Mr. Boulton, though they didn't look a thing alike. Something about the resigned expression. An expression she hoped she would not herself come to wear.

While Aggie couldn't love Mr. Bagger (she had decided with the certainty of youth that she would never love anyone again), she could be kind. No small feat, considering that he turned out to be the dull sort stuffed with information.

When he learned where the Chesters were staying, he said, "You will have noticed the groyne recently built west of the town is being extended toward those very houses."

"Groyne?" asked Aggie politely.

"The timber framework erected as a barrier. The sea wall."

"Ah, I understand."

"It's meant to prevent swamping of the town, but seaside settlements are precarious."

"Are they? Will the—groyne—not help, then?"

"The tide tarryeth no man," he returned ominously. "In addition to which, you'll notice the groyne also serves to trap pebbles."

"I did not notice that."

"Indeed, in a hundred years, I would not be surprised if most of the fine Worthing sand were gone, to be replaced largely by pebbly shingle."

"Fancy. That would be quite a change." And so forth.

No Aggie Bagger, then.

Mr. Ayscough was the master of ceremonies' next introduction, a pale young man not an inch taller than she. Would it be better to be Aggie Ayscough? she wondered. Despite his name, no cough afflicted him, but shyness certainly did. Aggie bore the brunt of conversation, and she soon thought she had not appreciated properly Mr. Bagger's steady flow of information. Still, she remembered what both Mr. Boulton and Tyrone had said, about it being difficult to approach a young lady and risk embarrassment or rejection, so she tried again to be kind.

"How do you like Worthing, Mr. Ayscough? My sister and her husband and I are but recently arrived."

"W-well."

"Do you hail from other parts? We are from Winchester—and Mr. Chester has a home in Dorset."

"I am from—er—outside Chichester."

"Ah! Then you must be very familiar with Worthing and, I daresay, Bognor. My mother spent some time in Bognor."

"Oh? Yes. Bognor."

Aggie had the unexpected thought that Mr. Ayscough was exactly the sort of gentleman who would benefit from hiring Tyrone. Tyrone could make him a list: Ten Questions to Ask When You Dance with a Young Lady. When one came to think of it, Mr. Bagger would also be improved by a lesson or two: Ten Subjects to Avoid When Speaking with Young Ladies. Item Number One: Groynes.

A smile curved her lips, startling Mr. Ayscough, who could truly not remember a time he made a young lady smile. Whether his partners were pretty or plain, he dreaded dancing with them, unnerved as he was by both bold girls and awkward ones. Nor could he be unaware of his own failings as a partner, but he was nearly thirty now, and his aunt threatened to cut him out of her will if he did not marry soon. Therefore, when Miss Weeks bestowed on him this astonishing sign of approbation, Mr. Ayscough was visited with an equally astonishing burst of confidence.

As the musicians brought the dance to a close, Aggie sank into a curtsey and then reached for Mr. Ayscough's arm, that he might take her back to Frederica. But no sooner did she touch his sleeve than he performed a sinuous twist, catching her hand in his own. Before she knew what he was about, he raised it to his lips.

"Mr. Ayscough!"

"Miss Weeks! Ch-charming Miss Weeks!"

Their eyes being on a level, her amazed blue ones stared directly into his.

"Miss Weeks, you have stunned me."

"Oh?" She gave an uneasy titter. "I might say the same of you. Now—where has my sister Frederica got to?"

"Will you tread another measure with me?"

"You mean right now?"

"Yes, at once."

"Pardon me, but I had rather hoped to catch Miss Weeks at liberty and nominate myself as a partner," came a voice from behind her. A voice she would have known anywhere, though it was the last one she expected to hear in the Worthing assembly room.

"Tyrone!" cried Aggie, her head whipping so fast to peer behind her she might have done herself an injury. "Whatever are you doing here?"

"I was—looking for you."

"In *Worthing*?"

"It's where your father said you were."

"And you *followed* me here?"

"Why wouldn't I? If I were looking for you."

Poor Mr. Ayscough glared resentfully at the tall and dashing interloper, whose inconvenient appearance so distracted Miss Weeks, but Tyrone had no more consideration to spare his rival than Aggie had. In fact, with her before him and not five inches of air between, Tyrone entirely forgot the bolt of wrath which scorched him when the upstart kissed her hand.

"Something is wrong," Aggie said slowly, an explanation for his sudden apparition striking her. "Is it Araminta or the baby?"

His puzzlement relieved her at once. "What? Minta—no."

"Well, then." She released her anxious breath, only to take and hold another. If Minta was safe, then what *was* he doing in Worthing? Had he come to announce his engagement? But why would he?

To either side of them couples formed for the next set, and Tyrone held out his hand. With the barest tremble, she placed hers in his, thinking that gloves might have prevented her feeling Mr. Ayscough's kiss, but against Tyrone's touch they were worthless. Without a backward glance, the two of them abandoned Mr. Ayscough to an embarrassed retreat and his aunt's pursed lips.

Aggie's heart hammered as she stepped through the figures. All power of speech had left her, and though he watched her steadily, he said nothing.

He must want to tell me of his engagement, she thought. *Does he think I need to hear it directly from him? Does he know I will be hurt?* It was too mortifying to consider. He had already robbed her of her pride by impersonating Mr. Boulton—was he determined to claim every last scrap?

She would not help him, she decided. If he wanted to crush her, he must do it himself. Therefore, no more questions about why he had come to Worthing.

But if small Mr. Ayscough's silence had forced her to speak, neither was she proof against Tyrone's.

"How—how is your book going?" At his blank look she added, "Your book of sample letters. Or—was that just a story you told me?"

"No!" he insisted hastily. "I'm sorry. I was thinking of something else. No—the book is real. I've been dropping it in bits and pieces with my cousin. I told you my cousin Benjamin was going to try to find a publisher?"

"Yes, you told me. Has he had any luck?"

"I don't know. I didn't ask. I was in a hurry and fairly threw them at him—whatever I had on me."

"Poor fellow. I hope he will indulge your caprices."

"Yes," said Tyrone, sounding vague. They were nearing the bottom of the room, and when they next took hands to exchange sides, he grasped her fingers convulsively. "I say, Aggie—do you mind if we steal away for a moment? Find some tea and-and-and a little privacy? There is something I would say to you."

She pressed her lips together. Oh, heavens. The moment was upon her. Could it not somehow be avoided? She twisted around looking for the Chesters, but Mr. Chester must have vanished to the card room, and Frederica was deep in conversation with a matron they met at Spooner's library. How could Freddie not even notice that Tyrone Ellsworth had appeared?

She gave a grim sigh and a nod, and the next second he had hold of her fingers again and was fairly *dragging* her off.

"Honestly, Tyrone!"

Every corner of the coffee room featured groupings of potted plants situated to obscure the benches between them, but Tyrone marched past all of these when he saw the sets of double doors standing ajar on the wall opposite.

"We can't go out there," Aggie protested under her breath. "My sister will have my head!"

"Just one minute," he ground out.

The doors opened on a terrace overlooking the shingle. Moonlight rippled silver on the restless sea, and despite herself Aggie breathed an appreciative "ahhhh!" Shaking her hand free of his grip, she ran to the balustrade to lean out. "Isn't it wondrous? I love it here. The world seems immense and one's problems so insignificant. I bathed for the very first time yesterday, and it was like someone dipped me in—in cold chaos—and I *loved* it! Tomorrow I will—"

But before Aggie could declare her future plans, his hands gripped her shoulders, and he spun her around. "*You're* wondrous," he uttered. "When I see you, I can't think of anything else."

And then his mouth was on hers—hard—and Aggie was so stunned she couldn't move, couldn't think. She had only ever been kissed in her life by one man—the loathsome Mr. Taplin—four years earlier in an impertinent little offering which made her heart flutter—and more recently by him in the coffee room, which filled her with rage, but this—! This was an attack. This was a *possession*. Somewhere in her spinning head she marveled. Light, indolent Tyrone Ellsworth—what was he *doing*?

But then she couldn't think, couldn't marvel. Her astonished paralysis was yielding, melting under the heat and pressure of his lips. He made a sound deep in his throat—or maybe she did. The balustrade dug into her back, but without it she would have sunk to her feet.

It was only when they were breathless that he pulled back, his eyes raking her face as if he would pull the truth from her. They were panting.

Aggie trembled and hated herself for trembling. Hated herself for wishing the kiss might have gone on and on and on. If the sea was cold chaos, the kiss was its burning counterpart, and she *adored* it. Adored it and hated it at the same time. It was as if, in the time since she fled Winchester, she had erected a dainty timber wall to keep out the might of the sea. She had walked along her wall, admired it, and imagined it would afford her protection, only to have Tyrone roar in like a flood and smash it to fragments.

He came here, an engaged man, and offered her this insult? It was not enough, what he had already done to her in deceiving her, but he must add this?

Desperately she blew on these feeble sparks of outrage, praying they would catch fire. She must fight back, or she would be lost.

Knocking away one of the arms which encircled her, Aggie strode several steps along the terrace, pressing gloved hands to her bosom to steady herself. Her heart was going like a mill-race.

When she could manage it, she turned back, her face calm. And when she heard her own voice, she could have punched the sky in triumph. For she sounded like her usual self, even mildly amused.

"Dear me," said Aggie. "Were you delivering a message on behalf of someone, or was that one from you?"

Chapter 27

She may break my heart—but damnit—I'm determined
she shan't keep her temper.

—Richard B. Sheridan, *School for Scandal* iii. 33 (1780)

"I deserved that," Tyrone said quietly. "I didn't mean to kiss you. I meant to talk to you. But when I saw you—"

She raised a skeptical eyebrow. Now that she had put space between them, her flying pulse began to abate, and sense returned, along with the memory of the last time she saw him. Bent over Miss Caraway, exactly as he had bent over her a moment ago. And Miss Caraway's breathless, "Oh, Mr. Ellsworth, yes!"

But no offer of marriage had preceded or accompanied Tyrone seizing *her*. Aggie supposed none could have. Miss Caraway was his intended bride, whereas Aggie was…nothing. And whatever Aggie might think Tyrone Ellsworth capable of, she doubted even he would engage himself to two girls in the space of a week. Why, then, did he dare kiss two girls in the space of a week?

Warily Tyrone watched the parade of emotions across his beloved's countenance, even as he cursed his loss of self-control. In giving way to passionate impulse he had set the cart before the horse and turned an homage to her desirableness into an insult. As if he had not insulted her enough already!

"Aggie."

She faced him, her arms crossed over her midsection.

"Are you—cold?" he asked.

"Why—do you want to put your arm around me?"

He bowed his head and took a long breath. "Aggie, listen to me. I've gone about this all wrong. But if you would hear me out…"

"I don't see that I have got much choice," she replied, but even as she spoke she knew she wanted more than anything to learn what was in his mind. Her shoulders drooped a fraction. Would she always, always be such a simpleton in love?

"Oh, thank God," he muttered. Then, with a lightning glance to ensure they were still alone on the terrace, he dropped to one knee.

"What are you doing?" cried Aggie, retreating a step and getting the railing in her back again.

"I—I'm asking you in my clumsy way to be my wife," he blundered out, awkwardly scooting forward a few inches on knee and foot to close the distance between them again.

"To be your—!" she choked. "How dare you? Get up at once!"

"Aggie, darling—please—you said you would listen!"

"Don't you 'darling' me!" hissed Aggie, shoving his shoulder so hard he lost his balance and tumbled to the terrace. "How *dare* you mock me thus? Is it not enough, how you have already wronged me? What have I ever done to you, Tyrone Ellsworth, that you should treat me like this?"

Scrambling to his feet again and running a desperate hand through his hair he said, "I never, never meant to insult you, Aggie! You cannot think how wretched I have been about—all that Boulton business. I have apologized to you, as you know, and asked your forgiveness, and now I have followed you to Worthing not to—offend you—again, but rather to make a full confession—"

Her hand flew to her mouth. "You mean there is *more* you have to tell me of the wrongs you have done?" Oh, heavens! What more could there be? Was she indeed the talk of the New College junior common room, the ready joke on every undergraduate's lips?

"Not a wrong—not a confession of a wrong—" Tyrone floundered. "A confession of my feelings. Because I did not tell you—I never told you yet—that I—I—I am in love with you, Agatha Weeks. Madly."

She hardly knew what to do with this. He did not appear to be lying—the jumble of his words, the wildness of his eyes did not bespeak premeditation— but how could it be otherwise? And if she believed him, would she be an even greater fool?

"I wanted to tell you straight off," he went on, taking advantage of her bewilderment, "when I realized I had lost my heart, but I thought in honor I should let Boulton offer for you again and be refused before I spoke, because I did not want to muddy the waters more than I already had. But then, when you found out my—my unfortunate deception—you were so angry I thought I had better let time pass, and never say a word, to improve my chances. And I would have—let time pass—only waiting felt impossible. I even wrote another apology, but I had no opportunity to give it to you, on paper or in person, for I went to The Acres after the music meeting, only to have your butler tell me you were gone! Gone! You will have to forgive me again, Aggie, when I tell you my first panicked thought was that you had eloped with Taplin—"

"Eloped!" she shrilled, all else momentarily eclipsed by this new outrage. "With *Mr. Taplin*? As God is my judge, if you *ever* mention that man again to me, Tyrone Ellsworth, I will murder you with my bare hands."

"Would you?" The fire in her eyes was so fetching he drew closer without intending to. "Would you really?"

Aggie felt her insides turn a somersault, her rage over the accursed Francis Taplin evaporating with mortifying swiftness. "You keep your distance," she whispered. She jabbed him with a feeble finger. "I mean it. Get away from me."

Instead he leaned an inch nearer, his gaze hot as a brand.

"Make me."

Aggie's lips parted. Her hands clenched in fists, that she wouldn't take hold of him and throw herself into his arms. She wanted so badly to believe he cared for her. She wanted so badly to yield, cost what it might.

Desperately she gave her head a shake. Her eighteen-year-old self had been willing to accept a kiss from Taplin, even though she knew they couldn't marry, but she was older now. Wiser.

Wasn't she?

He saw her wavering, and a slow smile spread across his handsome features. Reaching up, he took her face gently between his two hands, inclining his head toward hers.

No. *No, no, no—you can't!* Aggie managed not to scream this aloud, and she jerked away from him, croaking, "What about your betrothal to Miss Caraway?"

Tyrone's hands dropped to his sides as if they'd been chopped off. "My betrothal to Miss Caraway?" he echoed with convincing incredulity. "*What* betrothal to Miss Caraway?"

"Do you deny it?"

"I do! I deny it utterly. I haven't got the least idea what you're talking about, Aggie. I'm no more betrothed to Miss Caraway than I am to the princess Amelia."

"But Lord Downing says you are," she insisted, pinching herself frantically to keep unruly Hope in check.

"Then Lord Downing may go to the deuce," he swore rudely. "Pardon me, Aggie, but I've never met the man in my life, so he can't have said such a thing."

"My brother Mr. Chester heard it secondhand," she admitted. "It seems Lord Downing told a Mr. Cusworth that you were to marry Miss Caraway, but that it had not yet been announced."

"Nor ever will be," vowed Tyrone. "Where *can* the man have got the idea?"

She bit her lip, but the words could not be contained. "Possibly he saw you kissing her."

Tyrone roared with indignation, and Aggie hushed him hastily. "Do be quiet, or we will have everyone out here, and I must know all the truth."

"I never kissed that person in all my life, and I defy anyone to prove otherwise—"

"But I—I saw you myself," she said softly. "Kissing Miss Caraway."

"It can't have been!"

"It was the night of the music meeting, after we left the Kenners' home in the Close. I ran after you because Minta had taken Miss Caraway's fan, and I meant to return it, but when I came around the cathedral, I saw—you and Miss Caraway—embracing."

"You did, did you?" Instead of appearing conscious or abashed, he broke into a grin, crossing his arms over his chest.

Her chin lifted. "I did."

"Then you're blind as a bat at noon."

"I am not! You were bent over her, and she was clinging to you, and I heard her say—say Yes to you."

He snorted. "That's all you know. That dashed Miss Caraway tripped over her own shadow or something like, and I could hardly let her fall and crack her head on the paving stones. I suspected she and her sister Lady Downing plotted the incident between them, so if you heard her say 'yes' to me, it was most definitely not in answer to a proposal, you foolish creature. I merely asked if she were all right."

"Oh, Tyrone," breathed Aggie. "I must say I am relieved to hear it. But then, how could Lord Downing say what he is saying? And he must think it true, or surely he would not start such a rumor about his own sister-in-law."

"I haven't got the least notion, and I don't care right now. Aggie, tell me—if I am not engaged to Miss Caraway, would that change anything—for you? I mean—if I were to 'bend the supple knee' again, would you still be angry with me?"

She could not answer. Something lodged in her throat that was equal parts pain and joy. Tyrone was not engaged, and he loved her. Enough to pursue her to Worthing and throw himself at her feet. He loved her!

When she said nothing, hope leaped in him. He wanted to do everything at once: shout—kiss her—gallop about like an idiot—squeeze her to him until she cried for mercy—leap on the balustrade and sing—write her a cycle of sonnets—elope with her to Gretna Green.

"You forgive me, then?" he murmured.

Still she could not speak, but she gave one slow, unmistakable nod.

It was enough.

She was swept into his arms again. His lips were on hers, and their bodies pressed along their entire lengths, as if they could not be close enough. Aggie shut her eyes, dizzy with it all, the roar and hiss of the surf mingling with the roar and thump of the blood slamming about in her. His fingers were in her hair and hers wound about his lapels and neckcloth. He was kissing her mouth, her temples, her hair, her neck, and her lips again, and she was kissing him back, and heaven knew how long it might have gone on, if the doors to the terrace had not been thrown open and a scream and a bellow heard.

The scream issued from Aggie's sister Frederica and the bellow from Mr. Chester, both cries choked off as soon as the two remembered themselves. Tyrone released Aggie instantly, but his signet ring caught in her tresses, a mishap which prevented any pretense of innocence, and which prevented him turning fully to face the oncoming Chester wrath.

But Aggie broke into a giggle as she tried to disentangle herself, a giggle which grew into a whoop of laughter, she was so irrepressibly happy.

"Agatha, indeed!" snapped Frederica. "What is the meaning of this? Why—is it Mr. Ellsworth?"

"It is," Tyrone admitted, unable to suppress his own chuckle. "I'm afraid you've quite caught us."

"Sirrah," declared Mr. Chester in an awful tone, "release my sister at once."

"I'm trying to, you know," explained Tyrone, grinning. Twisting about, he offered Mr. Chester a lopsided bow. "Good evening to you, Mr. Chester, Mrs. Chester. I hope you will congratulate Aggie and me. We're going to be married."

Frederica gave another shriek, soon throttled, and her husband drew himself up to his full height, which, admittedly, was some inches shorter than Tyrone. He ignored the latter's bow and said sternly, "I'm afraid you're going to be no such thing. I cannot consent to have the family tainted by scandal."

By this point Aggie had shut her eyes, gritted her teeth, and *torn* Tyrone's ring free of the two hairs which refused to let go, and she wheeled on her brother-in-law indignantly. "Mr. Chester, my marriage requires my parents' consent, not yours."

But Frederica held up an imperious hand. "Linus is here *in loco parentis*. I promised Papa."

Mr. Chester ignored these feminine contributions, his eyes locked on Tyrone. "Sirrah, are you or are you not engaged to Miss Caraway of Winchester, sister to Lord and Lady Downing?"

"I am not," said Tyrone simply.

"It's all some sort of misunderstanding, Mr. Chester—"Aggie interposed, only to be silenced again by Frederica's hand and Mr. Chester's stonelike determination to ignore her.

Tyrone raised amused brows. "As Aggie said, it's all some sort of misunderstanding, Mr. Chester—"

"Young man, this is not a joke! Agatha's reputation is not a joke! You come here and—kidnap her—to this out-of-the-way place—"

"Oh, honestly, Mr. Chester," interrupted Aggie again. "I went willingly, and it's the terrace, not the world's end."

"—In order to make love to her without her family's knowledge or sanction?"

"That last bit is indeed true," conceded Tyrone. "Because it was Aggie's sanction I was most concerned with. Mr. Chester—I will repeat. There has been some sort of misunderstanding with Miss Caraway, which I will get to the bottom of, as soon as I return to Winchester. But I hold myself absolutely at liberty to win Aggie, if I can, and she has blessedly indicated that I can."

They could not help it—their joy burst out once more. Beaming at each other, Tyrone took Aggie's hand and lifted it to his lips.

Mrs. Chester sputtered helplessly. Mr. Chester's chest swelled with impotence. Glowering at his young sister-in-law, he barked, "We return to Winchester tomorrow!"

"I was just going to suggest that, sir," agreed Tyrone. "The sooner I may speak with Mr. Weeks, the better. And the sooner I can clear up this confusion, the happier everyone will be. I hope, Mr. and Mrs. Chester, that in a few short days you will be able to join in wishing us joy."

Mr. Chester hemmed his doubt and disapproval, and between him and his wife Aggie was hauled away from the impudent rogue, but not without her looking over her shoulder as she went and blowing him a kiss.

When they were gone Tyrone did caper some, and he vaulted over the balustrade for a long walk on the sand, both to share his felicity with the universe and to cool his heated blood.

Chapter 28

With scoffs and scorns and contumelious taunts.
In open market-place produced they me,
To be a public spectacle to all.
—Shakespeare, *Henry VI, Part I,* I.iv.497 (c.1591)

Tyrone no sooner descended from the Flyer at the George than he heard his name called. Turning, he saw his dark-haired cousin Benjamin weaving through traffic to catch him.

"Did you get my letter, or did it cross with you? Good news, cousin, you are famous!"

"Would that be good news?" Tyrone replied. "Come, tell your glad tidings somewhere more discreet." Giving brief directions for his valise, he led the way through Hammonds Passage to a small coffee shop on the corner of St. Clement's Street.

"Are you pressed for time?" asked Benjamin, when Tyrone consulted his pocket watch.

"I am, rather." Leaning forward, Tyrone flashed the grin he had trouble preventing nowadays. "Congratulate me, cousin. I am to be married."

"So I have heard," Benjamin replied, to Tyrone's patent surprise. "To Miss Caraway, sister of Lady Downing."

"Not you too, Ben! No!" Impatiently he waited for their coffees to be set down before adding under his breath, "To Miss Weeks of The Acres—once I speak to her father, at least. That's where I have been. I followed Miss Weeks to Worthing to offer for her, and she has accepted me. I haven't got the least notion where this rumor comes from that I am to marry the other one. Aggie said something about Lord Downing putting it about."

Benjamin clicked his tongue thoughtfully. "Heard it thirdhand myself. There's a muddle you'll have to clean up, and I don't envy you the task. But hearty congratulations on Miss Weeks. Minta will be glad of it. They've been thick as thieves for years."

"Indeed. I might have spared myself a good deal of trouble if I had been wise enough to notice Aggie earlier, but it's all coming right in the end. Or will be, once I extricate myself from the mysterious Downing knot. Come—what was it you wanted to tell me when you said I was famous? Is this about the book?"

His cousin slammed a delighted fist on the table, causing their cups to rattle. "It is! I have found a publisher. I described the whole enterprise and gave him copies of two sample letters, and he wants to buy it! Richardson's book had over a hundred letters, of course, and we proposed only twenty-six, but our focus is narrower. He wants to call it *Letters to Ladies: a Gentleman's Style and Form Manual*. What do you think?"

"I think it sounds grand. What does he propose to pay?"

"That's just it, Tyrone. He proposes to pay a hundred pounds for the book outright, but Austin and I would earn no royalties. Or we might take a risk and publish it on commission. Then Austin and I would have to repay the costs of printing and distribution out of the earnings—say £180, but anything above those costs would end up in our own pockets, less the publisher's percentage."

"Then why would you not simply take the hundred pounds?" Tyrone asked. "Unless you expect me to supply the £180 if it fails."

"It would never fail for the entire £180," Benjamin said practically. "And I think *Letters to Ladies* will prove a winner. So what do you say? We publish on commission, and if it succeeds, we share alike the earnings; and if it fails, we share alike the cost?"

"I already told you I don't need the earnings, but I am willing to shoulder a third of the failure," agreed Tyrone, shaking his cousin's hand on it. "I have got notes for letters N through Zed and will develop them shortly. When do you want them?"

"As soon as ever you might. Confound these love affairs of yours, Tyrone. You might write ten books if you weren't busy engaging yourself to every young lady in the kingdom."

"Well, I will jilt one of the young ladies, in any event. Or would it not be considered a jilt if I never engaged myself in the first place?" Digging in his pocket, Tyrone extracted a coin and tossed it down. "This should cover both of us. And now you've kept me long enough."

"Fine, fine. Perhaps the 'Letter to Miss M' could be written by an impatient lover, since that seems to be your mood." Benjamin clapped his hat back on and pushed back from the table. "And while you're at it, send another copy of the 'Letter to Miss C.' It was missing from the earlier batch. I have got the ones to Miss A, Miss B, Miss D, et cetera, but poor Miss C went astray."

Tyrone paused, his brow creasing. "It was not in the packet?"

"Unless you labeled it mistakenly. But I counted letters to Miss A through Miss M, and came up with twelve, not thirteen. What was the subject of Miss C?"

"It was a marriage proposal," Tyrone replied hoarsely. "A proposal to Miss C from 'A certain admirer.' You don't think—good heavens—what next?"

Benjamin took hold of his arm to steady him. "What, man? Speak out."

But Tyrone was remembering again the scene with Miss Caraway in the cathedral close, how she stumbled and clung to him and affected faintness. Lord have mercy! Could he possibly have out-Boultoned Boulton? Had he dropped the 'Letter to Miss C' in the churchyard, and Miss Caraway come upon it? He had carried both the packet and his prepared apology to Aggie that evening—no, no—it was too horrible to contemplate.

"Walk with me, cousin," Tyrone urged. "Even here there are too many people to talk candidly."

Benjamin whistled but followed Tyrone from the coffee shop readily enough. He thought the latter might unburden himself after they passed through the West Gate at a fiery pace, but it was not until they reached Cock Lane that Tyrone put his suspicions into words.

"You mean to say you think, while grappling with you, Miss Caraway may have come upon the 'Letter to Miss C' and understood it to be addressed to her?" Benjamin summarized.

"Exactly," groaned Tyrone. "She has probably been waiting for me to show myself and make it official, and in the meantime, the Caraway and Downing families have not troubled to keep the matter to themselves."

"They cannot hold you to it," Benjamin assured him. "A 'Miss C' might be anyone, and it is not signed by you."

"No," agreed Tyrone glumly. "There's that."

"It's not nothing," his cousin insisted. "To begin with, the girl's father could not drag you into court for breach of contract. They would have no ground to stand upon. Moreover, families like that don't want the scandal. They will settle for hating you from a distance."

"Splendid."

At the arched entrance to Hollowgate's drive the cousins stopped, Tyrone hoisting himself to sit on the low stone wall and Benjamin leaning against the post, studying the clouded sky thoughtfully. "The trick, you know, would be to give the Caraway-Downing faction a means of escape. Let them be the ones to call it off."

"It isn't *on*."

"I *know* it isn't on, you blockhead, and *you* know it isn't on, but the rest of the world thinks it is. But suppose you were to give Lord Downing a reason to declare he has forbidden the match after all? He need only say at the same time that it is all in confidence, and the whole county will know of it before you can say Jack Robinson."

"What would you suggest?" The corner of Tyrone's mouth lifted, as his natural good humor began to assert itself. "I might murder someone, though if I were hanged or transported I couldn't marry Miss Weeks."

Benjamin snapped his fingers. "Eureka! We might turn this contretemps to account, cousin, if you permit. Suppose we placed an advertisement in the *Chronicle* about the missing letter? We could say, 'LOST, on Thursday last in Winchester, in the vicinity of the cathedral, letter addressed to Miss C from a Certain

Admirer. The letter is intended for inclusion in forthcoming *Letters to Ladies: a Gentleman's Style and Form Manual* by a Gentleman (Hartrow-Keith, Whitehall). If found, please return to B. A. E. at the Signet, Winchester.' You see? Downing sees the ad and goes straightaway to Caraway House to say they have got it all wrong, and what Miss Caraway found was no proposal, but rather some page torn from a textbook. She weeps, bewails her fate, yields. Everyone rejoices in the unfortunate family's hideous error and flies to order his copy of the book."

"If the letter was on my person, Miss Caraway will surely suspect me as the writer of *Letters to Ladies*," Tyrone pointed out.

"She might, or she might think you had got hold of an advance copy. You are not 'B. A. E.' after all."

"And though Lord Downing might be convinced Miss Caraway deceived herself, he will still resent me for the confusion," Tyrone persisted. "That is, for his own indiscretion in sharing the supposed engagement with all and sundry."

Benjamin threw up his hands. "He might. It was an idea. It would get you out of the engagement, but I do not see how we might also get Lord Downing out of having embarrassed himself and his wife's family. A half a solution is better than none."

Tyrone nodded. "True. True in the main. I thank you, cousin." Rising from his seat on the wall, he said,

"But if I am to take such a step, I must consult Aggie on it. With her father's approval of our marriage, we will be in a stronger position to brave out Lord Downing's wrath. In fact, I would snap my fingers at it, then. I will send word when I have decided."

The cousins shook hands again, Benjamin returning to town and Tyrone heading onward to The Acres. He had intended to smarten himself up and shed his road dust before seeing Aggie again, but now he was too impatient to bother, and he contented himself with slapping at his breeches and sleeves as he walked and removing his hat to drag fingers through his hair.

For the moment Miss Caraway and her troublesome relations were forgotten, as Tyrone schemed how he might persuade Aggie to walk the grounds, in order to steal a few kisses. First things first, however: he must secure Mr. Weeks' approval.

"Good afternoon, Orton," Tyrone greeted the butler cheerily. "Would Mr. Weeks be at home?"

"Mr. Weeks this time, eh? He is, sir. If you would follow me."

"Aggie!" cried Tyrone, catching sight of her in the passage. She had just emerged from the very parlor to which Orton was leading him. "I'm here to speak with your father."

She nodded, putting a finger to her lips, and rushed toward him. Surprised, he held out his arms, willing enough to receive her, but she neatly slipped by, muttering "Abbey" under her breath as she passed.

Before he could acknowledge her message, Orton had the door open and announced, "Mr. Tyrone Ellsworth to see you, sir," and Tyrone had no choice but to walk in.

It must be admitted that Tyrone had taken entirely for granted Mr. Weeks' approval of the match. He was, after all, the brother of Aggie's closest friend, besides being wealthy and of respectable family. Mr. Weeks likely didn't care if Tyrone were attractive or not, but he was that as well, for good measure. And if Aggie married Tyrone, she would settle a mere stone's throw from her parents! Indeed, taken altogether and considering she had once favored Francis Taplin, Tyrone could be pardoned for considering himself a vast improvement.

But the Mr. Weeks who made him a regulation bow appeared anything but delighted. With a metaphorical thump Tyrone returned to earth. He returned the man's bow and took the chair indicated.

For a minute they sat regarding each other, Mr. Weeks with his hands on his knees, back straight and every hair of his beard motionless. Apparently, he was not going to smooth the path with small talk.

Very well, then.

Tyrone cleared his throat. "Sir, I have come to ask you for your daughter's hand in marriage. She has accepted me and made me the happiest of men, and we crave your blessing and permission to name a date."

Mr. Weeks must have suffered from a similar obstruction in his throat because he cleared his throat twice in return. "Mr. Ellsworth, I have known your family a long time, and it is with regret that I tell you I withhold my consent. It has come to my attention in the past couple days that you are spoken of as an already-engaged man in Winchester. Wait—" an upraised hand cut off the words bubbling to Tyrone's lips. "Agatha tells me it is a misunderstanding, and she cannot think how it came about that Lord Downing should so mistake himself—"

"Sir," Tyrone interrupted in desperation, "I have just learned how it came about." He wished he had had a chance to speak with Aggie, to know how much she told her father, but he would simply have to gamble on it.

Fortunately Mr. Weeks was too curious for the truth to silence him again, and he even relented so far as to lean toward him an inch or two.

"I'm writing a manual for letter-writing," blurted Tyrone. "Specifically, sample letters a gentleman might use to address a young lady. They are based on a— thoughtless little enterprise I maintained at New College, for amusement and to help my fellow undergraduates. Notes, poems, even proposals. Nothing scurrilous or intended to—to lead a young woman into—er—danger, but merely to—start the ball rolling, as it were, for someone unsure how to do it himself. The sample letters I've gathered are anonymous. Addressed to Miss A, Miss B, Miss C, and so on. And I'm afraid the 'Letter to Miss C' somehow was found by Miss Clementine Caraway. She must have assumed I intended to mail it to her or to offer for her in person, and she must have shared that conclusion with her family."

"You have *not* proposed to Miss Caraway, then?"

"I have not, sir. I love your daughter and only your daughter. And I—er—have got a plan to encourage Miss Caraway and her family to abandon their mistaken notion, though I'm afraid it will involve some unpleasantness for a time. But with your support, sir, Aggie and I can weather it. I know it." Briefly, he shared Benjamin's advertisement scheme. "You see? Miss Caraway will be disappointed, and Lord Downing angry for his premature sharing of the news, but it will all blow over in time, and all the sooner when Aggie and I marry."

"Ah," said Mr. Weeks. He lifted his hands from his knees and slapped them down again. "I confess I am sorry to say it, but I still cannot allow you and Aggie to marry."

"What? But sir—"

"You know what a cloud she was under some years ago, because of that Taplin person," he continued. "It was painful for her. Painful for all of us. And now—now that he is gone at last, and she no longer endures the pity and contempt and wagging tongues of the town—how could I possibly consent to her marrying you under such a cloud? No, sir. As I love my daughter, I will not consent to it. Mr. Ellsworth, I can only say that I like you and would have given my blessing under other circumstances, but under these I cannot. Should you find a means to extricate yourself from your difficulty, however, and should enough time pass that it was all forgotten, and should you still wish then to marry my daughter, you might try again at that date. But not now. Absolutely not now and not like this. That is my final word on the matter."

If Mr. Weeks had swung the fireplace poker and dealt Tyrone a blow to the kneecaps, he imagined it would have felt much the same. He could not respond—could not even breathe—for some moments. Oh, God! If he were successful in the *Chronicle* advertisement, how long would it take for it all to be forgotten? Not months, he was certain. It would be years. And if it were years, would Aggie still love him? He would love her always, but she had ceased to love Taplin in four years—suppose that were also to be Tyrone's fate?

He felt sick.

He never knew how he got out of the room or even the house.

But somehow he was standing on the steps. He stumbled down them, thinking he would go—somewhere. Away somewhere.

He was halfway down the drive before something caught his eye in the distance. Something white being waved. Only then did he remember Aggie's whispered "Abbey," for it was she, standing by the wall of the ruins, waving her shawl like a flag of surrender.

At once his stupor fell from him, and he was running. Aggie retreated behind the wall, but when he skidded around it, she hurled herself at him, sending them both tumbling to the grass.

"He said no, didn't he?" she gasped, between the kisses being showered on her. "No—stop, Tyrone—stop. We need to talk."

"We will, but I haven't seen you for two days, and after that interview with your father, I can't possibly talk unless you apply balm to my tortured soul."

"Ridiculous," she scolded. But she came to him all the same and submitted to one very long, very tender embrace. Then she shoved him away, smiling. "Now talk."

He talked. With Aggie perched on his knee, he told her every detail from the moment he stepped down from the coach at the George to the moment he found himself on the step at The Acres, like one cast out of Eden.

"I should go directly to the barracks and enlist, should I not?" he wound up. "Then I might stuff my head in a cannon for King and Country and be blown to bits. Because you'll forget me, won't you, Aggie—if we must wait years to be married?"

"You needn't go to the barracks," she replied. "I'll blow you to bits myself for thinking such a thing of me."

"But you didn't love Taplin after a few years," he argued, rubbing his cheek against her bare arm.

"Taplin never deserved my love from the outset," she retorted. "And did I not tell you I would murder you with my bare hands if you mentioned him again?"

"Then 'let me be put to death,'" he murmured, now brushing his lips up that same arm. "'I am content, so thou wilt have it so.'"

"Mm," said Aggie, "don't think to cajole me with your fine words." But he did get another kiss out of it. Then she shoved him again and stood up. "Look here, Tyrone, I think your cousin is right, and you should put the advertisement in the *Chronicle*. Only, you shouldn't instruct them to send the letter to 'B. A. E.' You should tell them to send it to 'T. Ellsworth.' Let them not mistake the matter."

"You think I should admit to writing the book?" he gawped.

"I do. I think it must be made clear as crystal that you are writing this book, which implies that you have got a sordid history of writing false things to women."

"But—but—that will make things worse!" protested Tyrone. "The bigger the scandal, the less likely Mr. Weeks will ever condone our marriage!"

"You want Lord Downing and the Caraways to think they've escaped by the skin of their teeth, don't you? How much better then, if they believe you've been writing such things and leaving them all over the kingdom to be misconstrued by countless innocent lady victims!"

He took a long breath, his brow still troubled. "You would choose a short, sharp pain over a long, drawn-out ache? It's true, I would look the worse, but perhaps then I would be more of a nine-days' wonder. You think that would be enough, if it were all concentrated? I don't know, Aggie. Your father might then say I am too scandalous altogether to be your husband."

"That is why I had better be tainted with the same brush," she said solemnly, taking hold of his hands.

"What do you mean?"

"I mean, if we are already married, my father cannot forbid it. No—listen to me, Tyrone. What if we were to elope?"

"Elope?" he barked.

"Hush! Someone will hear you. Yes—elope. I would leave a note to my parents saying Miss Caraway was not the only one deceived by your letters. You had written some such to me, on another's behalf, and when I learned *you* were the writer, it was too late. I loved you. I would say, 'Papa, Mama, forgive me, but I am running away to throw myself at Tyrone Ellsworth's feet. When you read this, we will be gone.' Then I'll climb out my bedroom window and run to where you wait with the carriage."

He was too stunned even to take advantage of their clasped hands. "But why would you need to say the part about being deceived by my letters? Why couldn't you just say you were so disappointed that Mr. Weeks refused his blessing, you were driven to it? He knows the truth already."

"Because, don't you see? The note is not really for my father. If I leave it for my maid Banniker to find, she will trumpet all over Winchester the bit about you writing letters! Then Miss Caraway and her family will think, *ah-ha*, poor Clemmy was not the only one fooled, and now that poor, pitiful Agatha Weeks—the one who chased after Francis Taplin four years ago—the pathetic creature has gone and flung herself at yet another scapegrace! They will think, but for the grace of God, there would go our Clementine."

"But Aggie—darling! I can't let you ruin yourself like that for me. I can't have people say you were one of the silly girls fooled by my letters."

"But so I was."

"No, Aggie, never. I meant every loving word I ever wrote to you, even if I pretended to be Boulton."

"That must have been what made your words so convincing. No, Tyrone, let it be said I was fooled and threw myself at you, and you gave in to temptation and eloped with me for my fortune. I don't mind—not if I have got you. And if Papa cuts me off without a penny, we'll still have your pennies. Mr. Ellsworth would never do you such a turn."

"True enough," conceded Tyrone. "He would be delighted by our marriage. And eventually your father would relent, wouldn't he? When the Downings and the Caraways forget how I supposedly wronged them, or when the world forgets how I supposedly did so." He shook his head ruefully, his smile both fond and sheepish.

"Oh, Aggie, it's such a scrape, but I think your plan just might work."

"I think so too," she said with decision. We'll do it, then? Because the shameful truth is, I don't want to wait years for Papa to come round."

"Nor do I." He bent and placed a gentle kiss on her mouth. "But this means our marriage will begin under a cloud."

"So it will, but sooner or later the clouds will part."

He gave her dear face a lingering look, his throat tight. "Oh, Aggie, I hope for your sake it will be sooner, rather than later. Though I promise you solemnly, if such a beginning can be redeemed by a lifetime of my love and devotion, you never, never will regret taking this step."

She enclosed both his hands between her own and carried them to her heart. "No," she promised him in return. "No, I never will."

And she never did.

◊◊◊◊◊

The adventures of the Ellsworth Assortment continue in *Miranda at Heart*.

◊◊◊◊◊

If you enjoyed Tyrone's story, please help other readers and leave a review!

◊◊◊◊◊

To join my mailing list and hear about new books, promotions, and other tidbits, go to www.christinadudley.com. I'll be delighted to send you this companion novella (ebook only) to my **Hapgoods of Bramleigh series**, *A Fair Judge*.

◊◊◊◊◊

◊◊◊◊◊

And have you read the Hapgoods of Bramleigh series of Regency romances?

Made in the USA
Las Vegas, NV
14 September 2023